YOURS IS THE EARTH

YOURS IS THE EARTH

Simon Munro Kerr

T

The manufacturer's authorised representative in the EU for product safety is Authorised Rep Compliance Ltd,
71 Lower Baggot Street, Dublin D02 P593 Ireland (www.arccompliance.com)

Troubador Publishing Ltd
Unit E2 Airfield Business Park,
Harrison Road, Market Harborough,
Leicestershire. LE16 7UL
Tel: 0116 2792299
Email: books@troubador.co.uk
Web: www.troubador.co.uk

ISBN 978 1836283 126

British Library Cataloguing in Publication Data.
A catalogue record for this book is available from the British Library.

Cover artwork by Claudia Munro Kerr

Printed and bound by CPI Group (UK) Ltd, Croydon, CR0 4YY
Typeset in 12pt Minion Pro by Troubador Publishing Ltd, Leicester, UK

In loving memory of
James Cole Munro Kerr. DSO 1880-1954, my grandfather
& Ector Orr Munn 1891-1993, my inspiration.

If you can fill the unforgiving minute
With sixty seconds worth of distance run,
Yours is the earth and everything that's in it
And – which is more – you'll be a Man, my son!

Rudyard Kipling

PART I

CHAPTER 1

The aeroplane, built of nothing more than canvas, spruce and wires around a willow frame, lurched violently in the turbulence of the approaching thunderstorm. The pilot glanced at his rudimentary instruments and checked the fuel. He finally admitted that he was indeed lost over this flat English countryside and, according to the gauges, had very little time to find his way home.

It was June 1913, and he was flying out of Pangbourne, now five thousand feet over Berkshire, testing the rate of climb and manoeuvrability of the prototype two-seater Avro 504 B biplane, powered by an eighty horsepower Gnome rotary engine. So impressed by its performance he had lost track of time. He moved the stick gently sideways and banked right, losing altitude at an impressive rate. He knew that he couldn't make it back to base; nothing for it but a forced landing to re-fuel.

At two thousand feet he crossed a railway, altered course to follow it and searched for landmarks. He could see a station ahead and, throttling back, lost more height in an attempt to make out the signs along the platform. He tore past at less than a hundred feet and read CROWTHORNE; it meant nothing to him.

A heavy wall of thunderheads was building up rapidly high to his left and lightning flashed violently, striking a tree in a field four hundred yards ahead. He banked away from the storm and there, emphasised by the dramatic light, he saw a vast group of interconnecting red brick buildings, with mansard roofs and two tall, distinctive towers. There were playing fields to one side and, on the other, a large stretch of water. He skimmed a broad-leaf wood and saw a startled expression on the up-turned face of a man in a cab, just as it drove through wrought-iron gates.

He scanned all sides as the rain began. To his right, beyond the extensive complex, he could see several rugby pitches. The goal posts, pointing skyward, were set too close for comfort and barred his way. He lifted the nose of the machine slightly, cleared the fields and banked for another approach.

Ahead was a cricket pitch, game in progress. Spectators thronged the boundaries and milled around the pavilion. Beyond was a broad expanse of grass, away from the crowd, ending in a wood. He was aware the game had stopped and everyone was looking up. He waved reassuringly, many waved back and suddenly they broke ranks and ran towards where he was going to land.

'Eddy, wait for me!' Two boys in white flannels and open necked shirts ran ahead of the rest. Edward Meade, tall, athletically built with wavy blond hair was just ahead of Jock Sinclair. Born on the same day, they had been friends from the first day of school and were now in their penultimate year. Allies in most things, they were both playing for the first XI against Harrow. Edward looked back, but said nothing nor slackened his pace.

A hundred yards ahead the 'plane touched down gently and rolled to a halt. The pilot switched off the engine and climbed down just as Edward rounded the end of the tail. A peal of thunder drowned the pilot's greeting and heavy, warm raindrops spattered the wings. The pilot removed his helmet and goggles, and Edward was surprised at how young he looked.

'Are you all right?'

'Fine.'

'Good,' Edward grinned, 'welcome to Wellington, why are you here?' The pilot looked mildly embarrassed. 'I'm sorry, I didn't mean to be rude, but I've never seen a plane before, only photographs.' Jock stopped beside him.

'Eddy, what's happened?'

'Nothing, we have a visitor' he said casually, 'I'm Edward Meade' he extended his hand to the pilot, 'and this is my friend, Jock Sinclair.'

'Alister Miller.' They shook hands warmly. The rest of the team and a lot of the spectators surged around the aircraft. Some of the spectators had umbrellas but everyone else was being soaked by the heavy rain.

The thunder was receding into the distance and Edward knew that the storm would soon pass and that he would have to return to the game.

'Are you going to stay?' he asked the pilot, confused by his own question but not wanting to lose contact.

'I'm afraid not, I must get back to the airfield at Pangbourne. I'm already overdue but I will need to re-fuel, as I'm very low on petrol.' Mr Robinson, their Latin master, stepped forward from the crowd. He was tall and angular with a disproportionately large, hollow-cheeked head that hung from his shoulders as if his neck had been broken. His long jaw was clean-shaven, and his thin grey hair was plastered to his head in patches.

'What's going on Meade?'

'Mr Miller is low on petrol, sir and needs to re-fuel to get back to his airfield.'

'This is a school Meade, not a garage and I hold you responsible for this outrageous behaviour.'

'Me, sir?'

'Yes, you sir! You led what I can only describe as a rout. You have shamed the whole school in front of our visitors.'

'I was nearest to the aircraft sir, the game had broken up because of the rain and I thought that the pilot might be in need of help.'

'Don't answer back boy, I'll see you in my study after the game.'

'It was my fault sir, 'said the pilot 'had I not run low on fuel none of this would have happened. If you can kindly provide me with a few gallons of petrol I'll be on my way.'

'We have no petrol here.'

'But we do, sir,' cut in Jock, before Mr Robinson could go any further, 'there are several tins of it in the groundsman's shed. He has it for the tractor, sir,' added Jock lamely whilst he shuffled his feet nervously.

'I wish you paid as much attention to your Latin, Sinclair, as you do to other people's business. So be it,' he turned to Jackson, one of Edward's contemporaries hovering at his elbow, relishing the possibility of another confrontation between Edward and Mr Robinson, 'Jackson, your *friend* Meade,' his voice dripped with sarcasm, 'is once again telling us what to do. See to it that this... this... aviator gets some petrol from the groundsman and make sure he pays for it. Give a full accounting to the Bursar and I will check with him that you have done so. The rest of you get back to the game.' He turned on his heel and strode back to the pavilion.

'Damn you Meade! How do you always get away with it, why should I be responsible for this? I don't even know what petrol costs!' Jackson's voice rose as his anger increased. 'Who do you think you are, you bloody colonial with your high and mighty airs, to tell Mr Robinson what to do?' Spittle sprayed those nearest to him as his voice cracked in frustration. Not another sound could be heard, Jackson suddenly realised that once again he had lost his temper with Meade, as those nearest to him looked at each other knowingly.

'I think sixpence a gallon should cover it.' said Alister Miller, reaching into his pocket for some money. The moment passed and Jackson, with a great effort, got control of himself.

'Sounds about right to me,' said Edward, 'and by the way, Jackson, I was born in America and they haven't been a colony for over a hundred and thirty years.' Dismissively he turned his back on Jackson and addressed the pilot while everyone else, with the exception of Jock, headed back to the game.

'Thank you for coming to my rescue, Mr Miller.'

'It was the least I could do and please call me Alister. I had no idea I would be the cause of so much resentment and anger. Do you have many more like him?'

'Man or boy?'

'Both, I suppose.'

'No, thank God, two is two too many.' He eyed the 'plane appreciatively and added almost to himself 'I'd love to learn to fly.'

'Come on Eddy, we must get back to the game,' said Jock, tugging at his sleeve.

'If you're serious about flying, come and see me when you can at Pangbourne. Anyone there will tell you where to find the field.' They shook hands.

'Thanks, I will.'

The game had re-started but Edward's attention was almost entirely focused on what was going on beyond the boundary. As he changed position after each over, he watched the re-fuelling and eventual take-off with great interest. He was amazed to see how easily the 'plane left the ground after a short run and could not help waving as the 'plane banked over the pitch and headed back to Pangbourne.

The school won by three wickets and, as they had already had tea, the players made their way to the changing rooms. First there and first through the showers, Edward and Jock stood before the small mirror by the door, each combing their hair into some semblance of order.

'I suppose you're going to see Mr Robinson now, I'll come with you if I may, it's on my way back to our study, you don't mind do you?'

'No, of course not, but we'll have to hurry.'

Within minutes they passed the dining room and headed down the long corridor past the ornate Victorian marble Roll of Honour for Old Boys. The names of those who had been in the Volunteer Corps and had fallen in the various campaigns in India and Africa were inscribed in gilt lettering. Meade glanced at the long sombre portraits of illustrious old boys, benefactors and past governors that looked down on them. At the end of the long gallery, they came to the large oak and leaded glass doors that opened out onto the quadrangle. The late afternoon sun cast long soft shadows on the flagstones. They quickened their pace along the north side of Chapel Quad and Jock trotted to keep up with Edward's long strides as they came to the far corner. The double doors ahead of them swung open and Mr Robinson stepped through.

'Meade, why were you running?' His voice crackled like dry tinder.

'I was not, Sir.'

'Don't argue with me boy, you know the rule.' He stuck his thumbs into his waistcoat pockets and drummed long bony fingers on his chest.

'Yes Sir.'

'Yes Sir what? I was running or I know the rule.'

'I know the rule, Sir.' He could feel Jock breathing heavily at his left shoulder.

'Then why were you running?'

'I wasn't running Sir.' Mr Robinson looked for a moment at Jock then back at Edward. He had never liked Edward and made no effort to do so. He was a man of dry, sarcastic wit who abused his position of considerable authority with impunity.

'A hundred lines Meade, on my desk before Chapel tonight. 'I must not run across the quad." Edward smarted at the injustice of the punishment and knew, as he opened his mouth, he was going to make it worse.

'That's not fair Sir, I was not running.'

'Two hundred lines.' Again Edward could feel Jock at his shoulder, his embarrassment, his indecision, his fear, his friend. Jock wouldn't say anything, Edward knew that, and he certainly wasn't going to give Mr Robinson the satisfaction of playing them off against each other.

'Yes Sir. I was on my way to see you.' He paused for a second, before adding, 'Sir.' He could taste corrosive anger in his mouth and hoped that it didn't show in his face. 'I didn't want to be late Sir,' he added and instantly regretted it.

'So, you *were* running.' Edward caught the sadistic edge in Mr Robinson's voice and watched him slowly remove a small black notebook from his inside jacket pocket. With his other hand, he took a silver pencil from another pocket. With great deliberation, he opened the notebook and glared at Edward.

'Then you lied to me.'

'Yes Sir.' Mr Robinson's eyes gleamed with triumph behind steel-rimmed glasses. Edward felt hot at the back of his neck, guilty in some incomprehensible way. His mind drifted, he felt dizzy, dominated by the gaunt vulpine figure before him who stood shrouded in an old musty gown. He tried to concentrate, his shirt stuck to his back with sweat. He had given up, and wondered why. He stared at the notebook.

'For lying to me Meade, you will have another two hundred lines on my desk before Chapel. 'I must not run across the quad and I must not lie.' He noted the punishment, replaced the book in his pocket and with his gown flapping, strode past the two boys. They stood and watched him go, his steel tipped heels ringing on the flagstones. Ten paces from them he turned and added 'In Latin, Meade.' Without waiting for an answer, he continued on his way.

'Excuse me, Sir.' cried Edward following him across the quad. 'Do you still want to see me in your study?'

'No, Meade, report to the Master instead.'

'I'm sorry Eddy, I should have said something. It was all my fault, I hate that man. It's not just you, he's like that with almost everyone.' They went through the large double oak doors into another long corridor at the end of which was the Headmaster's study. 'I wish I could do some of your lines for you, but he'd notice the difference in our handwriting.' The floor was highly polished oak and the walls were hung with large uninspired portraits of long-dead Headmasters. Edward laughed, as he glanced at them and wished the same fate on all masters, especially Mr Robinson.

'All right Eddy, I'll see you later. Good luck,' said Jock. He turned away, head down and his hands stuffed into his pockets.

Poor Jock, thought Eddy, he knew and yet he hadn't come forward. He wondered why as he faced the study door, straightened his tie, ran his fingers through his hair and polished the toe caps of his shoes on the back of his trouser legs. His mouth felt dry. He knocked tentatively and then again, harder.

'Come in.' The Master's voice sounded muffled through the heavy door. It was a large, high ceilinged room with long casement windows in two walls. A beautiful early Georgian knee hole desk dominated the centre of the room and stood on an antique, coral coloured, Aubusson rug, heavy curtains bracketed the windows and 19th-century English landscapes covered the walls.

'You sent for me, Sir?' The Master was looking out of the window and stood with his back to Edward. 'It's Meade Sir.'

'Come in Edward, how are you, my boy?' The Master turned away from the window and faced him across the desk. 'You played very well this afternoon and thanks to your batting we won. Please sit down Edward,' he waved to a chair on the other side of his desk, 'your brother is here, he came down by train earlier this afternoon.'

'Chadwyck or Gerald Sir?' he asked excitedly as he realised Mr Robinson had not reported him.

'Chadwyck, he's in the other room. I want to have a word with you first before I put the two of you together. It is sad news for us all, Edward, about your father, I regret to have to tell you that he died in Ireland on Tuesday. I'm most terribly sorry my boy, I understand it was very sudden and all over in two days.' The Master turned away and went back to the window. Edward sat with his head down and stared at the rug, he suddenly felt cold and wrapped his arms around his body. A small keening sound escaped him, his lips felt numb and he chewed on them, determined not to cry. His breath caught in his throat and his chest ached, at last he looked back to the Master and stood up.

'Please may I see Chad, Sir?'

'Of course my boy, he's in the next room.' He indicated the other door, 'you won't be disturbed.' Without a word, Edward crossed the room and opened the door.

'Eddy, how are you?' Chadwyck rose as Edward came into the room and the two brothers embraced 'you have grown since I saw you last, and your hair's much longer.' He tried to laugh but it lacked substance.

'I'm fine Chad, but God I'm glad to see you.' They held each other at arm's length and Edward tried to draw comfort from the contact. 'I still hate this place and its gratuitous discipline. I miss you all very much. I miss mother and Gerald and the horses and dogs.' He drew a deep shuddering breath. 'How did it happen Chad? He was so strong. Tell me what happened.' Chadwyck went back to his chair and Edward sat down opposite him.

'Bacterial pneumonia. Doctor Carrigan told me that father had had bronchitis before. We had been fishing all day in the rain, gone back to the house for supper and, as we were going out afterwards for sea trout, we did not bother to change. We sat by a roaring fire, steaming like old kettles and eating our supper as fast as we could.'

'I wish I had been with you, Chad, please go on.'

'It was much colder later, the sea trout were running well and we fished until after midnight. It was really our last night as we were booked on the boat out of Galway to New York on the Monday night. We have fished in the rain dozens of times and nothing ever happened to father before. He had been working very hard for the last two months in Washington on the railway merger and must have been very run down, he had no resistance to the bacteria. I am so sorry Eddy, I really don't understand it myself and I was there and saw it all happen.' Chadwyck paused to gather his thoughts, he couldn't stand the pain in his brother's eyes.

'Go on Chad, please tell me the rest.'

'Father was too sick to be moved, so the doctor stayed most of the day and did all he could to make him comfortable. Later he had to leave and a nurse came and took over. We did everything we could Eddy, but he never rallied, he remained like that all night and all day Monday, slowly sinking lower and lower.'

'Poor mother, she must have been distraught.'

'She was, I will never forget his eyes when he tried to say something to us, he just could not form the words. Mother couldn't stand it any longer and went to her room and I sat beside him all Monday night in case he did say something. But he didn't, Eddy, not a word for any of us, then very early Tuesday morning, he died.'

'Where's mother now?' He fought for control and tried to concentrate on the immediate future, he got up and stood looking out of the window.

'At The Connaught. We came back together on the packet boat and took a train to London. We brought father's body with us and I've arranged for him to be buried at Glen Lyon, on Saturday, according to his will. I've asked the Master to give you leave. We'll go back to London as soon are you are ready and have packed a bag.'

'What did the Old Man say about me going?' He watched a group of boys walking towards the cricket pavilion, laughing and joking with each other, and tried to think how his father's death would affect his life.

'That you could go of course, you're not in prison.'

'It feels like it, at times. Will I stay on here at school?'

'What would you like to do? We can discuss it with mother after the funeral.'

'I don't know. I really don't know what I want to do right now.' The boys had almost reached the cricket pavilion. They had disturbed the rooks that swept and soared above the chestnut trees, on the edge of the park.

'I suppose you're now head of the family Chad, after all, you're almost six years older than me. What are you going to do? Do you still want to go into the navy? What about Gerald, how is he? I haven't seen him since his twenty-first. You haven't mentioned him at all. Where is he, will he be at the funeral?' He dug his hands into his pockets and tried desperately to control himself, he did not recognise his voice, 'I never really missed father when he was alive but now, I miss him terribly. I can't believe I'll never see him again.' Tears streamed down his face, no sound, just pain. He wanted to use his handkerchief but didn't want Chadwyck to know he was crying.

'Please wait here a moment Eddy, I want a word with the Master.'

When he had gone Edward pulled out his handkerchief and blew his nose. Above, the rooks were still riding the thermals.

CHAPTER 2

With a great flourish of steam, the train eased alongside number four platform at Paddington Station and stopped, with great dignity, four feet from the buffers. Porters lined the platform, primed for well laden passengers. Chadwyck and Edward stepped out, and a paper seller followed them down the platform as they threaded their way through the crowd.

'Dope scandal shocks Ascot stewards. Read all about it!' he shouted and, as he approached he continued in a lower voice, 'Paper Guv?' Chadwyck fished in his pocket for a penny.

'Come on Eddy, let's find a cab. The sooner we get back to The Connaught, the happier I'll be about mother.' They paused at the barrier with their porter as he handed their tickets to the collector.

'Want a cab Sir?' asked the porter 'and where for?'

'Yes please, The Connaught.'

'Follow me, Sir.' They filed past the clock, bombarded from all sides by the cries of fruit and flower sellers. The repetitious sound of the slamming railway carriage doors, and the piercing blast of the guard's whistle, mixed with fragmented farewells of departing passengers. They came out through the high-vaulted main entrance to find themselves beside a long line of horse-drawn carriages.

'The Connaught, cabbie,' said the porter, 'and no long way round. These gemp'men may be furreners but they ain't no fools!'

The porter turned to Chadwyck and winked. 'Beggin yer pard'n sir, all cabbies is thieves if they think they'll get away wiv' it.' And more power to you, thought Chadwyck, when it comes to your tip, as he handed him the three-penny bit that he had always intended to give him. With Edward's bag lashed on the roof, they swung out of the station and headed for Hyde Park. The hooves rang on the cobbles and the babel of sound receded. Ahead of them was a large open Daimler, its driver clad in a long checked tweed motoring coat and cap. A young woman sat beside him wearing a very smart veiled toque, with small white feathered wings on the sides. The driver was having trouble with the timing and great clouds of black smoke, interspersed with the occasional backfire, belched from the exhaust pipe. The cab's horse shied towards the pavement, scattering a group of pedestrians.

'Bloody machine' growled the cabbie, 'there should be a law against 'em!' Edward laughed and watched enviously as the car pulled away from them into the park. They crossed the Park and went along Mount Street, turned left at Carlos Place and pulled up in front of the Connaught.

The top-hatted, green coated doorman approached the cab and saluted the brothers as they stepped down. A porter removed Edward's bag and disappeared through the service entrance. The doorman held one of wide double doors open for them.

'Good evening Mr Meade and good evening to you, Sir.' Chadwyck gave him a shilling and told him to pay the cabbie. They walked across to the hall porter's desk and Chadwyck asked him to make first-class reservations for his mother, Alice, his brother and himself on the night sleeper that left King's Cross for Inverness at ten o'clock. His father's coffin was already with the station master and arrangements had been made for it to travel on the same train.

'Come on Eddy, let's go and see mother and I'll introduce you to Alice. She is a neighbour of Doctor Carrigan's and he persuaded her to accompany mother for as long as mother might need her. If it's not too late we'll have some tea sent up to mother's suite.'

'I'll take care of all that, Sir,' said the hall porter as they turned towards the lift. On the fourth floor, they found the baggage porter waiting outside their mother's suite. Chadwyck rested his hand on Edward's shoulder. 'Mother will be very pleased to see you Eddy, but don't be too shocked by what you see.'

'Where's Gerald, Chad, you never told me?'

'I don't know, I sent him two telegrams to the house in Washington, one when Papa fell ill and the other when he died.' Chadwyck opened the door and they crossed a small hall furnished with delicate regency pieces. The porter stood Edward's bag in the hall and left. Their mother was sitting with Alice in front of a blazing log fire and the room was suffocatingly hot. Alice got up and Chadwyck introduced her to Edward. She smiled, bobbed them a courtesy and excused herself.

Their mother was dressed in deepest mourning in a long sleeved, full length black frieze wool dress with black lace gloves, a small black hat with a heavy veil. She appeared to Edward to be indescribably fragile and in awful contrast to the vivacious, life loving woman of just a few weeks ago. She didn't move at all, although she must have known they were there.

'Mother, I'm back. How are you feeling?' No response came; Chadwyck turned to his brother and, with an encouraging smile, eased him towards their mother. Edward crossed the room and knelt at her feet.

'Mama?' He picked up her two hands in his, they felt fleshless and cold. 'Mama, it's Eddy.' She appeared to be looking over the top of his head but he knew that her unfocused eyes were seeing far beyond her immediate surroundings. He squeezed her hands very gently. 'It's Eddy, Mama.' he repeated, but still no response. He stood up and walked over to his brother. He could feel the tears again in his eyes.

'I can't reach her Chad, I don't think she knows I'm here. She's so cold, her hands are like ice. Please Chad, go and talk to her. See if you can get through to her, I'm frightened, I've never seen her like this.'

'Edward's here mother, so now we can leave for Scotland.' Chadwyck had drawn up a chair and was sitting in front of his mother. Tentatively he stretched out a hand and touched her knee. 'Mother, did you hear me?' He raised his voice a little. 'Edward's here and now we must get ready to go to Scotland.' Slowly, she focused on him.

'Scotland? It's too soon to go to Scotland, we never go until August.' Chadwyck drew in a deep breath and glanced at Edward but he hadn't heard his mother, her voice was so low and childlike. 'The house won't be ready, it's much too soon to shoot. Why are we going to Scotland Chadwyck? Does your father know?'

'Yes mother, he's going with us.'

'Of course dear, well then, that's all right. What do you want me to do?'

'We're taking the train, the night sleeper as we always do, so we'll have dinner here and then we'll leave for King's Cross at nine o'clock. Have you had tea yet mother?'

'Oh yes dear.'

'Good, because I've just ordered some for myself and Eddy.'

'For Eddy dear? Is Edward here?'

'Yes mother, he's just arrived.' She turned her head, suddenly aware of her surroundings and Edward went over to stand beside his brother.

'Hello Mama, how are you?'

'Oh Edward, how tall you are. How tall and handsome and strong. You're almost as tall as Chadwyck now. Look at the two of you together. Come closer, let me look at you.' With great elegance, she lifted the veil away from her face, held out her arms towards him and Edward leant forward and kissed her on her chalk white cheek. There were great dark smudges beneath her eyes and their usual sparkling violet seemed washed out. He was shocked by her appearance but tried not to let his feelings show. 'We're going to Scotland early this year Edward, with Papa.'

'Yes mother, I know.' It was all he could say without crying, and, puzzled, he stepped back gratefully when the waiter arrived with their tea.

CHAPTER 3

All was not well with Gerald Meade; he was suffering from an appalling hangover on a bright, hot morning in Washington, the temperature already well into the seventies. Sunlight flooded his bedroom and scorched the sand, that he thought he could feel grating behind his eyes. In a vain attempt to alleviate the pounding in his head, he turned away from the windows. He could hear someone calling his name in the hallway outside and a moment later his host, Oliver Carruthers, resplendent in a magnificent Chinese silk dressing-gown, was standing by his bed.

'Get up Gerry, Armageddon is upon you! It's gone ten and judging by your appearance it is going to take all of two hours to get you ready.'

'Go away Oliver and leave me alone.' He grabbed a pillow and buried his head.

'No my old friend, this is your great day and I, as your best man, will make damn sure that it all goes like clockwork. I've got the ring, your train tickets to New York,' he tapped his chest, 'which, as you know, leaves Union Station at eight o'clock. Whatever happens, Gerry, you must not miss the train or you will not make your connection with the SS *Adriatic*, which sails on the morning tide from New York.'

'Yes, yes, Oliver you sound like someone from Thomas Cooks

and by the way, who the hell opened the curtains?' He rolled onto one elbow and stared belligerently at Oliver.

'My valet, an hour ago, in an attempt to get you going.' Gerald kneaded his bloodshot eyes, winced and carefully ran his fingers through his long, dark hair, as if he expected to find something missing.

'God, what were we drinking last night?'

'We?'

'Me.'

'As I remember anything you could lay your hands on.' Oliver took hold of the edge of the bedclothes and stripped them back. 'Up and at 'em boy, soak that ugly head of yours in cold water and repent your sins. I have told my man to bring up some coffee.' Gerald eased himself up and glanced cautiously around. 'They've gone, if you're looking for Sybil and Veronica. Hopkins chased them out, an hour ago.' Unable to hold his position any longer with any semblance of dignity, Gerald rolled out of bed and padded through to the bathroom.

He stood under the shower in the vast cast-iron bath and turned on the cold water, which drummed on his head and shoulders with enervating force. He looked at himself in the full-length mirror and inspected the ravages of the last twenty-four hours. There were deep scratch marks down his back and several purple bruises at the base of his throat. In the three years since he had left school he had put on a lot of weight, a fact that his father wouldn't let him forget. The thought of his father immediately triggered all the old recurring themes. Why hadn't he gone to university, like most of his contemporaries? Why wouldn't he get a job? Why was he always in need of money, if it wasn't to pay his gambling debts? Why, God forbid, wasn't he more like his bloody brother Chadwyck? He picked up a large bar of soap and, rubbing himself furiously, worked up a lather. Why was his father so hard to please? Why was it that nothing Gerald did was ever right in his eyes? Why, he argued, couldn't he enjoy himself when young. Plenty of time to work later and, as his father put it, show himself to be a man. In a sudden flare of temper he threw the soap across the room and stepped back under the shower. He'd show him, marrying Betty Wickham would solve all his problems.

He stepped out of the shower and wrapped himself in a large white towel. He found no one in his room but his frock coat and striped trousers had been laid out and a large silver coffee pot stood on a table by the bed. Before he had finished his first cup Oliver, debonair in checked trousers and a silk faced frock coat returned.

'How are you feeling, as awful as you look? It's almost eleven and we have to leave here by noon, to meet the others for lunch. A condemned man should go to his execution on a full stomach.' He prodded the scratches on Gerald's back 'You'd better keep yourself covered up for a while or you'll find these hard to explain.'

CHAPTER 4

After a subdued dinner at the Connaught, Chadwyck, Edward, their mother and Alice left the hotel and caught the night sleeper to Edinburgh, from King's Cross. During the night, Edward heard his mother crying softly through the partition and almost immediately the sound of a door opening and closing and then the gentle soothing sounds of Alice.

He woke at seven when the train pulled into Edinburgh's Waverley station and went to Chadwyck's compartment. The ornate iron columns and roof girders cast long shadows in the early morning sun, across the platform. They dressed quickly and left the train to stretch their legs and buy a newspaper. No sound came from their mother's compartment.

Half an hour later, they were having breakfast in the resplendent gilt and mahogany Pullman dining car, waited upon by a liveried steward. The sound from the wheels changed as they thundered over the Forth Bridge. Edward watched the graceful schooners two hundred feet below the bridge, as they trimmed their sails according to the wind and tide. Far to the east, he could see the docks of Leith and the kaleidoscope of commercial shipping dominated by one of the large outward-bound ships of the Leith, Hull and Hamburg Line. Alice joined them in the dining car, as they drew level with the island-studded Loch Leven to their right, and told them that their mother had had a fairly restful night and seemed reconciled to the purpose of their journey.

'Will mother be joining us for breakfast, Alice?' asked Edward.

'No, Edward, I've ordered a light breakfast to be sent to her compartment.'

'Did she talk to you about our father?' Chadwyck had been looking out of the window, with a distant expression but Edward's question caught his attention and he looked to Alice for her answer.

'Yes, late last night when she was unable to sleep. She cried for the first time since we left Ireland and it seemed to help. She talked about your father and you, Chadwyck and how she had come to rely on you. She blamed herself for shirking reality.' Alice paused and toyed with her tea before taking a sip. She looked from one brother to the other, for encouragement.

'Go on,' said Chadwyck gently, 'what else did she say?'

'She talked about your grandfather,' she continued in her soft Irish brogue, 'about the estate at Glen Lyon and about the church at Fortingal. She seems to have always been very happy there and I believe that those memories helped her during the night.'

'Did she talk about Gerald? Will he be at the funeral?'

'No Edward. She talked about Gerald with your father just before he died, but she hasn't mentioned him since.'

'What did she say to him?'

'I don't remember very well, it was something to do with the Whichers, or some such name.'

'The Wickhams, do you mean the Wickhams?'

'Yes, but it didn't make much sense to me and your father never answered her.'

'Please Alice, try and think what it was about the Wickhams. They are neighbours of ours in Washington.'

'Washington, that was it. Your brother had cabled your parents in Ireland and it was waiting for them when they first arrived. He wanted to marry the Wickhams' daughter, Betty, and it appeared from what your mother told me later that your father was vehemently against it and sent a telegram to your brother forbidding the marriage. I had completely forgotten about it, it was my first night there with your mother after Doctor Carrigan had to leave.'

'Why didn't you tell me sooner?' Chadwyck had raised his voice without meaning to and the people at the next table looked across. 'You never said a word,' he continued in a gentler tone, 'are you sure about this, Alice? That would explain why Gerald avoided me in Washington before we left for Ireland.'

'I think so, but perhaps it would be best if you talked to your mother when you have a chance.'

At Perth they changed trains and travelled on to Stanley on the Caledonian line, then the Highland line. The train took them through some of the most beautiful countryside in Scotland as they travelled along the river Tay, past Ballinluig to Aberfeldy.

Hector MacPherson, their Factor at Glen Lyon, met them with the estate Daimler. He stood by the car, clad in the kilt and holding his bonnet before him, while a gentle breeze riffled his long silver hair. His sombre, aquiline features conveyed both respect and great sadness. Behind the car stood a carriage to take the coffin directly to the church at Fortingal. The Reverend Duncan MacLeod was waiting for them at Glen Lyon House. He was a small, dark-haired Highlander, as conversant with a fishing rod as with the Bible and a great favourite of all three brothers, whom he had known all their lives.

Several of their father's local friends were also waiting and they all went through for a late lunch. Afterwards Edward joined his brother in the library, where he was sorting a large pile of letters and telegrams spread over the long leather topped table in the centre of the room.

'I saw these before we went into lunch, but thought you should open them. There must be something here from Gerry in answer to your telegrams.' Edward separated the telegrams from the letters and pushed them towards Chadwyck. 'When did you send him the first one?'

'I told you,' said Chadwyck gently, 'when Doctor Carrigan

diagnosed pneumonia and the second when Father…' he couldn't bring himself to finish and tore open another telegram. They scanned the wording of each in silence, messages of love and sympathy that brought tears to Edward's eyes, but not one of them was from Gerald. They stood side by side in silence for a long moment and Chadwyck put his arm around his brother's shoulders.

'Come on Eddy, let's go for a walk. The funeral's not till five, Mother will be resting and as long as we're back in time to change, it'll be all right.'

At the appointed time the family assembled in front of the house and drove the short distance to the church, in silence. They could hear James Cameron, the Estate piper, playing in the churchyard. Edward sat next to his mother in the car and took her hand; nothing to say. The Reverend McLeod led them into the tiny church, overflowing with friends and estate workers. In single file, they walked to the front and sat in the family pew. The coffin stood before them on trestles draped in rush matting, interwoven with dozens of freshly cut flowers. The family wreathes, ordered in London by Chadwyck, lay across the top. The sound of the pipes faded and the Minister rose from his chair and addressed the congregation.

* * *

'Dearly beloved, we are gathered here today to join together these two people in Holy matrimony.' Gerald glanced at Betty out of the corner of his eye. She was very lovely in her pale ivory coloured, silk and lace wedding gown. As she stood tall beside him, he almost felt for her what she so obviously felt for him. She seemed enthralled by the service, but his fleeting sense of pride and affection passed as he recalled the events that had led up to the moment.

He thought of the telegram his father had sent him forbidding the marriage and his masterstroke in sending himself another telegram, supposedly signed by his father, congratulating him and agreeing to it all. He knew his father would be furious when he returned but, by then, it would be too late. Henry Wickham's expression had been priceless when Gerald had told him that he had his parents' consent and their blessing. He had shown Henry the telegram that had conveyed their deepest regrets at being unable to attend the wedding. He recalled Henry's ill-disguised triumph at what he must have considered to be a great coup for his daughter and family. Pathetic, misguided, social-climbing snob, with more money than he could count. After all, thought Gerald, the money was the only thing that did count. Henry had immediately opened a joint bank account, in Gerald and Betty's name, as a wedding present, with more than enough money to take care of all of his gambling debts and their immediate needs.

The wedding had been a hastily convened affair, almost indecently so. Some of the bride's friends and relations had thought most improperly of her but, as his parents were due to land in New York in less than a week, he had had no alternative. It would have been most inconvenient, not to say embarrassing, for the Wickhams, to cancel everything at the last moment and, from his point of view, most regrettable to have to return all those lavishly expensive presents Aware that he was being addressed, Gerald, with as much regard as he would give to saying 'aye' to a collegiate vote, acceded to his vows.

'I now pronounce you man and wife.' Betty turned towards him and, in anticipation of the vicar's next words, swept back the veil from her face.

* * *

'Ashes to ashes, dust to dust…'

After the internment, everyone went back to the house. Victoria, flanked by her two sons, sat beside the fire in the drawing room in a high-backed Queen Anne chair, as one after another estate workers and household staff paid their respects.

Two servants moved around the room offering whisky, small oatcakes and cheese. Hector MacPherson approached Victoria, who graciously inclined her head so that he might sit on the broad leather and brass fire surround. For a moment he said nothing but stared at the crackling fire and absent-mindedly straightened the tassels of his sporran.

'Does taking orders from a woman bother you, Hector. That's what you're thinking about, isn't it?'

'No, ma'am, not at all.' He sounded shocked and couldn't meet her eye. She laughed for the first time since her husband's death, a gentle musical sound, leaned forward and touched Hector's wrist with her fingertips.

'I'm sorry, Hector. I don't know what made me say that. As long as I can remember, you have managed Glen Lyon for my late husband and for his father before him and I hope you will continue to do so for us for many years to come.' She withdrew her hand. Hector looked up and cleared his throat.

'As you say ma'am, and thank you for it.' He paused for a moment. 'I was going to ask, ma'am, if you would allow the men to erect a memorial up here by the house, rather than at the church, so that they can see it when they go about their work. Its form and wording can be decided upon later but it would be nice, ma'am, if I can tell the men now, tell them that is, that it would be all right with you.'

She held her hands tightly together in her lap and thought of all the memorable summers, over the last twenty-five years, since Malcolm Meade had first brought her to Glen Lyon on their honeymoon. She remembered the inherent gentleness and kindness of all those who had looked after them, some long-since dead and she felt very humbled by the simplicity and sincerity of the Factor's request. There was so much she wanted to say about it all, but perhaps it would be best to let them say it for her. 'Yes, Hector, I would like that. Please tell them now and thank them all.'

* * *

The reception was held in a magnificent yellow and white striped marquee, erected in the garden behind the Wickhams' house on

Scott Circle. Neither the Wickhams nor their friends remarked on the absence of the bridegroom's family. Only those that knew Gerald's parents well asked after them and, with considerable charm and tact, he managed to explain their absence.

After the speeches he and Betty went up to change into their travelling clothes; when they came down they were met by a milling, boisterous crowd of guests to see them off. The same carriage and four faultlessly matched greys that had brought them from the church stood before the great portico.

Showered with rice and encouragement, they made their farewells to the Wickhams, her brother and two sisters and ran the gauntlet to the carriage. Betty's cabin trunks were already in the second carriage, drawn up behind. Where the streets had been paved, the heat had made the tar tacky, in places running in shiny black rivulets. It made Gerald think of blood and he laughed aloud at the bizarre association and the irony of his situation. 'What is it, darling? I am glad you are so happy. Me too.' she squeezed his hand, 'I've never been happier.'

'I was just thinking that blood is thicker than water, or at least it's supposed to be.'

'What's funny about that?'

'Nothing really, it's more tragic than funny, because had it been so we wouldn't be here now.'

'I don't understand, Gerry.' She let go of his hand and turned away. 'You're talking in riddles. I don't know why but I don't like what you have just said.' She was off balance, uncertain of her mood and when she glanced back at him she saw a supercilious smile playing about his sensuous lips. She grabbed his hand in both of hers. 'You are teasing me Gerry, please tell me why you laughed?'

'It was nothing really, my dear, I was just thinking about the moment when that unsightly friend of yours, Olive, fell flat on her face trying to catch your bouquet.' Betty laughed as she remembered the moment.

'You are so cruel, Gerry, she can't help her looks.'

'Well she certainly won't improve them by banging her face on the pavement.' Betty laughed again and raised his fingertips to her lips. Within minutes they had travelled the short distance to the Meades' house in Lafayette Square. Gerald opened the door to the carriage before it had stopped and leapt down on to the pavement.

'Please wait for me Gerald, I want to come with you.' Without waiting for an answer, she alighted as soon as the carriage had stopped and ran up the steps to join him. The massive front door swung open as they reached it and Wilks, the Meades' butler, stood back to let them in, his stooped shoulders held back as he spoke gently to both.

'Congratulations from us all, Mr Gerald and best wishes to you Miss Betty, for your future happiness.'

'Thank you, Wilks. We are a bit late so please have my trunks loaded into the second carriage immediately. I am just going upstairs to collect one or two things and will be down in a moment, Betty please wait here.' He glanced at the four equestrian pictures, as he went up the curving marble staircase, two steps at a time. They were by Stubbs and his father had bought them at a Christie's sale, when they had been in London for George V's coronation.

'I am sure the reception must have been splendid, Miss Betty. The staff and I were outside the church and saw you come out. You looked very beautiful, if I may say, and very happy.'

'Thank you, Wilks. I am afraid I was so involved with my husband I didn't see any of you. Please forgive me and thank you all for coming.'

'I wouldn't have missed it for anything, Miss Betty.' She walked over to the large Georgian gilt mirror that hung on the wall between the library and drawing room doors. It was flanked by two ornately carved eighteenth century Chinese chairs. She studied her reflection carefully, checking the make-up over her honey-coloured eyes, flawless creamy skin and full, determined mouth. Satisfied, she made a tiny adjustment to her hat and sat in one of the chairs. Wilks had withdrawn deferentially to the other side of the hall. After a discreet interval he picked up a silver salver from one of the tables and approached.

'Excuse me, Miss Betty, I have some letters and two telegrams here for Mr Gerald. The telegrams arrived at the beginning of the week but Mr Gerald was staying with Mr Carruthers at the time and he had instructed me most emphatically not to forward his mail or advise any visitors of his whereabouts. Would you care to take them for him now?'

'Oh no, thank you, Wilks, he won't want to see any boring old letters just as we are leaving on our honeymoon, and telegrams are usually bad news and that's the last thing we want on such a special day.'

'Well, if you say so, Miss Betty. I am sure you are right. I shall keep them until your return.'

'We will send you a postcard from London.'

A door slammed at the top of the house and she looked up to see Gerald running down the stairs, with a Gladstone bag in one hand and a cane in the other. A pretty housemaid leant over the banisters on the top landing, smoothing her uniform down over her hips.

'Let's go,' he said. 'We have less than half an hour to catch the train and, as Oliver kept telling me, if we miss it we'll miss the boat to England.'

CHAPTER 5

Chadwyck and Edward, up early the next morning, breakfasted on porridge, kippers, thick brown toast and homemade marmalade, then walked over to the stables where the horses were already saddled and waiting. Two Gordon setters followed at heel. The brothers had decided the night before to ride out over the estate and make plans for the future before they discussed it with their mother. Cook had made them each a pack lunch and stowed it in a canvas game bag, which Chadwyck slung over his shoulder. Edward's horse, a sixteen-hand Welsh cob, was playing up and pulling back from the groom, who held on grimly to its reins, and tried to soothe it with gentle words.

'Whoa there boy, steady, steady there, steady.' The cob's ears were pinned right back on his neck and he had a wicked glint in his eye. 'Jason's a bit frisky this morning, Master Edward. Too much oats I'd say, and not enough exercise. Shall I bring you one of the other horses instead?'

'No thanks, Tom.' Edward eyed the cob with some apprehension but would have rather be thrown than accept a quieter horse. 'He'll settle down after a bit. As you say, he just needs a bit of exercise.' Before his remaining courage evaporated, Edward slipped his left boot into the stirrup and swung up. He gathered the reins in his right hand, slid his whip into his left boot top, as he certainly wouldn't be needing it and nodded to Tom to let go. Jason skittered sideways, hooves clattering on the cobbles, bucked twice, almost unseating Edward, and plunged out of the yard, past Chadwyck on old Major. Chadwyck increased his pace and called out.

'Pull back on the bit and come up beside me Eddy, we'll go down along the river and when we get out in the open, you can let him go and we'll gallop up to the War Memorial. That should take some of the steam out of him.' The ground was soft along the bank, and Chadwyck increased the pace, and soon they were galloping across the low ground, past the great beech and chestnut wood to the War Memorial that stood high on the hill looking away down Glen Lyon, towards Loch Tay.

Once in the open, Jason tore away from Major and the wind whipped through Edward's hair and snatched at the ends of his scarf. He could feel his lips drawn back from his teeth and felt free and alive for the first time in days. He looked back over his shoulder. 'I'll race you to the War Memorial,' he yelled, but didn't catch Chadwyck's reply, lost in the thunder of hooves and the wind in his ears. He won the race easily, slowed to a walk as the dogs caught up and circled the War Memorial to let Jason cool down. His coat glistened with sweat over his shoulders and neck and ribbons of saliva still clung to his bit and bridle. Chadwyck joined Edward on his second lap, Major looking none the worse for wear.

'Who was in charge?' laughed Chadwyck, 'I've never seen Jason move so well. Were you frightened?'

'No, there wasn't time to be. All I could think of was staying on. I love riding because it always seems to make me do more than I think I can.'

'You ride well Eddy, for a nipper.' He didn't want his brother to hear the pride in his voice. 'Come on, let's go up on the moor and see if we can find any grouse. I thought we'd stop at MacKay's shieling, it'll take almost two hours to get there.'

They talked about Glen Lyon and their family as they rode on, side by side, and Edward asked about their grandfather, who had died two years before Edward was born. 'When did he leave Scotland and why?'

'The family lost most of their money.' Chadwyck patted Major's neck as they came over a ridge and rested. 'His oldest brother gambled it away and they had to sell Glen Lyon and their house in London. Our grandfather had no alternative but to come down from Oxford, before his final year, because there just wasn't enough money to keep him there.'

'So what did he do?'

'He left for America in 1853, at the age of twenty-two and started alone, from scratch. He made a fortune in coal which led him eventually into substantial shareholdings in various new railroad companies. After the Civil War he returned to Scotland and bought back Glen Lyon.' They turned their horses towards Mackay's shieling and rode on together.

'Do you remember what he looked like?' asked Edward. The two setters, working the ground out to their right, flushed a covey of young grouse which curled away, flying low to the ground, until it disappeared in the distant heat haze. 'How old was he when he died?'

'Sixty-two, his last trip to South Africa broke his health. He was a tall man, I suppose that's where we get our height from, certainly not from mama.' He smiled at Edward. 'He had a lot of white whiskers like Santa Claus, not really a beard as he shaved the front of his chin. I remember watching him in the morning, I was only about four or five, and he shaved with an old sgian dubh, which he always said was much sharper than any razor he had ever owned. He used to strop it on a leather just as father does … did.' He glanced across at Edward, who hadn't seemed to notice the slip. 'I suppose you are shaving every day now, Eddy? I remember when mama was so proud of you, when you first started.'

'I don't remember watching pater shave.' He had heard; there was a great sadness in his voice. They lapsed into silence and rode on to the shieling, deep in their own thoughts.

Cook had packed some cold Roe deer venison, pickles, cheese, a great chunk of freshly baked bread, apples and two bottles of beer for lunch and they sat in the heather, the vast panorama of Glen Lyon laid out before them. They could hear an old cock grouse calling and watched a pair of eagles soaring high.

'What do you want to do, Eddy, about the rest of your schooling? If you stayed on, it would only be for another year. You could do that easily, couldn't you? I think you should,' he added, 'It would be wrong to move, at this stage, to a school in America. It's really a question of what you want to do later in your life. Pater wanted you to go up to Oxford, as our grandfather did. You've done very well in your exams so far and you're a great cricketer so I'm sure they'll take you like a shot.'

'I suppose you're right, Chad, I would like to go to Oxford, but I think there will be a war before I ever get there. I know Gerry really disappointed pater, in not going to Yale and perhaps Oxford will make the long slog at school worthwhile.'

'Good.' Chadwyck poured more beer into their glasses. 'Mama will be pleased because pater was very set on it, determined, for tradition's sake, that one of us would be educated in the old country.' Edward threw a crust of bread to one of the dogs which lay at his feet, the other was fifty yards away, following a scent.

'Are you going to go on to Annapolis and make a career out of the navy?'

'I don't know now, I'll have to discuss it with mama, although she was never really involved in pater's business affairs, and probably hasn't got much idea of what's involved. I'm sure the trustees and directors can manage without me, for the moment.' He grinned at Edward.

'What's the feeling back home about the situation between Britain and Germany?' The Kaiser is always at odds with the King, like most families I suppose.' He added, and laughed. 'If there is a war, I hope it doesn't start too soon because I want to be in it. I want to fly, Chad.'

'I know where you got that idea from. Come on, Eddy, drink up, it's time to head for home.' They caught their horses, retightened their girths, called in the dogs and set off across the moor at a leisurely pace. They returned to the house by a different route that brought them down on the far side of the village, past the churchyard. They dismounted and stopped for a moment at the family crypt.

'What's Gerry doing now, Chad? Wasn't he going to work in pater's office?'

'That was the plan, originally, but you know Gerry can never stick to anything for very long.'

'Are we going to tell mama that Alice told you about the Wickhams and the telegram?'

'Yes, at dinner would be best. I don't think she will approve of Gerry marrying Betty, knowing how strongly pater was against it. He would never have let them marry before Gerry was settled in a job and I think mama will stick to that.'

'You don't suppose Gerry could have gone ahead and married Betty anyhow, do you? That would explain why he isn't here now.'

'Don't be silly, Eddy, even Gerry wouldn't be that stupid. Come on, let's get back to the house and see if we've been missed!'

'You go ahead,' said Edward, 'I'm going to pick some roses for Mama in the walled garden.'

Chadwyck found Alice and his mother, who seemed very subdued, in the drawing room having tea. A card table stood by the fireplace with an unfinished game of canasta; the two women must have had a rather strained day but, before he could say anything, Edward joined them flourishing a magnificent bunch of roses.

'How are you feeling, Mama? These are for you,' said Edward. 'We had a marvellous time. I rode Jason and he went like the wind.' His mother smiled at him gently and Alice took the roses out to the pantry.

'We've just started tea, would you like to join us or would you rather change first? Alice and I have been playing canasta and looking through the old game books. Do you remember when we were here in 1904, Chadwyck? It was the first year you shot with your father and his friends and the best year for grouse so far this century.'

'Yes mother, it was a wonderful summer. I think I'll change first before tea, come on Eddy.' They left the drawing room, crossed the hall and started up the great oak staircase, to their rooms.

'I don't think we should mention Gerry tonight, Chad, let's leave it until tomorrow.'

CHAPTER 6

The next morning Chadwyck and Edward found their mother with Alice in the walled garden. They were strolling through the huge Victorian greenhouse, running the length of the south-facing wall. Victoria, entirely in black, was looking at the rows of peach and nectarine trees trained against the wall. Their blossom had fallen, the withered flowers on the ground. The new fruit, just forming, would not ripen until late August. It was pleasantly warm in the greenhouse compared to the chill in the garden, and Chadwyck suggested a family conference. They pulled up canvas-backed chairs around a wooden table, and Alice excused herself when the three of them sat down. Edward looked at Chadwyck to open the conversation.

'Eddy and I had a long talk on the hill yesterday, about our future and we wanted to discuss it with you, Mama, as we feel that anything that we do now must be agreed between us all.' Victoria got up and, in a haphazard way, started to rearrange the small pots of cuttings that stood in rows on the staging. He was about to try another tack when, without turning round, Victoria spoke.

'What were you talking about, Chadwyck?' He paused for a moment to choose his words carefully. 'So what did you talk about?' She asked again and turned back to face him.

'Eddy must get back to school, Mama. It's a critical time for him, he starts his exams next week.' She didn't answer but walked across to the water butt to fill a small, long necked, copper watering can. She returned to the staging and started to water the cuttings.

'Do you want to go back to school now, Edward?' Is that what you miss most at the moment?'

'No, mama,' he blurted, 'of course not, but what Chad says is true. I do have exams next week and if I miss them, everything I've done this year will have been for nothing. If I lose a year now I'll never make it to Oxford in two. I promised that to Papa.'

'I'm sorry Edward. I know life must go on, I've been telling myself that every day since your father died. His loss to you, albeit in a different way, must be as great as it is to me. We must arrange for you to return to school, as soon as possible.' She put the watering can down on the staging, touched her throat and tugged nervously at her high lace collar. 'What shall you and I do, Chadwyck? Have you made plans for us, too?' Chadwyck was on his feet in an instant and, in two steps, was beside her.

'Mama, come and sit down.' She allowed herself to be led to one of the chairs. 'What would you like to do? Would you like to stay here for a while? I'll stay with you, of course.'

'No, I don't think I want to stay here now, even with you and Alice. Perhaps later in the year, when the heather blooms and the fruit is ripe on the trees, then we'll come back and be with Papa.'

'Shall I make arrangements for us to go back to Washington?' She turned her head away and closed her eyes.

'I couldn't possibly face Washington now, the family and all our friends. I don't want to be in that huge house and miss your father at every move.' She opened her eyes and looked at her sons. 'Let's go away, Chadwyck. Let's go on a trip together, just as we did when you graduated from Groton. Let's go to Springbokfontein.'

'But it will be almost midwinter there, Mama, and do you feel strong enough for the long voyage?'

'I know, but I do want to go.' Her mood had brightened perceptibly, even a touch of colour in her cheeks. She got up from her chair and picked up the watering can again. It was empty. She was smiling.

'Don't you want to go with me, Chad?' She teased. She hardly ever called him that and he responded immediately. He rose, went over and put his arms around her. He could smell a light daytime scent, lingering in her hair. He squeezed her very gently by the shoulders, bent and kissed her proffered cheek. She was still smiling and it reached her eyes.

'Of course, Mama, you know I'll go to the ends of the earth with you.'

'It jolly nearly is the ends of the earth,' chimed in Edward.

'No, Edward, it's the most beautiful place in the world and when you leave school next year, I'll take you there. Your grandfather bought it in the early eighties when he went out to South Africa to see about his gold mining interests. His brother, your great Uncle Walter, who was one of the directors of Sir Donald Currie's Castle Line, invited him into the venture. They bought quite a few claims together and in those days it was a very rough and tumble life, with nothing like the organisation that exists today. People were claim jumping all over the place, rather in the way they did during the Californian gold rush.'

'Will you show me the gold mines when you take me there, mama?' asked Edward.'

'The claims were all sold to Cecil Rhodes. Your grandfather bought Springbokfontein with the proceeds because he loved South Africa and wanted to have a reason to go back.'

'When would you like to go, Mama? I'll go down to the post office before lunch and send some telegrams.'

'We'll go as soon as it's possible, Chadwyck. Telegraph the Union Castle Line in London and book us on the first sailing for Cape Town. We'll go south with Edward tomorrow, on the night sleeper, and by then we should have an answer from the shipping company. I'm very proud of you, Eddy and so glad that you're going on in the way that Papa wanted.' She stretched up, kissed him on the edge of his mouth, and turned to Chadwyck. 'Please send the telegrams and book us into The Connaught for Wednesday night, Eddy and I are going for a walk in the herb garden.'

The next afternoon they travelled south and Edward went back to school. Alice returned to Ireland and Chadwyck and Victoria moved into adjoining suites at the Connaught. Chadwyck confirmed their reservations on the *Kenilworth Castle*, due to sail to South Africa on Saturday morning. He had arranged for them to go down to Southampton by train on Friday afternoon and spend the night in their staterooms to avoid the frantic rush of a last-minute departure. After a light lunch on Friday they left the Connaught and Chadwyck escorted Victoria to a cab waiting outside the hotel. Chadwyck had already arranged for their trunks to be sent to Waterloo and loaded on to the boat train.

As he reached for the door, Chadwyck thought he saw Gerald's face, in profile, in a passing cab. He looked again but could see only the back of a blonde women, sitting beside a man and then only the rear of the cab as it moved away along Carlos Place towards Berkeley Square. He and Edward had not discussed Gerald's absence or the telegram with their mother, and he wondered whether Edward was right after all, and his brother had married Betty Wickham. He dismissed the idea as soon as he thought of it and jumped into the cab beside his mother.

It had been a pleasant time in London together, lunching with friends and going out to the theatre. Victoria was more settled and looked forward to their trip to South Africa. Chadwyck's great uncle, Sir Walter Meade, a confirmed bachelor in his early seventies, who lived alone in The Albany, had been delighted by Chadwyck's visit and had spoken on his behalf, with some emphasis, to the reservations manager at the Union Castle office. Chadwyck knew that they would have the finest accommodation and treatment available on their voyage to South Africa.

'Mama, I forgot to tell you that Uncle Walter gave me a package, wrapped in oilskin and sealed with wax. He told me not to open it until we arrived at Springbokfontein. He was most mysterious and said it was to do with the time when grandfather and he were involved in some diamond mine.'

'I know what you're thinking dear, and I hate to disappoint you, but it won't be a bloodstained map with an X marking the buried treasure. Uncle Walter may, at times, give the impression of being a gentleman adventurer but, in fact, he is a pillar of society and probity itself.' Chadwyck laughed at his mother's response; he'd decided not to mention possibly seeing Gerald or what Alice had told him about the telegram.

'It's so good to see you laugh, mama,' he took her hand and squeezed it gently, 'are you tired? We're almost at the station. In two hours we'll be aboard the *Kenilworth Castle* and in good time for dinner.'

CHAPTER 7

All the painful memories of his father's death ran through Edward's mind as he again stood outside the Master's study, straightened his tie and ran his fingers through his hair. He knocked on the door.

'Come in.' The Master's muffled voice just reached him from behind the heavy door. He opened it, stepped inside and closed it quietly behind him.

'Good morning sir, I was told you wanted to see me.'

'Good morning Edward, come in and sit down there, please.' He waved to one of the two armchairs, in front of his desk. 'I won't be a moment, I've just got to finish this.' He went back to the letter he was writing and Edward sat down. He gazed around the large room until his eyes settled on a magnificent seascape, over the mantelpiece. The Master glanced up from his letter and noticed his attention.

'Are you interested in pictures, Edward?' Edward nodded and the Master continued. 'That was done by Turner, in 1838 and was given to the school by an old boy. It's my favourite picture in this room. The vibrant colours give me great pleasure, when little else does.' He smiled kindly at Edward and went back to his letter. 'I won't be a moment, walk around and look at the others, if you like.' Edward got up and crossed to the wall by the door and looked at another seascape by Van de Velde. He heard the Master walk across and stand behind him.

'That's Dutch, Edward, late 17th century.' He turned away to one of the windows and stood looking out over the immaculately kept lawns, to the cricket field. 'I wanted to know if you have settled in again, after your recent tragic experience. I have a very good idea how you feel, and I know how difficult it must be for you to concentrate on your work.' He turned back and looked at Edward for a moment. 'Please sit down, Edward,' he said, before returning to his desk. 'I went through the same thing as well, my father died when I was even younger than you. I was at school at the time, of course, and I found it very hard to get back into the routine again.' He sat down. 'Is there anything I can do for you Edward, to make it any easier?'

'I don't think so sir, but thank you very much for asking.'

'You start your exams next week don't you, Edward. Are you confident of good results?'

'In most of them sir, except Latin,' he added with a self-depreciating grin. 'I'm not very good at Latin.'

'That's Mr Robinson, isn't it?'

'Yes sir.'

'Not one of your favourite masters, Edward? Not what you would call my Turner, if you get my drift, my boy?' He smiled at him encouragingly but Edward remained silent. 'He told me last week that you hadn't done some lines he gave you and he thought that I should know about it. He contended that you should have told him, before leaving with your brother, that you would be unable to do them.' The Master was watching Edward carefully as he continued. 'I told him that that was unreasonable but he was adamant and his attitude towards you seemed,' he searched for a word before finally adding, '…extreme.'

They looked at each other for a moment and the Master knew that Edward would not say anything, unless asked a direct question. 'Has something happened between you and Mr Robinson that I should know about, Edward?' Edward still didn't say anything and, with a trace of impatience in his voice, the Master continued. 'I would rather know about it now, than be faced with something more serious later. If you feel that Mr Robinson is picking on you I want you to tell me.'

'No sir,' said Edward after a pause, 'I don't think he treats me any differently than he does most of the other boys.'

'Good, well that's that then.' The Master stood up again. 'I'm glad we've had our little chat Edward, cleared the air, so to speak.' Edward stood up at the same time and the Master put a hand on his shoulder and walked him to the door. They shook hands and just as Edward was about to leave the Master said. 'Don't forget Edward, I'm always here to help you.'

CHAPTER 8

Over a late lunch, in the dining car on the Paris-bound train from Calais, Gerald and Betty conducted a post-mortem on the first few days of their honeymoon. The highlight, they readily agreed, had been when the American Ambassador had introduced them to King George V on Gold Cup Day at Ascot. They had stayed at Claridge's in one of the three royal suites and Mr Piovanelli, the manager had gone to great trouble to make their stay in London as enjoyable as possible. They had dined in the restaurant on their first night and danced to the haunting music of the Tzigane orchestra. The earlier excitement of their Trans-Atlantic voyage had been eclipsed by the seemingly endless round of parties in London. On their last morning at Claridge's, having stayed out very late the night before at the Cafe Royal, they had overslept and nearly missed the boat-train to Dover.

Two and a half hours after leaving Calais, the train pulled into the Gare du Nord. They had reservations at the Ritz, and one of the hotel cars was waiting for them. Betty, who had never been to Paris, plied Gerald with endless questions as the chauffeur forced the car through frenetic traffic. Finally, they drove into the Place Vendome and pulled up in front of the magnificent mid Victorian facade of the famous hotel. Great banks of beautiful flowers bloomed on either side of the imposing entrance.

The doorman stepped forward, resplendent in blue and gold

livery, and helped Betty from the car. They were welcomed by M. Pierre Joubert, the manager, who addressed them in faultless English, with only the slightest trace of an accent.

'Welcome to Paris, Mr and Mrs Meade, we are indeed honoured to have you as our guests.' He led them towards the lifts. 'Perhaps you will permit me to show you your suite? I have given you four twenty-one and two which overlook the Place. It is your father's favourite, Mr Meade and your parents always have it when they stay with us.' They reached the magnificent gilded wrought iron lift. 'How are they, Mr Meade,' he continued, 'I trust they are both in good health?'

'Indeed Mr Joubert, and thank you for asking,' said Gerald. 'They have always spoken, with great fondness, of their times spent here and I am sure my wife and I will enjoy our visit just as much.' He was amused to find himself copying the manager's speech patterns. The lift rose sedately to the fourth floor and M. Joubert led the way to their suite.

'I hope you will be very comfortable,' he said as he opened the door for them, 'my only regret is that you are not staying longer.' He led them from one room to the other and although it was not as big as their suite at Claridge's, it was exquisitely furnished and had a magnificent view over the whole of the Place Vendome.

'It's lovely Mr Joubert,' said Betty, 'absolutely charming.' She took her hat off, dropped it on a sofa, walked over to one of the windows and looked down into the Place. 'I'm so excited to be here Gerry, thank you for making it possible, I've always wanted to come to Paris, ever since I was a little girl and, for some reason, we never did and last year we went to Rome instead.' The porters arrived with their luggage and then left with Mr Joubert, who reassured them, once again, of his unfailing attention and devotion.

'What a sweet man,' Betty said, when the door closed behind him, 'very elegant and so courteous. I really love it here and I can't wait to meet Paul Poiret tomorrow. He used to make mother's clothes, when he was with the House of Worth and now that he has set up on his own, he has become even more revolutionary and his colours are just fantastic.' She couldn't contain herself anymore and she ran over and impulsively threw her arms around Gerald's neck. 'What are we going to do tonight darling, or will it be like our first night in London?' she added kittenishly.

'No my dear, tonight we are definitely going out.' She made a face of exaggerated disappointment. 'The hotel has tickets for us, for the ballet.'

'Oh, wonderful, what is it?'

'Stravinsky's *Firebird*, performed by Diaghilev's Ballets Russe.' Betty clapped her hands like a small child and her eyes danced with excitement. 'And to top it all,' added Gerald, 'Stravinsky is conducting the orchestra himself.'

'Heavens, what shall I wear?' wailed Betty, 'I've got absolutely nothing that will do.'

Gerald raised an eyebrow and looked through the communicating door to the dressing room, where a hotel maid was unpacking one of Betty's four trunks. She followed his gaze and laughed guiltily. 'Well, darling, *almost* nothing, but by the time we leave Paris I hope to have changed all that. M. Poiret's establishment is not going to be the only House I'll patronise.'

'Am I expected to accompany you on these outings?

'Of course, my darling, that's half the fun. You'll be made to feel like a Pasha, probably meet some famous actress or other, and anyway, I want your approval. From now on I'm going to dress just to please you.'

'You'd please me far more if you'd un…' she placed a finger on his lips.

'I thought you said we were going to the ballet?' she teased, and to change the direction of his appetite, asked, 'Where are we going to dinner afterwards?'

'Maxim's, I thought. My father took me there two years ago, in one of his better moods,' he added reflectively, 'when he thought I was going to go on to Yale. We had a lot of fun, many of the theatre people go there after the show. Now, no more questions because we don't have much time for you to get ready.' He couldn't resist emphasising the 'you.' She grinned and kissed him lightly.

'I'll race you then and, by the way, I'm starving. Lunch was days ago.' She went through to where the maid was waiting for her and Gerald ordered champagne and smoked salmon on the house telephone.

The following morning Gerald accompanied Betty to M. Paul Poiret's Salon, where she and Poiret discussed endless designs and materials in his startlingly individualistic and flamboyant colours, while Gerald lay back on a chaise and sipped Perrier Jouet. His attention had been fixed on the parade of models who, at a nod from Poiret, changed from one outfit to another from behind an ornate Chinese lacquered screen that, from Gerald's point of view, was more of a suggestion than a reality.

After lunch they had gone to the House of Worth, where Betty had spent a further two hours while they sketched designs of more evening and day dresses for her approval. That night they attended a ball at the American Ambassador's residence given in honour of Henry Stimson, Secretary of State for War, on an unofficial visit to Paris. After a late breakfast the next day, Betty and Gerald walked from the hotel to Cartier's, in the Rue de la Paix, to collect her wedding present, which he had ordered from Washington. It came as a complete surprise to her and she was very excited.

'You make me feel terrible, Gerry, because I haven't given you anything. We were so caught up with all the presents that everyone else gave us, that I never actually thought of getting you one.'

'Think nothing of it, my dear,' he said as they walked around the Place Vendôme, in the bright sunlight, 'it's only a little trinket and, after all, you are the only present I want. Packaged in as many ways as you can devise and given to me, as often as you can.'

'Oh darling, you say the nicest things but I know you're only teasing me. What is it anyhow,' she asked impatiently, 'please tell me?'

'Wait and see,' and he laughed, 'where would the surprise be, if I told you now.' As soon as they had introduced themselves, the unctuous directeur de ventes disappeared into the back of the shop and reappeared moments later carrying a red leather box. He placed it with great care on a large square of black velvet, which lay on top of his desk.

'Madame,' he said, like a conjurer about to perform his greatest trick, 'we pride ourselves at Cartier's in our self-imposed and unsurpassed standard of excellence.' He toyed with the box with his finger tips and continued. 'In this case I can say, in all modesty, that we have excelled ourselves.' Betty glanced quickly at Gerald with a fleeting smile and back again at the box. 'It isn't often that we are given the opportunity to face the sort of challenge that was set us by Mr Meade,' he beamed at Gerald with an expression of immense self-satisfaction. 'It was just by extraordinary good fortune that one of my colleagues happened to be in the Far East at a pearl auction,' Pearls, thought Betty, how clever of Gerry to know they're my favourite, 'when we received your husband's esteemed order.'

He turned the box round slowly, so that when he opened it, the lid would not hide the contents from Betty. With enormous restraint, she managed to keep her hands clasped together in her lap, while the directeur continued in his infuriatingly pedantic manner. 'So he was able to buy a pair of pearls, the likes of which I have never seen in thirty years in the business and will probably never see again. You can imagine, Madame, our excitement and, might I add, the endless, agonising decisions that we had to make before choosing exactly the right diamonds to complement your pearls.' Diamonds, thought Betty, my second favourite, and if he doesn't open the box now, I'll scream. 'We decided on platinum for the setting and you have no idea how many stones we discarded before we were totally satisfied with the ones we finally used. Hundreds, Madame, literally hundreds before we admitted to ourselves, that we had achieved the correct balance. Perhaps, if I were to let you see them, their own outstanding quality, beauty and elegance would say far more than even I.'

Mesmerised, Betty watched as his fingers slowly and very carefully opened the lid of the box. She yelped in delight and her hands flew to her mouth. For a moment, she could say nothing and then when she did the words tumbled out so fast that she was totally incoherent. Her eyes brimmed with tears.

'Oh Gerry, they're beautiful. I have never, ever seen anything so beautiful.' She watched the directeur gently remove the most exquisite pair of pendant earrings. They were made with a perfectly matched pair of black pearls, each the size of a robin's egg and set with magnificent diamonds at the clasp and drop that flashed fire, even in the subdued light of their surroundings. She looked at them in awe, speechless and unable to touch them as they lay in front of her on the black velvet square. Eventually, with great care, as if they might suddenly disappear without a trace, she picked up one of them and, turning to the looking glass that faced her on the table, she held the earring to her left ear. As she moved her head, the light splintered on the diamonds. The fluorescent depth of the pearl was accentuated by the pale tones of her flawless skin. She laid the earring down on the velvet square beside the other one and looked at Gerald. There was nothing more she could say and he saw it all, as two glistening teardrops rolled gently down her cheeks.

'They are very handsome,' said Gerald to the directeur. 'As you can see my wife is very happy with them and we thank you for all the trouble that you have taken.' Anticipating him, Gerald added 'Kindly have them sent round to The Ritz Hotel and locked away in their safe and send the account to my father's office in Washington.' The directeur's smug, self satisfied expression slipped a fraction, before he recovered.

'But of course, Monsieur, it shall be as you say.' Gerald nodded curtly, rose, offered his arm to Betty and without a backward glance they swept out of Cartier's.

Once on the street Gerald burst out laughing. 'Did you see his face when I told him to send the bill to my father's office? Priceless, my dear, like your pearls.'

'Are you looking forward to seeing the Allens at lunch?'

'The who, dear? Oh yes, the Allens, those frightful people from New York that you met at the ball last night.'

'That's right. And they are not frightful, she's sweet.'

'You make her sound like a beverage, my dear.'

'I didn't hear that,' said Betty tetchily. 'Let's walk to Fouquet's and see some of the sights.' And some of the girls, thought Gerald, eyeing a pair who passed on the pavement. So much more ... what, he thought, was the word he wanted, 'willing' perhaps, than those in Washington.

After lunch they went to see M. Poiret and the House of Worth. As Betty pored over designs and drawings, Gerald sat back comfortably on a chaise, drinking champagne and watching a string of models parade before him and a select group of clients.

'Did you enjoy that, darling?' she asked as they walked to the next shop on her list. 'Such nice people, and everything will be ready in three days and,' she added, 'in good time for the Marseille boat to Mombasa. Did you see the agent to confirm all is well with our booking?'

'No, my dear, but I'll do it tomorrow morning while you are having your fittings. Then I'll go to Mr Vuitton's establishment to buy you another trunk, or perhaps two.' He was looking away at another girl and missed the spark of irritation in her eyes.

CHAPTER 9

'… Grampius mons, Meade? Wake up, Meade, and answer my question.'

'Yes sir.'

'*Yes sir* is not the answer I want.' Mr Robinson stood in his favourite pose in front of his desk, thumbs stuck into his waistcoat pockets, shoulders rolled forward and his eyes locked with Edward's across the intervening rows of desks.

'No sir.'

'*No sir*, is not the answer I want, either. You'd think that after your little holiday, Meade, you would be fresh, rested and raring to go instead of fumbling over the apparent complexities of Latin nomenclature.'

'Please would you repeat the question, sir.'

'No Meade, I will not. Sinclair what's the answer?'

'The Grampian mountains, sir, or,' he added uncertainly, 'the battle of that name, fought in AD 72, sir.' Mr Robinson removed his thumbs from his waistcoat pockets and rubbed his hands together as if drying them. He nodded at Jock and moved slowly towards Edward's desk.

'You, better than anyone Meade, should know the answer to that, I'm told you were near there, recently.' He hovered over Edward and added. 'I want a hundred lines on my desk before Chapel this

51

evening. 'I must pay attention at all times in class.' And mind, boy, no excuses this time. After all, two deaths in the family in one month would be a bit much.'

Edward said nothing. He didn't have to. Mr Robinson and anyone else watching, could see what he was thinking. Suddenly the bell rang and Mr Robinson turned away, wrapped his gown about him and stalked out of the room.

'The bastard, the rotten, stinking, bastard!' Edward was choking with anger. Jock got up from his desk and came over.

'Forget it Eddy, don't pay any attention to him. We've got nets in half an hour before the match, we'd better get down and change.'

'I can't forget it, Jock, I just can't. I don't understand his hate. He's sick and I should have told the Old Man when I had the opportunity.'

'And now I suppose you're going to tell him?' Jackson had slipped up behind them, unnoticed and he continued in his provocative way. 'I can see you sauntering into his study now, with all the influence that you think you have, and saying 'Fine afternoon, Master. Something you should know about Robinson. He has such a strange sense of humour, always digging the knife in and twisting the blade. Makes us chaps so miserable."

'Belt up Jackson and mind your own damn business.'

'Make me Meade, go on, make me.' Edward looked directly at him, his eyes were ice cold and deadly, his voice a whisper.

'Any time and any place.' Jock stepped quickly between them and took Edward's elbow.

'Come away Eddy, he's not worth it. We'll be late for nets.' Edward allowed Jock to lead him towards the door.

'You're a coward Meade, a bloody coward, you're running.' Jackson was almost shouting. Several boys around him stopped what they were doing and looked across, in expectation. Edward shook his arm free and walked slowly back until he stood in front of Jackson.

'Five minutes, Jackson, in the yard behind where they are building the new changing rooms, at the bottom of Anglesey Gardens and bring a Second. Then we'll see who's a coward.' Jackson stepped back and all the colour drained from his face.

'I say Meade,' he stuttered, 'just a second, no need to be so hasty.'

'Five minutes, coward.' Edward left the room. There was an excited buzz of conversation around Jackson and he realised that there was no way he could get out of the fight, without losing face.

The yard was jammed with boys, jostling and shoving for the best positions, forming a ring in the centre. Edward, dressed in rugby shorts and shirt and barefooted, stepped into the crowd with Jock behind him. The crowd roared in anticipation and approval and parted to let them into the centre.

'Eddy, put the gloves on please, you know what the Old Man will do if you don't.'

'No Jock, I'll wait and see if Jackson's wearing them and if he is, I will.' They felt a palpable excitement in the air and in the press of humanity about them.

'They're with you Eddy, every one of them, you can feel it.' Jock grinned lopsidedly at him. 'Jackson has had this coming for a long time.'

'That's right, Jock, we're all for Eddy,' a boy beside them called, 'and speak of the devil, here comes Jackson.' The crowd parted again to let him and his Second, Webb, through. Neither was carrying gloves.

'Chuck the gloves, Jock, and go and talk to Webb. Tell him there will be no rounds and no quarter given or expected. Whichever way it goes, we'll end it in one. If he agrees, tell him we start the moment you are behind me.'

The crowd fell silent as the Seconds talked, straining to hear. Jackson had turned his back on Edward and was talking to one of his toadies in the crowd. He shuffled nervously from one foot to another and ran his fingers through his blonde hair. He was two inches taller than Edward and at least twenty pounds heavier. His back was broad and well-muscled, as were his arms, but there was a noticeable slackness around his gut. He was also dressed in rugby shorts, shirt and was barefooted. Webb waved his arm in protest and argued with Jock. He pointed to Jackson but Edward couldn't hear what was said and didn't care. He stood there with his arms folded across his chest his legs spread wide apart and felt the cold of the newly laid cobbles through his feet. Webb shrugged and turned back to Jackson. The last comments and cries of encouragement from the crowd died. Jock walked back towards Edward.

'It's as you said, Eddy, and watch his left. He'll hook very low, I've seen him box before. You must keep your distance, avoid his head and shoulders and work on his stomach, he's soft there. Whatever you do, don't let him grapple. Good luck.' Edward dropped his arms and stepped forward to meet Jackson in the middle of the ring. Edward noticed a sheen of sweat on Jackson's brow, as they stood facing each other, and that his eyes were unsteady and flicked from face to face around the ring. Edward extended his two hands to shake and Jackson grabbed his wrists, dropped onto his back, pulling Edward off balance, and brought his right foot up into Edward's gut. With a sickening lurch he felt his feet leave the ground as Jackson swung him in a high arc over his head and brought him crashing down onto the cobbled courtyard behind him. Edward's shirt was torn from his back in shreds and he felt the sharp edge of a cobblestone cut deep into his shoulder. All the air was knocked out of his body. The crowd growled and surged in disapproval.

Edward forced himself up onto his knees and as he came to his feet he watched Jackson warily. He knew that he had to get up before Jackson took advantage of the situation. The sticky warm feel of blood running down his back cleared his brain. Jackson started towards him with a triumphant grin on his face, confident of an early kill. With a great effort Edward regained his feet and stepped towards Jackson, who stopped in surprise. Edward began to circle the perimeter of the ring, flexing his fingers and slapping his biceps to regain the feeling in his arm. Jackson followed him and swung a vicious left hook to Edward's head. He ducked and Jackson was thrown off balance. Edward side-stepped and kicked Jackson as hard as he could with the heel of his left foot on the side of Jackson's knee and heard the cartilage tear. Jackson went down with a howl of pain, rolled heavily on his side and staggered to his feet.

'Foul,' he yelled, as he swung round and appealed to the crowd.

'Fight by your own rules,' someone shouted back, 'you fouled first.' Edward could feel the strength return to his right arm. He raised his two fists in the classic defensive position and moved towards his opponent.

Jackson was confused and Edward could see the fear in his eyes. He retreated, limping away from Edward, until he stood with his back to the crowd. Edward hit him hard with a left to the head and followed with a right which Jackson took on the hard muscle of his shoulder and Edward remembered Jock's words. He side-stepped and feinted to draw Jackson from the edge of the ring. There was no point in trying to pin him to the 'ropes,' as he would have in a conventional ring, because the crowd just moved back and made way for them.

Jackson moved forward and threw another mighty swing with his left. Edward ducked below it and landed three hard jabs to the stomach, left, right and left again. He heard the breath forced out of Jackson's mouth and felt the sudden limpness in his body. Edward stepped back, just as Jackson's slack hands dropped onto his shoulders. Edward straightened and hit him hard with a right to the head, followed by a left cross to the mouth.

Jackson dropped to his knees and brought his hands up to his face. Blood, from his nose, oozed between his fingers and dripped onto the cobblestones. He stared at the blood blankly and Edward stepped back, breathing deeply. He watched Jackson for a moment and was about to ask him if he had had enough when Jackson lurched to his feet and swung his head from side to side, spattering blood over the spectators. He was making a deep growling sound in his throat, his co-ordination was gone and he shuffled, simian like, across the intervening space. He didn't bother with his guard, he just advanced inexorably towards Edward, who danced out of his way.

'Stand still, you bastard. Stand still and fight like a man.' His top lip had been split by Edward's left cross and one of his front teeth was hanging loose. He sucked on it with his bottom lip and spat it out at Edward's feet. A fine spray of blood and saliva bloomed on Edward's chest.

'Give up Jackson, I don't want to hurt you anymore.' The spectators voiced unanimous disapproval at the suggestion and Edward saw the bloodlust in their eyes. With extraordinary speed, Jackson suddenly swung a left hook at Edward and caught him high on the side of his head as he ducked, a fraction too late. He staggered back, feeling as if he'd been hit by the boom of a gybing sailboat. He shook his head from side to side to try and clear it and felt vomit in his throat. There was a terrible pain behind his eyes. Had he not ducked at the last moment Jackson's left would have connected with his chin and laid him out, unconscious.

Jackson, howling with pain, was hopping from one foot to the other and nursing his left hand with his right. Edward felt his legs going but knew that he had to stay on his feet or the fight would be given to Jackson. He moved back into the centre of the ring and, with an enormous effort, squared off in front of Jackson.

'Don't hit me, please don't hit me.' Jackson blubbered, through broken lips and dropped to his knees. Edward turned away in disgust and Webb stepped forward and helped Jackson to his feet. He then led him away and it was all over, Edward felt nothing. No triumph, no elation, nothing, just an emptiness, a feeling of shabbiness and regret, at the pointless, primitive futility of the whole affair.

'Well done Eddy, that'll bring him down a peg or two, and I think his hand is broken.' Jock raised a hand tentatively to Edward's forehead. 'More important, how's your head? I can see a lump on it already.'

'It hurts like hell and I feel sick. Let's get out of here.' Jock threw a coat over Edward's shoulders and steered him through the parting crowd, which roared with approval.

'Do you want to go up to the San to get your back seen to, you've got a deep cut and it's bleeding badly. You should probably have a couple of stitches put in it.'

'No, I want a shower and I'll fix it myself with your help. I've got some tape in the changing room. Jackson will be up there now telling some story about his broken hand, so if I turn up too you know what would happen to us both.'

'I'll tape it for you Eddy, but I don't think it will hold and it certainly won't if you're going to play cricket this afternoon.'

'No chance of that, I can feel my shoulder stiffening up already. None of this would have happened if it hadn't been for that bloody man Robinson.' He pulled the coat around his shoulders and, turning to Jock, said in measured tones, 'I will not let him, or anyone else, ever get to me like that again.' Jock looked at him in awe and was frightened by the intensity of his friend's emotions.

CHAPTER 10

After almost three weeks of great luxury and lavish hospitality, Victoria and Chadwyck arrived at Cape Town aboard the *Kenilworth Castle*. The voyage had been an exhilarating combination of rest and stimulation for Victoria. She no longer cried herself to sleep every night, even though she still felt the same dreadful emptiness when she thought of her husband, and then the pain that swept through her was almost tangible. At other times, with the help of new friends and every officer on board, her spirits rallied. Chadwyck had more time to himself for his own grief and instinctively they developed a system whereby one would help the other when in need.

After they had crossed the Tropic of Capricorn, the temperature fell, and when they came down the gangplank at Cape Town Victoria was swathed in a full-length sable coat with a high collar. They were met by Jan Viljoens, their manager at Springbokfontein and driven straight out to the estate. The colourful panorama of Cape Town, obscured by the long trail of dust, faded in the wake of their vehicle.

Springbokfontein, built in 1820, boasted one of the great vineyards in South Africa. It extended some ten thousand acres and stood ten miles southeast of Cape Town towards Arguillas. They had almost sixty acres under vines and the rest of the property was used for rearing horses to supply the constant demands of farmers up country. The original dwelling formed the nucleus of the present house, two storeys with a colonnaded portico running the full width. Two ancillary single-storey wings ran back from each end, forming a courtyard with a charming stone fountain. Beyond and behind stood various storerooms and staff quarters.

Victoria and Chadwyck ate in the long panelled dining room, warmed by a crackling log fire in the great stone hearth, and after coffee Victoria retired. Chadwyck went to the library and stood looking for a long moment, while he sipped his port, at Uncle Walter's package. He chose a small Zulu dagger from the mantelpiece, cut the string and broke the wax seals. Inside he found an oilskin pouch that contained a thick sheaf of old documents and two faded sepia photographs. One was of his grandfather and Uncle Walter standing beneath a massive tree, with a very distinctive twin-headed kopje towering some five hundred feet above the plain in the background. On the back, in faded black ink, was the name 'Groot's Farm' and the date 1891.

The other photograph was of a group of men on horseback, standing around an incongruously smart coach to which were harnessed four white mules. Chadwyck easily recognised his great uncle and grandfather standing to the right of the group. On the back, in the same hand, was written: 'Mr Rhodes and entourage,' with the date 1890.

With mounting excitement, Chadwyck spread the documents out on the table. He picked up the first and taking his glass went back to his chair to study the document carefully. It was a sheaf of six pages, pinned with a rusty clip. They were a merchant's invoice, written in a bold copper plate, for a wide range of equipment: a Dutch wagon, camping provisions, clothing, dry food stuffs and many other items, to the amount of £41.17.4d.

He got up, laid the documents back on the table with the others, threw a log on the fire and went over and poured himself another glass of port, before returning to the table to look at the two remaining documents. One was a well-worn black leather notebook and the other appeared to be a title deed. He took them both back to his chair and stretched his legs out to the fire. He put his glass and the notebook on the low table beside him and opened the other document. It was written in Afrikaans and, in frustration, Chadwyck realised he'd have to ask someone to translate it for him. It was the title deeds of a farm of one thousand acres, and there was an indistinct plan attached to the back. He picked up the black leather notebook. He compared the writing with the signatures on the deed – it was obviously written by his grandfather too.

It started as a diary, with abbreviated entries. After a few pages Chadwyck came to a passage that reflected his grandfather's feelings about the appalling conditions in which he and his brother were living. He complained in turn of the heat and the flies and later in the year of the blessed rain, which soon turned his life into a muddy nightmare and put an end to long unproductive days searching the ground systematically and without success.

This was followed by references to his failing health and then came a section of dates, one following the other, in chronological order, with cryptic notes and numbers haphazardly spread across the page. Small drawings of directional arrows with compass bearings and, on at least three occasions, a childlike sketch of the twin-headed kopje in the old photograph. There were many references to his brother being away on business, to either Cape Town or Kimberley, to meet Cecil Rhodes, and of the increasing demands Rhodes made on his time. In several places he referred to the long solitary nights with the dismal prospect of nothing better to look forward to than another day's fruitless searching. Chadwyck turned the pages slowly and became depressed by the obvious futility of the project. Why did the two of them continue, he asked himself, what were they trying to find. He turned another page and started to read it, almost aloud.

'Walter due back in the next few days and I still haven't found anything more than that first stone. I am now convinced that it was a fluke. Will welcome Walter's return as he has so much more confidence than I do. He really believes that there is a pipe here and that we will find it. I sincerely hope he has learnt something new from

Rhodes's mining engineers, without giving away the reasons for his interest. I wonder what he tells Rhodes when he absents himself to join me here, I'm sure they'll follow him one day, just to find out. Walter is convinced that it was a wise move to buy this farm, and at times I agree with him, and at others I feel it was a waste of money. Thank God Malcolm is making such a success of our business interests in America and no longer needs my help. I miss his company but I know he is far too busy and practical to spend time on a wild goose chase like this.

I've lost Maud's last letter, which is a terrible blow, as I'm never so happy as when re-reading her news about life at home with our children. Washington must be beautiful just now, with the blossom on the cherry trees. Tomorrow I'm going to go out and find that peg that Walter knocked into the ground, beyond the big tree, measure out the distances and start digging. I'm tired and my legs still hurt a great deal.'

Chadwyck closed the book, rested it on his knee and stared at the fire for a long time. Finally he put the documents back in their oilskin pouch and got up slowly. He went over to the far wall which was lined from floor to ceiling with books, removed a large leather-bound volume at random and slipped the pouch behind it.

The next morning, coming down to breakfast, he found his mother already up and organising the household. She looked well rested and something of her old self was there in the way she took control. For the rest of that week, he and Jan Viljoens spent a lot of their time on the estate. Jan showed him everything about the vineyard, from new plantings right through the whole fermenting process to labelling and casing the bottles.

Chadwyck was fascinated, so involved that the depressing words of his grandfather's diary finally slipped into the back of his mind. At lunch time he would go back to the house to be with his mother and on several occasions she managed, cold as it was, to join him for a picnic on one of the vineyard terraces overlooking the sea. In the evenings they sat in front of the library fire for hours and talked about his Grandfather and Springbokfontein and eventually, with increasing ease, his father.

'Your father loved South Africa and if he had not had so many business interests in Washington and London he would have spent a lot more time here.' She looked back to the fire so that Chadwyck could not see the tears in her eyes.

'But he did come here, mama, I remember when he brought me.'

'Oh yes, as often as he could, but it was never for very long.' She got up from beside the fire, walked across to the bookshelves and stood, quite by chance, looking at the book behind which Chadwyck had left the oilskin pouch. He wondered whether to tell her about it but decided that it would only distress her unnecessarily. She walked slowly along the shelves, gently touching the spines.

'Your father and I were very happy here. I want you to think favourably of Springbokfontein when you get back to Washington and take on the responsibility of your father's affairs.' He went over and stood beside his mother and he put his arms gently around her shoulders.

'I will Mama, it has come to mean almost as much to me, as it does to you.'

One morning at breakfast, towards the end of the following week, Chadwyck broached the subject of great uncle Walter's package and his grandfather's diary. 'But surely, Chadwyck, you don't want to go to that dusty, Godforsaken place to see some miserable farm of no commercial value. I can't imagine what your great uncle Walter was thinking about when he gave you that diary, knowing that the failure of it all greatly contributed to your grandfather's death.

'I want to go, Mama,' he said gently, 'because I know that if I don't, I'll always regret it.' Before she could say anything he leant across the breakfast table and patted her hand. 'You'll be fine here,' he continued, 'all your old friends now know you're back and there's been a constant stream of visitors. I'll be back in a week and with a bit of luck might find out why my grandfather and uncle Walter spent so much time and effort on the place. Perhaps I'll have a better understanding of

his diary and feel less despondent about the apparent futility of it all.'
She looked at him with great love and understanding and could see
the determination in his eyes, so like his father's, and she knew that
nothing she could say would change his mind.

'Take care, Chadwyck and come back soon.'

CHAPTER 11

Very early the following Monday morning Jan Viljoens drove Chadwyck to the station in Cape Town to catch the Kimberley train. He would have to change at De Aar Junction and again at Naauw Poort Junction, then north to Springfontein. From there another change for Jagersfontein, to stay for a day or so for a thorough search of records relating to the farm and to his documents.

A long and uncomfortable journey of more than six hundred miles, with many stops for coal and water at the various junctions. Almost twenty-four hours later, tired, dirty and in far from the best of spirits, he arrived. It was very dark, the moon had set and the sun would not be up for at least another hour. Picking up his grip in one hand and draping his heavy overcoat over his shoulders he walked stiffly to the Station Hotel. The streets lay deserted, bar a few stray dogs, who scattered on his approach. A sleepy-eyed night porter finally appeared and arranged a room.

He walked slowly up a single flight of stairs to his room. He had sent the night porter off to organise hot water for a bath. Two boys staggered in carrying large copper pots of steaming water, which they emptied into the hip bath in one comer. He undressed and slipped into the hot water, feeling tension soaking away from tired and cramped muscles. Ten minutes later, as the water began to cool, he soaped himself thoroughly, washing the caked dust from his body, dried himself with a threadbare hotel towel and slipped on a long flannel night-shirt before getting into bed.

He slept for six hours and was woken at noon by somebody banging saucepan lids in the kitchen courtyard beneath. Half an hour later, dressed and having pocketed his grandfather's diary, he went downstairs, fractious and hungry. Easing his way through a group of farmers in the lobby he crossed the square in search of a restaurant. The first was very basic and the second no more than a bar. On the point of asking directions, he came to the corner of the square and saw an attractive place a few yards down a side street.

Shown to a table near a window, he scanned the menu and wine list. He ordered ribs and a baked potato and a half carafe of Cape wine. He was very surprised to see Springbokfontein wine on the list but decided against it on his own. While he waited for the ribs he pulled out the diary and turned to the page where his grandfather had written about supplies and what he had bought when he and his uncle first started. A long shot, but perhaps there was somebody still working there who might remember them and perhaps they could help him find a wagon and horse to rent and some camping gear. Failing that he would go to the Land Registry and ask there where to get a map and directions to Groot's Farm.

He finished lunch, thanked the waitress and took his bill to the cash desk by the door. A man in his early twenties, dressed in riding breeches, boots and a leather jacket, came into the restaurant and picked up a newspaper on the cashier's desk. Chadwyck pocketed his change, doffed his hat and addressed him.

'Do you happen to know where I might find the premises of Cathcart and Company?' The man looked at Chadwyck's tailored English clothes and handmade boots.

'You're obviously new to these parts?'

'Obviously, otherwise I would not be asking.' Chadwyck noticed that the man's eyes narrowed slightly and that he had his full attention.

'Touché, forgive my impertinence. My name is James Flynn, at your service,' and he swept off his hat in an exaggerated, cavalier manner.

'Chadwyck Meade.' They shook hands. He was slightly taller than Chadwyck and, by his grip, a lot stronger.

'What can I do for you? You've obviously had lunch but would you care to join me?'

'Yes indeed and perhaps you will share a bottle of wine with me?' They went back to Chadwyck's table, which the waitress had already cleared and Chadwyck ordered a bottle of wine from his own vineyard. Without looking at the menu, James ordered lunch from the waitress, who obviously knew him well.

'I eat here whenever I come into town which, at the moment, is only about twice a month as we're very busy at the farm right now.'

'Cattle or sheep?' asked Chadwyck as he sipped at his wine, not quite cool enough.

'Cattle and you can't be such a stranger if you know that we don't mix them up here. Where are you from?' Chadwyck thought for a moment before answering and wondered how guarded he should be about his background.

'I just came up on the train yesterday from Cape Town. My mother and I are staying with friends there for a month or so and I wanted to have a look at the country around here. A great uncle of mine has a small farm about twenty miles north west of here.'

'Our farm is that way too.'

'He bought it about twenty-five years ago. It's known as Groot's Farm. I thought I might go out and have a look at it tomorrow.'

'That marches with us to the north of our place and it belongs to a couple of Englishmen that left when I was a baby. How were you thinking of getting out there?' The waitress returned with his order.

'I was going to rent a horse and cart tomorrow and a pack mule and take supplies with me for a couple of days.'

'That is a bit risky, if you don't know the country. Why not come out to our place this evening and spend the night with us? I'll point you in the right direction in the morning.'

'That's very handsome of you, but I don't want to be any trouble. Have you been up here long? Chadwyck refilled their glasses.

'The family has been here for ages.' He sipped his wine and glanced at the bottle. 'Not bad wine this, you picked a good one.'

'I've had it before, it's an old favourite. How about you?'

'I've been back just over a year, now. Came back after I finished at Stellenbosch.'

'The university at Cape Town?'

'Yes that's right. It was my grandfather who came here first and bought the place just before they found diamonds here in Jagersfontein. We never found any diamonds though. Not on our patch.' He continued, between mouthfuls, as Chadwyck sipped his wine and watched him closely. 'Nobody did, there were claims all over the place but not a thing. But, when it was all over, the others had nothing so we were lucky to be farming cattle. My grandfather bought up all the farms around us and we now have about twenty thousand acres here.' He continued to eat as he talked and Chadwyck filled their glasses again.

'Jagersfontein has about 3,000 miners now, and over the last thirty years their predecessors dug the hole. It's massive; Kimberley has one too about the same size, about forty acres and almost seven hundred feet deep. They are still mining it but now they're about to start underground with a vertical shaft and horizontal drifts.'

'I'd like to see it. I can go and find it while you're picking up supplies.'

'You can hardly miss it. The original miners in the mid-seventies came through here from Port Elizabeth on their way to Kimberley but they didn't find much and had problems with lack of water and the supply of food and equipment.'

'Who did the actual digging and with what.'

'A very diverse cross-section of humanity, both white and the blacks who were made up mostly of the Sotho, but the trouble with them was that they all returned to their kraals for crop planting and harvest. They used picks and shovels and dynamite, and towards the end of the last century they had steam shovels and locomotives.'

'You said they didn't find much?'

'In the seventies and eighties, but by the early nineties the two main companies, United and New Jagersfontein, had amalgamated and within three or four years they had dug up the two biggest diamonds ever found, anywhere. It wasn't until 1905 that the Cullinan was found at Kimberley, twice the size of the other two put together. Farming is hard work but there's good money in it. I hope you will come back this evening; you'd enjoy meeting my people and seeing what it's like. Tomorrow you can go on and see your farm and I will come with you, if I can get away.'

'I accept,' said Chadwyck as he finished his wine, 'and you will pick up your stuff from Cathcart and Co.?' Chadwyck couldn't resist and was amused by James's reaction.

'You asked me that at the door. How the hell did you know about Cathcart if you've only just arrived? The place isn't even called that anymore. It was bought up by Simpson years ago, when I was a boy.'

'My uncle and grandfather bought some stuff there when they first came out.'

'What sort of stuff?' asked James as he set down his knife and fork and wiped his mouth with a napkin. There was a very keen interest in his eye.

'Oh, just things, provisions, I don't remember now. What time do you want to leave?'

'About four. I've got a few more things to do in town but I should be ready by then.'

'Fine. I'm staying at the Station Hotel, could you collect me there when you're ready?' The two men got up from the table, Chadwyck picked up the bill and paid it on their way out. They shook hands on the street.

'Which way do I go to the mine?'

'Straight across the square past the Reform Church and keep going, less than ten minutes from here and I'll see you back at the hotel. Thanks for lunch.'

'My pleasure, you're buying dinner.' They both laughed.

* * *

There was a pair of piebald horses hitched to a wagon, which was covered with a brown tarpaulin and tied to a rail in front of the hotel. He found James inside the lobby stretched out in front of the fireplace, boots on the fender, reading a newspaper.

'I'll get my bag and be down in a couple of minutes.'

'How did it go?'

'I'll tell you about it on the way out.'

'Right, I'll wait for you by the wagon.' He folded the newspaper, dropped it on the chair and headed for the front door while Chadwyck climbed the stairs to his room. Two minutes later, he came down with his grip and stopped by the desk.

'I'll be back in two days and I'll be keeping my room. Take this on account and please give me a receipt.' He dropped a sovereign on the desk and accepted the clerk's receipt.

* * *

The wagon edged slowly through the streets, Chadwyck sitting beside James on the sprung seat. In fifteen minutes they had cleared the last of the houses and a long, straight, dusty road lay ahead to the north. To their left, the sun was low in the sky.

'Should be there before dark,' said James, cracking the whip over the horse's head to get a bit more speed.

'Tell me more about the mine. Did you find anyone to show you around?

'Only Red, whom I've already mentioned, also known as Henry Fielding, to give him his due. An interesting man with Scottish antecedents, so we had some common ground; he had just arrived from Kimberley, where he worked for the last three years.'

'Trying to get a job here, I suppose. How old is he?'

'Late thirties, almost my height, a lot heavier, but light on his feet. He wanted to be taken on at foreman level, which he said was not going to be easy but added that he didn't like taking no for an answer.'

'Why did he leave Kimberley?'

'I asked that and he told me that the mine he worked for played out and he was laid off.'

'Did you believe him?'

'Yes. We walked the perimeter, it's all fenced in and then we went back to his digs for a drink in the local bar because I wanted to pick his brain about the rudiments of open-cast mining.'

'What did you learn?'

'About him or mining?'

'Both.'

'It's hard dispiriting work with no certainty of success, but he has seen enough of the upside to want to go on with it. He told me that he specialised in controlled blasting, which I suppose saves a lot of manual labour and cost.'

'How did you leave it with him?'

'I told him I'd be in touch when I got back to town.'

'Why?'

'I like him and perhaps I might need him.'

'Did you tell him that?'

'No.'

'Foreman of the Groot Farm Diamond Mine!' said James, and roared with laughter.

'One never knows how things will work out, and the more options one has the easier it is to pull it together.'

'I'm sorry Chad, I'm a romantic and always subscribe to the happy ending. You're quite right, let's be positive. We *are* going to find diamonds on Groot's Farm.'

Chadwyck looked at him out of the corner of his eye but James was looking straight ahead. Chadwyck was glad he had said 'we.'

The sun had now dropped behind the hills and the long shadows thrown across the plain by the steep sided kopjes dissolved into dark smudges. A herd of blesbock, interspersed with zebra, grazed half a mile away. They had caught their wind and one or two of the herd were watching them carefully.

'I haven't told you the full story James, I'm not hiding anything, there just didn't seem time. My grandfather brought Groot's Farm on the advice of my great uncle Walter who was working for Rhodes at the time, firmly convinced they would find diamonds.'

'Did they? We never did at Rietfontein but that's not unusual, as you can find them in one place and there will be no sign of them a mile or two away.'

'As far as I know they found only one stone at the very beginning, but there's something about his diary that makes me think they knew where to find diamonds, and for all I know they did, that's why I came up here to have a look for myself.'

James nodded and cracked the whip. Far away in the distance Chadwyck could see, in the last of the light, the outline of farm buildings by the Riet river. They passed a group of giraffes clustered around a low acacia tree, necks stretched to the limit reaching for succulent shoots.

'Here we are,' said James as they finally approached two rough stone gateposts standing like sentinels. Half a mile on they pulled up in front of a large sprawling house, solidly built of unbaked bricks and rough-hewn timbers with a deep veranda running along the front. The roof was heavily thatched in sun-bleached reed.

A pack of hunting dogs came charging out of a kennel, from the left of the house, to greet them. A short distance away, scattered in haphazard fashion, stood a dozen or so shacks that were servants' quarters and storerooms. A black boy of about fifteen, naked except for a tattered pair of shorts, ran forward and took the horse's head.

'Evenin' Baasie.' He called in a singsong voice, his eyes rolling.

'Lo Sesi! Feed and water the horses and unload the goods and ask Caachy to help you.' He turned to Chadwyck. 'Welcome to Rietfontein. Come on in and meet the family.' Chadwyck jumped down, grabbed his overnight bag and walked past Sesi who grinned at him shyly. 'Leave the bag on the veranda, Chad, they'll take it to your room and unpack.' The front door swung open and warm, bright lamp-light flooded out, silhouetting a huge man standing on the veranda, towering above Chadwyck as he climbed the steps.

'Well hello James, who have we here?'

'This is Chadwyck Meade, Father, a newfound friend and an erstwhile neighbour.'

'Meade, my god, not Walter's boy? Don't tell me the old buzzard finally married and produced you?' He thrust out his hand and gripped Chadwyck's, lifting him off his feet onto the veranda as he clapped his other hand around his shoulder. 'Welcome to Rietfontein. Chadwyck. Damn me, it's good to see a Meade again. Come on in and I'll find us some whisky. Dinner will be ready soon.' He pushed Chadwyck ahead, through the doorway into a high-ceilinged room, which ran the full width of the house and was the best part of forty feet in length. Six doors led off it and, in the middle of the far wall, was a massive stone fireplace in which a log fire crackled merrily. The floor was of broad, hand hewn and pegged sandalwood planks, partially covered with a variety of zebra and kudu skins.

Deep, comfortable leather chairs were scattered around the fire and a fifteen-foot long stinkwood table, large enough for twenty to sit in comfort, stood at the far end of the room. The walls were hung with dozens of mounted trophies. Two elephant tusks, more than a hundred pounds apiece, stood on either side of the fireplace and the biggest buffalo head that Chadwyck had ever seen hung over the mantelpiece.

'Jenny, where are you? Come and meet Chadwyck, Walter Meade's pup.' Chadwyck looked to James for help, without success. Just as Johnny spoke a door that led out of the back of the house opened and his wife walked into the room. Her trim figure, clad in buckskin riding breeches, leather calf-length boots, a plain white shirt and an embroidered waistcoat, vibrated with boundless energy. A great mass of raven black hair cascaded from beneath a broad-brimmed slouch hat, as she removed it along with her leather gloves, which she used to slap the fine powdery dust from her legs. As she came closer, Chadwyck noticed her exquisite bone structure and extraordinary dark green eyes. She extended her hand and gripped Chadwyck's firmly.

'How do you do, Chadwyck.' He was taken aback by her well-modulated English accent, in sharp contrast to her husband's exuberant manner. 'How's your father, we've never met but I've heard a great deal about him from Johnny.'

'How do you do, Mrs Flynn, I…'

'Oh, please call me Jenny, we're very informal here.'

'Thank you. I was about to say there's been a misunderstanding. Mr Flynn…'

'Johnny,' she smiled.

'Johnny, of course, Johnny assumed that I was Walter's son, but actually he is my great uncle and he never married.' Before she could answer, Johnny cut in.

'The old dog, I knew he'd always escape that fate, although I'll never understand how he did it because he was one of the most attractive men you'd ever meet. I would have bet anything that some woman would have got him in the end.'

'Hush, Johnny and let Chadwyck continue.' Johnny grinned fondly at her and waved him on. Chadwyck paused and then changed the subject.

'James and I met by chance over lunch today. I appreciate his kindness in asking me out here.' He faltered, he sounded very stilted to himself. Jenny took his arm and led him towards one of the doors on the other side of the room.

'Come with me Chadwyck, I'll show you to your room. I'll get one of the boys to fill you a bath. Take your time, relax and change, and we'll have dinner in about an hour.'

'But Jenny, he never did tell us who his father is.' Chadwyck turned at the door and looked across the room to where Johnny lay sprawled back in one of the large leather armchairs by the fire. 'If Walter never married, then you must be Duncan's grandson because you're too young to be his son. That would make his son your father, is that right?'

'Yes sir.'

'For God's sake don't call me sir, Chad. So how is he? Malcolm, that's his name isn't it, I remember meeting him in Johannesburg with your grandfather back in the early nineties.'

'He died in Ireland, Johnny, almost three months ago.'

'Oh, damn it boy, I am sorry. Trust me to put my foot in it again. I'll bring you through some whisky while you have your bath.' Chadwyck saw compassion in Jenny's eyes, before she turned and led him from the room.

By the time Chadwyck had bathed and dressed, the rest of the Flynn family had assembled. They were sitting around the fire, and two of James' brothers, as like as two peas in a pod, were locked in combat over a chessboard, struggling with a game that had been going on for days. The great stinkwood table was laid for eight with two splendid silver candlesticks, fine china and glassware. James got up from where he was talking to his father to introduce Chadwyck to the rest of the family.

'I hope you're ready for this, you get the whole lot in one go.' He led Chadwyck over to the fire and stopped in front of a very beautiful dark-haired girl, who looked up from her book. Her eyes were almost the same colour as her mother's although the green was not quite so deep and Chadwyck noticed honey coloured flecks around the irises. Her dark hair was gathered at the nape of her neck and was rich and lustrous.

She was wearing a long white cotton and lace dress. 'This is Big Sis as opposed to Little Sis, otherwise known as Adelaide.' Chad leant forward and shook hands.

'It's always good to meet someone from the outside world, I so envy anyone who has been to England.' To Chadwyck's surprise her voice was exactly like her mother's.

'Pay no heed, Chad, that's all she can think of, how to get out of here.' Chadwyck was startled to see her stick her tongue out at her brother, it seemed so incongruous.

'You see what I mean, she's as bad as her baby sister.' James leant quickly forward and kissed her on her cheek. 'Pax, Sis, I love you.' He led Chadwyck across to the other side of the room. 'Here we have my two younger brothers, Frederick, who's seventeen and sometimes answers to Fred, if he answers to anything, and Hugh, who is also seventeen, but the younger of the two and never answers at all. Frankly, I don't know how they can stand the sight of each other, it must be like looking into a mirror all the time.

'You're not nearly as funny as you think you are, James.' Hugh got up from the table and extended his hand. 'How do you do Chad, welcome to Rietfontein.' Fred remained where he was and waved casually at Chadwyck. They were absolutely identical and Chadwyck searched their faces to find some distinguishing marks.

'Can you tell the difference between them Chad, I keep threatening to break one of their noses so we can tell them apart, but I never seem to get around to it.' He playfully cuffed Hugh on the shoulder. 'Come on, dinner's ready, let's go and eat and, by the way, has anyone seen Sophie?' A door flew open at the far side of the room and slammed back against the wall.

'Sorry I'm late everyone, Belle made an awful mess of my bloody plaits and I had to do it all again myself.'

'Don't talk like that Sophie, I've told you before.'

'Yes Mummy.'

'Come over here and say hello to Chadwyck.'

'Ooh, a man.'

'And behave yourself, child.'

'Yes Mummy, what's for dinner?' She looked at Chadwyck, speculatively, as if there was some connection. She then promptly bobbed him a short curtsey, smiled enchantingly and held out her hand. 'I'm Sophie, how do you do?' Chadwyck took her hand and smiled down at her. She was fair-haired, like James and her father, with long plaits. She had a light complexion and a dusting of freckles on the bridge of her nose and cheekbones. Her eyes were blue and she wore a three-quarter length faded denim dress, of the same colour.

'How do you do Sophie, my name is Chad.' She smiled back at him, broke away and ran to her mother.

'Can I sit next to him, Mummy, please? He's so handsome.'

'I don't know darling, wait and see. We'll put your father here at the end of the table, I'll sit at the other end. Chadwyck you sit here on my right and Adelaide I'll put you on his other side. The rest of you sit where you normally do.' Johnny said a short grace and Jenny clapped her hands twice as they sat down. The door, which led through to the kitchen quarters, opened and two servants came in with soup plates and a large tureen.

'If you don't need me here Father, Chad and I could go out to Groot's Farm tomorrow morning to show him around.'

'That's a good idea, James, and take Caachy with you.'

'May I go as well, Papa?

'No, my girl, you'll stay here. Anyway the Schwartz children are being brought over to play with you tomorrow.'

'But that's not fair, Papa, they're awful, I never have any fun.' The servants removed the soup bowls and went back to the kitchen. James got up and walked round the table filling everyone's glass with wine, with the exception of Sophie's. She was drinking lemonade. The next course was a huge roast of beef and Johnny carved it from the head of the table while the two maids served the vegetables.

'I think we'll take one of the small wagons tomorrow, Father, and some camping gear and a couple of spare horses. We can do some shooting while we're out there and stay overnight. We might even be able to find the pride that has been helping themselves to our cattle and give Chad a crack at bagging his first lion.'

'That's fine James, I can spare you for one day.' While Johnny continued to give James advice on the proposed trip, Jenny turned to Chadwyck.

'Is this your first trip to South Africa, Chad?'

'No, I came here three years ago with my father, just before going up to Harvard. He wanted to show me Springbokfontein and give me some idea of the extent of his business interests. My parents were always very happy there and I suppose that's why mother wanted to come back now.'

'Is she alone now or did one of your brothers come out with you?'

'No, she's alone. Eddy, my youngest brother, had to go back to school after our father's funeral and, to be quite honest, Gerald could be anywhere. I haven't seen him for a couple of months.'

'Tell me about Eddy,' chimed in Sophie, 'he must be about my age.'

'I'm afraid not, Sophie, he's more the age of Hugh and Frederick.'

'Oh,' she sounded disappointed, 'but I bet he's not as stupid as they are, I bet he's really intelligent, like you, and that would make Gerald about Adelaide's age, wouldn't it?' She grinned wickedly at her sister. 'There you are Sis, a serious rival for Tim.'

'I don't think so, Sophie. The last I heard of Gerald he was determined to marry Betty Wickham, in Washington. I have a nasty feeling, in fact, that is possibly why he wasn't at our father's funeral. I think he and Betty probably ran off together.'

'Ooh, how romantic, they eloped. What's nasty about that, Chad, I wish someone would elope with me.'

'Hush Sophie, you're incorrigible,' chided Adelaide, gently.

'Don't discourage her, Sis, I think it's a splendid idea,' said Hugh.

'And the sooner the better,' added Frederick.

The conversation turned to more general topics and Adelaide questioned Chadwyck closely on life in London and Washington, the new plays and fashions. After dinner Chadwyck and James followed his father through to the study and the twins went back to their chess game. Sophie, in spite of stalwart opposition, was finally sent off to bed.

Johnny offered Chadwyck a cigar, which he declined so he took one himself. They were in a much smaller room with a distinctly masculine stamp to it. Two walls were covered with floor to ceiling bookcases, overflowing with a very diverse selection. Chadwyck remained on his feet and browsed. A lot of them were finely bound first editions about African exploration and others, the journals and diaries of big game hunters such as Baldwin, Cornwallis-Harris and Gordon-Cumming. The third wall was dominated by a glass-fronted gun case in which stood a great many shot guns and rifles interspersed with revolvers, hanging from their trigger guards.

'You have some splendid books here.'

'Help yourself to any you might want to read.'

'Thank you,' said Chadwyck, picking up a silver-framed photograph. 'This is you isn't it, and who's that beside you?'

'Oom Koos, an old friend, we go way back.'

'You were a lot younger when this was taken.'

'We were, it was before Jenny and I married.' He smiled and, changing tack, picked up a large cut-glass ship's decanter from a nearby table and three large glasses. He splashed a generous measure of the fine amber liquid into the bottom of each, handed one to Chadwyck, another to James and raised his own. 'The King's health and happy times for us all.' He drank deeply and went and sat in a comfortable leather chair by the fire. Chadwyck and James sat opposite and they talked about farming in South Africa and the flourishing horse market, brought on by the Rebellion.

'Probably best to get some sleep now and we'll fix all the gear and guns tomorrow. Up at six, if that's all right. I'll see you're called and take any book you like if you want some reading matter tonight.' Chadwyck walked over and took Baldwin's book, which he had noticed earlier and bid the two men goodnight.

Outside the study, he could hear a piano being played with consummate skill. He turned left and followed the sound until he came to a closed door at the end of a long passage. He knocked and a woman's voice invited him in. He opened the door gently and stepped into the room. The floor was richly carpeted, heavy velvet curtains covered the windows and a large fire burned in the grate. A Steinway grand stood to one side of the fire. Adelaide sat in profile to him, at the keys. She had changed into a long ivory coloured, silk peignoir and her black, burnished hair caressed her shoulders as it fell freely, almost to her waist. She went on playing and Chadwyck stood, transfixed, watching the firelight flicker on her face and neck. It was the only light in the room and she was playing from memory. After a moment he started to leave, mumbling apologies. She immediately stopped playing and turned her head towards him.

'Don't go,' she smiled at his awkwardness. She had beautiful even white teeth and a single dimple in her left cheek, which he found irresistible. 'Please sit by the fire and I'll play for you.' Chadwyck closed the door, crossed the room and sat on the leather covered brass fender. He was still holding the book and his brandy glass. He placed the book on the floor and raised the glass in a toast to her.

'You play beautifully. It was Mozart wasn't it?'

'Yes, how clever of you.'

'It was just a lucky guess.' He took a sip of his brandy and then offered her the glass. 'Would you like some? It's very rude of me to be drinking alone.'

'No thank you, it makes me sneeze but on you go, it looks like Papa has given you enough to last all night.' He laughed and relaxed a little. She turned back to the piano.

'What would you like me to play? Chopin, Rachmaninoff or one or two of Mr Kipling's barrack-room ballads?' This time she laughed, a truly uninhibited sound, when she saw the expression on his face. 'It's all right, I was only teasing, I'll play something from Rachmaninoff's new opera *Francesca da Rimini*. If you don't like it, stop me and we'll think of something else.' She started playing and Chadwyck crossed his long legs, lay back against the mantelpiece and closed his eyes. He let the sound sweep over him and concentrated on the image of Adelaide, as he'd first seen her, at the piano. She stopped playing and when he opened his eyes he found her standing beside him.

'Were you asleep, Mr Meade,' she asked with an impish twinkle in her eye, 'or just overcome by my brilliance?'

'The latter,' he said slowly when he found his voice, 'but perhaps I should be off to my bed. It has been a long day and James and your father have planned an early start. I don't think I have ever seen anyone as beautiful as you were just now, sitting at the piano in the firelight. That memory will always remain with me.' She looked at him for a long moment, the firelight flickering in her green and tawny flecked eyes, then she leant forward and touched his cheek with her fingertips, so gently that he thought he must have imagined it.

'You're a very sweet and beautiful man,' she said, 'and I shall never forget what you just said. Now come, I'll show you to your room, or you might get lost again.'

CHAPTER 12

Gerald and Betty left Paris by train for Marseilles. Once there, thanks to her grasp of the French language and undoubted flair for organisation, their many cases and cabin trunks were soon retrieved from the train and loaded into two taxis for the short journey to the pier, where the SS *General* was docked. They were welcomed on board by their cabin steward who, convinced that he would get a good tip, made light work of organising their luggage. He then showed them to their magnificent adjoining staterooms, which were located on the promenade deck, on the port side of the boat. They had noticed while embarking, that their fellow passengers were very cosmopolitan. Fresh-looking English civil servants, on their first posting to East Africa, side-stepped politely men of the cloth and missionaries. To Gerald's great surprise, a crocodile of nuns already dressed in tropical whites, preceded them up the gangplank.

Gerald threw himself into a chair in Betty's suite and watched while she and a maid started to unpack.

'Did any go to the hold?'

'Any what, dear?'

He hated it when she called him dear. 'Trunks, dear.'

'Why do you call me *dear*, you know it irritates me?'

He said nothing and put his feet up on the end of her bed.

'Of course they did, this is just what I need on the voyage.' She opened another trunk and spoke to him over her shoulder: 'Why don't you go and unpack.'

'I have already done it.' He got up and, with his hand on the door knob, added 'I'm going to find the nearest bar and I'll see you there, when you have finished.'

The German crew cast off the lines and, with a lot of noise and billowing black smoke, the SS *General* moved off. She made her way slowly, with the help of two tugs, out of the busy port into the open sea.

The last of the afternoon sun threw long shadows across the city and highlighted subdued tones of the russet and gold stone buildings, which belied the squalor of the streets and made up, in part, for the odoriferous port. As the boat came round onto her new course and headed east, bound for Naples, Gerald and Betty sat for a while in silence, watching the sun sink into the sea in a blaze of colour. They then went to their respective staterooms to dress for dinner. They had been invited by the Captain to join him at his table.

The first-class dining room was situated on the main deck, and ran the full width of the boat. It was sumptuously decorated, with deep purple carpeting, and extravagant yellow and grey curtains and furnishings. Smartly uniformed stewards stood attentively around the tables, covered with rich linen tablecloths and sparkling crystal and silverware. By the time Betty and Gerald arrived, most of their fellow passengers had already assembled. A young officer, who smiled politely in greeting, approached them from across the room.

'Herr Meade? May I present the Kapitan's compliments to you both,' he clicked his heels and bowed. 'Will you and your charming wife,' he said, turning to Betty, 'please accompany me to the Kapitan's table.' He turned smartly on his heel and led the way. As they approached, the Captain stood up and towered over them. He had thick wavy dark hair and a long beard, which hid his mouth and most of his chest. He took Betty's hand, which seem to disappear completely in his and raised it to his lips.

'Mrs Meade, I have been looking forward with great anticipation to meeting you both from the moment I saw your names on the passenger list. Your parents have travelled with me and other boats of the East African Line for many years now and it is a great privilege to have you, so like your beautiful mother, with us now.' He turned to Gerald and shook hands. 'You sir, are very welcome too. Mrs Meade, will you please sit here on my right,' and he held back the heavily embroidered purple and gilt Empire style chair. 'And you Mr Meade are over there between Mrs Ehrhart, the charming wife of our new Ambassador to Egypt,' and he smiled broadly at the woman in question, 'and on your other side, Mr Meade, you have Signora Agnelli who, regrettably, is going to be with us only as far as Naples.' Gerald took his place and the Captain sat down and devoted his undivided attention to Betty. An orchestra was playing quietly in the background and Gerald noticed a small dance floor in front of it. As they brought the first course the Ambassador's wife leant across and put her hand on Gerald's arm.

'The Kapitan tells me, Herr Meade, that you are on your honeymoon,' she simpered, her eyes almost lost in the folds of flesh around them and her multiple chins trembled in excitement, making the endless ropes of pearls bounce alarmingly on her matronly bosom. 'How romantic, it makes me think of when Joseph and I were on our honeymoon, so long ago. That is Joseph, there, Herr Meade, on the other side of your wife, don't you think he looks very distinguished?'

Gerald glanced across politely and was surprised to see that, in fact, the Ambassador was extremely distinguished, with iron grey hair, dark, almost black eyes and strong, well-defined features. Dressed in tails and bedecked with ribbons and orders, he appeared to be at least ten years younger than his wife. The incongruity of the match surprised Gerald and, as he looked back at his companion he wondered, very briefly, what that honeymoon of so long ago had been like.

'Indeed, madam, he is most distinguished and you are right, we are on our honeymoon. We are bound for Mombasa where we will stay for two weeks with some friends of my wife's family, outside

Nairobi and then on to Cape Town. And you, no doubt, will only be going as far as Port Said?' and then hopefully, he thought, I'll have someone more attractive to sit next to.

The stewards cleared away the first course and some of the passengers got up to dance, while they waited for the next. At the end of the main course, Gerald excused himself and asked Betty if she would dance. With a lovely smile, she accepted and he led her to the floor.

'How's the Ambassador's wife?' she asked.

'A little of her goes a long way, and him?'

'Charming.'

'He would be, I think she must be very rich.' Betty raised an eyebrow but said nothing. Gerald regretted his remark and, as they started to dance, he tried to think of something to retrieve the situation.

'It was such a good idea of yours to let your father book this passage.' He almost added *and pay for it*, but instead said, 'he and your mother seem well known to the Line.'

'They travel a great deal and my father always tips outrageously.'

'I'm glad, because we'll reap the benefits.' She looked up, a speculative smile touching the corners of her mouth, 'Come on,' he added before she could answer, 'Let's see what the next course is.' He led her back to the table.

At noon the following day, they could see the mountainous outline of Corsica to the north, and the long verdant coast of Sardinia stretching away to the south. By the time lunch was over, they were threading their way carefully through the Straits of Bonifacio. They went out on deck in the bright hot sun and watched the dozens of small, colourful sardine boats scattered about. They waved to the wiry nut-brown Corsican fishermen casting their almost invisible nets. The picturesque port of Bonifacio nestled in the folds of a mountainous backdrop on their port side. To the south the spectacular Cape Testa raised its proud head against the dazzling blue sky.

That night they went to bed quite early as they were docking at

Naples at nine the next morning. They wanted to be up on deck in time to see the sun rise over the island of Ischia. They would then pass the island close on their port side and swing round into the twin bays of Naples, divided by the point of Castel dell'Ovo. They had been told that, behind it, they would see Pizzo Falcone and over to the left, high up on Sant' Elmo, would be the ancient castle with its commanding views over the town.

The next morning it was exactly as they expected, except that nobody had mentioned Vesuvius. They could now see its spectacular outline in the distance, with its head lost in the clouds. They steamed slowly towards the Porto Grande, impressed by the extraordinary activity all around them. The pilot boat came up alongside, and two tugs positioned themselves to nudge the SS *General* into her berth. The old town spread back from the port, rising as it went, towards Capo di Monte. They were scheduled to sail again at six for Port Said and Gerald and Betty decided, like a great many of the other passengers, to go ashore for lunch and see some of the city.

Betty had done her homework and, as they went ashore, she told Gerald about the ambitious rebuilding program going on for the last twenty years. They were widening the streets and improving sanitation. About seventeen thousand houses and more than sixty churches had been razed to the ground.

They took a horse-drawn carriage, bedecked in black in such a way that Betty thought more appropriate at a funeral, and drove through the new part of town. They intersected the Via di Roma and down into the plaza, across which they could see the Royal Palace, an amazing extended edifice with three lines of pillars, one above the other, Doric, Ionic and Corinthian. They passed the Cathedral, which had been started in the thirteenth century by Masuccio, and had since been altered and added to so often that its original simplicity had long since gone. Betty soon noticed that Naples did not have nearly so many beautiful fountains as Rome. They stopped for a delicious lunch, at a typical restaurant, with tables spread out over a wide pavement. Afterwards, they drove back past the magnificent palaces of the Orsini, della Rocca and Franca Villa families to the pier and boarded the SS *General*.

With a tumultuous send off by a brass band and hundreds of cheering locals the boat, festooned with streamers, was towed away from the pier and set her course south for the Straights of Messina. That night there was a Gala dinner in the first-class dining room and the Captain, exuberant as ever, made a long and extravagant speech to welcome the new passengers. After dinner when everyone was in fine fettle the ship's doctor, escorting a beautiful woman with luxuriant auburn hair, piled high on her head, and with startling grey eyes, approached their table. The Captain rose somewhat unsteadily to his feet.

'Kapitan,' said the doctor, 'may I present Miss Daphne Frobisher, who joined us at Naples. She is the daughter of Admiral Sir William Frobisher, C in C of The British Mediterranean Fleet, based at Malta.' The Captain took her hand and bowed low over it.

'How do you do, Captain.'

'Delighted to have you on board Miss Frobisher. How is your father? Is he with you or have you left him on Malta? It has been some years since we last saw each other.'

'Actually, my father's away with the Fleet at the moment and that's why I've been staying with friends in Rome. I have no plans to return to Malta, in the immediate future.'

'Just as well my dear, as we're not scheduled to call there but, of course,' he added with a piratical smile, 'it would be my pleasure to put in to Valetta, if you so wished.'

'How very sweet of you Captain, but I'm looking forward to seeing Egypt so, with your permission,' and she smiled coquettishly at him, 'I'll continue the voyage with you.' He beamed and waved an expansive arm around the table.

'Allow me to present you to my guests.'

The men rose to their feet and the captain introduced them all by name. When he reached Gerald he added, 'Perhaps, sir, you would like to dance with Miss Frobisher and I will have the pleasure of dancing with your lovely wife.' Gerald excused himself and with his most charming smile, offered his arm to Daphne.

'My pleasure Miss Frobisher.'

'Oh do call me Daphne, it's Gerald isn't it?' They reached the floor and joined in the waltz, that the orchestra had just begun. She moved easily within his arms as they circled the floor, her beautiful grey eyes watching him, with an amused expression. Her scent intoxicated him and although they were not quite touching, he could feel the heat of her body. Over her shoulder he could see Betty watching him closely as she danced with the Captain. He wanted to say something amusing to impress Daphne and, as if reading his thoughts, she tilted her head back and laughed, the impact was electrifying. The words died in his throat and he swallowed painfully. She was very aware of the effect she was having on him and she delighted in his discomfort. She parted her lips as if to speak and, enthralled, he watched a slow secretive smile spread across them, exposing small, perfectly formed teeth. He increased the pressure on her back involuntarily and felt her body brush against his. All too soon the music stopped and the spell was broken.

'Thank you' they said in unison.

'We should go back' said Gerald hoarsely.

'Must we?' She looked at him in such a way that he knew he must, or there would be no going back. With his right arm still wrapped fondly around her slender waist, he led her back to her own table. Later, knowing that he should not have stayed so long with Daphne after their dance, Gerald approached Betty and asked her to dance. She refused and insisted he escort her to her stateroom. Once there, she closed the communicating door between their rooms firmly and locked it. Gerald returned to the Captain's table and made her excuses. He glanced briefly at Daphne as he addressed the ambassador's wife, she was talking to the man on her left.

At six o'clock the next morning Gerald was awoken by a hue and cry outside his stateroom, on the promenade deck. He slipped into a silk and brocade dressing gown and stepped out onto the deck to be confronted by the most incredible sight. To the southwest Mount Etna was erupting, with a vengeance.

It was still dark, which made the leaping, dancing column of fire and molten rock that spewed from the crater even more terrifying. The whole mountain was brightly illuminated, as was the base of the great black cloud of ash that hung above. He watched in awe as it grew and spread higher and higher into the sky, where it was caught by the prevailing winds and swept out across the Mediterranean. Tendrils of molten lava coursed down the slopes smashing their way through everything in their path: houses, trees and roads. The sun was rising and the light increased as they came closer and closer to the volcano. The sound was ominous and threatening and Gerald felt the hair on the nape of his neck stand on end. He ran back to find Betty because he knew that she would never believe him if he tried to describe what he had just seen. The corridor was crowded with excited passengers and he ran straight into Daphne Frobisher. She was wrapped in a gossamer thin lace peignoir and was just coming out of her stateroom, which was on the starboard side and almost opposite his own. They stood holding onto each other, silhouetted in her doorway.

'What's happened, have we hit something?' she held his arm tightly. There was a look of excitement, rather than fear, in her lovely eyes.

'No, it's all right,' he said as he put his other arm around her, which seemed the most natural thing to do. 'It's old Mount Etna, putting on a splendid show for us.'

'How terribly exciting' she said, her eyes danced mischievously as she moved closer and gazed up at him. He could feel the warmth of her body against his. A sudden slamming sound made Gerald glance across the corridor and he saw the 'Do not disturb' sign on Betty's door handle, swinging from side to side.

'Please take me onto the promenade deck, so that I can see it all for myself. After all,' she added, 'it wouldn't be proper, now would it,' and she giggled, 'for me to be out alone, dressed like this?' He glanced again at Betty's door and felt exasperated by what he considered to be her unreasonable reaction.

'Anything for propriety,' he grinned, 'I'd love to,' and with his arm still around her, they went out on deck.

After breakfast Gerald went back on deck with a pair of binoculars, borrowed from one of the ship's officers, to watch Mount Etna as they sailed past her and steamed into the Straits of Messina. Although it was no longer erupting he could see the red-hot lava as it forced its way down the slopes and onto the level ground, where it spread out and lost some of its momentum. A mixture of steam and smoke hung above and vast quantities of black and grey ash still rose from the main crater.

He hadn't seen Daphne at breakfast and he didn't relish facing Betty. He knew that whatever he told her, she wasn't going to believe him. They were soon in sight of the ancient city of Messina which they passed on their starboard side while over on the port side the far less impressive town of Reggio, slipped away behind them. Gerald knew that that would be their last landfall before they reached Port Said in three days' time.

By noon there was still no sign of Betty and Gerald went to her stateroom to try and get her to join him at lunch. He found her door locked and she did not answer when he knocked and called out her name. He was not worried, in fact, rather relieved that she preferred to sulk. He retraced his steps, went down to the first-class dining room and sat at one of the small tables in the bar, off to one end. A steward took his order for a pink gin and he leant back in his chair to watch the comings and goings of his fellow passengers. He ordered a second drink, finished it and got up to go over to his table just as Betty, looking very pretty and vivacious, swept into the dining room on the arm of the Captain. They were both laughing and obviously enjoying each other's company. He walked over rather stiffly and nodded to them both, as he took his place. Two other couples were already at the table.

'Oh, there you are, Gerald,' said Betty, 'I was looking everywhere for you. The Captain had kindly invited us up onto the bridge and I couldn't find you, so I had to go alone. Didn't I, Captain?' she touched his arm and smiled at him. There was a brittle, forced gaiety to her voice that Gerald realised was probably not obvious to anyone else. He was surprised by his sudden feeling of tenderness towards her and decided to do everything he could after lunch to make her happy.

That afternoon she ignored him and refused to speak to him, beyond saying that she would not be joining him at dinner. There was no anger in her voice, just disenchantment. So he made her apologies to the Captain that evening and to all intents and purposes, dined alone. He watched morosely as Daphne and her friends enjoyed themselves at their table. Finally, he shook off his mood and, prompted by the old axiom that if you have the name you might as well have the game, he got up and went over to ask Daphne to dance. One of the men at her table had beaten him to it, so he didn't stop but veered away and left the dining room. Feeling a little sorry for himself he knocked again on Betty's door.

'Please open the door, I want to talk to you.'

'Go away, Gerald, and leave me alone.'

'You're being very unreasonable and if you don't open it, I'll ask the steward to do so.'

There was silence for a moment and then he heard the key turning. He opened the door, but she had already turned her back on him and walked over to the writing desk, where she sat down.

'I know what you're going to say Gerald and I'd just as soon not hear it. You know I saw you coming out of Miss Frobisher's stateroom with your arms around her and nothing you have to say will change that.'

'What! I was not in her stateroom, Betty, and what you are thinking is simply not true. Had you not slammed your door you would have realised I had come to collect you and had bumped into Daphne in the melée.'

'Oh, it's Daphne is it? So I was right and you expect me to believe that it was just a coincidence, with all those people about, that it should be Miss Frobisher,' she added scornfully, 'and that you felt it necessary to hold onto her in such a blatantly affectionate manner.'

'I wasn't holding on to her, as you say, it was just that she was frightened by the noise of the volcano and grabbed my arm. Before I could excuse myself you had jumped to the wrong conclusion and slammed the door and I knew you wouldn't open it.'

'But you could have tried Gerald, that's the difference, instead of going out onto the promenade deck, in such...' for a moment she was at a loss for words, 'such a blatant manner. You still had your arm around her as you passed my window and crossed to the other side of the boat where, fortunately, I could no longer see you.'

'For God's sake Betty, why do you go on like this? It was a chance meeting. She suddenly popped out of her cabin and I literally bumped right into her and that's all there was to it.'

'Well it certainly didn't take much to divert you from your original plan. Couldn't you have fought your way free and collected me as you said you were going to do?'

'I didn't think my chances with you were very good at that moment,' he tried to smile, 'but you're quite right I should have tried,' he added in a gentler voice, 'and I'm sorry, I'm truly sorry that I didn't.' He went over and stood close to her but made no attempt to touch her. She got up and faced him and for a long while she looked steadily into his eyes.

'Jealousy is a terrible thing, Gerald. It is the cause of more damage than anything else in any relationship between two people who love each other. It is so unfair because it has nothing to do with the relative degree of love, of one for the other. It is more like an allergy that you either have or, if you are lucky, you don't. I have it and I hate what it's doing to us. Please try and understand that and help me.' She laid the palms of her hands on his chest and pushed gently against him, rocking backwards slightly on her heels. He noticed her eyes were slightly unfocused and her breathing became fast and very shallow.

'Kiss me,' she whispered, so quietly, that he hardly heard her. He took her gently in his arms and then, with sudden passion, kissed her.

She tasted of honey and, with desperate strength, she clung to him. 'Make love to me, my darling,' she cried into his mouth. And so they did, where they were, on the floor of her stateroom.

For the next three days they remained in their staterooms and the only person who saw them was their steward, who brought them their meals and made their apologies to the Captain. Only when they were due to arrive at Port Said did they surface, long before most of the other passengers. They stood wrapped in a blanket and each other's arms by the ship's rail and watched the sun rise over the Nile. The lights of Alexandria went out, one by one, as they made their way into Port.

The Ambassador and his wife disembarked, with one or two others and two British army officers and a very fat Egyptian merchant, joined the first-class passengers. The whole of that day The SS *General* moved slowly southwards, through the sweltering heat of the Suez Canal. Flyblown, noisy settlements were scattered haphazardly along the shore and Kantara, the largest of them that disappeared into the heat haze behind them, wasn't much better. Later, with Ismailia astern on the other side of the canal, they soon reached the Bitter Lakes where the heat wasn't quite so sultry. Vast numbers of duck and wildfowl flew over the ship as they passed through the lakes and the many boats that were anchored there.

By the following morning, when most of the passengers had lost all interest in their surroundings, they cleared Port Suez and sailed on into the Gulf and beyond into the Red Sea. The heat started to build up again and even the slight breeze caused by the passage of the ship through the water was not enough to bring relief to the lethargic company. For four days they sailed on in the same conditions. Fewer people attended meals, simply because they couldn't be bothered to dress and everyone, including the ship's officers, became short tempered and irritable. Finally they reached the Straights of Bab-el-Mandeb and passed Perun Island on the port side. Gerald, with the use of his borrowed binoculars, could see a large Union Jack, hanging limply against the flag pole on the fort. Finally, with the first breath of air in almost a week, they broke out into the Gulf of Aden. The next day they docked at Aden, just before breakfast and left before lunch for the last leg of their voyage, which would take them another four days.

Betty felt debilitated by the heat, and begged Gerald, who was not nearly so affected by it, to spend more time with the other passengers. She assured him that she would be much happier resting quietly in her stateroom. That evening as they headed south around the Horn of Africa, Gerald dressed for dinner and joined the others to find that Daphne had been moved to the Captain's table and was sitting on his right. It appeared that the younger of the two army officers, who had come aboard at Port Said, was already well acquainted with her and during the whole meal she hardly said a word to Gerald.

He left the table as soon as he decently could and went back to Betty's stateroom, to find her stretched out on top of her bed in a thin cotton shift and breathing gently as she slept. The fan above the bed rotated slowly and stirred the turgid air. He took his jacket off and sat in an armchair beside the bed and watched her sleep. After a while, as she didn't wake, he slipped through the communicating door and went to bed. The following evening was a lot cooler, during the day they had passed Cape Guardafiii on the mainland and the island of Abd-el-Kuri on their port side, with the hazy outline of Sokotra to be seen far beyond it.

They went down to dinner, having enjoyed a lazy afternoon together in their stateroom. When they reached the Captain's table, Betty was obviously surprised to see that Gerald was sitting next to Daphne but she said nothing. After the main course, the young army officer, with perfunctory permission from Gerald, asked Betty to dance. Daphne turned to Gerald and smiled invitingly at him. He had no alternative and she accepted his invitation with a provocative laugh. After a few minutes Gerald managed to position Daphne and himself so that they were dancing beside Betty. With great gallantry, Gerald excused himself from Daphne, leaving her in the care of the army officer and took Betty in his arms. She remained there, in one way or another, for the next three days, while the boat ran on south. Only the distant port of Magadoxo broke the stark, mountainous Somali coastline. On the last night, before they reached Mombasa, the Captain excelled himself at dinner by making a magnificent speech in Betty's honour. Gerald and Betty danced until there were only themselves and the orchestra left and one stalwart steward, who looked as though he was asleep on his feet.

'Come, my darling, to bed,' said Gerald, 'in the morning, Mombasa.'

'It is the morning,' she laughed, 'but I'm all for bed.'

CHAPTER 13

With a sharp, eye-straining intensity the sun rose rapidly out of the Indian Ocean as the SS *General* steamed slowly into the haphazardly buoyed Mombasa roads, to take up her station. Gerald and Betty stood at the rail of the promenade deck and looked down at the bustle of activity in the forepeak. An officer was directing four deckhands, working the anchor windlass. One of the seamen swung a mallet and knocked a large iron pin out of a shackle and, with a loud clattering sound of its chain, the starboard anchor dropped thirty feet into the sea, with a resounding splash. The chain continued to run out until, on another order from the officer, two sailors secured it.

'What are they doing, darling?'

'Dropping the hook my dear is, I believe, the colloquial expression.'

'The anchor? Are we stopping?'

'It seems so, we have arrived at Mombasa.'

'Don't be silly, darling, we're in the middle of nowhere, we're miles away, how're we going to get ashore?'

'You'll see,' said Gerald, smugly, having found out the form from one of the officers on deck, 'All in good time, now let's go and have breakfast.' An hour later the first of the surf boats, to ferry the passengers and luggage ashore, had already tied up alongside the suspended gangway. Stewards, struggling with luggage of all shapes and sizes, moved up and down the steps, squeezing past each other to load. When it was full it cast off, loosened a lateen sail and, taking advantage of the offshore breeze, sailed towards the beach. It was soon lost in the mist, not yet been burnt off by the sun.

By noon all the luggage was ashore and the boats lined up to take the passengers off the SS *General*, before she continued on her way to Zanzibar for bunkering. From there she would continue down the coast, calling at Mozambique, then round the Cape of Good Hope to Cape Town and on up the west coast of Africa to Hamburg. Gerald and Betty watched two of the passengers step gingerly into the surf boat.

'They look very small, Gerry and it seems such a long way to the shore.'

'Don't worry, if our luggage made it, so should we.'

'Mr and Mrs Meade, how glad I am that I could leave the bridge to say goodbye to you.' The Captain, dressed in immaculate whites, appeared beside them. 'I hope you have enjoyed your voyage with us. It has been a great honour for us to have had you on board.'

'Thank you, Captain,' said Betty graciously, 'we have enjoyed ourselves enormously,' and she looked at Gerald coquettishly causing the Captain, who never missed a trick, to laugh heartily.

'Your charming excuses, Madam, your indispositions, I remember them well. Perhaps for you it was the best part of the voyage, but for me it was the most lonely and disappointing,' Betty laughed delightedly and took hold of Gerald's arm, 'and do not worry, Mrs Meade, you will be quite safe. Once you are through the surf and have reached the beach, you will be carried shoulder high, in a sedan chair, by four natives and I don't think they've ever dropped anyone, in all the years I've been on this run.' He laughed at her expression of astonishment, as he turned away and when he reached the bottom of the companionway, he looked back and added 'By the way, I've signalled my colleague on the SS *Tabora* and he is very much looking forward to the pleasure of your company between here and Cape Town, in two weeks' time. Auf Wiedersehen.' He clicked his heels, turned and climbed up back to the bridge.

'Come on my dear, let's try this one. How do you like the look of the skipper?'

'He looks like a pirate Gerry, with that patch on his eye.'

'He'd probably look a lot worse without it.' He took her arm and they carefully descended the swaying ladder to the surf boat.

There were already two passengers seated on the thwarts and they waited for two more to join them. Then with a flourish the skipper waved to the deck hand to cast off, pulled the tiller hard over until the breeze caught the sail and they pulled away from the side of the ship. Once clear, the breeze heeled the boat over and the bahareen very politely, and with elaborate pantomime, rearranged the passengers to trim the boat.

When they were two hundred yards from the SS *General* they were almost deafened by the ship's siren as it sounded three times. They could make out the great white figure of the Captain, magnificent curly beard blowing in the breeze, as he stood on the bridge wing and waved farewell. The mist had cleared and they could see the whole of Mombasa spread out before them, seeming much larger than it had from the ship. There were a great many people milling around on the beach, everything unloaded from the boat stacked in chaotic piles next to narrow tramlines that carried gharris from the town to the beach and back. The surf boat approached at an alarming rate; about fifty yards off, the skipper called out in pidgin English.

'Hold on very tight,' he dropped the sail and for a moment the boat began to lose way until the surf caught them. With a great surge they were carried forward in a headlong rush up onto the beach and left in about a foot of water, as the sea ran back. Immediately two chairs, each slung between two long bamboo poles and carried by four natives, were brought out. They were held clear of the water, but low enough for the first of the passengers to board. The natives were singing in their deep, melodious voices. The first chair was swung up onto their shoulders and they carried the passenger, in great style, till they reached the dry sand. The second chair was already carrying the next passenger ashore when the first returned for the third. In short order all six of them were high and dry on the beach.

'That wasn't so bad, darling, in fact I thought it was rather fun.'

'I loved it Gerry, I think one should always go ashore like that,' Betty's eyes shone with excitement; she looked very beautiful in a pale cream hat that shaded her from the hot sun, 'and just think of it, in two weeks we can do it all again, the other way round.'

'If you have never met the Cunninghams, how will they recognise us? But,' he added on reflection, 'I'm sure your cousin Annabelle has described us in great detail.'

'Look darling, over there, that tall thin, distinguished looking man with that magnificent moustache, I'm sure that's Arthur Cunningham, and that must be Annabelle's aunt Gladys right behind him.'

'Where? There are dozens of people over there.'

'There, silly, talking to the man in uniform. We'll walk over to them and see what happens.' As they approached, the man in uniform saluted and left and the couple turned and looked directly at them. 'Betty Wickham,' the woman exclaimed, 'I'm sorry, I mean Betty Meade, you must be Betty and Gerald Meade.' She was so certain that she stepped forward and embraced Betty without waiting for an answer.

'That's right,' said Betty, 'how clever of you to recognise us and how very kind to come all this way to meet us.'

'We were delighted to, weren't we Arthur?' she turned to her husband but, before he could say anything, she continued, 'we spotted you as you came ashore and I said to Arthur, didn't I Arthur, that lovely couple must be them, they look so happy, so much in love. Don't you remember dear?' She turned back to him, 'just before Captain Watson came up and spoke to you?'

'Of course I remember, my dear, the way you talk anyone would think I was senile.' He swept off his hat and shook hands with Betty and, rather unnecessarily, added 'Arthur Cunningham, and very glad to see you both. I hope you had a pleasant voyage, it's always so beastly hot in the Red Sea. Not much better here for that matter.' He pulled out a large spotted handkerchief and dabbed at his bone-dry forehead. 'Don't have to worry about your baggage, you know, I told Watson to take care of it. He'll have it all in our compartment under guard, for when we leave for Nairobi at ten tonight. Meanwhile, how about some lunch?' He offered Betty his arm and the four of them walked towards an open vehicle, of indeterminate age and make, which was surrounded by small naked black children and guarded by a grizzled old native driver.

'We've been staying with the Shaws for the last two days,' said Gladys 'after the most frightful train journey; Arthur always says he'll never do again. Roland Shaw is a district judge here in Mombasa and he and Audrey are expecting us to lunch. They have a simply delightful house, right on the beach.'

The driver chased the children away and opened the doors. Arthur sat in the front and the other three climbed into the back. With a great deal of horn blowing, they left the beach and followed the tram lines past the Law Courts, drove through the centre of town, leaving the old fort on their left and took the coast road to the Shaws' house. It was a most attractive sprawling bungalow, surrounded by a lovely garden full of an incredible profusion of flowers and plants.

After a delicious lunch of many different types of fish and fruit, Roland Shaw went back to the Law Courts and Arthur took Gerald and Betty fishing, in the Shaws' boat. By six they returned and, in the comparative cool of the evening, walked up the beach towards the house, leaving the boatman to take care of the catch. They could see the two women on the veranda overlooking the sea, no sign of Roland.

'Any luck?' called out Gladys when they were still twenty yards away. Betty was flushed with the sea air and thrilled at having caught her first fish.

'It was such fun,' she said as she approached the veranda, 'and we had a marvellous time. Your husband was so patient with me and finally I caught a fish, you'll never guess what it was.'

'You're right,' said Gladys, caught up in her excitement, 'but I can see that you're bursting to tell me, whatever I say.'

'It was a yellow fin tuna and it was absolutely enormous.'

'Twenty pounds is hardly enormous for a yellow fin,' said Gerald laconically.

'Don't be such a wet blanket Gerry, you said you were very proud of me.' She turned back to Gladys. 'It was one of the most beautiful things I've ever seen, when I finally got it into the boat. Its colours shimmered like precious stones and it had a bright golden stripe which ran all the way along the side of its body, from its eye to its tail. When it took the live bait, we were using, it charged off like a dervish and I was absolutely terrified. It fought so bravely and afterwards I was really rather sad when I saw it dead in the bottom of the boat and all its radiant colours had gone.

'That was very clever of you dear,' said Gladys, 'did anyone else catch anything?' 'Gerald boated a pompano,' said Arthur, 'about the same size.'

'No it wasn't,' contradicted Gerald, 'you said it was almost thirty pounds at the time.'

'That's true, it was much bigger than mine,' said Betty, totally unaffected, 'and just as beautiful. It was a lovely gold and silver colour, with streamers on its fins. It ran back and forth, just under the surface, so I could see it all the time, the water was so clear. It was all terribly exciting and I'm absolutely exhausted.' They climbed onto the veranda and, as it was too late for tea, a houseboy offered them drinks.

'Any sign of our other guest, Gladys?' asked Arthur, once they were settled with their drinks, in comfortable reclining chairs. 'She should be here by now.'

'No dear, but don't worry, there's plenty of time. You know perfectly well she was spending the day with friends of her father's and they're going to drop her off here in time for dinner, about half past seven.'

'I love meeting new people,' said Betty, 'we've met so many

interesting people everywhere we've been, ever since we left Washington.'

'Not just to dinner, dear,' said Gladys, 'she's staying with us for the next two weeks and will be travelling with us on the train tonight.'

'Oh,' said Betty, 'that'll be fun. What's her name?'

'Surely you met her, my dear?' said Arthur as he glared at the whisky in his glass. 'You spent the last two weeks with her on the boat.' Betty looked quickly at Gerald but he was staring out to sea. 'Beautiful girl, daughter of an old school chum of mine, although I haven't seen him for years, not since he became so important.'

'What's her name,' repeated Betty, in a very controlled voice. Gerald could feel her staring at him, although she had addressed her question to Arthur.

'No good asking Arthur dear, he has trouble remembering mine.' Instinctively, Gerald knew who it was and that Betty would never believe he hadn't known about it all along.

'Let me guess,' said Gerald, standing up and handing his glass to the houseboy for a refill.

'No, Gerald,' cut in Betty, as she stood up, 'you don't need to guess, you know.' She stood for a moment in front of him and he was startled by the expression in her eyes. She moved even closer, so that no one else on the veranda could hear her. 'You knew Gerald and you didn't have the guts to tell me.' She looked at him with such intensity that he felt sweat breaking out. He didn't dare answer because he was afraid of her reaction. He tried to hold her gaze and, although he didn't look away, he knew that, at that particular moment, she wouldn't have believed anything he said. After what seemed an eternity, she turned away to Audrey. 'I'm suddenly rather tired after all that fresh air,' her voice was only just under control, 'I wonder if I might go and lie down until dinner?'

'But of course, dear, how thoughtless of me.' Audrey stood up beside her and took her arm. 'Come with me, one of the guest rooms at the far end of the veranda is made up and should now be pleasantly cool.' Gerald watched them go and took a large gulp of his whisky to regain his equilibrium.

'It's been a long day for us both,' he said lamely. He heard a car draw up on the other side of the house. 'That must be the Judge,' he said and hesitated when he heard a woman's voice approaching.

'Good Heavens, Mr Meade, what an extraordinary surprise,' she hadn't yet seen the Cunninghams, 'what on earth are you doing here? I didn't even know you had come ashore at Mombasa.' Gladys stepped forward.

'How lovely to see you, Daphne,' said Gladys, 'I knew you must have met on the boat but how strange that you never knew you were both staying with us. Come closer and let me look at you. You're absolutely lovely, isn't she Arthur? It's beyond belief that an old stick like Willie could have such a beautiful daughter.'

'He's no more of an old stick than I am, my dear,' Arthur bridled in defence of his friend and moved towards Daphne, 'but Gladys is right, you are very beautiful.' He leant forward and kissed her on both cheeks. 'Welcome to Africa, my dear, I'm very glad to see you again, you now seem so much more grown up than before. I remember you as being very shy and your hair was…'

'That's quite enough of that, Arthur. Don't listen to a word he says dear, come and sit over here and tell me all about Malta and the voyage.' An hour later dinner was served on the veranda. A pale and subdued Betty joined them, but she neither looked at, nor spoke, to either Daphne or Gerald throughout the entire meal.

* * *

At two minutes past ten, the train pulled out of Mombasa. 'This must be something of a record,' said Arthur, 'I can't remember this train ever leaving on time before.' He was sitting in one of the two window seats, facing forward, in a first-class carriage which they had to themselves. Betty was opposite him and Daphne sat on his left, Gerald and Gladys faced each other, on the corridor side of the compartment. Bedlam reigned over the rest of the train, as the other passengers fought and struggled for positions in the third-class carriages, crowded by their baggage and livestock.

'How very thoughtful of Audrey to have made up this food hamper for us,' said Betty as she tapped the basket that lay on the seat between her and Gerald.

'It's ours actually,' said Arthur, 'we had it for the trip down and you'll be very glad of it, my dear, long before we get to Nairobi. It's a fourteen-hour run if we're on time and, if anything goes wrong, as it invariably does, God knows how long it will take us.' He smiled at her, tapped his jacket pocket and added, 'and I've got something special here to help us through the inevitable delays.' The door opened and an emaciated Indian merchant poked his head in, obviously looking for a seat. He hurriedly withdrew under the combined fire of Arthur and Gerald's unwelcoming looks.

The long train, mostly made up of freight wagons, had one first- and four third-class carriages at the end and was pulled by two steam engines, coupled together. They had more than three hundred miles ahead of them and would climb five and a half thousand feet from sea level to Nairobi. The freight wagons contained an extraordinary assortment of agricultural machinery, fencing wire and cages of assorted livestock. There was also a very handsome Hereford bull from England that Arthur told them had been bought by a neighbour and had travelled out with them on the SS *General*.

'What's the first stop,' asked Betty, when they had been travelling less than ten minutes.

'Voi, my dear,' said Arthur, 'in about four hours, and then an hour or so later Tsavo, if we're lucky. It'll probably stop several times before, for one reason or another, but at least at Tsavo we'll have half an hour to get out and stretch our legs.'

'You and Gerald can do that dear,' said Gladys, 'but we'll stay here and guard the compartment.'

'Good idea, otherwise we've no idea what we might find when we get back.'

'Wasn't it at Tsavo that they had all the trouble with the lions, when building the line?' asked Gerald.

'Quite right,' said Arthur. 'It was back in '98 when Colonel Patterson, who was one of the engineers, finally got the men back to work after he had killed most of the man-eating lions. They had become so fearless that for a month the Company had had to stop work entirely. About thirty Indians, over a hundred natives and even one or two Europeans had been killed.'

'Were they really man-eaters?' asked Daphne.

'They ate them all right,' answered Arthur. 'They'd run in at night, break through the thorn barricades while the coolies were sleeping and grab one or two, blanket and all.' Daphne caught her breath and Gerald saw excitement in her eyes. 'The lion would pick up the poor chap like a dog would a bone and bound off into the night with him. They never went very far because the rest of the camp could usually hear them crunching away on the bones. If he was lucky the man was dead but the unlucky ones were pinned to the ground while the lion, with a tongue like coarse sandpaper, licked the skin off them, so they bled to death.'

'Really Arthur, must you go into such unpleasant detail?'

'Sorry dear, but the really interesting part of it is that, if there were any remains at all to be found, it was the head of the unfortunate fellow. If any of his friends had the guts to run after the lion, in an attempt to rescue him, they usually found nothing but the head because the lion always started at the other end.'

'Arthur, I think that's quite enough.'

'Well my dear, it made it a lot easier for the authorities to work out who had been eaten and who had just run away, in fright.' Gerald laughed and Betty looked as though she was going to be sick.

'I think I'm going to try and sleep,' said Gladys, 'and the rest of you can enjoy Arthur's colourful stories.' She settled comfortably into her corner and pulled a light travelling rug over her legs.

* * *

104

By midnight the train was still on schedule and almost halfway to Voi. Both Gladys and Arthur were asleep and Betty, Daphne and Gerald exchanged a few desultory remarks that punctuated long, rather strained, silences.

When they stopped at Voi, Gerald got out and, stepping over sleeping bodies in the corridor, reached the end of the carriage and climbed down. There was no platform. It was after two in the morning and very cold. He walked briskly up to a shed beside the line, which he assumed to be the station, to see if he could find something hot to drink. There was nobody around. Everyone was working on the train. Some loading and unloading luggage while others were helping the fireman direct the long hose from the water tower into the boilers. Several others, having formed two chains, were loading cord-wood into the tenders, for the next leg of their journey.

He looked up at the sky, it spread from one horizon to the other, a great black velvet inverted bowl that completely covered the world, through which shone countless minute fragments of light, scattered like dust in the wind. Some stars seemed close enough to touch, others were way beyond that and the rest stretched away in all directions, into infinity. For the first time in his life he felt humbled. When they stopped again he would bring Betty out to show her and again try to convince her, once and for all, that he hadn't known about Daphne being a guest of the Cunninghams. Doors were slamming shut all down the train and a man in uniform blew a horn, which was echoed by the train's whistle. Gerald returned to their carriage empty-handed and made his way once again over the still sleeping bodies in the corridor.

At Tsavo they all got out except Gladys, who remained behind to guard the compartment. A few of the passengers in the corridor had already left so it was easier to reach the door at the end and, to Gerald's surprise, there was a platform. Arthur gave Daphne his arm and led her towards the station building, a lot more substantial than that at Voi. Gerald and Betty walked away from the immediate area of the train and beyond the light cast by the flickering oil lamps that were scattered around the station.

'Where are we going?' she asked nervously. 'Isn't this where all those poor people were killed by the lions?'

'I want to show you something.' They stopped about fifty yards from the track and the noise made by the porters, natives and passengers was less intrusive. 'Look,' said Gerald.

'Where, I can't see a thing.'

'Up there,' he pointed with his left hand in a great sweeping gesture to take in as much of the sky as he could, and with his other arm around her shoulder he continued, 'have you ever seen anything like that. Have you ever seen anything quite so magnificent, so grand, and awe-inspiring?' Betty looked up in silence and her head fell back against his shoulder. She had left her hat on the train and the sweet smell of her hair filled his nostrils.

'You're right,' she said after a moment, 'it is awe-inspiring and it makes me feel very small.' Some of the tension eased from her body as she leant back against him. He had dropped his left arm to his side and very gently, frightened that she would move away, he slipped it around her waist. She continued to gaze at the stars and, if she moved at all, it was towards his embrace. They stood there gazing at the sky and listening to the night sounds of the African bush, around them. He brushed his lips against her hair. He desperately wanted to make her believe him but, at the same time, he didn't want to spoil the moment.

'My darling,' he said. She sighed as he rarely called her that. 'I honestly didn't know that Daphne Frobisher was staying with the Cunninghams.' She stiffened slightly and then relaxed again.

'I don't want to talk about it,' she finally said, 'just hold me as you are and make me feel that you love me because that is what I need more than anything else right now.'

'But, my love, we must talk about it. If we don't, you'll only bring it up later, and you'll be hurt and angry all over again, and I don't want that, believe me, I really don't want that.' She pulled away and turned to face him. Her face was taut and very pale, with hard lines around her mouth. The spell was broken and he wished that he had not insisted.

'I asked you to help me Gerald, the other day on the boat and I thought then that you understood me. You are not helping me by insisting on your innocence. Is it so hard to admit that I'm right? To admit that you did know, or are you frightened of what I might think of you for having lied to me?' He took her firmly by the shoulders and pulled her towards him so that her heels were off the ground. She was surprised by his strength.

'For God's sake stop this. I only wish that you could ask either Arthur or Gladys and they would tell you that Daphne Frobisher was as surprised to see me at the Shaw's house, as I was to see her. Coincidences do happen and this is just one of them and nothing more. I think I do understand something about jealousy and I will do all I can to help you, but I can only do so if you let me.' He was almost shaking her by the shoulders and he suddenly saw that he was hurting her. He took a deep breath and tried to control his anger. He slackened his grip and felt that she was going to fall. He supported her gently and with great feeling added. 'Please, my darling, believe me.' She wouldn't look at him, she seemed completely detached, with a distant look in her eyes that he found unnerving. He held his breath until, eventually, she did look at him.

'I'm sorry Gerald, I wish I could.' The train whistle blew sharply, three times in succession. He still held her there for a moment, there was so much he wanted to say and now, there was no time to say it.

'Hurry, or we'll miss the train.' Still holding her hand they ran back to the track.

An hour and a half later they rattled through Mtato-Andei and at Makindu stopped to refuel and to fill the boilers. Gerald and Arthur got out but the women stayed in their compartment. It was extremely cold outside and would get colder, the higher they climbed. A hint of light to the east, the false dawn, relieved the night. In an hour, the sun would rise over the distant horizon. After Makindu they ran on to Simba where Gerald got out alone and saw the evocative, snow-capped Mount Kilima N'jaro, seventy-five miles to the south. It was washed by the first rays of the morning sun that had just broken over the surface of the Indian Ocean.

When the train pulled out of Kiu, Betty was woken by the sudden jolt of the carriage. Arthur too, appeared to be dozing and Gerald moved into the empty seat next to Betty. Neither of them said anything as he took her hand and they watched the sunrise. They could see more and more of the landscape around them. Gerald wanted to re-establish the mood that they had felt earlier, back at Tsavo, but, certain that Arthur was still awake, he knew that anything he said was bound to sound stilted. The train continued to climb towards Nairobi and Gerald could feel Betty's hand relax in his. He squeezed it very gently but there was no response and he dozed off to awake, with a start, when the train stopped again. A moment later the guard walked past the window on his way to the engines. Betty stretched and looked at Gerald.

'What's happened, why have we stopped?' she whispered. The others had not stirred.

'I don't know, we are not at a station. Perhaps we have broken down.' Gerald looked across to Arthur for confirmation but he was asleep. He turned to Betty. 'Would you like to go forward and see what's happened?'

'No thank you. I'm very comfortable here.' She squeezed his hand to emphasise her meaning. 'What was it you were going to say before we had to run for the train?'

'Nothing I haven't said already, it was just how I was going to say it. It is important that you believe me.' He paused, searching for something in her eyes and then added, 'We could always stay at the Norfolk Hotel instead of going to the Cunninghams.'

'You really mean that Gerry, don't you?' He nodded. 'Perhaps after all I've been very silly and you really didn't know she was staying with Aunt Gladys.' She leaned forward and kissed him gently on his mouth. 'Just the two of us together at the Norfolk is a lovely idea but, I'm afraid we can't, it would be rude.'

'All right. We'll stay with them for just a few days and then we'll leave early, on some pretext or other. I can't wait to get to South Africa and show you Springbokfontein.' She smiled at him and some of the old light was back in her lovely eyes. Knowing, in this instance, that discretion was the better part of valour, he said nothing and sat there beside her, relaxed, as she lay back with her head on his shoulder while they waited for the train to move again. He listened to her breathing; as it slowed until he knew that she was asleep and then, he too slept and sometime later, half awake, he was aware of gentle movement. Finally, after a further three hours, they reached Nairobi. They found the Norfolk Hotel car waiting, as Arthur had made the reservations before leaving for the coast. They felt tired, crumpled and dusty and were very glad that there would be time to rest, before dressing for dinner, their first decent meal in twenty-four hours.

CHAPTER 14

Chadwyck was already awake when he heard a discreet tapping on the bedroom door. The windows were open, the curtains drawn back and it was pitch dark outside. The tapping was repeated, slightly louder than before.

'Come in,' he called. The door opened and the face of one of the kitchen maids peered round.

'Mornin' Massa Chadwyck, here's your chai.' She was holding a large steaming mug of tea on a small wooden tray in one hand and an oil lamp in the other. She crossed the room lightly on bare feet and placed both the lamp and the tea tray on the table, beside his bed. 'It's a lovely mornin' Massa Chadwyck.' She smiled broadly and her teeth flashed in the lamp light.

'If you say so and thanks for the tea.' She smiled again and left. He sat up in bed, picked up the mug in both hands, leant back against the pillows and sipped gingerly at the scalding, sweet brew. He hadn't slept well and he recalled random thoughts and images which added to the confusion that he already felt. He wondered why he hadn't dreamt of Adelaide instead, so much for his promises. He sipped again at his tea and his head began to clear. There was no other sound that he could hear in the house and he wondered if the others were up. He was just about to get out of bed when there was another, much louder, knock on the door.

'Chad, may I come in?' It was Sophie.

'No Sophie, you can't, I'm getting dressed.'

'No you're not, I'm coming in.' She opened the door. He couldn't help the smile that spread across his face.

'Sophie, you're impossible. How did you know I wasn't getting dressed?'

'I was out on the veranda when Belle brought you your tea.' She walked around the room picking up his clothes from where he'd dropped them. 'You'll make some poor woman an awfully messy husband, someday.' She looked at him archly from the foot of his bed where she had casually draped his trousers.

'Out, Sophie, and go and see if James is up.'

'Oh, please Chad. Don't send me away, I wanted to ask you something.'

'What?' He knew what it was going to be before she opened her mouth.

'Take me with you, you won't regret it. While you're having breakfast, I can slip out the back and wait for you on the road out to Groot's Farm. Nobody will miss me until the Schwartz brats arrive and then, it will be too late, we'll be miles away.' He didn't have to answer, she could see from his expression that it wasn't going to work. 'OK, then I'll go and ask James, and I thought you were my friend,' she flung at him, as she slammed the door shut behind her.

He swung out of bed, shaved and dressed quickly in cavalry twill trousers, a wool shirt and a bottle green pullover. He threw the rest of his stuff into his grip and left it at the foot of the bed. He opened the door to find James coming down the corridor towards him.

'There you are, did you sleep well? We'll have breakfast in the kitchen.' It was warm and well-lit with tantalising smells of grilled bacon and freshly baked bread. Johnny was already halfway through his breakfast when James and Chadwyck sat down beside him. A large steaming pot of coffee stood in the middle of the table and James poured some into two mugs.

'Help yourself to sugar and milk.' One of the maids put a plate of three fried eggs and at least half a dozen rashers of bacon in front of Chadwyck.

'I've given you one of the small wagons James, because I'm going to need the big one today. The small ones are faster anyhow and you're not taking that much gear. Caachy should have it loaded by now and I suggest you take the .416 Rigby and the .318 Wesley Richards as a backup and a couple of shotguns in case you come across any sand grouse or francolin, for the pot.'

They finished breakfast and went out onto the veranda. It was beginning to get light and Chadwyck could just distinguish the outlines of the servants' quarters. 'We'll be leaving soon,' said James as he stood by the small wagon checking the load.

'Right, I won't be a minute, I'll just get my bag.'

'It's already here, but come and give me a hand with the guns.' They went back to the study and James unlocked the gun cupboard. He took down the two rifles and slipped them into leather and canvas cases. From a drawer in the cupboard below the guns he took out ten rounds of ammunition for each of the rifles and from another drawer two boxes of twelve bore cartridges, for the shot guns, which he emptied into a leather cartridge bag. He gave the two flat boxes of .416 ammunition to Chadwyck and put the other two boxes of the .318 into his own pockets. He picked up a heavy leather case from the bottom of the cupboard and handed it to Chadwyck. Here are the shotguns. Put them and the cartridges in the wagon and I'll bring the rifles.'

The cook had prepared a large hamper of food and in another box there were some emergency rations which would last at least a week. On either side of the wagon, were slung two large ox-skin water bags that contained about five gallons each. It was now much lighter and Chadwyck could see Caachy coming towards them from the stables. He was leading two sturdy looking chestnut geldings of about fifteen hands.

'I think that's about it. Do you want to ride or do you want to travel on the wagon?'

'I'll sit with you on the wagon.'

'Good idea, we'll keep the horses fresh for later. Caachy, tie the horses to the wagon.' He turned back to James. 'I'll just go and get Castor and Pollux.' Within minutes he returned with two of the dogs that had greeted them yesterday. They were tall, finely muscled with brindled grey and tan thick wiry coats, bred for speed and endurance. 'That's Castor.' James pointed to one of the dogs which Chadwyck noticed had a white blaze on its throat.

'l will expect you back by noon tomorrow, James, so don't turn this little jaunt into a full-blown safari.' Johnny waved them goodbye and went back into the house.

Once they'd cleared the gates James swung the wagon round and they headed northwest towards Groot's Farm. Caachy and the two dogs ran alongside the wagon.

'We should be there in less than two hours. We can have a look around, a bite to eat and then try to make sense of Walter's map.'

'Did you see Sophie this morning?' Chadwyck asked.

'No, why?'

'I didn't think you would, but we may see her soon.'

'What the hell are you talking about?'

'She came to my room before I got up and asked me to take her with us. Said she'd wait for us out here on the road. When she got nowhere with me, she said she'd try you.' James laughed.

'Well if she is waiting I'll send her back. That doesn't mean she'll go of course but I'm damned if I'll waste time taking her back. She might try to follow us, but I doubt it.' Chadwyck realised that the younger Flynn children were much more independent and self-reliant than he, or any of his friends, had ever been at that age. After a further two miles there was still no sign of Sophie and Chadwyck no longer thought of her and her idle threat. The sun was beginning to clear the eastern horizon and soon the bone chilling cold of the night would disappear. Caachy ran on effortlessly beside them. He carried a short hunting spear and a buffalo hide shield was slung over his left shoulder. His back was draped with a civet skin kaross which he discarded as the day got warmer and stuffed into a leather pouch that hung from his waist. The dogs, working as a pair, followed up on the early morning scent of a porcupine. When they found their quarry they kept their distance, as they had both learnt manners, from an earlier encounter.

Chadwyck tried to read his grandfather's diary as they went but he found it impossible to focus in the jouncing wagon. He closed it and folded it with the other documents back into the oilskin pouch and put it in his pocket.

They rode on in silence for another half hour, each occupied with their own thoughts. There seemed to be more game about the further they got from Jagersfontein. Chadwyck watched great herds wheel and scatter as they caught their scent. It seemed they were not bothered by the wagon and horses but as soon as they got the scent of man, they were off.

'Adelaide seems so nostalgic for London, and yet she told me last night that she's never been there. She ought to go, she could stay with Uncle Walter, he'd be so proud to show her around. It would add years to his life.' James laughed.

'I agree, but she won't.' They went on in silence.

'Why on earth not, what's keeping her here?' James glanced quickly at Chadwyck and paused as he chose his words carefully.

'She's unofficially engaged to a friend of mine, a chap called Tim, he is a pilot, but our fathers, I suppose quite rightly, won't let them make it official or marry until he's shown his colours in his father's business in Cape Town. His father made a fortune in shipping and Tim is trying to get his old man to put up the capital to start an airmail service in South Africa. He wants to get a contract from the government to deliver mail in the colony out of Cape Town. He already has a 'plane and flies all over the place with it. He covers the cost by doing charter work just to prove to his father he can make it pay.'

'How long have they known each other?'

'Years, most of their lives in fact but only continuously since Adelaide was at boarding school in Cape Town.'

'Will they marry?'

'Chad, you've been smitten badly.'

'Don't be so bloody silly. I just thought the excitement in London would be good for her.' James wasn't convinced. 'What's that ramshackle place up ahead?'

'That, my friend, is the new suitor's stately home,' James roared with laughter, 'that's Groot's Farm. What more could a bride want?'

James drove the wagon into the area between the two buildings and pulled up in the shade of an acacia tree. He hitched the wagon to a low branch and walked over to the nearest building with Chadwyck right behind him. There was a metal bar across the door and Chadwyck guessed it opened outwards. The bar was slung on two metal brackets and fastened at each end with a four-inch nail.

'Very basic but effective for keeping animals out' said James as he withdrew the nails and removed the bar. He pulled the door open and they went in together. They could see where the windows were by shards of sunlight shining through the shutters. There were three windows and once they were opened the musty smell began to clear.

'Let's open up the other one so we can work out which was used for what.'

The other building was smaller with the same type of door. Inside it was fresher and with more light coming from the far corner where part of the corrugated iron roof was missing. There was no fireplace or range as they had seen in the other building so the smaller one was obviously used as a storeroom.

'I'll get Caachy to unload the wagon into the other building and collect some firewood, we will need a lot for tonight because I saw quite a few lion tracks around the buildings.'

'Are you thinking about the horses? We could lock them in here for the night.'

'Not a bad idea as long as the lions don't try to get through the broken roof.'

They walked back to the other building, followed by the dogs and Chadwyck carried a wooden table and two chairs outside. Chadwyck retrieved his satchel from the wagon and pulled out Walter's papers and a notebook.

'I'm going to redraw Walter's map and then we can pace it out.' James sat beside him and started to roll a cigarette while Chadwyck drew the two buildings in their relative positions in the centre of the page.

'There is no compass point bearing on the map but that doesn't matter because the first line is a continuation of the front of the larger building and runs for 140 paces. I assume as Walter is about my height so I should be within two or three paces when we walk it out.'

'What's this ninety on the corner of the building?'

'Degrees, a true right angle.'

'Of course, there's another ninety at the end of the 140 so the line goes off at a right angle to the first line and runs for 170 paces.'

'We are going to have to get the right angles spot on or we could end up way off.'

'How are we going to do that?'

'Easy. I'll show you later, the dubious result of years of expensive education. Let's get going and please ask Caachy to bring the canes.' He stuffed the drawings into his satchel.

'I'll get the mallet and rope.' They met at the corner of the building.

'James, you stand at the other end of the front of the building and line up my cane, sighting along the wall.' He stood with his back to the corner of the building and stepped out twenty paces. He took a cane from Caachy and held it upright.

'Tell me to move to the left or to the right, James?' James squinted along the front of the building to line up the cane.

'There's nothing in it, perhaps ten inches to your right?'

Chadwyck moved the cane and James called out, 'That's it.' Chadwyck drove the cane firmly into the hard ground and made sure it was standing vertically.

'Stay there, James and we will do it again. We know the first cane is true so line the second cane with it and the front of the building.'

Chadwyck paced out another twenty steps, turned and held the cane upright in front of him.

'About a foot to your right.' Chadwyck moved the cane. 'A bit more, that's it.' Chadwyck drove the cane in.

'One more and then you can move up to the first cane.' Within ten minutes they had placed seven canes and reached the 140 mark.

'Now I'll step out ten paces at approximately ninety degrees and lay a cane on the ground,' Chadwyck moved as he spoke.

'Next I backtrack ten paces from the 140 mark towards the building, measure off fourteen paces on the rope and lay the rope from that point to the end of the stick on the ground.' He knotted the rope at the fourteen pace mark and gave one end to James.

'Put your end of the rope at the tip of the ten-pace mark.' It overshot the tip of the cane by six inches so he asked James to move the tip six inches to the right and waved Caachy over to bang in another cane.

'And there you have your right angle. Please stand behind the 140 cane and we'll mark out 170 paces to the next right angle.' Half an hour later they had passed the next right angle and reached the spot marked on the map. 'Allowing for a margin of error, this spot must be within ten paces in any direction of their dig,' said Chadwyck, dropping his satchel to mark the spot. The dogs lay down beside it.

'I don't see any signs of digging. It's untouched and look here there is a seam of quartz.'

They slowly circled Chadwyck's bag, spreading further and further out and searched the ground. The sun was noticeably hotter and they both had a drink from their water bottles.

'Caachy, drive in an iron rod by Chadwyck's bag and we'll head back for something to eat and a bit of shade.'

They followed the canes back and Chadwyck pulled them out as they went. At the next right angle, James had Caachy drive another iron rod into the ground, deep enough so that it didn't move when James kicked it. They did the same at the first right angle and were soon back at the farm.

By three o'clock with some help from the dogs, they had finished a delicious beef stew made for them at Rietfontein, washed down with beer. The temperature had dropped noticeably.

'What should we do now' asked James, 'go back and look again?'

'Yes. I want to be certain before I write to Uncle Walter. I've checked his map again and gone through his notes and I'm certain it's the right place and can't understand why we couldn't find some sign of digging, even though it was more than twenty years ago.'

'Right. I'll tell Caachy to set up our cots in here, find more firewood and feed the horses. We will take a pick and shovel and work together.' They retraced their steps to the third iron rod but after more than two hours they had found nothing. They had dug four two-foot wide trenches of about six or seven feet long, down to a depth of two to three feet within a ten yard radius of the iron rod. It had been very heavy going and no sign of disturbed earth or any indication of previous digging.

'That's it, we've done out best. Let's go back and see what that whisky tastes like.'

'They look like graves, should we fill them in? The mortal remains of our hopes and prayers.'

'The rains, when they come, will do that Chad and don't sound so maudlin. We knew it wouldn't be easy, we'll try another approach tomorrow.'

* * *

They were already in bed by ten when Caachy came in and talked quietly to James in setswana.

'What did he say?'

'He's worried about the horses. There's a pride of lions prowling around the farm and he believes the horses will break their halters. I think I'll put them in the other building.'

'I'll give you a hand.' They took the three horses and tied them close to each other onto two iron rings attached to the wall. They barred the door and the three of them walked back. A lion grunted out by the first iron rod and another answered even closer.

'Those could be the ones helping themselves to our cattle. I think we should get closer acquainted at first light.'

CHAPTER 15

Chadwyck awoke to the smell of fried bread and bacon. It was still dark.

'How many eggs do you want?'

'Two please, coffee smells good.' He swung his feet to the floor, pulled on his breeches and boots and walked over to the table.

'Always a good idea to tip your boots out before putting them on first thing in the morning.' He paused. 'Spiders and scorpions.'

'Why didn't you tell me before I put them on?'

'Didn't need to. I had already done it just before you woke up.' James easily avoided the left hook that Chadwyck swung at him.

'Now you'll remember next time.'

After breakfast they left the wagon horse tied up, took the other two and saddled them up. It was just getting light and James sent Caachy out to find the lion tracks out by the first rod and work out which way they had gone.

'You take the .318 and I'll take the .416. Have you even shot a .318?'

'No. Nothing bigger than a .270 when stalking in Scotland.'

'More kick and more weight to absorb it. Both rifles are recent developments and we only took delivery last year. Just hold steady, lean into it and you'll be fine.' They put the rifles into their saddle scabbards alongside their water bottles and biltong. Without a word Caachy appeared behind Chadwyck and spoke to James.

'He said they moved off last night when they couldn't get into the other building and had headed in the direction of the twin-headed kopje. He thinks they would have killed during the night and will now be lying up.'

They rode out side by side towards the twin headed kopje. Caachy trotted ahead of them in his usual effortless way. On the other side of them Pollux and Castor worked the ground. In less than an hour they had halved the distance between the farm and the kopje, which they kept to their left, as they rode on in a northerly direction. The ground rose ahead of them and after a while the farm buildings appeared far behind them, like matchboxes on the veldt, with the lone acacia tree standing over them. In the distance they could see the thin ribbon of the Riet river working its way west and south in the direction of the mighty Orange river. There was a lot more cover on the slopes, mostly wild mimosa and a tall bush, with grey leaves and a pungent aromatic scent. Caachy pointed out some vultures, wheeling in the sky a mile ahead of them and said something to James.

'Something dead has attracted that lot up ahead. We might be lucky, it could be a lion on a kill.' James pulled a twin leash out of his saddlebag and handed it to Caachy, who secured the dogs. 'We'll move around a bit further north, so that the wind is in our favour. Keep slightly behind me and to my left, check the load in your rifle and leave it in the scabbard. No talking from now on in, but watch me for hand signals.' Caachy moved ahead of them with the dogs straining on their leashes.

After ten minutes of positioning into the wind they turned to make their final approach to where the vultures were still wheeling in the sky. Every so often one of them would drop to the ground, out of sight and a moment later it would be back in the air again. James leant across towards Chadwyck.

'There's definitely something on the kill, or else they would all be down on the ground.' They moved forward carefully behind Caachy until they were less than two hundred yards from the vultures. Caachy signalled with his hand, palm down, the finger tips fluttering. He then rolled his hand over, clenched his fist and extended one finger. James dismounted and handed his reins to Chadwyck.

'Wait here, I'll be back for you. I'm going forward for a closer look with Caachy, he says it's a single lion. I want to have a look and work out the best approach.' James moved forward until he passed Caachy and Chadwyck watched as they disappeared together into the thick mimosa scrub. Neither of them made a sound and Chadwyck remained motionless until they returned. James then signalled to Chadwyck to dismount and stood close beside him to whisper in his ear.

'It's a splendid old lion. Well on with his meal of what could be either a blesbok or a bush buck. Too much of it has been eaten to be sure. He's down in a vley, and totally unconcerned, except for the occasional rush at a vulture. He doesn't know we are here. We're down wind and he hasn't scented us. Caachy will stay here with the horses and dogs and you and I will go forward to a point about forty yards from him, where you should be able to get a clear shot.' Chadwyck nodded silently and James continued. 'I will be slightly behind you and to your left and will back you up. Take your time and wait till he's broadside on, preferably standing. Shoot him just behind and above the elbow. That should get him in the heart and lungs and hopefully end it in one. If he doesn't go down reload and fire again immediately and then reload. Don't talk when we're up there or he'll hear you. If he should have turned towards us and you can't get a broadside shot, fire at the middle of his chest, just below the chin. Do you understand?' Chadwyck swallowed hard and nodded.

'Don't look so worried, if anything goes wrong, I'll think of something. He spoke briefly to Caachy who nodded and took the horses' reins. At a signal from James the dogs lay flat and silent. He touched Chadwyck's elbow and led the way towards the lion. After they had gone about fifty yards James leant across and whispered in Chadwyck's ear.

'We're now in dead ground and will be until we get to the firing point I told you about. He can't see us so there's no need to crouch but be careful where you put your feet, a broken stick could spook him.' Taking great care where they trod they reached the rock outcrop, overlooking the vley. They moved up side by side avoiding the skyline and got into a position where they could both see the lion clearly. He was a magnificent beast with a thick shaggy mane, pale tawny in colour, flecked with silvery grey and liberally smeared with fresh blood. He had immensely powerful shoulders and strong heavily muscled hind quarters and was lying sideways on to them, less than forty yards away. One massive paw was clamped over the carcass and the other pushed against the ripping and tearing motion of his jaws. Chadwyck glanced sideways at James, who cautioned him to wait.

After five very long minutes, during which time the lion never moved except to tear another great mouthful off the carcass, Chadwyck looked enquiringly at James who glanced up at the vultures, back at Chadwyck and shrugged. His meaning was obvious. The vultures had seen them and were too cautious to land, so the lion wasn't about to move again. Chadwyck raised the rifle to his shoulder and, keeping it off the rock behind which he lay, he took careful aim and gently squeezed the trigger. The report and recoil was far greater than Chadwyck had expected. As fast as he could he reloaded and brought the rifle down to bear again. The lion was on its feet, lashing his tail furiously. Chadwyck fired again as the lion leaped forward, over the remains of the carcass and disappeared behind a rock, even before James could fire his first shot.

'Gut shot. Too far back but he won't go far and the dogs will soon catch up with him.' James yelled something to Caachy. Chadwyck reloaded and within a few minutes Caachy brought up the horses and dogs. 'Right Chad, now listen carefully and I'll tell you what we are going to do. We'll ride on close together, so that we can back each other up. The dogs will be out in front and they will pick up the lion's scent and blood spoor. He will be bleeding and in considerable pain and from the noises he and the dogs make I'll know what's happening. With luck, the dogs will turn him at bay and hold him there, until we can catch up. If they don't bay him we'll just have to follow until he stiffens up and stops. He'll be quite fearless but hopefully the dogs will distract him enough for you to get a clear shot. If you can't and he's more than seventy yards away when you first see him, back off because if he charges your horse can outrun him. If he's less than seventy yards and charges, you must stand and shoot. He'll cover that distance in three seconds and you won't have time to do anything else. If you get thrown and lose your horse, take to a tree and, if you can, take your rifle with you. That goes for you Caachy, now, up that tree and stay there until you hear from me.' James took the leash from Caachy and loosed the dogs. Chadwyck and James leaped onto their horses and followed the dogs, which had already passed the kill, and were off on the lion's scent, belling lustily. By the time they came out of the far end of the vley the dogs were a hundred yards ahead of them. James pointed out large splotches of blood on the ground. Once clear of the vley, they increased their speed and closed the distance with the dogs. Two hundred yards ahead of the dogs, they could see the lion bounding across an open patch of ground, swinging its head from side to side as he kept track of his pursuers.

'I don't seem to have slowed him up much,' yelled Chadwyck.

'You have, he's badly hit. The dogs should be able to turn him at the foot of that cliff.' A moment later they came out onto their side of the open ground and although they could no longer see the lion or dogs, they could hear all three giving tongue. 'They've done it, they've got him cornered,' shouted James, 'Slow down we don't want to go rushing in before we know what's happened.' Chadwyck reined in his horse and they dropped back to a trot. 'Check your load.' James did the same. 'Now stick close behind me and we'll head towards that infernal din.'

The dogs had worked themselves into a frenzy and were dancing, just out of reach, around the lion who snarled and feinted, in an attempt to break away. The riders slowed to a walk and approached very cautiously. They could see nothing but the sound of battle intensified and James knew, by the howling of the dogs, that the lion was becoming bolder and was unlikely to remain at bay much longer. When they cleared the last of the cover the scene that confronted Chadwyck was almost exactly as he had imagined it.

Forty yards ahead of them, the wounded lion faced the dogs and spat hatred and defiance at them. The lion was backed into a hollow depression against the high cliff that stood over him and the weaving, growling dogs. The lion suddenly sprang forward in a savage attempt to swipe one of the dogs with his massive forepaw only to be checked by the other, tearing at his flank.

'We'll separate here, Chad, as he can't face both of us at the same time. I will go to the left and try and hold his attention without provoking a charge and you go to your right until he is broadside on to you and when you can, shoot. Quickly now, he won't hold much longer.' Chadwyck nodded and James turned his horse away, holding the .416 loosely in his right hand, as he moved sideways around the edge of the depression, His eyes never left the lion. Like a hawk, he watched his tail to catch the moment it stopped slashing from side to side, for he knew the lion would then charge, with flattened ears and tail rigid as an iron rod.

Chadwyck gentled his horse carefully to his right and held the .318 by the fore-end in his left hand, with the stock resting on his thigh. Both horses, like all their breed, were skittish and restless at such close proximity to the lion, even though they had been well trained, were normally rock steady and used to being shot over. Within seconds, Chadwyck was in a position to shoot. The lion was almost broadside on to him and still focused on James and the dogs.

He dropped the reins from his right hand, swung the rifle into his shoulder, took aim and fired. The detonation of the rifle, in the confined space beneath the overhanging cliff and the nearness of the lion, panicked the horse. It reared up, throwing Chadwyck to the ground, spun on its hind legs and bolted. With a blood curdling roar the lion whipped round towards Chadwyck and in a blur of speed, charged. He knew he hadn't missed but he'd have to shoot again, within the next two seconds, or it would be all over for him.

He still had the rifle in his hand and, having favoured it when he fell, he knew it wasn't damaged. He reloaded and tried to bring it to his shoulder as he lay twisted and in great pain on the ground. He was mesmerised by the murderous intent and the sheer unadulterated hatred that blazed deep in the lion's eyes. Roaring continuously, the lion charged with terrifying speed and Chadwyck's senses reeled from the foul, fetid smell of the animal, as it came to within yards before he was able, in the microsecond that remained, to fire again. The stock tore into his chest, as he had been unable to get it into his shoulder and the breach smashed against his cheek. Fractionally before he fired, he'd heard another shot and just as he pulled the trigger he saw the lion flinch, in its final leap. Chadwyck tried to roll sideways, in a desperate effort to get out of its way and the lion crashed to the ground close to where he had been.

'Don't move, Chad, stay where you are!' James' voice crackled with tension. Chadwyck couldn't have moved, even if he'd had to. He heard James work the bolt of his rifle and reload. One of the dogs was whimpering, hurt when it had been bowled over by the lion's final charge. Fascinated, Chadwyck watched the lion, less than five feet from where he lay, staring straight at him, with wide open eyes. A trickle of bright red blood oozed from its right ear. There was no movement in the eyes at all and slowly the light faded from them. An opaque sheen replaced the terrifying malevolence that had been there just a moment before. Chadwyck could feel James circling behind him, as wary as a leopard.

'It's all right Chad, he's dead.' Up you come.'

'I can't move. I think my leg is broken.'

Caachy had already gone to recover Chad's horse, so James dismounted, flung the reins over the horse's head to make it stand and hunkered down besides Chadwyck.

'What happened? Where does it hurt?'

'He reared as I fired and I went over his back and he pivoted on his hind legs, and at that point must have trodden on me as he bolted.'

'Where do you think it's broken?'

'My left leg. It's swelling up and hurts like hell.'

'Do you think the skin has broken?'

'I don't know but there's no blood. May I have some water, please?'

'Of course.' James pulled his water bottle out of his saddlebag, unscrewed the top and held the lip to Chadwyck's mouth. Spluttering at first, he finally managed to swallow a couple of mouthfuls.

'Can I move you to ease the pain?'

'You might bring my left arm round from behind my back.'

'Is it dislocated?'

'I don't think so but it's gone to sleep.' Very gently James lifted Chadwyck's shoulders and pulled his arm around so that it lay on his chest.

'I'll put a saddle bag under your head and shoulders because you are lying downhill.' He went back to his horse and unstrapped one of the saddlebags.

'Here comes Caachy and he's got your horse.' With Caachy's help, James made Chadwyck more comfortable while he gave Caachy instructions before he slipped away with just his spear and shield.

'I'm just going to check on the dogs to see if they are losing blood and then I'll be back to tell you my plan.' Within minutes James was back.

'How are they?'

'They'll do. Castor has a an eight-inch wound on his flank but he has been licking it since they settled and its clean and only weeping slightly. The dog's tongue is a cure all for them and Pollux is unscathed, a lucky outcome as they held the lion at bay for almost five minutes.'

'May I have some more water, please?'

'Of course. I've sent Caachy back for the wagon and told him to bring back one of the camp beds and the other mattress and all the blankets and sheets, also the rope, one of the water bags, and half a dozen canes. Oh yes, and the drum of alum, because I am leaving him here to skin out the lion and taking you back to Rietfontein. When we get there, I will send one of my brothers to fetch Doctor Marais from Jagersfontein. Once we have you home, I'll send Sesi and another man back with the wagon to bring in Caachy and your lion skin, meanwhile I'll rig a groundsheet that I have in my saddlebag over you to give some shade.'

They waited for Caachy and tried to ignore the proximity and smell of the dead lion. Within an hour, Caachy was back with the wagon and between them they had Chadwyck trussed up on his back on the camp bed with a temporary cane splint holding his left leg straight. From the knees down, his legs were strapped together with wet strips torn form a sheet and his boots strapped together to stop his left twisting. They had doubled up with the other mattress and remaining blankets to absorb the impact of the rough ground.

Chadwyck couldn't help crying out when they lifted him onto the camp bed and James was glad to see there was no blood on his breeches.

'Now we'll put you head first on the wagon so that I can keep an eye on you and rope you down to the floor to stop you rocking about.' This done, he took the groundsheet from beside the lion and rigged it from the back of the bench seat, to the sides of the wagon. 'That will keep the sun off you.' He then hitched the two horses to the back of the wagon.

'Caachy, you stay here and start where you can, skinning the lion. I'll send the wagon back with two men as soon as I can. Take this rifle, in case any of the others of the pride return and, when the wagon gets near to where they think you are, they will fire a shot and you answer them.'

'Have you any questions?' Caachy just looked at him without a word.

'I'm sorry. I'm way off balance.' Caachy smiled, extended his hand and they tapped fingertips.

CHAPTER 16

After what seemed an interminable time to Chadwyck, they arrived at Rietfontein.

'Hugo, quick as you can, ride to Jagersfontein and tell Doctor Marais that it is a broken femur and bring all he needs to set it and something for the pain. Tell him that at this point I don't think we should go on for another two hours to Jagersfontein Hospital, at least until he has seen Chadwyck. Now scat and take care.'

Johnny and James picked up the camp bed and carried it into Chadwyck's room and set it on the floor. Jenny and Adelaide followed them in and sat on the bed.

'Doctor Marais will probably want him on the kitchen table, but we can move him there if that's where he wants him. It's cooler here and a lot quieter.'

'How do you feel Chad?' asked Adelaide as she got up and lent over the camp bed, putting her palm on his forehead. 'I think you have a bit of a fever. I'll make you some chamomile tea,' she added, as she stroked his hair back with her fingertips.

* * *

'Take him through and put him on the kitchen table.' Adelaide caught Chadwyck's eye and they both smiled. Doctor Walter Marais,

'Bones' behind his back, was a veteran of the Boer War, who had spent most of three years in field hospitals close to the fighting with a penchant for amputation in all shrapnel cases, but was vindicated by very high survival rates amongst his patients.

'You have done a good job here James. Good idea to have bound his feet together.'

Doctor Marais cut away at the canes and Chadwyck's breeches. His thigh was inflamed and bruising but the skin was unbroken. He gently probed along the femur.

'James, give him a strip of biltong to bite down on. Clean lateral break, which is the best it can be from my point of view. I can set it here and won't have to take you into Jagersfontein for x-rays, wondrous machine and so simple but nobody knows its side effects.'

'How long will it take to mend?' asked Jenny.

'Two months without moving and then I'll come over and remove the cast. It will be another two months of crutches with therapy to rebuild the muscles. I'll leave it to you girls to take care of the emotional mend.' Only James laughed. 'Now, I'll need a big bowl to mix the plaster and I'll prepare a sterilized dressing for Chad's leg. How do you feel? Not what you expected on your first day in our backwater burgh. Look on the bright side, things can only get better.'

'Where's Daddy?' asked Adelaide.

'I asked him to put a couple of iron roofing sheets under Chad's mattress. We don't want him bending in the middle.' This time no one laughed.

When the plaster was set they moved Chadwyck back to his bedroom. Someone had moved the bed around so that he could look out over the garden, to the blue hills in the distance.

'He mustn't leave that bed, absolutely no weight on his left leg. Bed pans and bottles, I'm sure Adelaide and James can sort it out between them. Sponge bath occasionally and he might want to grow a beard. Light food, no curries or alcohol and plenty of water. I'll send a nurse out in three days to check the dressing and when it itches, and in time it will, try using a knitting needle.' He headed for the door.

'Before you go Doctor, may I first thank you very much for coming out here so quickly and fixing me up, and secondly, would you very kindly send a telegram to my mother in Cape Town, if I write it now.'

'Good idea,' said Jenny, 'I'll get you some paper and a pencil.' A few minutes later Johnny saw Doctor Marais to his wagon where he pulled a bottle out of his bag, 'Give him a little of this if he really needs it to sleep.'

'What is it?'

'Laudanum, and if he runs a high fever, send somebody for me.'

'Thank you Walter, and please put it on my tab.' At that moment, Caachy arrived and Johnny walked over to see the lion skin.

'Peg it out in the end barn Caachy and finish treating it. Make sure the doors are shut and I'll tell Chadwyck it's here and in good order.'

For the next three nights, Chadwyck found it difficult to sleep because of the constant pain. His leg was inflamed and the skin felt very tight and was hot to the touch. Last thing at night, Jenny gave him a spoonful of laudanum, which managed to ease the pain so he could sleep.

Johnny and James were out on the farm almost all day, and Jenny and Adelaide took it in turns to bring him meals and do their best to entertain him. On the second evening Johnny had set up a small bookcase in Chadwyck's room and filled it with some of the hunting books from his study so that, when he was alone, he had something to take his mind off his immobility.

* * *

On the third morning, after Doctor Marais's visit, Adelaide came into his room brandishing a mirror and a cutthroat razor. Chadwyck was propped up in bed and studying the map in Walter's diary. Adelaide handed him the mirror.

'Hold this so you can see what I'm doing to you. Are you sure you don't want to grow a beard, Chad? It's the fashion now and so much less work for me and less risk for you.'

'No, go ahead.'

'Then tip your head back, please.' Chadwyck was holding the mirror at right angles to the map.

'Hang on a second,' he angled the mirror towards the map. 'I think I've got it, what a sly old fox. The map is a mirror image.'

'What are you talking about?'

'The place they were digging. It's all backwards. Look over my shoulder and you'll see what I mean. We were digging about 350 paces from where we should have been. A huge discrepancy when one is concentrating on an area ten yards by ten. I must talk to James about this. The prime markers are still there so it won't take him long to find the real spot and I'll write to Uncle Walter for confirmation. I can't believe I'm stuck here for three months. We'll all be at each other's throats by then.

'Not me. I'm already beginning to enjoy my hold over you.'

'Sheer happenstance my dear, nothing more.'

'Don't show ingratitude or I might…'

'You might what?'

'Nothing, dear.' He picked up his pad and pencil.

'Dear Uncle Walter, I broke my leg badly and now grounded for three months immediately after James Flynn and I followed your map to nowhere! I've now realised it's a mirror image and James will try again with any further help you can provide. With love, Chadwyck.'

CHAPTER 17

Soon after the sun was up and long before anyone else from his party was to be seen Arthur Cunningham, impatient to continue the journey on to their farm, prowled the garden of the Norfolk Hotel. He hoped Gladys would soon be down so that at least they could have breakfast together before he went out to check on whether the car and wagon were ready for the journey. It was a three-hour drive to the farm if all went well and he didn't want to think how long it could take if something went wrong. The wagon, with supplies that he had bought before going down to Mombasa and the Meade's luggage, that was not needed immediately, would reach the farm sometime that night.

He went into the dining room, which opened off the garden, and was shown to a table where he sat alone to wait for the others. By the time they were all assembled he had read every morning paper available and, having finished his breakfast and no longer able to control his own impatience, he excused himself. As he stood up he told them, in a voice that brooked no argument, that they would be leaving in half an hour and that he would have everything loaded and ready to go.

They arrived at Kashmir, as their farm was called, in memory of their time in India, late for lunch. A house boy unloaded the car and took all the luggage to appropriate rooms while Gladys led them straight into the dining room, where lunch was already laid out.

After lunch, she suggested that everyone might care to rest. This met with the obvious approval of Betty, who would have happily gone to her room before lunch. Leaving Arthur in close conversation with Daphne, who was hanging on his every word, Gladys left the table.

'Come with me, you two and I'll show you your room,' she smiled at Betty and added, 'forgive me, my dear, for not doing so before, but we were so late for lunch and Arthur gets very angry, if we eat late.' With the door closed and Gladys gone, they stood just inside their room and looked around. They could see their suitcases beside a wardrobe, in the adjoining room.

'Hardly The Ritz, my dear,' said Gerald. 'Not even up to the SS *General*'s standards. Oh well, beggars can't be choosers, at least you don't have to pay for this place.'

'Keep your voice down, Gerald and don't sound so spoilt. Money's got nothing to do with it, the Cunninghams are good friends of my family and they have a comparatively hard life out here, considering they lived in the lap of luxury in India.'

'Then, my dear, why don't they...'

'I know,' she interrupted him, 'go back to India. You're being childish and I'm tired so please make yourself useful and find out where the bathroom is.' Gerald went out into the corridor and walked towards an open door at the end. She heard him roaring with laughter and a moment later he was back at their bedroom door.

'Do you want me to tell you this or do you want to see it for yourself?' Before she could answer, he continued. 'I think it would be best if you saw it for yourself, because I'm sure you won't believe me.'

'Don't be silly, Gerald, why on earth shouldn't I believe you?' He looked at her and raised his left eyebrow and she knew very well what he was referring to. 'Tell me.' She really didn't want to start on Daphne Frobisher, again.

'The room is of a reasonable size and contains three items of furniture, if you can call them such. Firstly, a broad heavy wooden plank with a hole in the middle over a longdrop which I imagine is the lavatory, a table with a large porcelain hand painted, floral patterned ewer on it and a copper bath, of generous dimensions and reminiscent of a medieval throne, that is totally unconnected to any form of plumbing whatsoever. That, my dear, is the bathroom and doubtless shared by all.' He laughed in that same thoughtless way at her obvious discomfort. His infuriating attitude annoyed her intensely and she couldn't help herself.

'Even if I didn't, at first, believe what you said about Daphne Frobisher, I think concocting this nonsense, simply to annoy me, is puerile beyond belief.' She swept past him to see for herself. He followed her down the corridor and leant against the door frame. She stood just inside the bathroom and stared in silence before walking slowly back to their bedroom. He followed her in and dropped into a chair, as she stood at the mirror gazing at her reflection. 'I am sorry, I apologise, you were quite right about the bathroom but that has got absolutely nothing to do,' she continued, headlong, 'with the fact that you two were far too familiar with each other on the boat, for you not to have known that she was coming here.

'For God's sake Betty, drop it. I will not discuss this matter with you anymore. I have told you a dozen times, that I did not know that she was going to stay here and I thought you had accepted that on the train. For that matter,' he added wearily, 'what possible difference does it make to us, whether she is here or not?'

'Don't try that on me, Gerald Meade,' she almost screamed at him. 'It's been all you could do to keep your hands off her since you met and, for that matter, how do I know that you did?' Gerald slowly rose from the deep, chintz covered armchair where he had been sitting with his feet propped up on the windowsill and walked over and stood in front of Betty.

'Meet her on the boat, or keep my…?' he trailed off, no longer interested in provoking her. 'I am sick and tired of your carping, bilious little attacks on me and anyone you think I might have associated with. I've had enough of your snide innuendo and uncalled-for remarks. I'm going to find Cunningham and perhaps he'll show me round, before we dress for dinner. I suppose they do dress for dinner here,' he added as an afterthought, 'I suggest that you, my dear, try to contain yourself, rest perhaps, and I'll see you later.' As he quietly closed the door, Betty tore her hat off her head, scattering tortoiseshell pins in all directions and hurled it across the room. Instead of Cunningham, Gerald found Daphne on the veranda.

'Hello, what a pleasant surprise.' He moved towards her. 'Have you seen Arthur?' She was sitting in a deck chair and reading a magazine which she dropped on the floor, as she got up.

'No, but he should be here any moment. He told me he wanted to show me around the place.'

'Good, that's what I wanted to do, if you don't mind my joining you.'

'Of course not, don't be silly.' She gave him a dazzling smile. There was a long pause as he discarded various gambits, he was acutely aware of her proximity.

'What an extraordinary coincidence,' he said, finally, 'that we should both be staying here now and not have known about it before.'

'Not really, after all, we hardly spoke to each other on the boat,' she lay her hand gently on his arm as she continued, 'let alone got to know each other.'

'Unfortunately,' he said without thinking, 'that's not how Betty sees it.'

'What on earth do you mean?' She asked, searching his face and his soul, as he felt it, with disconcerting candour. The houseboy passed them, struggling under the weight of one of Betty's cases. Gerald stood aside to let him through.

'Take it straight on in,' he said, 'and put it in the dressing room.' The boy nodded and Gerald turned back to Daphne. 'Well I've started, so I might as well finish. Betty thinks that you and I ...' he stopped, unable to continue, so he changed his tack, 'Betty thinks that I...' She burst out laughing.

'What you're trying to say,' she choked, 'is that your wife thinks that you and I ...' She couldn't finish either, because she was laughing so much.

'Afraid so,' he said, rather lamely, 'that's about it.' He heard the boy knock loudly on their bedroom door.

'Bwana told me to come right in. So sorry missy, I put your case in wrong room.'

The boy grinned and went through to the dressing room and dumped the case by the wardrobe.

'He would,' she said to herself and then added when he came back through the bedroom, 'where's Bwana now?'

'He's out on the veranda, talking to other guest.' Betty stormed out of the room, past the startled boy and marched down the corridor. She could hear a woman laughing and then Gerald's voice, although she couldn't hear the words and then the woman laughed again. She came to the end of the corridor and out onto the veranda. She saw Gerald at the far end, standing very close to Daphne and saying something in a low conspiratorial tone.

He looked up suddenly and their eyes met. She hesitated for a moment and then walked back to their bedroom, with as much dignity as she could muster. She could hear Daphne laugh again and felt that Gerald must be talking about her most recent outburst. Just as she reached their bedroom, the door opposite opened and Arthur Cunningham stepped out.

'Gerald's looking for you,' she said and slammed the door behind her. She went over and threw herself face down on the bed and pounded on the pillows, with clenched fists. She evoked every misfortune she could think of, to torment the hapless Daphne. Arthur stared blankly at the bedroom door, shrugged his shoulders eloquently and walked towards the veranda. His American wife's friends were even more American than she, he thought, there wasn't one of them he'd yet met who knew how to behave properly. Thank God for men's clubs, the sooner Berkeley Cole opened the one he kept talking about, the better.

'Ah, there you are Daphne. Gladys asked me to come and see how you are. Recovered, I hope, from that long voyage. Beastly hot the Red Sea, no wonder they wear nothing but night shirts up there. I hope you weren't too surprised, Meade, by our little shenanigans at the hotel last night? It always seems to end up like that when a few of us get together. Hate to think what the breakages will be on my bill, but I've never known them to overdo it.'

Gerald laughed as he recalled the outrageous spectacle of himself as the horse and Cunningham as the knight teamed up against Culpepper and Cole in a jousting match in the bar, where they spent five hilarious minutes trying to unseat each other with billiard cues, while scattering furniture, bottles, glasses and people in all directions.

'I see that you do remember it, so you can't have been as drunk as you appeared.' He turned to Daphne. 'I'm so glad, my dear, that you and the other women had already gone to bed. Come now, I'll show you round and afterwards Gladys will join us for a dish of tea and I hope your lovely bride will too, Meade, although,' he added as he pulled on one end of his moustache, 'she seemed a bit on edge just now.'

'She's just tired from the journey Sir, I'm sure she will.'

'That's good then, you must have noticed it's a lot cooler here than it is down on the coast. Beastly hot place, Mombasa, only go there when it is absolutely necessary.'

'You are so right Arthur, may I call you Arthur?' She looked up at him guilelessly.

'Of course you can, my dear.'

'It's the first bearable weather,' she continued, 'that I've enjoyed since leaving Naples.'

'I trust your parents are well. How much longer will your father be stationed at Malta? I suppose the old boy's too long in the tooth to be promoted?'

'Nonsense, Arthur, he's not even as old as you are.' Gerald noticed Cunningham flinch. 'He's got another year, and you're not really that old.' She hugged his arm reassuringly, so that he smiled just enough to make his moustache twitch.

'I suppose you two must have had a lot of fun on the boat.' Gerald and Daphne looked at each other and started laughing. Cunningham looked cross. 'Can't see what's so funny about that.' Daphne started to hoot with laughter, she couldn't control herself. 'What on earth is the silly girl laughing at?' He appealed to Gerald.

'It's nothing, sir, it's just…' and Daphne started again.

'Just what, for God's sake?'

Well sir, we were talking about that when you found us.' Gerald shot Daphne a furious look to make her stop. Tears were streaming down her face and she was dabbing ineffectually at her eyes with a small lace hankie, smearing her make-up.

'I still don't know what that was, but from what I can see, it must have been hilarious.' Daphne was going to start again and Gerald thought he would strangle her, if she did. He tried desperately to think of something to change the subject.

'I suppose it was pretty wild when you first got here, Sir.' They were walking across the open sun-baked ground in front of the house towards the edge of the nearest banana plantation.

'It still is, my boy. Every week I have to shoot something that's got into one of the animal stockades and nipped off with a calf or goat. Lion or leopard usually and wire fences are not much good because what animal can't hop over them, walks right through them, like the rhino. They and the elephants play havoc with the plantations. A year's work can go down the drain in one night.' Daphne finally had control of herself and gazed up attentively at Cunningham.

'You're so brave, Arthur, to tackle all this.' The moustache twitched again. The plantation was irrigated by a complex system of ditches and two men, working with hoes, were opening and closing the earth sluices as they directed the water into one channel after another. Daphne turned away from the plantation and looked across to the house and outbuildings. Over to the left was an area about the size of a tennis court, with a thick thorn and wire fence around it.

'What's that Arthur?' she asked, pointing with a long elegant finger. She'd taken off her hat and held it in her other hand, as the sun was now quite low and the worst of the heat had gone. Gerald noticed that as she raised her arm, her tailored shirt accentuated the firm, well rounded contours of her body. He appreciated her narrow waist and flaring hips, the way her dark hair was piled on top of her head and the delicate lines at the nape of her neck. A strand of loose hair fluttered in the light breeze, that played around them and caught between her lips.

'Oh that's Gladys' garden, bless her. Works terribly hard at it and then some idiot leaves the gate open, a stray beast gets in and she has to start all over again. Won't give up though, she's determined that we have our own vegetables here.' Gerald wasn't listening, he just wanted to touch Daphne, his mouth felt dry. The impulse, triggered by her scent, was almost irresistible as he watched her hook the errant strand of hair from her mouth. Unexpectedly, she turned and looked directly at him from beneath heavy lids. He started, as if she had read his mind.

'I bet you've never worked in a kitchen garden, Gerald,' her mood was irrepressible, 'and why should you,' she continued, 'when you, and I for that matter, have always lived with shops just around the corner.' She put her hat on and turned back to Arthur. 'May we go in for tea please, I'm terribly thirsty.' Gerald's mouth was still dry and he needed something a lot stronger than tea.

Tea was served on the veranda and Gladys joined them. There was no sign of Betty. They sat in cane chairs and chatted about colonial life. Gladys told them how different she had found it all to begin with, from their life in India. They had spent most of their married life there, since she had left her family in Washington and they had only recently moved to British East Africa. Gerald sat across from Daphne and once, when he looked up suddenly, he caught her looking at him with a small, enigmatic smile on her sensuous lips.

'Dinner is at eight.' Gladys told Daphne, when tea had been cleared away. 'We do dress, just to maintain standards and I've invited the Culpeppers, who are one of our nearest neighbours. They started farming at about the same time as we did. The Gilbeys who are staying at the Norfolk, while their house is being built, are also coming.'

'They are old friends of ours from India,' added Arthur. 'In fact, I think they came here because they couldn't live there without us.' The moustache twitched again.

'Don't talk nonsense, dear,' she turned back to Daphne, 'I've also invited young William, who's General Drysdale's son and is up here on leave, from Cape Town.'

'He has quite a reputation with the girls, I'm told,' said Arthur, 'but Gerald and I will look after you, my dear.' He beamed at her. 'He's also staying at the Norfolk and will be coming out with the Gilbeys and all of them are staying with the Culpeppers for a couple of days.' Gladys got up and the others followed and went to their separate rooms. Betty was asleep and Gerald closed the door silently. She had removed her dress and was stretched out on the bed. He went through to the dressing room where he found that his luggage had been unpacked and his clothes hung away. He opened the wardrobe and riffled through until he found one of his tuxedos. He took it out, hung it on the back of a chair and then found a shirt, tie and clean underclothes, which he threw on the bed.

He stripped off his clothes, shrugged into a silk dressing gown and tucked his feet into brocade slippers. He flung a towel over his shoulder, picked up his wash bag and went out into the corridor, by the dressing room door. He found a line of steaming hot water pots standing beside the copper hip bath and emptied all but the smallest into the bath and that, he tipped into the ewer and started to shave.

Afterwards, he soaked himself in the bath and thought about Betty and all that she had said about him and Daphne. It was almost as if Betty's latest attack on Daphne had triggered what had happened between them. Something certainly had happened that afternoon and he knew that Daphne was equally aware of it. The water was very relaxing and he sank as deep as he could into the bath. In fairness to Betty, he admitted to himself he had, of course, noticed Daphne but for that matter, so had every other man on board. Only a blind man or one who was senile, or both, would have missed her.

He washed and rinsed his hair and the rest of his body, stepped out of the bath and briskly rubbed himself dry. He put on his dressing gown and went back down the corridor to his dressing room, dropped his sponge bag on the table and moved quietly through to the bedroom. Betty was sitting at her dressing table, gazing at herself in the mirror.

'The bathroom is all yours, my dear, should you want it. One of the house boys went in to change the hot water as I left.' She ignored him and touched the skin delicately beneath her eyes. He could see that she had been crying. He went back to the other room and started to dress. Damn women, why were they always so emotional, never on an even keel, so that one never knew where one was with them?

'Gerald,' she called, 'I will not be at dinner.' He finished tying his tie and then went through to the bedroom. 'Did you hear what I said? I don't want any dinner. I'm not hungry. I don't feel like being polite to people I don't know and I certainly don't want to have to sit across the table and look at you.'

'Just as you wish, my dear, I'm sure Gladys will be very disappointed but, on the other hand, Daphne will be delighted.' He went back into the dressing room, secured his cummerbund and slipped his feet into a pair of patent leather shoes. He ran his silver-backed brushes through his hair, took his tuxedo jacket from the back of the chair and put it on. He left quietly by the dressing room door. There was not a sound from the bedroom.

CHAPTER 18

'Doctor Marais's nurse is coming out to see you this morning and I think Tim is coming sometime today to meet you. You can compare notes. He broke his arm last year in a flying accident,' she finished shaving him and handed over a damp towel, 'Not a drop of blood to be seen.' She straightened the bedclothes over his right leg.

'How are you feeling, did you eat all your breakfast?'

'Yes nanny.'

She smiled as she held his eyes briefly. She's nervous, he thought. Tim probably.

'You mustn't fuss so, but I love it, you mustn't get me used to it.'

'Why not? It's usual for a woman to look after a man, or women after men in general' she added, and he caught her eye again.

'Tim is coming out today.' He took her hand as she straightened his pillow.

'I know, you told me that when you came in. Are you nervous?'

'Why should I be nervous?'

'Because I have the feeling you somehow want my approval, a non family opinion.' She looked straight at him, her colour high, and very gently freed her wrist with her other hand.

'Of course not…well yes I suppose so…in a way. You are so worldly and I'm well…'

'Unworldly?'

'Well yes, I've never been out of South Africa. A lot of my school friends toured Europe, some even went to America but I've always been here. I'm not complaining but everything I know, have learnt, has been from books and studying skills such as needle point, painting in watercolours, ballroom dancing, chess, and playing the piano and violin.'

'You play the violin?'

'Yes, a treat in store for you' she laughed and clapped her hands.

'Pull up a chair and tell me about Tim.'

'He's young, well…my age, but he seems younger. I've known him all my life. We were children together until his father moved his whole family to Cape Town. He has coastal cargo ships running around the southern half of Africa. Made a lot of money in the War and he is insistent that Tim joins him in the business.'

'And Tim doesn't want to? James told me he wants to start an air postal service.'

'Exactly, so you know all about it.'

'No I don't, that's all I do know.'

'He wants to run an air service between Cape Town, Kimberley and Johannesburg to begin with and then build on that. All the mail from the UK comes from Southampton to Cape Town on the Union Castle boats in two weeks and then it gets bogged down in unreliable train and coach services. He could carry at least 300 pounds of mail in one flight from Cape Town to Kimberley and on to Johannesburg in one day.'

'How would it be paid for?'

'That's easy. There would be a two-tier rate out of England and the same system here in South Africa.'

'Air mail and donkey mail.' She laughed and Chadwyck felt her enthusiasm.

'He's fiercely independent and takes on odd charter work so he doesn't have to toe his father's line.'

'You mean go to work for his father?'

'Yes.'

'I was going to do that too, having finally finished University, well two in fact, but now it's rather different.' She took his hand at her side of the bed, wanting to say something but unable to form the words. 'I miss him terribly but I know I will have help from all sides when I feel I am ready to take his place. No I don't mean that. I mean follow in his footsteps, that's not right either. It's a vast multifaceted, multinational operation that I was going to be part of, climbing to the top in time but now…I don't know, I am at the top and thank God for the board of directors who have run it very successfully for years and can continue to do so without my help.'

'Would you like some water?' She filled his glass from a carafe on his bedside table. 'Is this why you've come up to see if there is anything to the diamond story?' He sipped the water and watched her over the rim of the glass. 'You weren't ready for what you have told me, you want time to think and do something on your own before falling back into the comfortable arms of an existing empire?' He smiled at her and she was more relaxed.

'I wouldn't call it an empire but I think you're right. I haven't talked about it, I came close to discussing it with my mother at Springbokfontein before I came up here but she knows nothing of business and right now any mention of my father would distress her unnecessarily.' She took his glass and put it back on the table. 'Anyway we are talking about you, not me.'

'Not much more to say really.'

'You were telling me about Tim, about his independent streak.'

'That's a good way to describe him, independent, but I have had no way to compare him or his thinking until you arrived. It's not the same with James and my father. They are country folk with different values and we are family, peas in a pod, but Tim is different because he has lived in a different world, at University and in Cape Town. He has even been to England last year with his father, when he finished University.'

'Do you miss him when he is away?'

'No not really' she answered immediately. 'I've convinced

myself it's a negative, counterproductive emotion. I can't see myself withering away from unrequited love.'

'You'd have to love him to do that.'

'I don't but I'm always very pleased to see him. He makes me laugh like you do and he's gentle and considerate.'

CHAPTER 19

Gerald crossed the veranda and went through the open double doors into the large lamp-lit drawing room. The beautiful silk oriental rugs, tiger skins and regimental swords and colours that were hung on the walls gave it a distinctly Indian look. A magnificent oil seascape, of an East Indiamen at anchor in Hong Kong Bay, hung over a broad, deep fireplace in which several large logs were burning. Most of the furniture was Georgian, good quality and well cared for and had obviously come from England originally. Its elegance contrasted sharply with the rustic effect of the highly polished, hand-hewn timber floor and the joinery work of the windows and doors. Cunningham, who was dressed in a beautifully cut bottle-green velvet smoking jacket, was standing by the fireplace and arguing with Culpepper.

'Ah, there you are Meade,' he glanced with some surprise at Gerald's tuxedo. 'What a splendidly casual looking outfit, American no doubt.' Before Gerald could answer, he continued. 'You'll remember Culpepper from last night,' and he waved a hand in Culpepper's direction. 'His recollection of the outcome of our contest differs from mine. I'm sure you'll agree with me that, although it was a very close-run thing, we won.'

'Nonsense,' said Culpepper, tugging on the lapels of his black dinner jacket, 'if Cole heard you say that, he'd blackball you from the club.'

'What club? He hasn't started it yet and if he insists he won, I wouldn't want to be a member of it anyhow.' Gerald laughed and shook hands with Culpepper.

'Then the best way to settle it would be to have a return match as soon as possible.'

'Capital idea,' said Cunningham. 'What can I get you to drink?'

'Scotch please,' said Gerald and added, 'on its own.'

'By that you mean whisky, I suppose?' said Cunningham and Culpepper laughed. Gerald walked across and took the large crystal glass that Cunningham held out for him.

'Thank you, Sir.' He cleared his throat. 'I hope I'm wrong and Betty won't disappoint us, but I don't think she will be joining us this evening.'

'That would be a great shame, my boy, Culpepper was just saying how much he was looking forward to meeting her again, although I don't think he would have said it with such enthusiasm if his wife had been here. She and my wife will be with us shortly. Women always seem to have things to talk about that they won't share with us.'

'And why not, Cunningham, haven't we things to say to each other that we'd rather they didn't hear?' Gerald sipped his whisky and wondered if they always called each other by their surnames, as if at school. The sound of a car horn cut across Arthur's answer. A Napier, with gleaming brass lamps and polished coachwork, pulled up in front of the house. The chauffeur switched off the lights and leapt out and held open one of the doors.

A young man in mess kit, stepped out and with an ingratiating smile held out his arm to a very elegant looking woman in her mid-fifties, who emerged from the car, wearing a full-length black evening dress. She wore a six stranded pearl choker, at her throat and carried a mother-of-pearl and silk fan. She was followed by a stockily built man in a burgundy-coloured smoking jacket, that fitted a shade too snugly around his stout figure. He had thin white hair, a florid, fleshy complexion, and was clean shaven. Arthur put his drink down and went out to greet them.

'Perfect answer to a ticklish question, Meade, the old boy doesn't like to lose.' Culpepper who was about fifteen years older than Gerald, stood with his back to the fire and swirled the last of his whisky round his glass and drank it. He was almost the same height as Gerald, solidly built and obviously, by his complexion, spent most of his time outside.

'Arthur tells me you're farming here.'

'Yes I am and bloody hard going it is too. Emily and I came out here five years ago after I left the army. She's South African you know, so she's used to the life, unlike one of those delicate English roses, who would never last the course.' Gerald could hear the new arrivals talking loudly around the car and at the same moment Gladys and Emily Culpepper came into the room.

'Gerald, there you are, you do look dashing. Let me introduce you to Emily.' Gerald moved round Culpepper and stopped dead in his tracks. Daphne was standing behind Gladys, and he hadn't seen her come in. He couldn't breathe. The fresh, laughing young girl of that afternoon had suddenly become a devastatingly attractive woman. 'Gerald, this is Emily,' Gladys repeated. He stepped forward, as if in a dream, and shook hands.

'How do you do, your husband tells me that you are from South Africa.'

He wasn't looking at her, he was looking over her shoulder at Daphne, who had moved into the room and was standing by the fire. He didn't hear Emily's answer, only the roaring in his ears as he stared at Daphne's legs, which were outlined by the firelight, through her dress. She was watching him with a mischievous look in her slate grey eyes and with that same enigmatic smile, playing at the edge of her mouth.

'We're going there soon,' he hazarded.

'Oh, where?' asked Emily. He looked at her, for the first time.

'Why, South Africa, of course. You were talking about South Africa, weren't you?'

'No Gerald,' said Gladys, 'you were.'

'I'm awfully sorry.' Gerald let go of Emily's hand and smiled weakly at her. 'I must have missed what you said.' He was certain he heard Daphne laugh. He could feel his face flushing.

'When are you going to South Africa?' asked Emily in her soft, gentle voice.

'Yes, Gerald, do tell us. When are you going to South Africa?' Daphne came up beside him and laid her fingertips casually on his arm. 'I might come with you, instead of going back to boring old Malta.' She smiled wickedly at him and ran her fingertips along his sleeve until, as if by accident, she touched his wrist.

'In a week or so, I suppose. It really depends on Betty.'

'Betty?' said Emily.

'My wife,' said Gerald. Emily looked at Daphne and then back at Gerald. 'This is Daphne,' said Gerald, introducing her, 'Daphne Frobisher,' he added, by way of explanation.

'Oh,' said Emily, 'how do you do. I heard you were just married,' she stammered, looking back at Gerald, 'on your honeymoon and when I saw you two together, I thought…' Daphne laughed, a deep, exultant laugh and squeezed his arm.

'Gerald, you're blushing, how sweet, how simply delightful.'

'I'm most awfully sorry,' said Emily and was saved from further embarrassment by the noisy arrival of the Gilbeys. Arthur made the introductions and offered everyone a drink. Culpepper had already helped himself. William Drysdale made an obvious move for Daphne, much to Gerald's annoyance. Cunningham, Gilbey and Culpepper stood in one corner and Gerald, as he watched Daphne flirt with William, heard them discussing the events of the previous night. He knew that she was doing it on purpose to see what his reaction would be, so he turned away and spoke to Gladys and Emily. If William continued to lean on Daphne anymore, thought Gerald, he'd have her on the floor. How could he break it up without being rude to his hostess?

'That must be the General's son, you spoke of this afternoon. We haven't been introduced yet.'

'How very remiss of Arthur.' She turned her head. 'William, my dear boy, come and meet Gerald Meade, from Washington.' He looked cheated, Gerald was delighted. William offered Daphne his arm and led her across. Gerald shook hands and could feel William putting every ounce of strength he had into his grip. Daphne stood at his side and enjoyed the contest. William was an inch or so taller than Gerald and painfully thin. He had pale blue eyes, a weak chin and mouth and a large nose that dominated his face. Scented pomade held his lank, straw-coloured hair firmly in place.

'Well, we all seem to be here now, except for Betty.' Gladys glanced at Gerald.

'I mentioned to Arthur earlier, Gladys, that she won't be joining us and she asked me to make her apologies. She's still very tired from the voyage.'

'I'm so sorry to hear that, perhaps Daphne could go and see how she is.'

'I don't think that would be a very good idea, Gladys.' As he spoke, Daphne enthused.

'But of course I'll go, Gladys.'

'No, really there's no need. If you'll excuse me, I won't be a moment.' Before he could reach the door, it opened and Betty walked into the room. Her presence was electrifying and they all stopped talking at the same moment as she crossed the room, in absolute control of herself and everyone else. She was dressed in white, almost shocking in its intensity and breath taking in its simplicity. It was more the idea of a dress than the reality. A confection created by a genius and crafted by a magician. It flared upwards from her tiny waist covering, as if by suggestion, her breasts and shoulders, while leaving her back and arms almost completely bare. It flowed downwards, with sweeping, pleated lines to the floor. It was made of silk and lace and shimmered with thousands of hand sewn seed pearls. She had bought it in Paris and Gerald had never seen it before.

Her burnished, corn coloured, hair was painstakingly coiled high on her head and swept vertically up from the tips of her delicate ears.

It was held in place with an exquisite tortoiseshell peineta. At her flawless, creamy throat she wore a fabulous diamond necklace that her father had given her as a wedding present. She wore nothing at her wrists and no rings at all. Gladys broke the spell and was the first to speak. 'My dear, you look absolutely lovely. I'm so glad you are able to join us.'

'Thank you, I'm sorry I'm late.'

'But you're not,' said Arthur, collecting himself with a great effort and coming forward to stand proudly by her side. 'Let me introduce you to dear friends of ours from India, Lionel and Harriet Gilbey.'

Betty stood where she was and everyone gravitated towards her. They were suddenly all talking at once. Gilbey stepped forward, bowed low over her hand and kissed it. She gave him a brilliant smile, which she held while greeting his wife and the Culpeppers. William Drysdale, squirming like an over-excited puppy, in anticipation of being introduced, was rubbing his sweating palms on the seat of his trousers. Gerald saw Daphne glance quickly at herself in one of the two ormolu mirrors that flanked the fireplace. She fidgeted nervously with that same errant strand of hair, that had seemed so devilishly attractive that afternoon.

With conflicting thoughts of compassion for Daphne and confusion with his own feelings for Betty, Gerald turned away from the group that thronged about his wife and addressed Daphne. As casually as he could he asked her about life on Malta. He caught her appreciation of his gesture in her eyes and some of the bravura returned. Like an outclassed filly she was trying desperately to claw back the ground she had lost, fighting to regain a position of pre-eminence. Gerald was amazed at her resilience and she was still talking about Malta when a houseboy slipped into the room and spoke quietly to Gladys.

'Dinner is ready everyone. Please will you all follow me.' Arthur offered his arm to Betty and followed his wife through to the dining room. The Culpeppers and Gilbeys followed them and, before Gerald could move, William had swept Daphne away in pursuit. Gerald was left standing alone in the large empty room and all he could think of was that Betty had removed her wedding ring. Gladys led the way into the dining room and, without looking back, she started to call out the seating arrangements.

'Gerald, dear boy you sit here on my right. Gerald.' She turned to look for him. 'Where on earth is Gerald?' He appeared at the door, just as all of them, except Betty, turned towards him. 'Ah there you are, dear boy. Why are you hanging back? Don't be bashful, come and sit up here beside me.' She tapped the back of the Sheraton dining room chair to her right. Daphne made a sound that could have been a laugh and covered it with a remark to William. Gerald, feeling rather foolish, noticed Betty's head snap up and knew that it wasn't going to be easy to get them to talk to each other. Gladys hadn't noticed anything and blithely carried on.

'Betty you will be sitting to Arthur's right.' Betty smiled at her sweetly and moved round the table. Arthur held out her chair for her with a gallant flourish and she sat down. 'And Harriet you, of course, are on Arthur's other side. The bad side, my dear. You do remember?' The two women smiled secretly to each other in reference to Arthur's deafness. 'And Lionel, of course, you are here on my left.' He was already standing behind his chair. 'Now let me see, what can I do with the rest of you. William, I know you are dying to sit next to Daphne but you'll just have to contain yourself, dear boy, because if I let you, it would mean Emily would have to sit next to her husband and, we can't have that, can we?'

William looked crest-fallen and Gerald suddenly realised what was about to happen. He looked across the table at Betty and knew that she too had seen the inevitability of it. For a moment, he thought she was going to leave the room. 'So that puts Daphne beside Gerald, Emily opposite her and you George, will be between Daphne and Harriet.' Culpepper rubbed his hands in glee and moved in that direction, before Gladys changed her mind.

They sat down and two of the houseboys, who had been standing like bookends at either side of the serving table, started to take round the first course. William was very rudely sitting with his back to Emily and staring at Betty who was in animated conversation with Arthur. As Lionel, who was on her other side, was talking to Gladys, Gerald could see that poor Emily was going to have a rather thin time of it. He lent across and smiled at her in an attempt to make up for his earlier rudeness but, before he could say anything he had to lean back to allow the houseboy to put down a plate. It was game paté decorated with sprigs of freshwater cress and tiny wedges of lemon. The second boy held a silver salver in front of him on which stood a wicker basket of hot buttered toast wrapped in a napkin. By the time the houseboys had moved on to Daphne, Emily had been drawn into conversation by Gladys.

Daphne, who had been talking to George, swung round in her seat when the first houseboy put her plate down and her knee brushed against Gerald's leg. He looked directly at her. She moved away instinctively on contact but, as he started to talk to her, she allowed her leg to fall back against his. He kept talking but faltered badly when he heard one of her shoes scrape against the other and he knew what would happen next. He moved away from her slightly, reaching for another piece of toast, which the houseboys had left in the centre of the table. As he did, he caught the surprise in her eyes, which was followed immediately by a spark of amusement. He picked up the basket of toast and offered it to her.

'A little more, perhaps?' She glanced down between them and then laughed.

'Such impetuosity.' When she looked back at him there was no mistaking her meaning. He could hear Arthur talking to Harriet and he knew without looking that Betty was watching them. He turned towards Gladys.

'Would you like some toast, Gladys?'

'No thank you, dear boy, it's cold and I've asked them to bring some more from the kitchen.' She turned back to Lionel. Gerald could feel Daphne's silk-stockinged toe on his instep as she gently removed his shoe while she talked on about how dull life was in Malta, when the Fleet was a sea. One of the houseboys returned with more toast and Gerald followed him with his eyes, as he passed behind Betty, so that he could look at her without being too obvious. She was staring at the top of the table between them as if she could see right through it and knew every move that Daphne was making. The houseboy offered her toast that she refused, with a polite smile. She looked directly at Gerald and he was numbed by the coldness of her eyes. William said something to her but she ignored him. There was only the two of them, locked in a private world of their own.

Although he realised the gravity of the situation, his feelings were strangely ambivalent. She was very beautiful, very rich but so unreasonably possessive. It seemed absurd that she could instil in him such a sense of guilt over something, that seemed to him, so trivial. He was flattered by women's attention and he knew that they found him attractive, surely his wife must know that too and could make allowances. What was the point of the game if nobody had any fun playing it? Must there always be a winner and a loser and why did one always lose a little when one did win? He suddenly realised that Daphne's foot was no longer on his, she had turned away to Culpepper and he realised that Gladys was talking to him.

'Gerald you haven't been listening to a word I've said and I'm not about to repeat it. Stop glaring at your lovely bride and pay a little attention to your ageing hostess.' Betty was still looking at him in a strange dispassionate way, as if she didn't know him but had met his sort before. With a great effort he turned to Gladys, he'd heard threads of her conversation and knew she had been talking about motor cars. He fished wildly in his mind for something intelligent to say and looked to Lionel for help,

'What car do you drive, old boy, in Washington that is?' he obliged.

'A Packard, Sir. A twelve horsepower Packard, it's an open tourer. My father gave it to me for my eighteenth birthday. He drives a Rolls.' What a stupid, pretentious thing to say, he thought, as if it mattered what car he drove. He could hear William braying like a donkey, as he told Betty about soldiering in South Africa and how much he regretted missing the opportunity that his father had had, in giving the Boers the pasting they deserved. Stupid arrogant sap. God help the British Empire if he and the likes of him, were going to be the next in charge.

'What was that, Meade?' Lionel asked. Gerald started.

'I think, Sir, I said God Save the British Empire.' Lionel looked at him blankly. Daphne laughed and the rest of the table fell silent.

'How very sweet, dear boy,' said Gladys, 'but of course, you are half British aren't you?'

'I'll second that, Meade,' said Arthur, from the other end of the table.

'Can't think what it's got to do with motor cars,' mumbled Lionel, as he tried the claret that had been poured, in readiness for the next course. Gerald knew that they were all watching him and could feel his face flushing again. He realised he'd have to say something because, until he did, nobody else would. Arthur was holding his wine glass in front of him in anticipation and, with a lurch, Gerald got to his feet and picked up his own glass. He looked around at their expectant faces. Betty, who was studying her clasped hands on the table in front of her, was the only one who wasn't looking at him. 'I know my timing's a little out but I just wanted to thank you,' and he gave Gladys his most gallant smile, 'and Arthur very much for inviting me here as the newest member of the Wickham family and to tell you how much I appreciate your kindness to us both. As you just said, Gladys, I am half Scottish and at times like this, I feel very proud of it. So here's to you all and,' he emphasised the word, 'to the British Empire and long may you all last!' He raised his glass and the men got to their feet. 'The British Empire.' They choroused and drank in unison. Gerald looked at Betty, she was now looking at him but he still couldn't read anything in her beautiful, ice-blue eyes. They all sat and Gladys beamed at him.

'Thank you Gerald, that was very thoughtful of you. I'm sure you and Betty will have a marvellous time here and Arthur and I will do everything we can to make sure you do.' He smiled at her and mumbled something in appreciation. He felt dizzy and mildly nauseous. The conversation seemed to be getting louder and more confused and with it thrumming in his ears, he felt as though he was underwater. One of the houseboys brought in the main course, which was roast guineafowl and a marvellous selection of Gladys's fresh vegetables and then cleared away the first course, while the other refilled their glasses. Gerald drank deeply from his and slowly the room returned to normal.

He looked at Daphne and was surprised to find that he no longer felt the same excitement he had before. She was talking to Culpepper and, although she must have felt his presence, she ignored him and yet, at the same time, somehow managed to convey the feeling that a man that had been discarded by his own woman, was of no interest to her. So he talked to Emily of trivial things while his mind tried to make sense of his feelings.

Never once, during the rest of the meal, did Betty look at him. Somehow he kept going as the wine was taken round again and the glasses refilled, the plates removed and replaced by others. Dessert followed the fowl and was in turn followed by a savoury, until he found himself on his feet again and the women had gone. After large quantities of port and very good cigars, the men went through to the drawing room to find that Harriet was ready to leave and Betty had gone to bed. Once the Gilbeys had gone, taking the hapless William with them, the Culpeppers soon followed.

'Come on, my dear, it's been a long day,' said Gladys and Arthur rose to his feet and followed her before stopping at the door.

'Don't worry about the lamps, the servants will take care of them after you have gone to bed.' Daphne was lying back in one of the armchairs by the fire and Gerald stood by the window and drained his glass of port.

'Good night Daphne.' He put his glass down carefully on a pie-crust table and left the room. She said nothing. When he reached his bedroom Gerald found Betty sitting in a chair by the window, reading a book.

'I thought you'd gone to bed.' He was surprised and at the same time pleased that she was still up.

'Well, as you can see, I haven't.' She spoke to him in a voice that one used with a troublesome child. He took off his tuxedo jacket and casually threw it on the bed. 'Pick that up, please. I'm sleeping there and you're not. I've made up my mind Gerald that it was a terrible mistake to have married you. I foolishly allowed the emotional side of my heart to overrule the practical side of my mind. I can see now that it won't work, you're not ready for marriage.' He opened his mouth to say something, to somehow stop her saying what he didn't want to hear. 'Don't interrupt me Gerald. I want you to arrange passage for me, as soon as possible, so that I may return to my family in Washington.' Her voice was now flat and lifeless as she continued. 'I shall stay with them and you must decide what you want from life and know, without any doubt, what you are going to do before you ever again try to involve me in it. Until you do that Gerald, there is no future for us together. Now please leave me, I have a splitting headache and I must rest.'

He moved towards her but she got up and walked past him towards the door. She stood there, firmly holding herself together with the last of her strength and looked at him steadily until he picked up his jacket and left the room.

CHAPTER 20

'Nurse here Miss Adelaide, to see Bwana Chad.'

'Thank you Lily, please show her in.'

The maid stood aside and the nurse brushed past her. She was small, plumpish and dressed in a white starched uniform that almost reached her ankles. She had grey ringlets pinned close to her head and appeared to be in her early fifties. She bustled into the room in a no nonsense manner.

'Good morning Adelaide, you are looking well. I'm Fiona Logan, one of Doctor Marais's nurses' she said as she stood in front of Chadwyck. 'Mr Meade, I presume, and I am very pleased to meet you. I have this for you,' and she handed him a telegram. 'It was delivered to the hospital now that you are registered with Doctor Marais.' She spoke with a soft west Highland burr, which immediately made him think of Glen Lyon.

'Thank you and I am very pleased to meet you, a fellow Scot.' He noticed her eyebrow rose imperceptibly.

'Well we are probably more Irish than Scottish but my father's family originally came from Glen Lyon, where we still have a house.'

'Oh I know where Glen Lyon is, I'm from a wee bit further west, near Oban. I came out here early in the war with a field hospital attached to the Second Battalion of The Black Watch. When the War was over I stayed on to help with the concentration camps, a terrible business, women and children rounded up in Kitchener's scorched earth tactics, a very shameful moment in our history.' She was carrying a large bag, which she placed on the floor close to his bed.'How are you feeling? Have you had trouble sleeping?' She knew it hurt, she hadn't even asked if he felt pain.

'I have had to take small amounts of Laudanum at night but when I'm awake I can, more or less, contain it.'

'Have you finished the bottle Doctor Marais left you?'

'No I've still got a little more than half left.'

'Good. I brought you another bottle but go easy on it because it can be very addictive. Now let me take your temperature and pulse.' She produced a thermometer from her apron and stuck it under his tongue. With her other hand she scooped up his wrist and peered at the watch clipped to her chest. 'Very satisfactory, you are young and will mend well.' She shook the thermometer and returned it to the pocket in her apron. 'Now I'm going to test your reflexes. I have here two needles and I'm going to touch one or two of your toes at the same time and I want you to tell me which ones. We'll call them one to five, the big toe being one. Do you understand what I'm going to do?' Chadwyck nodded. 'And I'll put this pillow on your chest so you can't see what I'm doing.' Adelaide laughed and went to stand beside Nurse Logan who pulled out a notebook and pencil.

'One and four' said Chadwyck.

'Good.'

'Two.'

'And the other one…'

'Just one needle on number two.'

'Very good. Now.'

'Both on three.'

'You'll do. Now I've brought you a few things on loan. Two bed pans and two urine bottles. They are the old tin type from the war, perfectly serviceable and they don't break like some of the new glass ones. I have also brought you a hoist so you can use a bedpan. Have you had any bowel movement yet?'

Chadwyck shook his head.

'I thought not but you will soon.' She dipped into her bag again and pulled out two ropes with handles on the ends and a box of laxative powders. 'If not, take one of these in the morning. Have someone tie these ropes to a ceiling beam, three feet apart and directly above your pelvis. Move the bed a bit if you need to. This will enable you to raise your body six inches off the bed to slip the bedpan under you, which someone must do for you. You must concentrate on lifting your body without moving your legs,' she smiled at him and he nodded in understanding.

'Well that's me done. Doctor Marais will be pleased with the reflex test. Have you any questions?'

'No nurse and thank you very much for coming out to see me.'

'I'll be back this time in two weeks but if you develop a fever. Send for Doctor Marais immediately.'

'I will and thank you again.'

Adelaide came back to his room after seeing Nurse Logan to her wagon.

CHAPTER 21

The day after the dinner party at Kashmir, Betty had spent all day with Gladys and completely ignored Daphne. Arthur and Gerald had gone into Nairobi to find out about Betty's return to Washington, having both failed to dissuade her when she appeared after breakfast. That evening they tried again and when Betty wouldn't change her mind, they admitted that they had made a tentative booking, on a north bound boat for Cherbourg, which was due to call at Mombasa in three days' time. Once at Cherbourg, she would connect with a French liner to New York. After dinner Gerald had tried again and when she remained adamant he insisted that he would go with her. They had argued bitterly and finally she had told him that she didn't give a damn what he did.

When Gerald came down to breakfast the next morning, he found himself alone in the dining room. He could see that Arthur had already had breakfast and supposed that he was somewhere outside, organising the men on the farm. There was no sign of anyone else around except one of the houseboys who was clearing away the dishes.

'Jumbo bwana,' he bobbed his head and grinned. 'Coffee or tea, please bwana?'

'I'll have coffee, orange juice and scrambled eggs.'

'Right away bwana,' and he scuttled out of the room. Gerald

walked across to the window and looked out towards the plantations, where he could see men working in the irrigation ditches. A rider, under a large slouch hat, was heading towards the house with a canvas bag swinging from his shoulder. Gerald sat at the table as the boy returned with a steaming pot of freshly brewed coffee and a large glass of orange juice. He poured coffee into Gerald's cup and left the pot on the table.

'Eggs very soon, bwana,' he said and left the room again. Gerald sipped his orange juice and reflected on the traumatic events of the night before. He could hear two men talking on the veranda and a moment later, the other houseboy came in with a handful of mail, and put it on the dining room table, within reach of Gerald.

He eyed the pile as he sipped at his orange juice and, when his curiosity got the better of him ,he turned the letters over, one by one, reading the envelopes until, surprised, he found one addressed to himself. It was a small manila envelope, sealed, heavily waxed and post marked Washington, two days after he and Betty had left. He looked at it with apprehension and for the first time in more than a month thought of his father and family. He nudged it, like a chess piece, with his fingertips and moved it to one side of the pile. The houseboy came in and set a plate of scrambled eggs in front of him. He toyed with the eggs, totally absorbed in his thoughts. He was in no hurry to open the envelope.

He drank his coffee and the houseboy who was standing behind him, refilled his cup. He buttered a piece of toast and left it lying on his plate, got up from the table and went over and stood by the window again. He dug his hands deep into the pockets of his flannels, looked out of the window and hunched his shoulders, in a defensive manner. He looked back at the table, resentful of the envelopes' existence. He walked back and stood behind his chair and picked up the manila envelope and slit it open with a knife from the table. It was from Bayard Braithwaite, the senior partner of Braithwaite, Chambers and Caldicott, his father's solicitors in Washington.

Dear Gerald,

I assume that you are, as yet, unaware of the fact that your father died in Ireland and was subsequently buried at Glen Lyon, on the same day that you chose to marry Betty Wickham. I have since learnt from Mr Wickham that you showed him false documentation, supposedly from your father, conveying his consent to the marriage and his regrets at being unable to attend.

Your mother and Chadwyck are now at Springbokfontein and I think the least you and your wife can do is go there as soon as possible and have the decency to explain your behaviour to them in person.

The enclosed unopened telegrams I know to be from Chadwyck, as he sent me one after your father had died. I deplore the fact that you chose to ignore the telegrams when they were offered to you in Washington before your precipitous departure.

I can only add how glad I am that your father never knew of your latest wilful act of disobedience. I, as his Executor, have strict instructions with regard to your Trust, which I will naturally follow to the letter. There is no provision in your father's will for you to receive any monies by way of capital or income. As you well know, he expected you to earn your own living as you had repeatedly refused to go on to university, as was his wish.

Yours sincerely,
Bayard Braithwaite

He picked up the telegrams, walked slowly over to the window and sat heavily on the window seat. He was breathing with difficulty and his hands trembled badly. The peace and beauty of his surroundings were in stark contrast to the chaos of his mind. He turned away and stared numbly at Braithwaite's letter. Slowly, already aware of their contents, he opened one of the telegrams. It was postmarked London and dated the day before his wedding.

'It is with the greatest sorrow that I have to tell you that our father died of pneumonia, early on Tuesday morning, in Ireland. He will be buried on Saturday at Glen Lyon. May God be with us all. Chadwyck.' He sat and stared at the telegram. He smoothed it repeatedly, with the palm of his hand, on his knee and soundlessly he began to cry. Great tears splashed onto the paper so that the ink smudged and started to run. He didn't hear Betty come into the room, he didn't even move when she put her hand on his shoulder. She stood beside him, and looked at him intently for a moment before putting her arms around him. She gently sat beside him so that his head rested on her shoulder. She could feel his hot tears on her skin. She made soothing, calming sounds deep in her throat and stroked his cheek and neck.

'Gerry, what's the matter? What has happened?' He didn't answer but moved his hand so that she could take the telegram. The ink was so smudged that she had to read it twice before she could understand it. She leant across and picked up Braithwaite's letter and read it. She could not believe its callous tone and forced herself to read it again. She dropped the letter and went back to stroking his cheek. She could still feel his hot tears on her throat.

'I'm so sorry, Gerry, so very, very, sorry. I wish we had waited. You never told me that your father was against our marriage. Why Gerry, why didn't you tell me? Did you think I wouldn't wait? Didn't you know how much I love you?' He didn't answer. She thought of Braithwaite's statement about Gerald's finances and everything suddenly made sense.

She felt empty inside and couldn't prevent herself from feeling pity and contempt for him. She suddenly realised that her father had literally bought Gerald, for no other reason than to enhance his own social standing. She felt a searing, blinding hatred for her father, appalled that he should put his petty ambitions before her happiness and future. She wanted to move away but couldn't, to run from the house and scream at the sky, but didn't. She just sat there with her arms around her poor, sad, weak husband. The man she loved. Finally he stopped crying and raised his head and looked at her, in a way she had never seen before. She saw pain and humility in his eyes and his expression had matured dramatically.

'I never opened the other telegram Betty. There were two in the envelope from Braithwaite but I only opened one. I don't think I can bring myself to open the other, will you please do it for me?' He edged past her and collapsed into one of the dining room chairs. She bent down and picked up the telegram from where it lay on the floor and opened it. It was from Ballynahinch, in Ireland and dated the Sunday before their wedding.

'Father is dangerously ill with suspected pneumonia. Please come soonest. I need your support. Love Chadwyck'

She picked up the other telegram and Braithwaite's letter and slipped them into her bag. She looked across at her husband, where he sat slumped in the chair. As you need mine, my love, she thought, as you need mine. Betty went over and stood behind him and rubbed his neck soothingly but he didn't respond, he was miles away, dejected, in a world of his own. Thoughts and emotions tumbled like dice across her mind but through it all she could see that, because of what had happened, she couldn't possibly leave. She knew that she had committed herself to him and she knew herself well enough to know that she would see it through. She heard a door slam somewhere in the house, which cut across her thoughts and at the same moment Arthur and Gladys walked into the room.

'Good morning, you're up bright and early,' he stopped short. 'I say, my dear,' he continued, 'You look devastated, what on earth's the matter?'

'We need your help, Arthur, terrible news. We have to get down to Cape Town, as soon as possible. We've just learnt from the Meades' lawyer in Washington that Gerry's father was buried in Scotland the day we got married and that his mother and one of his brothers are in their house near Cape Town. We need to get the first boat we can out of Mombasa.'

'It's all so confusing, Arthur, I thought Betty was going to go back to Washington.'

'I know, my dear, but this is more important.' He patted Gladys gently on the shoulder.

'I'll go in to Nairobi after breakfast and get you booked on the first boat to Cape Town and if you write it now, I'll send a telegram to your mother in law, filling in your expected arrival once I know it. I'm very sorry you will be with us such a short time but I'm sure it's the right thing to do.'

CHAPTER 22

'Nurse Logan is such a dear. I have known her for years. I wonder where Tim is. He is expected to lunch and should be here by now. Have you opened the telegram?'

'No. You open it' said Chadwyck, handing it to her. 'It is almost certainly from my mother.'

'It is. I'll read it to you.'

'So very sorry to hear about your accident. Please convey my sincerest thanks and appreciation to the Flynn family for all their help and kindness. I received a telegram from Gerald today. He is in B.E.A. with his wife, Betty. They are taking a boat to Cape Town, arriving the end of next week. I have your address and will write to you now. All my love, Mama'

'My God she must be shaken to the core. How could he do it? Eddy and I thought it a possibility, the only possibility to explain his absence at the funeral. He knew it was against our father's wishes. How did he arrange it with the Wickhams? Although they wouldn't have needed much convincing.'

Lunch came and went and after they had finished eating, Adelaide excused herself and went to her room. Just before sundown Chadwyck heard Johnny and James come back. He could hear them discarding boots and hats and a moment later, with a perfunctory knock, James came into his room.

'All alone? Where are Tim and Adelaide?'

'Tim hasn't arrived and I think Adelaide is in her room.'

'He was supposed to be here to lunch or soon after, what could have happened to him.'

'I've no idea.'

'Something is wrong. Something has happened. He is always so reliable.' There was a knock on the door and Adelaide came in.

'Do you know where Tim is, James?'

'No. We will just have to wait and see. Speak of the devil, there he is!' They could all hear the sound of a horse being pulled up in front of the house.

'Don't move Chad, we'll be right back.'

'Very funny.'

A moment later they were back. Tim followed them in and approached Chadwyck's bed.

'Hello, I'm Tim, James has told me quite a bit about you.' He was not as tall as Chadwyck expected, about Adelaide's height, but his grip was firm, without being assertive. Chadwyck liked him on sight and smiled, hiding a tinge of jealousy, a novel emotion.

'Don't believe any of it, I made it all up.' They both laughed, leaving James on the back foot. 'But Adelaide...' she looked up apprehensively, or perhaps not ' did tell me something about you.' Chadwyck had chosen 'something' with care, rather than 'a bit'. He watched Tim's reaction with interest.

'All good, I'm sure, she's crazy about me.' Tim said, confident, like his handshake, without being assertive.

'Nonsense, I'm just fond of you, like a favourite sweater.' Chadwyck smiled and none of them knew why.

'Sit down Tim,' said James, and tell us what kept you.'

'I've lost my 'plane.'

'How can you lose a 'plane?'

'It's gone, James, burnt to a cinder.' Adelaide was very pale, as she had already realised the implications.

'How did it happen?'

'I was servicing it with Henry's help in his barn near Fauersmith when two dogs playing knocked a lamp over and set fire to a huge pile of hay next to one of the wings. In seconds the wing was blazing and more hay fell from the same pile across the floor, carrying the fire with it. Henry dragged me out of the barn because he was convinced the petrol tanks would explode, which they did moments after we got out. There was nothing we could do. We just stood at a safe distance and watched the whole barn burn to the ground. Thank God it was not close to the house so nothing else was damaged.' Adelaide, who had started to cry, excused herself and left the room while Chadwyck wondered why she didn't comfort Tim.

'When it had burnt itself out and cooled off a bit, Henry and I went back to see if there was anything we could salvage. Nothing, just the profile of the frame in ash on the ground and the engine so distorted by the heat that it was unrecognisable.'

'Was it insured? Chadwyck asked, and the other two looked at him in surprise.

'No' said Tim 'we hardly ever insure anything up here. Sometimes the premium can be almost as much as our profit margins.'

'When did you last eat?' asked James.

'I haven't since breakfast.'

'Right. Supper should be ready soon and you shall stay the night and we will sort something out in the morning.'

After supper, James came back with a tray for Chadwyck and pulled up a chair while Chadwyck ate.

'Sis says you got a telegram from your mother telling you that your brother did marry and that they are on their way to Cape Town.'

'That's about it and I'm glad Mama will have at least one of us with her because I feel very bad for having, in effect, abandoned her. What will Tim do now?'

'Not much he can do. He will have to go back to Cape Town and fall in with his father, who will compensate Henry for his barn but certainly won't give Tim money for a new 'plane.'

'Adelaide and I spoke about him earlier today. Do you think she wants him to start up an air mail service?'

'I don't really know but I think she wants him to do what he wants to do and she will support him anyway she can.'

What do you think of the idea? Do you think he can make a go of it? You have known him a long time. Does he finish what he starts?'

'Yes. He can be as stubborn as a mule and will fight for what he wants.'

'Do you think he will be interested in a partnership with me? I'd put up the money for a new 'plane and some working capital, say eight thousand pounds, with a fifty-fifty split. When he has made his first fifty thousand pounds, I'll sell back thirty per cent of the shares to him at par and retain twenty per cent to keep my hand in and be there should he need me.'

'I think he would jump at an offer like that.'

'And you think he can make a go of it?' James hesitated for a moment knowing his answer would lock him in.

'Yes. I think the concept is sound and I think Tim has the ability to pull it off.'

'Then discuss it with him tonight and if he wants to go ahead with it, please ask him to look in on me and we will talk it through.'

'Thank you Chad, and good night.' He picked up the tray and left.

* * *

A week later, Tim came back with a simple agreement in duplicate for Chadwyck to sign and went away with a cheque for eight thousand pounds. He had been told of a Farman H.F.16 that was almost new and for sale in Cape Town by a friend of a friend who was getting married but without the 'plane, a non-negotiable condition of the bride-to-be. He was very excited by the idea because it was ideal for what he wanted. It was a two-seater pusher 'plane with the engine behind the cockpit that had been built in France in 1912. It had the largest load capacity for a plane that size, about 900 pounds, so with just a pilot it could easily carry more than 500 pounds of mail.

'Just the job for the job Chad' he had said, with a great grin on his face, 'and thank you for making it possible' he had added, 'I won't let you down.'

* * *

Chadwyck had been almost a week on his back when James came into his room with a telegram.

'This arrived for you.'

'Open it please, and read it.'

'Sorry about your leg but very glad and proud you worked out my simple ruse. I could have told you when I last saw you in London but I wanted to draw you in so that you felt you had earned it. Letter follows. Affectionately, Walter'.

'That's good news. It confirms your theory and fits in perfectly because I came to tell you that Pa has given me two days off so I thought I would take Caachy and two more men out to Groot's Farm and measure out the mirror image.'

'So you will be gone Tuesday and Wednesday which will give you Thursday to go into Jagersfontein to register the claim if you find anything. I have Uncle Walter's deed to Groot's Farm and a notarised document making the farm over to me from Uncle Walter, so you can register it in my name and we'll sort out the company structure later. Whatever I need to sign you can bring back with you.'

'Hold on a second. Let's see if we find anything first.'

'With this,' Chadwyck waved the telegram, 'I have a strong feeling you will if you find an old ant bear burrow there, or the remains of one, because it was in the excavated soil that Walter found the garnets. Come back when you have had supper and we'll talk about it while I have mine. Also please tell Johnny to keep the two men you take out tomorrow here on the farm until you get back from Jagersfontein.'

'Why?'

'Just a precaution but from now on we must go cannily. We don't want to start a rush before we have a legal claim in place.'

CHAPTER 23

The next morning, Chadwyck heard James and the men leave and soon afterwards Adelaide brought him his breakfast. She put the tray down on the table and fussed around his bed, straightening the covers and plumping up his pillows.

'Wish you were with him, I bet.'

'Good morning Adelaide, how kind of you to bring me my breakfast.'

'Sorry, that was a mean thing to say. Good morning Chad, I have our breakfast. I thought we'd share it, a little idle chit chat to help pass the time.'

'What's the matter? You sound brittle, not your usual self.'

'I woke early from a bad dream, very confusing and rather frightening. A large group of people in black that I didn't know, seagulls and the sound of waves breaking on the shore. It was very blurred and when part of it came into focus it switched to another image.'

'Do you often dream like that?'

'No, I hardly ever dream.'

'Where's your father?'

'What's that got to do with it?'

'Nothing. I just wondered whether he went with James to Groot's Farm.'

'No you didn't. You just wanted to change the subject. Here, I've cooked us scrambled eggs and some bread baked this morning. He's gone to Jagersfontein to do some shopping and see his lawyers.'

'What are you going to do today?'

'Enjoy our breakfast and then go riding. Hopefully that will clear this cloud from my head.' When they finished she restacked the tray, bobbed him a brief curtsy and a broad smile, 'See you when I get back.'

'I'll look forward to it and, on your way through the kitchen, please ask Moses to bring me the bed pan.' She smiled and he picked up *African Hunting and Adventure from Natal to the Zambesi* by Baldwin, one of the earliest of its kind and he had almost finished it.

* * *

Later that morning, Chadwyck heard a horse rein in abruptly at the front of the house and Johnny's voice shouting for one of the boys. A moment later there was a brief knock on the door and Johnny burst into the room, closely followed by Jenny.

'He's dead, what a bloody waste of a young life, what a damnable waste,' Jenny clung to his arm.

'Johnny, please sit down and think before you say anything else.' Chadwyck knew immediately what had happened and exactly what Jenny meant. He said nothing and waited for Johnny to continue.

'Where's Adelaide?'

'She went riding,' said Jenny 'She should be back soon.'

'Roland Elliot telephoned my lawyer to leave a message for me when I just happened to be there. So we spoke on a bad connection but I think I got most of it. Tim and Charles Fleming, the owner, took his plane up for a test flight yesterday afternoon with Charles at the controls and he got into difficulties, something about climbing too steeply and stalling. The plane went into a tailspin and spiralled down. Charles was unable to pull it out and they crashed into the base of a cliff. A moment later the fuel tank exploded and the whole plane was engulfed in flames. They were both killed and Roland said they would have died on impact before the fire.' Johnny slumped into a chair, his head between his hands. He then looked up at Chadwyck. 'Tim wasn't even at the controls.' Chadwyck said nothing, he didn't see why he should accept responsibility for Tim's death just because it was his money that provided the cause.

'How was Roland?' asked Jenny, 'and what else did he tell you? I need to know as much as possible to tell Adelaide.'

'He sounded ghastly and said the funeral will be the day after tomorrow. I think we should all go. We can get a train tonight and be there by tomorrow evening.'

'What about Chad? Doctor Marais said he couldn't leave his bed for two months.'

'He'll be fine here,' said Johnny and turned to Chadwyck. 'I don't blame you in anyway Chad, I think Jenny thought I would but I don't. It was a kind and generous offer on your part and made with Tim and Adelaide's happiness in mind.' He held out his hand and Chadwyck took it. 'Now I must send someone out to bring James and his men back, I think I'll write a note rather than send a message.'

Chadwyck watched them leave and felt deeply for Jenny, who would have to tell Adelaide. After lunch Chadwyck tried to sleep when he heard a light tap on the door. It was Adelaide and she came and stood by his bed. She looked very pale and her eyes were red rimmed from crying.

'I've come to say goodbye. We are all going into Jagersfontein to catch the train to Cape Town.' She held out her hand and Chadwyck took it in both of his and found it icy cold.

'I'm terribly, terribly sorry, I couldn't find words to express my feelings to your parents and it seems to be the same with you. I just wish we could turn the clock back and re-think the plan. I wish I could give you something to comfort you because I can't be with you at the funeral.' He relaxed his grip on her hand but she clung on to one of his.

'The dream, Chad, that's what it was telling me.'

'Don't think about the dream. It's always very easy to make one's dream fit the circumstances, after the fact.' She squeezed his hand and withdrew hers.

'I'll tell you when we get back if the graveyard is by the sea.' She gave him a crooked smile and added, 'I'll miss you.'

'I'll miss you and take care on your travels.'

CHAPTER 24

At lunchtime, two days after the funeral, the Flynns arrived back at Rietfontein. Chadwyck had finished Baldwin and started on *Travels and Adventures in South East Africa* by F. C. Selous, a first edition published by Rowland Ward. There was a tap on the door and James came in.

'How did it go? It's a long journey there and back.'

'It was fine. The women are a bit tired but we are all glad to be home. How has it been for you? A bit lonely?'

'No, I've been well looked after. How was the funeral?'

'Masses of people and he was buried at the local church about twenty miles from Cape Town, near his parent's country house. A very simple service by the graveside, overlooking the ocean.'

'How's Adelaide?'

'Not good. She has become very introspective.'

'She…well we all, feel responsible for aiding and abetting Tim's plan. Only his father was against it. We talked about it a lot coming back on the train and my parents are in favour of accepting your invitation and sending her to London for a couple of months in Uncle Walter's care. They can come back together and we'll get him involved in the mine.'

'Let's find it first, did you have time to do anything before you were called back?'

'No, we got delayed on the way out. We came across a dead steer, a lion kill left for the hyenas from the night before which the herd boy hadn't reported and, as there were fresh tracks, I followed them up for a couple of hours. We had only just reached Groot's Farm when Pa's messenger caught up with us.'

'Good, so no one else knows about the mirror image?'

'No, and I won't be able to go out again for at least a week. A lot to catch up with here.'

'That's for the best because by then Walter's letter should have arrived. I'm sure it will contain a lot more information now that I have cracked his code.'

'Do you want to bring Red in when I go out?'

'No, wait until you have found something and register the claim.'

'Tim's father wants to return your money. Tim hadn't yet bought it when he died. I think he has arranged something with Pa.'

'I'd like it to go towards a memorial, something private between Adelaide and Tim's family.'

'He may not accept it, he's very proud and deeply affected by Tim's death.'

'Then we'll invest it in the mine and issue shares in the name of Tim's family.'

There was a light tap at the door and Lily put her head round the edge.

'Lunch is served, Master James,' and she was gone.

'Please ask Adelaide to come and see me this afternoon if she feels up to it. I'd like to talk to her, it might do some good. I'd like to help. I'd like to be able to do something.'

Lily brought him his lunch and after picking at it he went back to his book. There was another tap on the door and Chadwyck thought it might be Adelaide, but it was Lily coming to collect his tray. He lay back and thought about Adelaide and what he could say that might help to settle the situation, get her to accept the facts and eventually get over it.

An hour before supper Adelaide came to his room. She was still dressed for riding.

'You sent for me, Sir?'

'Don't be silly and come and sit down. I am so glad to see you. I have missed you.' She paused for a moment and then pulled up a chair on his good side.

'I've missed you too. You kept popping into my mind at the most inappropriate moments.' She laughed deep in her throat and he noticed that her voice was husky.

'Did you have a good ride?'

'Yes. I needed to get my feet on the ground, or at least my horses.' She laughed and started crying. He lent across and took her hand, she didn't resist. 'I'm sorry, I'm doing rather a lot of this now.' She pulled a large spotted handkerchief out of her jodhpurs with her other hand and blew her nose in a most unladylike way. 'That's better,' and she wiped the tears from her cheeks.

'I know what you have been doing. When you were far from the farm you gave your horse his head and yelled and yelled for all your worth at the open sky.' She looked at him in astonishment.

'How could you have possibly known that?' With surprising strength she gripped his hand and then dropped it and started massaging her throat.

'Because of your deep husky voice and because I know I would do something similar in the same circumstances. Did it make you feel better?' She thought about it and picked up his hand.

'Yes, my head is clearer.'

'Good, then you must go out and do it all again tomorrow and the day after, by which time nobody will understand a word you say, until you realise that one can usually live with memories, but one shouldn't try to live on hope alone. Tim has not gone, he has just moved from one to the other. She turned his hand over and peered at his palm.

'Do you read fortunes?'

'No, and tell me what you think of my suggestion.'

'I'll do it because strangely it made me feel better and you suggested it. I can't believe you worked out what I was doing.' She returned her attention to his palm and, in an old crone's voice continued 'I see a long life and a great fortune. What's this, a beautiful wife and many children.' She couldn't keep it up and started laughing. 'I think many children will suit you and I'll do my best to find you a beautiful wife.' She kissed his palm and let go of his hand. 'Thank you Chad, I must go and get dressed for supper. I'll come back later.'

CHAPTER 25

———

'You are a very popular fellow. There are two letters for you today.'

'How are you feeling?' She sat on his good side.

'Bloody miserable. I'm just dragging myself around doing chores, and if there is nothing obvious, I mope.'

'Have you tried yelling recently?'

'No and it doesn't help anymore.'

'Please read the letters. I find it so exhausting.' She looked at him quizzically and then smiled. 'That's better.'

'Which one first?'

'I don't mind,' he said glancing at the envelopes, 'One is from my mother and the other one is from Uncle Walter.'

'Ladies first,' and she slit it open with a penknife from her pocket.

'Springbokfontein
Cape Colony
September 1ˢᵗ 1913
My darling Chadwyck,

I hope this finds you well and in good spirits. Thank you very much for your last two letters and for taking the trouble to answer all my inquisitive questions but I care very much about you and need to know that you are being well looked after.' She looked up at him.

'Will you tell her I'm doing my best, a proper job?' He made a grab for the letter but she easily whisked it out of his reach. She cleared her throat and, mimicking what she thought Victoria might sounds like, she continued…

'Gerald and Betty arrived yesterday in Cape Town from Mombasa. They seem quite happy with each other but I can't forget how he used to talk about her and her family behind their backs.'

Seeing what was coming, Adelaide dropped the impersonation and continued.

'I know why he married her but it was so unnecessary. Gerald, as well as you and Edward, will inherit a great deal of money each from your grandfather. It has been held in trust for you all and will be made over as and when you reach your twenty-fifth birthday. I tried to get your father to tell you but he wanted you to work for your living with him, of course, as a safety net.

I am tiring of life here without you and missing my friends in Washington. I have been away for more than four months so I have booked passage for myself, Betty and Gerald on a boat for New York leaving Cape Town on the eighteenth of this month.

Take good care of yourself and I pray your leg mends well. Please thank the Flynns for their unstinting kindness and generosity, I consider myself greatly in their debt. I will write from on board and again when I get home. Please keep in touch with Edward, he needs your love and support, he is still very young.

With all my love, Mama

She really loves you. I'm glad Gerald and Betty are with her now. It's not your fault you can't be there, I know it troubles you.'

'Aren't you interested in what Uncle Walter has to say?'

'I hadn't realised it before but you are quite transparent, when your guard is down.'

'Remind me to keep it up, now read on'. She smiled enigmatically at him and picked up the other letter.

'The Albany
Piccadilly

London
11th August 1913

My dear Chadwyck,

Thank you for your telegram. I am very sorry to hear about your broken leg. A serious matter and I hope you have a good doctor to set it properly. Your grandfather also broke his leg in a riding accident and always had a slight tilt to one side afterwards. It gave him considerable pain when he was older and the weather was against him. Exercise as much as you can once the plaster comes off.'

'You don't sound at all like Uncle Walter.'
'I only do impersonations of women' she grinned, 'And stop interrupting.'

You will be looking for a very old dry riverbed. We dug down beside an ant bear burrow for about four feet through sand to red earth and found several garnets when we sieved the soil. Always a good sign, because one usually means the other should be close by. We dug on down and sideways for about ten yards from the garnets and then another four feet deeper. We found eight small diamonds which, when we had them cut in Cape Town, weighed in at nearly six carets. We had dug into a fissure or dyke running to or from a pipe. It was only about four feet wide where we found it. It is now more than twenty years since then so it might not be so easy to find. I paced it out and later measured my average pace at thirty-two inches so, with a modern tape, you shouldn't have any trouble on that score.

Try to find somebody in Jagersfontein with mining experience who knows how to handle the diggers. You will have to build a camp at the farm and bring in quite a lot of machinery. I have enclosed a list of stores and equipment that you will need to get you up and running. There will be a lot of new tools and such like since we were there so you must make your own decisions on what you think is best. Start small and build it up. Pay your men well and they will be less likely to steal from you. If they bring you a good-sized stone, that's been missed first time round, reward them. That way they will get a bonus without the risk of trying to sell it themselves.

I wish I could be there with you but I am now getting very old and would be a liability. Please keep me posted and if you need any contacts with DeBeers when it comes to selling stones, let me know. There are still one or two in senior management, who cut their teeth when I was with them.

Good luck and God bless you.

Your proud and affectionate uncle, Walter.

P.S. If you need extra working capital, please let me know. W.'

'That is great news. We must get James and a couple of men out there as soon as possible. Where is James?'

'Out on the farm with Johnny.'

'Do you often call him that?'

'Not to his face but it makes me feel more grown-up.'

'Please ask them to join me after supper and I'll show them Walter's letter and try to persuade Johnny to let James go tomorrow for a couple of days.'

CHAPTER 26

'I'm sure I've found it Chad. It matched the details in Walter's letter and where we were digging had been dug before.'

'Show me what you found.'

'Adelaide told you.' He fished in his pocket and pulled out a dull pale grey stone about the size of a robin's egg.

'No she didn't. I could tell by your face.'

'I'm not certain but I have seen the real thing before and it is very similar.'

'Was it alone?'

'No, there were two bigger ones but I left them behind.'

'Very funny. I meant garnets. Any sign of them?'

'No just this,' and he handed it over to Chadwyck.

'I don't know, I've never seen an uncut one to compare it with. You will have to take it to someone who knows. Perhaps Red, if you can find him, because I have been thinking of the next step while you were away. The first thing is to register the claim in my name and tie it in with Walter's title deeds and his notarised document making the farm over to me. We can work out a company structure later. We may have to offer Red, if he wants to join us, a small percentage.'

'I think Red is a good idea. Do you think we can get any references on him?'

'Unlikely. We'll just have to make up our minds while we talk to him. We can put him on trial for three months and, if it works, we'll lock him in. I'll need to transfer funds out here, so give me your bank details and I'll write a coded telegram to my bank in Washington.'

'It will have to be my father's account, I don't have one.'

* * *

The next evening James was back in Chadwyck's room. He had found Red, who had confirmed the stone, and shown keen interest in their plans. James had also registered the claim and sent off Chadwyck's telegram to his bank.

'What did you arrange with Red?'

'He is coming out tomorrow afternoon and I invited him to stay the night. That will give us all a better chance of sizing him up. If we agree to go ahead, I can take him out to Groot's Farm so he can see what we need to get started.'

'Did he say anything more about the stone?'

'Definitely the real thing but you never know what you have got until you cut it. We talked about the logistics and he asked about the farm buildings. He said they could be made into bunkhouses and that we would have to build a new kitchen and mess hall.'

'Did you find the spring by the diggings?'

'Yes but it is not very strong.'

'With canvas and pitch we can build a small pan. You will need to find a traction engine with a blade and a couple of dumpers, possibly in Jagersfontein but more likely in Kimberley.'

'We will also have to build a bath house and longdrops, so we are going to need a handful of carpenters and several wagonloads of lumber.'

By the time James went to his bed, Chadwyck and he had decided to make Red an offer, after he had seen the ground.

* * *

'How did it go?' asked Chadwyck, once James and Red were seated at a table pulled up beside Chadwyck's bed. 'What's your first impression, Red?'

'Good, it looks very promising. You should bring in a geologist to survey the ground and plan the whole operation. You need to find someone full time because he is always needed on site, to decide the direction of the dig as it goes, based on what is excavated.'

'I know just the chap,' said James, 'he's a Rhodesian friend of mine from school. His father is Colonel of the Grey's Scouts, in fact he co-raised it with George Grey in '96 during the Matabele rebellion. At that time they were attached to the Bulawayo Field Force.'

'And what is his name and where might he be now?'

'Jack Ripon. You just missed him. He's got a job with de Beers and he came through here two days before you arrived, on his way to Kimberley.'

'So he has just started there?'

'Yes, I can telephone his office when I go into town tomorrow.'

'Please do, sound him out and see if he might be interested in joining us. Now Red, we would like to offer you your previous foreman's wage for a three-month trial to see how it goes and, if we are all happy, carry on and, at that point, you will also have a ten per cent share in the company. You probably want to think about it.'

'No, I have already done a lot of thinking over the last two days and I would like to accept your offer. Thank you both for giving me this opportunity.' He shook hands with Chadwyck and then James, who went for the whisky, to celebrate.

CHAPTER 27

'We have a geologist, it's all set.'

'Do I have anything to say in the matter?'

'Of course, but it is all set.'

'So you said, but please start at the beginning.' James came round to the other side of Chadwyck's bed and pulled up a chair.

'I telephoned him in Kimberley from our lawyer's office in Jagersfontein and luckily caught him on the point of leaving. He said he was bored stiff and had nothing to do.'

'Why? I would have thought that he had his hands full, just learning the ropes.'

'Not so, he told me that head office had got their wires crossed and somebody had extended the contract of the man he was replacing by a month, so he has been told to hang around and stay out of trouble.'

'Can he get away?'

'Exactly what I asked him.'

'And he asked why and what did you tell him?'

'I told him about you and Walter and finding the old diggings. I told him about Red, his commitment and recommendations. I told him we needed him.'

'And what did he say?'

'He said that he will be here in three days.'

'Just like that, what else did he tell you?'

'That they are not paying him yet so he feels under no obligation to them. He said that he will tell them that he is taking leave and that he will report back, before the month is up.'

'Did either of you mention money?'

'No, I thought I'd leave that to you.'

'That's unusual, is he rich?'

'No and perhaps I did say something about matching de Beers' pay.'

'Anything else?'

'Well, I also mentioned something about a stake in our company.'

'Something he won't be getting from de Beers. Now I know why he will be here in three days.'

CHAPTER 28

He lay awake, his leg hurt and he didn't want to take any more laudanum, at least not for a while. He heard the door latch click and lay still. Soundlessly, on bare feet, Adelaide approached his bed. She stood for a moment at his side and appeared to be at the point of leaving.

'Hello,' he whispered, 'I couldn't sleep. Sit here on my good side.' She perched on the edge of his bed and he was very aware of her scent.

'Nor me, I'm afraid.' He waited a moment in case she continued.

'Of the indiscriminate way we live and die. Why here or there? Why him or her and not another?'

'We're conditioned by life to accept death and react with a well-worn response. But when I heard Tim had died, I was unprepared and had no response.'

'Don't blame yourself for that.'

'I'm not but I know that you are.' He said nothing more and he felt her shift slightly on the bed.

'May I lie down beside you? I want to comfort you and myself' she added. Before he could answer, he felt her move again and she lay on her back beside him with her head on the pillow next to his. He could smell her hair but it didn't touch him because it was tied back at the nape of her neck. 'If you hadn't given him the money he would now be in Cape Town working in his father's office. Please don't blame yourself Chad, if that had happened, he could have been run over by a tram and killed on his first day at work.' They lay quietly together with their own thoughts.

'Thank you,' he said finally because he couldn't think of anything more to say.

'He died happily because he was doing what made him happy. If it had been the tram he would have died in miserable and unhappy circumstances.'

'Why are you frightened?'

'Because I'm confused, I'm not feeling the confidence I'm used to . The little girl in me is wondering why and is frightened because she doesn't have the answers.'

'To what questions?'

'Why did I have to have it my way? Why couldn't I have done what he wanted?' He didn't say anything so after a moment she continued. 'He wanted to make love to me and I wouldn't let him and now I don't know if I was selfish or sensible, nor will I ever know.'

'Did you want to make love?'

'Yes,' she whispered and started to cry silently. 'May I get under the covers? I am cold.'

'Of course,' and without rocking the bed she was on her feet, he flipped back the covers and very gently she lay down on her side facing him having taken his hand and moved his arm beneath her neck. Her nightdress was an old favourite, well worn and plain white. He was very aware of the softness and warmth of her body against his. She put her right hand on his chest and then moved it onto her hip. She was still crying silently. He could feel her tears on his arm.

'Please don't cry. Nobody gets it right all the time. Life itself is a lesson from which we all learn, some more than others.'

'That's true I suppose,' she sniffed and rubbed her nose on his shoulder, 'I hope you don't think I'm a loose woman. I was frightened and somehow knew we could comfort each other.' He laughed gently. Most of the pain had left his leg.

'Of course not. Back home this is called Tarrying, it was in common practice amongst the poorer people in the eighteenth and nineteenth century.'

'Why Tarrying?'

'It was an accepted way for two young people to get better acquainted.'

'That's not possible, the parents wouldn't allow it.'

'The parents, usually of the girl, arranged it if they approved of the boy as a future son-in-law.' She giggled and then hiccupped. She had stopped crying. 'You probably did it here then because it was supposed to have started with the Dutch.'

'But didn't they, well…didn't they?'

'Not easy. In England it was called Bundling because they were both fully dressed and the girl was bundled into a sack which was tied at her feet and waist.'

'I don't believe you. You are making this up.' She put her hand back on his chest and laughed, 'you're teasing me to cheer me up. How do you know these things?'

'An enquiring mind.'

'Your nightshirt is very scratchy.'

'Good Scottish flannel. You don't want to be found here in the morning when they bring me my tea.'

'I won't be, I'll slip out later. Please let me stay,' and she moved her hand back to her hip.

'How can I say no, you have me pinned down.'

'Hey ho,' she said, kissed her fingertips and brushed them across his lips. 'Good night' and within minutes her breathing changed and she was asleep.

His leg woke him in the early morning and he was alone except for a very faint trace of her scent.

CHAPTER 29

In Washington, Victoria was holding court. 'I had a letter from Edward yesterday, it's on my desk if you want to read it. He's finished his exams and thinks he's done quite well.'

'What's he going to do at Christmas, Mama?'

'He's going up to Glen Lyon, with Jock Sinclair, and apparently two other school friends are joining them later. Hector MacPherson will look after them and organise some stalking and low ground shooting.' She turned to Henry Wickham and they started to talk about the Christmas Charity Gala. Victoria had invited Henry onto the committee and, although raising a few eyebrows amongst her more conservative friends, it pleased Gerald to see his mother involving herself, once again, in society. It would be her first public appearance since his father's death.

He watched Henry Wickham as he talked, so complacent and self-satisfied, he thought; only an earthquake would shake that equilibrium and self-esteem. Working for him was bearable only because they hardly ever saw each other. He was either at one of his clubs, while his lieutenants ran his various businesses, or on the golf-course, the latest craze in Washington, trying to broaden his social base. As for himself, Gerald saw a great deal of his bachelor friends and frequently dined with them, before going on to gamble. His losses were sometimes spectacular but there always seemed to be sufficient funds in the joint bank account to cover them. Betty, surrounded by her own friends and living only a short distance from the comfort of her parents, was putting a brave face on it, but he knew it wouldn't be long before she put her foot down. He glanced at her and returned her smile and thought that, as long as the status quo remained unchanged, he could do a lot worse. She was very beautiful, very rich and loved him very much indeed, but for that matter so did several other women. Now that his father's estate was almost probated he too would be rich and, contrary to frequent threats, he had not been disinherited. After the dessert they all remained at the table for coffee and Gerald was delighted, as he didn't relish drinking port alone with Henry, while the women retired. The butler returned, bearing a magnum of Champagne and five glasses and stood stoically by the sideboard.

'What's this, Wilks?' Victoria seemed surprised. Everyone stopped talking and looked at the butler.

'I hope you will forgive me,' said Betty sweetly, 'but it was my idea, I have some wonderful news and I wanted to surprise you all.' Victoria clapped her hands in delight.

'Of course, my dear, how very exciting. I love surprises.'

'I saw Doctor Jenkins this morning,' Betty announced, 'and Gerald, my darling,' she could not contain herself any longer, 'I am with child.'

CHAPTER 30

Adelaide came into Chadwyck's room and found him asleep. The window was open and a light breeze moved the curtains. Chadwyck's nightshirt had rucked up high on his left side. She stood silently by his bed without moving with her mouth slightly open. She suddenly became aware that he was watching her.

'May I touch it?' and before waiting for a reply, she lent forward and touched with the tip of her fingers. It spasmed and she snatched her hand back to her throat, as if avoiding a snake strike.

'Why did it do that?'

'Natural reflex.'

'Oh look, it's getting bigger.' He pulled down the edge of the nightshirt. 'When we were much younger, James and I used to share a bath. But his was much smaller and had no hair. That's the only other time I've seen it except with horses and other animals, but that's different.'

'Aren't we supposed to be doing exercises?'

'Yes of course. Moses has made you parallel bars to hold you up while you walk. I'll get him to bring it in.'

Five minutes later, Moses and Jacob staggered into the room carrying a very solid looking pair of parallel bars about three feet high and at least twelve feet long. When they had gone, she helped him swing his legs out of bed and stand up. He felt very unsteady and tiny beads of sweat broke out on his forehead. The ends of the bars were about three feet in front of him. She stood on his left and took his elbow.

'Grab hold of the bars and walk to the other end slowly, and place your feet carefully. Good, now turn around and do it again. How does your leg feel?'

'It's throbbing a bit and my balance is not quite right.'

'Now walk to the end again and then we will go on together to the cheval glass.' At the end of the bars she took his left hand in hers and swung his arm over her shoulder. He could feel her hip against his and she put her other arm around his waist. 'Stand as straight as you can and look up as you walk. Good, now stand straight in front of the glass and square your shoulders. Do you feel unbalanced or off-keel?'

'No.' She stood before him, then squatted down and took his left calf in her hands and started to massage it towards the knee. 'Do you feel any numbness or tingling?'

'No.' Very gently she moved her hands above his knee and continued with the same probing massage.

'What are you doing?'

'I'm looking for any aberration or splinters of bone but I'm sure Doctor Marais would have found anything when he took the plaster off and examined you.' She looked up and smiled at him. 'Anyway, I just like doing it. Now let's get you back to bed but not before I have put a towel over the sheet. I'm going to massage both your legs to nourish the skin.'

He lay back on the bed, glad to have his weight off. She picked up a bottle of olive oil she had left on the bedside table and kicked off her shoes. She pulled up the hem of her dress and put her left foot next to his. 'Try and lift up your leg and put your ankle on my knee.' He could feel the sweat break out again on his forehead.

'I need a little help.' She gently lifted his foot up and put it on her knee.

'Thank you.' She unscrewed the bottle and poured some oil into her hand, replaced the bottle on the table and rubbed her hands together. She started working up his calf, around his knee and dug her fingers into his quadriceps.

'You have lost a lot of muscle tone and quite a lot of weight, which I suppose is a good thing for the moment.' She put more oil onto her hands and went on massaging his leg.

'Have you given any thought to your parents' idea of going to London and staying with Uncle Walter?'

'Yes, but no, I want to stay here and look after you.'

'Walter will be more fun.'

'I don't think so. See if you can lift your heel off my knee.' He did, but only with her help. She lowered his leg gently to the bed and walked around to the other side.

'Now lift your good leg.' He couldn't until he lent forward and put his hands behind his knee. 'Well done,' she said as she ran the open bottle along the length of his leg and went to work with a will. 'Why am I always wet when I am with you? Is it normal?' His leg tensed and she stretched forward massaging his thigh, in such a way that he could feel her breasts on his foot. 'You haven't answered my question.' She watched him with the hint of a smile playing in the corners of her mouth, while he cleared his throat.

'No, not with most women, I suppose but you're lucky, it's a good thing.'

'Do you want to feel?' and she pulled the hem of her dress higher.

'No, well…no. Father always told me never to start something I couldn't finish.' She snorted.

'Wise parent, I suppose' she slapped the inside of his thigh with the flat of her hand and pulled her leg from under his. "You're done for now and I'm off to have a cold shower.' She laughed at the expression on his face.

CHAPTER 31

It had been a long day and his fourth trip out to Groot's Farm. He had been exercising for two months and had rebuilt most of his wasted muscles. His leg felt strong and straight, Doctor Marais had done a great job on it. The house was very quiet and he was on the point of dropping off when he heard the door open and close. Adelaide came over to his right side, put something on the bedside table and slipped in beside him.

'I want to tarry a while and discuss progress at the mine.' She was on her side and squirmed closer while he put his arm beneath her neck. Her hair was loose and when she pulled it back, it caught between his lips and tickled. 'I like to tarry and the mine can wait till tomorrow.' She was soon asleep and he must have dropped off soon after her.

He woke with moonlight flooding across the room and her naked back. She was kneeling between his legs and held him in her mouth. He took her head gently and pulled her forwards until her mouth was inches from his and her nipples brushed against his chest. She ran her tongue around her lips.

'Please kiss me Chad,' and he did, aware that it was for the first time. The cart before the horse and he almost laughed as she broke away.

'We must stop, you could become pregnant.'

'Not with this,' and she lent across him, trailing a nipple across his mouth and held up something small from the bedside table.

'What is it?'

'It belongs to James. He has a box full of them in his room. He knows a widow in town with a young daughter who lives with her grandmother.'

'How do you know?'

'I followed him once when he thought I had gone to the hairdresser.' She rolled away, 'I've been told it hurts, a lot, but I won't make a sound.'

'It shouldn't, you've been riding all your life.' When he was ready, he moved a bit so she could straddle him and as she did, he put his hand between her legs, she was very wet. She grunted, almost imperceptibly and bit her lip so when she lent forward to kiss him, he could taste her blood. Intuitively she seemed to know what to do and he let her find her way. She managed to keep most of her weight off his leg. In time she slipped off him and he noticed some blood on the bottom sheet.

'It doesn't matter, I'll swap it with mine after Lily has removed your breakfast tray and they'll think I had my period early.' She snuggled up beside him and kissed him again, 'I love your mouth. I must be very careful with Mama in the morning. She'll probably guess anyhow because of the silly grin that will be on my face.'

'We'll tread carefully. When you first see her tell her how happy you are with my progress and with what you have been able to do for me,' she giggled and after a pause he continued, 'I will back you up by saying the same thing in my own words. A near truth is much easier to sustain than a gauche denial.' She nodded, slipped out of bed and picked up her nightdress.'You are so beautiful naked in the moonlight. I can imagine you like that playing your violin.'

'Now?'

'No. Tomorrow will do.' She made a face, lent over and brushed her lips against his. 'Good night and don't forget what I said about near truth.'

'I won't, and sleep tight.'

CHAPTER 32

A lot had changed at the mine while Chadwyck had been confined to his bed. The work on the bunkhouse and a new kitchen was almost finished. Jack had completed his survey and marked out the perimeter, in part, of the pipe. He, James and a couple of men had started digging and Red had done several controlled blasts to loosen up the yellow ground. At the end of their second week they had come across a spread of garnets.

'When will the machinery get here?' asked Chadwyck.

'The grease tables should be here by the end of this week with the water pump,' said Red.

'And the materials needed for the pan?'

'It's all coming at the same time from Jagersfontein.'

'Good. What's the situation, Jack, with the jaw crusher and traction engine?'

'We're using the traction engine to bring the crusher down from Kimberley. They left at the end of last week and should be here in a week or possibly ten days, depending on breakdowns.'

'Let's go look at the spring. I want your advice on the best use of the ground around it. We need to set up a continuous and controlled flow for the grease tables, which can then run back into the pan and be pumped up to a feeder tank.'

Two hours later, the four of them walked back to the buildings,

Caachy carrying the camp chair that Chadwyck had been sitting on whenever possible.

'When do you think the bunkhouses and kitchen will be finished, Red? And are you going to build a separate cabin for yourself and an office, as I suggested?'

'They should be finished by the time the traction engine gets here. They have already started on my cabin, over there, you can see the corner of it beyond the kitchen block.'

'What about bedding and kitchen equipment?'

'That will be here with the pump and grease tables, by the end of this week.'

'And the men?'

'I've lined up eighteen for the moment and they are standing by to start as soon as the traction engine and crusher get here.'

'Good, let's have some lunch and then I think I'll head back, my leg has had enough for one day.'

CHAPTER 33

Towards the end of his treatment, Adelaide and Chadwyck had got into the habit of riding out most mornings until they had covered every corner of Rietfontein.

'Let's go down to the river, below the dam.'

'Good idea.'

'How much longer before I can break out of a walk? It must be very tiresome for you.'

'It appeals to my controlling instincts, to curb your enthusiasm.' He looked back at her and she grinned at him in an irresistible way.

'Silly question.'

'Not at all, but there is a minimal chance of being thrown if you walk and trotting and cantering put a lot more strain on your thigh.'

Half an hour later they tied their horses to a tree and walked along the river, with the flow. He put his left arm around her shoulders and she lent slightly in towards him.

'We'll walk down a way, do your exercises and then you can carry me back.'

'Yes, yes and no.' He squeezed her shoulders and she turned her face up to him.

'Kiss me, I'm feeling deprived.'

'Please.'

'Alright. Please me, I'm feeling deprived.' He kissed her and she stood on tiptoes and wound her arms around his neck. 'We should have brought a blanket.'

'Shameless child, we must concentrate on my exercises.'

'I'm not shameless, I'm just enthused.' They walked on and his gait was almost even.

'I think I love you. I've never said that to anyone other than family but I do. I've been thinking about it ever since we first made love and I don't just think, I know.'

'Me too.'

'What do you mean 'me too'. I'm serious Chad, please don't make fun of me, well at least not about this.'

'I'm not making fun of you. Me too means, me too. I love you and want to marry you but I don't know whether I should ask our mothers first or should we just keep it to ourselves.'

'Oh Chad.'

'Steady, you'll have me over. Perhaps I can get down on my good knee as a new exercise.' She started to cry silently and held his head in her hands. He took hold of her wrists and kissed both of her palms, one after the other.

'Adelaide Flynn, now think very carefully before you answer this one, will you marry me, Chadwyck Meade, to have and to hold from this day forth and all the rest of the good and bad bits, until death us do part.'

'Yes,' she said simply, 'Yes, yes, yes.'

'Good, good and good but let's keep it to ourselves for the moment.'

'No, we must tell everyone, starting with the horses.'

'Not before we have done my exercises?'

'No! well yes, it will give you time to change your mind but after that there is no going back.'

'I'm not going to change my mind. Now kiss me and convince me you mean what you say.' They walked on in silence, each with their own thoughts, until they reached the shade of an acacia tree where they sat down on a stone slab next to the river.

'We have been engaged for almost ten minutes. How does it feel?'

'Good, fantastic. It has given me purpose and a direction in my life,' he paused and after a moment added, 'that sounds a bit pompous but I don't seem able to simplify it.'

'No, it's best. You didn't have time to think about it. It's a true feeling and not contrived.'

'And you?'

'Much the same, I was drifting in a protected bubble and now you have given me the key to the outside world.' They looked at each other and both laughed at the absurdity of their remarks; at the same time they knew them to be true.

'I will speak to your parents when we get home.'

'That's the first time you have called it home, you have always said the farm or Rietfontein.'

'Acquisitive fellow, I can't help it.'

'Chad, when can we get married?'

'After an appropriate interval.'

'What's appropriate about an interval?'

'Decorum and conformity.'

'Piffle!!'

'First we must announce our engagement then after say two months, decide a date for the wedding and then after the wedding a minimum of a further nine months before announcing the birth of the first of a string of offspring. That's conformity.'

'Do you want a string of children?'

'Yes.'

'Well let's elope and we can start right away.'

'No, because that puts another slant on it and, whatever we might say later, the children would suffer. Also I don't think your parents would be very happy. I know my mother wouldn't like it, especially after what happened with Gerald.'

'Would she come to the wedding?'

'Probably not but we can go to America on honeymoon for three months and that way you can meet all the family.'

'What about your brothers?'

'Edward is still at school and we can see Gerald and Betty when we go to Washington. Tomorrow I will write to them all and uncle Walter. Now let's go home and tell your parents.'

CHAPTER 34

A week before the wedding, Jenny declared she had everything in place. They had celebrated Christmas quietly in Rietfontein and Chadwyck recalled how he had found Jenny first when they returned from the river and had asked her permission to marry Adelaide. Her answer was still as clear in his mind as the moment she gave it.

'Oh Chad, dear sweet Chad, I can't think of anything that would make all of us happier than that.' She arched her spine, threw back her head and laughed, the very essence of life and happiness. 'You will never know what I feel right now Chad, what a mother can feel for her daughter and I thank you for it, from the bottom of my heart.' She kissed him fleetingly on the mouth, 'You are a lovely man Chadwyck Meade and Adelaide is a very lucky woman.'

And then again, before dinner, when everyone had gone to their rooms to dress, Adelaide had found him working in her father's study.

'A moment, my Lord, if I may be so bold.' He was sitting at the desk with his back to her and he grinned with delight, at the interruption and her mood.

'Away with you, wench and petition my Chamberlain.' She approached silently and stood behind his chair. He continued writing, anticipating with pleasure, her next move.

'You're such a spoilsport Chad, you're becoming very stuffy in your old age.' He grinned again and waved his free hand in a dismissive gesture. She flounced round the desk, placed her elbows on it, cupped her chin in her hands and stared intently at him. For a full minute he held his own deadpan expression until, unable to control himself any longer, he burst out laughing.

'I give up,' he threw his hands above his head, 'I surrender.'

'Hurrah, victory at last. Now that I've got you where I want you, I'd better make the most of it.' She walked round the desk and held out her hands. 'Please come with me, my lord.'

'Where?'

'Wait and see.' She teased. He got up and held her hands gently.

'Well, now that you've had your way, it's my turn.'

'But I haven't,' she started to protest. He drew her gently towards him so that he had his arms around her waist and her hands behind her back, at the same moment he sat back, against the edge of the desk. Her lips were only inches from his, and her breath caught in her throat. The banter in her eyes slowly gave way to a look of profound love and tenderness. Her eyelids drooped so that all he could see were her long dark lashes against clear white skin. She seemed to have stopped breathing and very slowly she raised her mouth towards his and her eyes closed completely. Her delicate scent was intoxicating and, using all his self-control, he gently released his hold on her.

'That's better my dear, now that I have you where I want you, lead on.' Her eyes snapped open, the colour drained from her cheeks and she raised both hands, as if to strike him.

'You are a devil,' she hissed at him 'and I hate you. You will never do that to me again.' She pounded on his chest, as hard as she could and, to his amazement, he saw that she was crying.

'My dearest, please don't cry,' he caught her hands as she raised them again to strike him, 'please believe me I didn't mean…' She tried to wrench her hands free.

'Leave me, let go of me.' He held her firmly, again realising that he never wanted to let her go again. She pulled back as hard as she could against his grasp and was aware of the contact of his body against hers. Her dark green eyes blazed with fire and he was shocked by the intensity of her feelings. He held on and suddenly she collapsed, so that he found himself supporting her entire weight. He drew her towards him and she moaned deep in her throat, as her head came forward onto his shoulder. She took a shuddering breath and brought her head up very slowly, her eyes appeared fathomless and she was breathing deeply, through slightly parted lips.

'I love you, Chad.' She brought her hand up and with the tip of her index finger, traced a line around his mouth. Inexorably, her lips moved towards his and, as they touched, she withdrew her finger and he felt her tongue on his. He swept his other arm around her neck and was rocked by the passion of her kiss. Her whole body was trembling and an intense hunger raged through him. He wanted her more than anything he had ever wanted before in his life and, feeling it, she broke away.

'No Chad,' she said involuntarily, 'I mean yes, no, I don't … I don't know what I mean. I have loved you from the moment I first saw you. Crazy as it may sound, I thought Tim died, because of it.'

'Hush my darling, don't say that, there were several reasons why he died and that certainly wasn't one of them.' He kissed her again, with less passion, and a great deal more tenderness.

'But, it's true Chad, I knew after that first night at Rietfontein that I would never marry Tim, but I didn't really have the opportunity to explain it to him properly and, when I tried, he misunderstood me completely. Now, in a way, I'm glad that he did.'

'Then I too, my love, am equally to blame because, I have loved you since that same moment.'

'Oh Chad, say it again.'

'What? If we don't go and get dressed now we'll be late for dinner.'

'Chad, I'll kill you.' He caught her beautiful face between his hands and her kiss touched his soul.

'I love you,' he said, 'more than life itself.'

They had held a party on New Year's Eve for family and neighbours when Chad and Adelaide had announced their engagement.

For most of the first week in January they had argued for and against an early wedding and finally compromised on the first Saturday in April. Everyone was happy except Sophie and Adelaide, who found themselves alone in the elope camp.

'I'm almost certain my mother won't come, but at least she will have the time to think about it.'

'Do you think uncle Walter will come?'

'Who knows but he's probably keen to see the mine.'

'You are teasing me, Chad, aren't you?'

'Yes, my love and you wouldn't last long as a salmon.'

'What do you mean?'

'Because' he said, slipping his arm around her waist, 'you rise beautifully to every fly I put over you.'

Uncle Walter was unable to come, but dozens of Flynn friends from all over southern Africa did come and were put up by the nearer neighbours. As expected the party went on for a week but Adelaide and Chadwyck left on the fourth morning for Springbokfontein and their honeymoon.

CHAPTER 35

Ever since Alister Miller's forced landing by the cricket pitch at Wellington, Edward had thought of nothing but flying. He arranged to meet Miller again at Farnborough, before picking up Jock Sinclair and going north to Glen Lyon, for Christmas. He had not realised when they first met that Alister was a commissioned officer in the Royal Flying Corps. He found him waiting in the officers' Mess, where they shook hands warmly and Alister introduced him to his brother officers.

'I've arranged to take you up in one of the B E 2 trainers. That is, of course,' he added with a grin 'if you are still game.' Edward's expression of anticipation and excitement was all the answer he needed. He handed him a sheepskin jacket, helmet and goggles 'Put these on, they should fit. You will find it very cold, once we are airborne.' He led the way to the 'plane, standing ready at the end of the grass runway. A ground crew was standing by and helped Edward into the forward cockpit.

'How far will we be going and how high?'

'We'll take it up to five thousand feet and go over your school, if you like, and then I will show you what this beauty can do.' Edward grinned in appreciation and, for the next hour, they flew out over Wellington and back again in gin-clear air on a cloudless, crisp December morning. Edward thrilled with every new manoeuvre and, shouting at each other through the intercom, he asked endless questions. For a short while Alister allowed him to take the controls, in level flight. By the time they landed Edward was determined to learn to fly.

Over lunch, in the Mess, he questioned Alister on all aspects of flying. The more he learnt, the simpler it seemed to be and Alister, convinced of his sincerity, finally agreed to arrange for one of the instructors to give him private tuition. Excited by the thought of his newfound freedom, Edward caught the train to London and took a cab round to the Sinclairs' house in Phillimore Place.

'What time does the train leave for Perth?' asked Jock as he opened the front door.

'Hello to you too! 9.30 from King's Cross, and we'll be there for breakfast and at Glen Lyon by lunchtime.' They moved into the hall.

'You know I've never fished and I'm not much of a shot, Chadwyck dropped his bag at the foot of the stairs.

'You'll learn. You've got two weeks to try it out and if you don't like it, you have the library which is full of good books.'

After dinner the two of them took the night train to Perth and spent two enjoyable weeks, stalking and fishing at Glen Lyon.

On the third of January Edward received a telegram from Chadwyck announcing his engagement to Adelaide, informing him that the wedding had been set for April the fourth, at Rietfontein. The following day Edward sent a reply to Chadwyck, to congratulate him and regretfully make his excuses. That afternoon he and Jock took the train to Perth to connect with the night sleeper to London. Jock went on to his parents for the remainder of the holidays and Edward took a room at the Tumbledown Dick in Farnborough. For five days he applied himself, with total dedication, to absorbing all he could learn on the theory and practice of flight. During which time he clocked up ten glorious hours in the air with his instructor and, on his last day, flew solo for the first time.

CHAPTER 36

At the beginning of the Spring holidays Edward retrieved his new Napier Roadster from the garage in Crowthorne and drove Jock Sinclair over to the Central Flying School at Farnborough, where they met Alister Miller. During the term Edward had talked a great deal about flying and Jock, carried by Edward's enthusiasm, was determined to learn. Almost every day there had been something in the newspapers about Germany's military manoeuvres. Speculation had turned to certainty: there would be a war in Europe and Britain would, inevitably, be involved.

There was a prevailing mood of great excitement and anticipation throughout the country. The whole thing was looked upon as a glorified cricket match on a grand scale. There was no doubt in anyone's mind that Germany had over-stepped the mark and that they would get the drubbing they deserved, a short sharp lesson that would be over before Christmas.

They took rooms in the Tumbledown Dick again and spent as much time as possible at the airfield. Jock was assigned the same instructor and, although lacking Edward's flair, he showed promise. After his first lesson he and Edward were invited to the officers' Mess, in the new block, for a drink.

'How did it go Jock?' Alister asked, 'I'm afraid I was too busy in the office to come out and watch you over the field.'

'Fine, I loved it. It was even more exciting than I expected.' They saluted him with their glasses.

'There have been a few changes since you were last here, Edward' said Alister. 'The long accommodation blocks around the perimeter seemed to have sprung up, like mushrooms, overnight.'

'I preferred the old Mess,' said Edward, 'it had more character. I suppose, because of the way things are developing in Europe, all this is necessary.'

'Yes we've come a long way since Lark Hill on Salisbury Plain, when we were under the command of Major Sir Alexander Bannerman. In those days all the 'planes had been French.'

'Such as Farmans, Nieuports and Bleriots,' cut in Edward, 'don't look so surprised Alister, I read about it in the books you lent me.'

'Last year the War Office decided that the Royal Flying Corps was to consist of seven squadrons of twelve 'planes each and a reserve of a further twelve 'planes with twelve pilots for each squadron. So far there are only four squadrons in commission and a fifth is in preparation.'

'Where will you find the pilots?' asked Jock and then added, 'apart from us two, of course.'

'Don't worry we'll keep tabs on you, we are going to need every pilot we can get.'

'Where are the squadrons based?'

'Number 1 is here, 2 at Montrose and 3 and 4 at Nertheravon, on Salisbury Plain, headquarters of course is here.'

* * *

Two weeks later they drove up to London and spent the rest of the holidays with Jock's parents. Edward had developed his flying skills to an extraordinary degree and had been able to push any 'plane he flew to its limits. On two occasions he had engaged Alister Miller in simulated combat and got the better of him. Even though he didn't have enough time to travel to and back from his brother's wedding, he still enjoyed a great feeling of achievement and well-being. He promised himself that he would work harder than ever during his last term, pass his exams to the best of his ability and get back to flying the moment he left Wellington.

CHAPTER 37

Edward found it very hard to concentrate on exams during his last term. Almost every day, the events in Europe made headlines. Leave had been cancelled for the armed forces and a great deal of unprecedented political manoeuvring was going on in Whitehall. The Lords of the Admiralty were at odds with each other and with Asquith, who was both Prime Minister and Minister of War. Some still entertained the idea that the joint German and British Fleet Manoeuvres, planned the previous year for that summer, should go ahead.

It was a leaden June afternoon and Edward, feeling entombed in his study, decided to clear his head and get some fresh air. He went downstairs and set out around the perimeter path of the main building. Feeling hot, he loosened his collar just as he rounded a corner and came face to face with Mr Robinson.

'You are improperly dressed, Meade, and I have been told that you have parked your automobile in the staff car park.'

'Yes, Sir.'

'Why, might I ask, and, for that matter why do you have such a machine?'

'Is it against the rules, Sir?'

'No,' said Mr Robinson, rather reluctantly.

'So why do you ask?'

'You are being impertinent, Meade.'

'No Sir, I'm just answering your questions and to answer your other question, there is nowhere else to park it.'

Mr Robinson rocked on the balls of his feet and ran his right index finger around the inside of his collar. 'I have never liked you Meade, you are too privileged for my taste. It is not too late to have you expelled, you know. I just have to write my report to the Master and you will be out,' he snapped his fingers, 'Just like that!'

They both turned to the sound of the sash window behind them, as it was being fully raised. The Master looked out, an inscrutable expression on his face.

'Perhaps now would be a good moment, Mr Robinson, to make that report.' He paused and then beckoned him in: 'If you please...', and he closed the window with the finality of a guillotine.

When they got back from flying at Farnborough on Sunday evening Edward learnt that Mr Robinson had left the school after lunch that day. The rumour was that he was seriously ill and had had to go into hospital, for observation. As he only had two years to go before retirement, it was generally felt that he would not return. Many of Edward's contemporaries greeted him with the news and congratulated him as if he had been solely responsible for Mr Robinson's departure. The rest of the term was an uneventful slog of, seemingly endless, exams interspersed with prolonged bouts of study, far into the small hours. He was determined to pass his exams with flying colours.

* * *

At the beginning of the summer holidays he and Jock went back to their old rooms at the Tumbledown Dick in Farnborough, and spent as much time as they could improving their flying. Towards the end of July Alistair Miller invited them both into his office.

'War within a week,' he said 'and we need every man we can get to join the RFC.'

'Surely not,' said Jock 'Eddy wants to go up to Oxford, and I think

217

it is just a lot of sabre rattling and if there is a spat, it will be over by Christmas.'

'No Jock, this has been brewing for years. One spark will set it off and then there will be a domino effect that will roll around Europe, sucking in almost everyone. I think Alister is right and it won't be over by Christmas. I would like to join but I'm not speaking for Jock. What do I have to do to sign on?'

'In your case nothing but your signature. You have your pilot's licence, sufficient flying hours to become an instructor and God knows we need them but I can see that you want to be in the thick of it when the balloon goes up and that goes for you too, Jock.'

'Of course I'll join, somebody has to look after Eddy.'

* * *

On the day Victoria received a cable from Edward that he had joined, Betty gave birth to a girl in Washington. She was christened Edwina Victoria. Three days later Chadwyck sent his mother a telegram telling her that he and Adelaide were expecting their first child, in February. On the same day Austria–Hungary declared war on Serbia, a month after the assassination of Franz Ferdinand by Gavrilo Princip, at Sarajevo. Four days later Germany declared war on Russia and two days after that on France. The following day, Great Britain declared war on Germany.

In less than two weeks, more than two million men were mobilised.

PART II

CHAPTER 38

The morning papers were spread over one end of the breakfast table in the Meades' new house on the Avenue of the Presidents, in Washington. Their address was about to be changed back to Sixteenth Street, by dint of public outcry, much to Henry Wickham's chagrin and Betty's annoyance. She had just had great quantities of writing paper and invitations printed. Her father had bought the house for them as a wedding present while they were on their honeymoon. He had arranged for the entire place to be redecorated from top to bottom and it now, in Gerald's opinion, looked like something out of The Arabian Nights. He was having breakfast alone; he rarely saw Betty before leaving for the office. He picked up the *Washington Post* and scanned the headlines.

'General Sir John French is appointed Inspector General of the British forces.'

There followed a brief outline of his career and an uncommitted editorial comment on his appointment and, beneath it, was another headline.

'Admiral Sir John Jellico is appointed to supreme command of the Home Fleet.'

It was also followed by a resume of his career and a report that the *Konigin Louise*, a German mine-layer, had been sunk off Harwich the day after Britain declared war on Germany. The following day HMS

Hampton was sunk in the North Sea by a floating mine, with the loss of a hundred and three men. The article was continued on page eleven. Gerald shuffled the paper, turned to the appropriate page and sat down at the head of the table. Sykes, their butler, approached with a silver pot of steaming, freshly made coffee.

'Good morning, Sir,' he filled Gerald's cup and put a silver cream jug down beside it, 'Mr Wickham telephoned and told me to ask you to attend a meeting at the office. It's at ten o'clock with him and some business associates.'

'Thank you, Sykes, please bring me my scrambled eggs now.' Damn, he thought, as the butler left. He looked at the clock on the mantelpiece and realised that he would have to go straight to the office, instead of stopping on his way, as planned, at Lily Swan's house. He had telephoned her last night when he realised that he had left his watch, a birthday present from Betty, on the table beside her bed. He started to read the newspaper again, on page eleven.

'Two English warships attack Dar-es-Salaam Harbour.'

HMS *Astraea* and HMS *Pegasus* entered Dar-es-Salaam harbour, early in the morning, on the eighth of August and sank a German armed patrol boat and destroyed the wireless tower, with gun fire. The German Governor, Doctor von Schnee, surrendered the city without resistance and negotiated an informal treaty with the Captain of the *Pegasus*, supposedly in the hope that the International Exhibition, scheduled for that month and in preparation for the preceding two years, would still take place.'

Gerald put the paper down beside his table mat and started to eat his breakfast, Sykes poured him another cup of coffee and he turned back to the paper. He read on, turning over ideas in his head about how he and his father-in-law could profit by manufacturing equipment for the Allies.

'Lieutenant Colonel Paul von Lettow-Vorbeck, who was appointed by the German General Staff in 1913 as Commander of German East Africa's Schutztruppe, is reported, by our correspondent in Zanzibar, to have disregarded the conditions imposed on the Governor by the

British. He has ignored the terms of the Congo Act, which required the German Colony to remain neutral and has enlisted the help of Lieutenant Horn, Captain of the armed steamer *Hedwig von Wissmann*, to obtain and retain control of Lake Tanganyika. It is reported that he has also carried out an attack on Taveta, in British East Africa, which was successfully accomplished by the German forces, under the command of Major Kraut. At the outbreak of war Lettow-Vorbeck had only two hundred and sixty Europeans and less than five thousand native askaris under his command.

'Drawing on his experience gained in South Africa with the Boers, he has trained them in guerrilla bush tactics and is quickly gaining a reputation with the British as an accomplished adversary. The British forces, which consisted of both battalions of the King's African Rifles, was engaged in a pointless action against unruly natives in Jubaland at the time of the attack on Taveta. When news of Lettow-Vorbeck's success was known to the authorities, volunteers were immediately called for from amongst the English settlers. Two new regiments, one of which will be mounted, are presently being raised and will be commanded by Major Wavell.'

Gerald finished his breakfast, collected his hat and left the house. As he came down the steps his chauffeur leaped out of the car and held the door open. At ten o'clock exactly he walked into Henry Wickham's office, without waiting to be announced, and enjoyed the look of surprise on Henry's face at his punctuality.

CHAPTER 39

It was late September and Chadwyck was sitting in Johnny's study going over the mine accounts when Adelaide put her nose round the door.

'Daddy's back and he has brought all the latest papers he could find.'

'Come in, my love, and we will find out what is going on in the world.' Adelaide fanned the papers like playing cards and gave half to Chadwyck. He moved to the armchair by the fireplace and she to the sofa. For five minutes there was silence, except for the rustling of the papers.

Chadwick spoke first. 'Something here about a convoy of Indian troops under Brigadier Stewart, arriving in Mombasa to reinforce the K.A.R. in Kenya. Seems they are having a lot of trouble with the German general, Lettow-Vorbeck. It goes on to say that the German fellow intended to pull off a joint land and sea attack on Mombasa with their cruiser *Konigsberg*.'

'That's the ship James was talking about last night. And look, I found a whole column on it, exciting stuff, would you like me to read it out?' Chadwyck smiled at her and nodded.

'14th September 1914
Zanzibar
Peter Hutchence

This evening, the German cruiser *Konigsberg* encountered HMS *Pegasus* undergoing repairs in Zanzibar Harbour. She opened fire at 2,000 yards and kept firing as she steamed closer. The *Pegasus* was raked from stem to stern and her gun turrets, bridge and fo'c'sle were torn apart by successive salvos. When the Konigsberg stopped firing, not a single gun on Pegasus was left in action. Sailors, sheltering from the bombardment, appeared on deck to tend the dead and dying and the *Konigsberg* opened fire again.'

'How does Mr Hutchence know all this?'

Chadwick moved uncomfortably and mumbled something she didn't hear. 'Eyewitness, I imagine, and he'll be a stringer for one of the papers.'

'The ship's ensign, which had survived the first salvos, was shot away from its mast and two Marines, disregarding the relentless shell fire that scythed the decks, carried it aloft. Defiantly they held it there until one of them was killed, only to be replaced immediately by another. When the *Konigsberg* sailed away, *Pegasus*, battered beyond recognition, was listing badly but still afloat. Of her compliment of two hundred and thirty-four officers and men twenty-four had been killed and a further fifty-five wounded.'

'Why Chad? Did they have to kick them when they were down?'

That's war, he thought, but didn't say it.

'We'd probably do the same.'

'No, we wouldn't,' she said emphatically. 'Oh, I forgot to mention when I came in that lunch will soon be ready.'

'Then we had better go through. We can come back to these later.'

The *Konigsberg* never reached Mombasa. She was spotted by HMS *Chatham*, a cruiser of the Cape Flotilla under the command of Admiral King-Hall and pursued relentlessly for two weeks, before she was able to evade her pursuers and take refuge in the Rufiji river delta. There her Captain, Commander Looff, ran her in against the bank in such a way that her guns could bear on any vessel that approached from the sea. At the same time he had the crew prepare for siege by digging trenches on the landward side, along the river approaches.

Unable, due to her draught, to pursue the *Konigsberg* into the endless miles of confusing channels HMS *Chatham* scuttled two colliers to block the main northern channel, in an attempt to keep the *Konigsberg* bottled up in her refuge. The Captain of HMS *Chatham* realised that it would be almost impossible to determine the exact position of the *Konigsberg* because the estuary was under German control. He signalled Admiral King-Hall to that effect and requested aerial reconnaissance.

At that time there were some eighty 'planes under the command of the Royal Naval Air Services in Britain but there was nothing in East Africa. Of the two known civilian pilots in the colony, both had joined Lord Delemere's Scouts. Admiral King-Hall signalled Durban and the Admiralty approached H. D. Cutler, a civilian pilot, who was barnstorming with two decrepit Curtis amphibians in South Africa. He was immediately commissioned as a flight sub-Lieutenant in the Royal Naval Air Service. He and one of his 'planes were shipped aboard the HMS *Kinfauns Castle*, an armed converted liner requisitioned from the Union Castle and delivered to Niororo Island.

The first flight was a disaster, as he was flying visually without a compass and lost his bearings over enemy held territory, during a rainstorm. Desperately short of fuel, he headed out to sea to avoid a forced landing and possible capture in German-held jungle. He landed by a small island, damaging one of the floats and was picked up by one of the lifeboats from the *Kinfauns Castle*.

On his second flight, two days later, he found the *Konigsberg* twelve miles from the sea. He flew over her, at five hundred feet, to gather as much information as possible and was fired on by a machine gun on the foredeck. Two bullets tore through the port wings and, realising the importance of his intelligence and the need to get back to base with it, he banked steeply and dropped to less than a hundred feet to put a small mangrove covered island between him and the enemy.

He followed the course of the river and flew back to Niororo Island, where the information was radioed to H.M.S. *Chatham*, in Mombasa. He had marked the position on his map and, although certain of his information, he was unable to convince his superiors. The Admiralty pointed out that their charts of the river estuary showed that, in their opinion, it was quite impossible for a vessel of almost three and a half thousand tons to be in such shallow water and so far into the delta. They insisted that the position be re-established by a trained observer, before any further action could be taken.

To do this it was necessary to ship the other Curtis up from Durban so that one aircraft could be made from the two, in the hope that the resulting machine would be able to carry a second man. When this was done Lieutenant Cutler took off again with Captain Crampton as his observer; when they returned unscathed Cutler's original position for the *Konigsberg* was confirmed. That evening Captain Looff, knowing that he had been spotted and concerned for the safety of his ship, moved the *Konigsberg* one and a half miles downriver. He again ran her close into the bank so that at low water she was aground. She was again lying in such a way that her main armament covered any approach made from the sea. Admiral King-Hall, before taking action and anticipating such a move by the German Captain, sent Lieutenant Cutler with Commander Fitzmaurice, as observer, up again to confirm the *Konigsberg*'s position. Once more they were fired on but not hit, and they returned safely to base with the new position.

Bad weather set in before Admiral King-Hall could mount an attack and it was not until mid-December that Lieutenant Cutler could fly again. On this occasion he went up alone to re-confirm the *Konigsberg*'s position. A mile and a half up the river his engine started to miss, due to a block in the fuel line, and before he could do anything about it the engine cut out and he was forced to put down on a sandbar in the river. He immediately came under fire from German troops on shore. Putting the aircraft between himself and his assailants, he worked feverishly to clear the blocked line as bullets ricocheted off the engine block. By the time he had cleared it a platoon of twelve German askaris, led by an officer brandishing a pistol, were only fifty yards from him. Setting the controls he moved to the front of the aircraft to swing the propeller in a desperate attempt to start the engine. It fired and then, to his bitter disappointment, backfired and before he could try again the Germans were upon him.

Leaving two askaris to guard the aircraft the German officer, surrounded by his men, marched Lieutenant Cutler back to his headquarters. The Captain of one of the two British armed tugs left to guard the river mouth saw the Curtis come down. He radioed Niororo Island and, on their orders, steamed upriver to find the aircraft and if possible rescue the pilot. Seeing no sign of Lieutenant Cutler through his binoculars, the Captain steamed on upriver and brought his craft alongside the 'plane. He winched it on deck, under constant fire from the enemy, while the German officer, back at his own H.Q., toasted his prisoner's health and his own good fortune at capturing the first British aviator in Africa. Against mounting opposition, the tug fought its way back out to sea, bringing to bear its own not inconsiderable firepower on the German shore batteries.

CHAPTER 40

'There's a bit here about Africa, Eddy' Jock waved a week-old copy of the *London Gazette* at him. They were sitting side by side, in deck chairs, on the grass verge outside the Officers' Mess, behind the British lines at Vauxcéré, in northern France.

'You read it to me Jock, I'm too tired.' They had just come back from an aerial reconnaissance, along the railway line that led towards Soissons.

'It's about a German cruiser called the *Konigsberg*, seems she steamed into Zanzibar and destroyed HMS *Pegasus*, one of our cruisers, while she was undergoing repairs. Typical of the bloody Hun to take on a disabled ship and one that wasn't ready for action.'

'Don't be daft, Jock, we are at war, just in case you hadn't noticed and it's not typical. Remember that German pilot yesterday, in one of their new Fokker Morane machines, came out of nowhere when we were coming back from that recce over their trenches? He turned and flew back across our nose and threw us a salute, instead of the contents of his Lugers' magazine.'

'Well that's different, he was an officer and one of us.'

'Christ Jock, you sometimes say the bloody stupidest things I've ever heard. He wasn't one of us in any sense of the word, he was one of them, the enemy and the sooner you get that into your thick skull the better. No wonder the skipper won't give you your own kite.'

'Why are you so angry, Eddy?' There was a plaintive note in his voice. Two other members of the squadron came out of the Officer's Mess and Edward lay back in his chair and closed his eyes. He was too tired to reply but, in his own mind, he tried to answer Jock's question.

After they had joined up at the end of July, contrary to Alister's predictions, they had done six weeks basic training together on Salisbury Plain. He had felt that he was standing still, that he already knew what they were trying to teach him and Jock, in the close confines of the camp, repeatedly got on his nerves. Eventually the other pilots, navigators and observers finally caught up with him, they had been taught aerial photography, little realising at the time how different the reality would be from the simulation.

On the fifteenth of September, two days after the battle of the Aisne had begun, their squadron had been moved to Dover and across the Channel to Calais, in company with a reserve battalion of the Northumberland Fusiliers. They had travelled by train to Chantilly where they had changed trains and, still in company with the same battalion, travelled through Senlis on to Catterets where they had been met by an R.F.C. driver in a requisitioned delivery lorry, still proudly bearing the name Derry and Toms. From there they had driven, at a snail's pace, through hopelessly congested country roads to the airfield outside Vauxcéré. Since then they had spent the last three weeks flying at least two missions a day along the front, which stretched for almost a hundred miles from Compiegne to Tahure, east of Riems.

Four French armies and the British under Sir John French faced four German armies under Field Marshal Josias von Heeringen. Many times during their reconnaissance they had been fired on from the ground, both by artillery and rifle fire and, on two occasions, minor damage had been done to the fabric of the B.E. 2 aircraft. The observer, in his case Jock, sat in front of him and, when not actually taking photographs, acted as look-out and, when attacked, defended them. He was armed with nothing more than a .455 Smith and Wesson revolver. Edward also had his own and knew, as did all pilots, their alternative use in the event of crashing and almost certainly burning to death. Parachutes had been deemed unnecessary, as bad for morale apart from the fact they were bulky and there wasn't room for them in the cockpit.

Jock's attitude was typical of most of his fellow officers. They were unable to take it seriously. Perhaps it was because nobody in their squadron had, as yet, been killed. He knew of several deaths in other squadrons; perhaps only when it happened to them, would they finally realise the deadliness of the situation. If another optimist told him that it would be all over by Christmas, he would knock him down.

'C.O. wants to see you, Eddy' One of the two pilots that had come out onto, what the Senior Flight Sergeant was pleased to call, the lawn and stood over Eddy, blocking the weak autumn sun.

'What on earth for, Clive? It can't be half an hour since we were debriefed.'

'Who knows, dear boy, but a couple of keen types have just arrived and one of them thinks he's your new observer.' Edward's eyes snapped open and Jock, who was talking to the other pilot, stopped in mid-sentence.

'You're joking, Clive, he can't do that. Come on Jock let's go see the Old Man.' Edward heaved himself out of his deck chair and they went in to see their skipper.

Squadron Commander Bill Benson stood with his feet braced apart and his hands held in front of him, in an attempt to restore order. 'I say, chaps, one at a time please or, better still, me first. You are quite right Eddy, but I don't know where you got your information from because I only knew about it myself a few minutes ago. Jock gets his own machine and you each get a new observer.' He pulled nervously on the end of his moustache. He was a small, wiry man with coal-black hair and, although only five years older than them, had proved himself in all aspects of flying and was regarded with great affection by all his men.

'For God's sake Bill, Jock is not ready to fly his own kite.'

'Nonsense Eddy, he's done almost as many hours as you have.' He tapped Jock's service record, on his desk.

'But not as a pilot.'

'It's the C.O.'s decision, Eddy, you worry too much,' cut in Jock. 'Before we left England I had flown almost as much as you had. When we got here, I put in a request for pilot the moment I found out I was your observer. It's all right Eddy,' he grinned reassuringly at him, 'the Hun won't get me.'

The following morning, Jock and two other pilots with their respective observers took off on a routine recce along the enemy lines. Edward was unable to fly, his machine not airworthy according to his mechanic. Following pre-determined, individual flight patterns the three planes set off to their appointed sectors. Twenty-seven minutes after take-off, Jock Sinclair's plane was shot down by a British field battery and both he and his observer were killed.

* * *

'Come in Eddy and take a pew. I've just got a report from Archie.'

'Archie, Sir?'

'Yes, it's what we've dubbed the Anti-aircraft batteries, I'm surprised you haven't heard it before.' Bill Benson sat down heavily behind his desk, he was nearing exhaustion and it showed on his face. The squadron was being asked to fly almost continuous sorties to build up a photographic map, over a large section of the front, of the German artillery and troop movements. 'Do you remember what Jock said yesterday about the Hun not getting him? He was right, damn it, but I bet he never thought it would be our own anti-aircraft gunners.' He took off his leather helmet and flung it, in frustration, at the back of a chair. They had just come in from a mission and it was almost dark outside.

'Are you going to write to his parents or shall I, and what the hell are we going to say?'

'Please sit down Eddy, I know how you feel. I know you feel

responsible but the responsibility was mine and I'm very aware of what you said yesterday.' He emphasised the you and Edward slumped into a chair and threw his helmet onto the desk.

'He was exactly the same age as me, to the day and I have looked after him since we were thirteen. How did it happen, Bill?'

'In the report that I have here from Captain Wilson of the Royal Artillery, who was the officer in charge of the battery concerned, Jock had flown well over no-man's land and was following the German lines. Their artillery opened up on him and, for what seemed to Captain Wilson a very long time, he held his flight pattern regardless, while his observer was photographing the German positions. It was the appearance of a German Gotha, LD5 biplane, which came down on him from above that made him break off the pattern and head for home. The German, in a new and very fast machine known as the Falcon, was very close to him and they were firing at each other with revolvers, as the Hun swept past him.'

'Was Jock hit?'

'Not as far as I know because he turned out of the way and tried to climb above the German, who was well ahead of him and almost over our lines. At that point, our Archie opened up on the German but Jock, who was completing his turn to gain altitude, came up behind the German and directly into the field of fire and it was he that was hit by our artillery, not the German. Most of the port wing was torn off and there was no way he could control his descent. The machine fell like a stone from about two thousand feet and burst into flames when it hit the ground.'

'So he and his observer are still out there, in no-man's land?'

'No Eddy, I don't think so. According to this,' he nodded at the report on his desk 'there was a lull in the firing immediately after it happened and a German stretcher party went out, under a white flag and appeared to be carrying something with them, on their return. The Hun is pretty good at letting us know about this sort of thing, so we will probably hear something soon.' Neither of them spoke while Bill took a bottle of brandy and two glasses from a drawer in his desk and splashed a generous shot into both of them. He pushed one across the desk towards Edward, stood up and raised his own. 'Here's to Jock, Eddy. He was doing what he wanted and that,' he added bitterly, 'is more than can be said for a lot of us.' Edward got to his feet and raised his glass.

'I will not drink to Jock's memory because he is still real to me but, by God, I will drink to our success at avenging his death and to the total destruction of the Hun.' He spat out the last words and emptied his glass, in one. Bill, stunned by the raw power of his anger, refilled their glasses in silence.

CHAPTER 41

'I have a letter here from Jack, and he wants me to join him in B.E.A. A company of Greys Scouts has been detailed to gather intelligence on the *Konigsberg*.' It was the end of a long day and they were sitting in Red's office at the mine.

'How long ago is it now since he left to join his father's outfit?'

'Must be almost two months,' said James.

'Why?'

'Why what?'

'Why does he need to gather intelligence on the *Konigsberg*? Surely that's the Navy's job.'

'Not anymore, he says she is aground in the Rufiji delta.'

'So what more does Jack need to know? She can't go anywhere penned in by the fleet, and how is he anyway?' Chadwyck got up and poured them both a drink; it was almost dark and soon it would be time for supper.

'He seems fine, half the letter is about a girl he met on leave in Nairobi called Daphne Frobisher who knows Gerald, whatever that might mean.'

'Almost anything,' said Chadwyck sitting down again and they both laughed, 'so what are you going to do? I thought we were all going down to Springbokfontein next week for Christmas and New Year.'

'Well, if it's all right with you partner, I would like to join Jack. Red can take care of the place and my father can help out.'

'What about the campaign in German South West?'

'I think Botha can manage without me.' He grinned lopsidedly and Chadwyck knew that he had struck a nerve. He suddenly realised that James had been fretting for quite a while to have a crack at the Germans. He immediately thought of Edward and his last letter about Jock's death and how he too was frustrated by the stalemate on the Western Front.

'Why didn't you say anything about this before James? I don't mean Jack's outing but you obviously want to take an active part in the war.'

'I suppose it was because of General Beyers and his damned revolt, I didn't want to leave the place until that had been sorted out. Did you know he was drowned last week, trying to escape across the Vaal. It was all so pointless and such a pitiful end to a brilliant career. He had been on the run, around here, ever since Botha overthrew his commando at Rustenburg and, to think that at the time that De La Rey was shot, almost exactly three months ago, he was Commandant General of the Active Citizens Force.'

'Do you know why De La Rey was shot and what it was all about?' James refilled their glasses before answering.

'It was an accident, a case of mistaken identity. He and General Beyers were on their way to a meeting, to spark the revolt. It was really Beyers and De Wet's plan to start the revolution, backed by Hertzog and old President Steyn. They were using De La Rey, because his support would have carried the day. I still cannot believe he was involved in a revolt against the Union of South Africa.' He stretched out his legs and put his feet up on the desk, swirled the whisky around his glass and took a deep swallow 'If ever I had a hero, Chad, he was it. It's strange really because he and Pa were on opposite sides during the Boer War but he was an outstanding general and when it was all over he threw himself, body and soul, behind the peace process and the formation of the Union. Before the war he stood up to Kruger and told him that he was mad to think that he could take on the might of the British Empire and, that whatever he did, he could never win. He told him that most of what the Boers wanted could be achieved by negotiation. I think it was the only time that Kruger didn't get his way, he just sat glaring at Oom Koos and said nothing.'

'Oom Koos?'

'De la Rey's name, to his intimates.'

'Intimates, James?'

'I met him, he came to the house many times and had long talks with father about the war, that went on way into the night. Kruger had implied cowardice in his attack on him and Oom Koos' answer had been that he, Kruger would leave the field before him and, do you know Chad, he did.'

'You still have not told me how he was shot,' said Chadwyck gently, not really wanting to break in on James's thoughts but now curious and very moved by what he had said.

'It was just damn bad luck. The police were looking for an armed gang that had murdered two of their colleagues, run by a bastard called Foster. He had escaped in February from Central Prison in Pretoria and joined forces with two others, Carl Mezar and an American, called John Maxim. The police had set up roadblocks around Johannesburg and Bayers, thinking they were for him and wanting to get Oom Koos to the meeting, at all costs, ignored two of them and drove right through. At the third they did the same but one of the policemen fired at the back of their car, supposedly to puncture a tyre but the bullet ricocheted off the road and the nickel jacket went through the back of the car hit Oom Koos and lodged in his heart.'

'What was it all about?'

'It is a long story Chad and it really does not make much sense to most of us but it must have meant a lot to the insurrectionists, some seven thousand of them were taken prisoner by Botha's troops. Come on now, let's go eat, I'll tell you about it later.' Over dinner the three of them discussed the latest developments at the mine. They were finding some good diamonds and, although Chadwyck thought it bad for morale, he had finally agreed with Red that a security fence should be erected around the mine. They had adopted the old practice of offering a reward to any native who handed over a significant diamond found in the blue ground before it was processed by the crushers. They also arranged transport, usually a horse, and gave the man a pass back to his own village, which ensured indemnity from prosecution and explained how he came to be in possession of a relatively large amount of money.

The system, in general practice since the early nineties, offered the workers a safer alternative than trying to approach the illicit diamond buyers on the outside. Even so, despite guards on the gate, and Red, James and an overseer keeping a constant eye on the diggings, it was impossible to prevent the occasional diamond from being smuggled out. They had made a deal with one of the subsidiary buying syndicates, once been part of Wernher, Beit and Co., to take their entire production for the year at a predetermined price, based on carat weight. After dinner Red went out to check the natives on their side of the compound. James and Chadwyck remained at the table drinking whisky and talking about their families and the war.

'You were going to tell me about the revolution and why it started.'

'It was a form of 'Gewapende Protest,' a deep-seated practice that is almost a way of life to the Boers which, with your newfound knowledge of Afrikaans, you will know means violent protest.' Chadwyck smiled at the jibe; he had been studying the Boer's language and customs since May.

'I thought that was something of the past, go on.'

'It was, but it's so fundamental that it will probably never change. In the old days, when they had serious differences of opinion they would form commandos, laager the women, children and stock and go out on manoeuvres, armed to the teeth but with absolutely no intention of killing each other. It was an accepted way of settling their differences without either side losing honour. After a while they would return to their farms and they and their neighbours, who had been on opposite sides, would co-habit peacefully as before and work for the common good.'

'You mean to say that neither side fired a shot in anger and no one was killed?'

In the old days, yes, because a white man, whatever his beliefs or crimes, was too valuable to his peers, as a white man, to allow him to be killed. Every one of them was needed, when it came to defending themselves against their enemies. I know that you are now going to say that this was different, and it was. The difference was the German factor and their war.'

'What was Colonel Maritz's part in it?'

'He was appointed as commanding officer of the north-western districts of Cape Province, along the German border in August and it is now known that he was in constant touch with the Germans and would have eased their way into the Union, in conjunction with General Bayers and the rebels. In fact it was Bayers who insisted on his appointment, against the recommendations of the Ministry of Defence.'

'It still doesn't make sense James. Why would the Boers, who are now part of the Union, which they helped to establish, want to revolt against it?'

'As I said before, it was the timing of the thing and a great many of them were influenced by the Prophet, van Rensburg, who had a proven record of second sight. He kept referring to the fifteenth and originally the rebels thought he meant the fifteenth of August but when nothing happened then he changed it, when taxed, to the fifteenth of September, claiming that a month here or there made little difference. The extraordinary thing was that he lost little credibility and the ordinary folk in the Transvaal still believed in him, implicitly.'

'That was the day that the meeting was set for, at Potchefstroom Camp, where General Beyers would trigger the revolution, with De la Ray on the platform beside him?'

'Exactly, but as you know it did not happen as he planned. By then General Beyers had resigned, as had De Wet and, without Oom

Koos, the revolution went ahead.' They sat in silence for a while and James refilled their glasses. Chadwyck raised his in a salute.

'So you, beloved brother-in-law, have now got itchy feet and want to join the scrap, before it's all over.'

'Yes, but I think it's far from over, it is now on such a scale and involves so many nations that I think it will go on for a long time.'

'Why B.E.A., why not join Botha's lot in German South-West? There's talk of conscription so they'll probably get you, anyhow.'

'In that case I will definitely go to B.E.A., the climate is better and so are the girls.'

'Seriously James, what did Jack tell you about this caper?'

'Not much, except he wants an answer right away. It seems that the *Konigsberg* is bottled up in the Rufiji delta and they need confirmation of her exact position. She has apparently moved since she was last spotted and without that information they can't attack her from the sea, which would be the only feasible way of destroying her.'

'Why doesn't Jack recommend they do it from the air?'

'The weather is against them and the second part of his mission is to prevent the Huns taking the guns off the *Konigsberg* and converting them for use as field artillery.'

'When would you go?'

'As soon as possible. I would take a boat out of Durban to Zanzibar and the Navy would get me onto Mafia Island for a rendezvous.'

'Have you discussed it with your father?' James nodded. 'I take that to mean he agrees with your going.'

'Yes. Mother is a bit upset but, as you pointed out, conscription, if they bring it in, will get me and I would rather volunteer than be called up.' The door swung open and Red came in, having finished his inspection of the compound.

'Come and join us Red, and have a drink. Have you two discussed James's hare-brained scheme? I know you can do without him, but we probably shouldn't let him know that.' Red splashed some soda onto his whisky and sat down at the end of the table.

'He did mention it, but if he goes I will need another pair of eyes to watch that lot.' He nodded towards the compound, behind him.

'Look you two, stop talking about me as if I wasn't here and, if that's all I am, just a pair of eyes then I might just as well not come back again.'

'For God's sake, James,' cut in Chadwyck and there was a sudden ominous silence, 'you are tempting fate.'

'Take it easy, Chad. I didn't know you were so superstitious, why not come along and keep an eye on me.'

'You know perfectly well why not.'

'I know,' he grinned, 'big Sis, big being the operative word. When is she due?'

'In seven weeks. It's going to be a big baby and I hope to God that it will all go well.'

CHAPTER 42

'Where's Sophie? Lea, please go and find her or we will miss our train. Chad, are you sure Jan Viljoen's expecting all of us?'

'Every last one of you. I sent him written instructions right after we made our plans. So he and his team will have pulled out all the stops.'

'Such a pity that Johnny has to come back so soon.'

'When do the twins go back to school?'

'On the 17th of January and Sophie, if Lea can find her, starts her new boarding school the next day.'

'And,' said Chad with a grin, 'you will stay on and look after us. What did Doctor Marais say when you and Adelaide saw him yesterday?'

'Nothing much, He gave me a letter of introduction to a Doctor Clarke in Cape Town, a colleague of his and a well-known gynaecologist. He has already written to him with Adelaide's records.'

'Why, is he worried about her?'

'Not really, he was just a little concerned, something about the position of the baby. "Nothing to be worried about," he told me. "Normal procedure and you can't do better than Doctor Clarke."' Before Chadwick could answer, Adelaide came out of the house, helped by Lea, with Sophie in tow.

The twins were already at Springbokfontein when they arrived, collected from school by Jan. Chadwyck was delighted to be able to finally entertain the Flynns after all they had done for him.

They had found a large packing case waiting for their arrival, full of presents for them all, from Victoria. Chad and Adelaide had stayed with the Vanderbilts in North Carolina on their honeymoon and had enjoyed partying with their friends around their new pool. From that moment on Adelaide had pleaded with Chadwyck to build one at Springbokfontein, until she had finally got her way. It was a great success, especially with the children.

When they gathered with friends and neighbours for their New Year's Eve party, the mood was muted by the war news from the Western Front and the appalling casualties beginning to affect the first of the South African volunteer troops, fighting and dying there with the British Army. People were starting to know someone whose husband or son had been killed or, even closer to home, members of their own families. No longer did anyone believe that it would be 'all over by Christmas'.

At the end of that week, Johnny went back to Rietfontein and the rest of the family stayed on with Chadwyck.

Two weeks before the baby was due, Jenny and Adelaide went into Cape Town for her second consultation with Doctor Clarke. Adelaide had put on more than two stone and was suffering from the hot weather. Her feet would swell up and she found herself very unattractive in Chadwyck's presence. Doctor Clarke's hearty manner irritated her, as did most things now. She kept telling herself how every woman she had met that knew him as a gynaecologist had, without exception, sung his praises.

CHAPTER 43

Every effort had been made to make the Officers' Mess, on the airfield at Vauxcéré, as festive as possible for Christmas and New Year. It was a parody of their true feelings; none felt like celebrating. The optimists were finally becoming reconciled to the enormity of the conflict and the likelihood of it going on for years. Since Jock's death, three others had been killed and Bill Benson was waging a fiercer battle over supplies than he was with the enemy. Edward had become morose and introspective and his commanding officer had readily endorsed his application for transfer. Edward's natural ability and murderous intent towards the Germans had made his flying reckless and a bad example. His skill and determination were wasted on the mundane routine of reconnaissance and aerial photography, so Bill, emphasising his extraordinary ability, had recommended a special assignment.

On the first of January his orders came through and he was asked to report to the skipper's office. He had just returned from the early morning mission, severely shaken when an enemy 'plane had fired on him, when over the German lines. His starboard wing had been badly shredded and the fuel tank holed. He was still wondering why it had not caught fire as he knocked on Bill's door and went in, without waiting for an answer.

'They have beaten us to it Bill, I have just been shot up in the air. What the hell are our armourers playing at? My mechanic tells me it will take him two days to get my kite back in the air.' He stalked up and down the small office, rubbing the palms of his hands together in an effort to dissipate his anger and frustration. 'It was a bloody two-seater, a Fokker I think, with a light machine gun mounted behind the cockpit and operated by the observer. If they can do it why can't we? It's bad enough being shot at by both sides from the ground, but we haven't a chance if they can shoot at us in the air and we can't fire back.'

'Settle down Eddy and tell me all about it.'

'I just have, for Christ's sake. If I had not dodged when I did the bastard would have had me. Pistols are no good against L.M.Gs and we have got to do something about it, now.'

'We are working on it Eddy and have been since it first started, as you well know. The French are developing a synchronised gun that will fire through the propeller but it is not easy and, right now, it is doing more damage to their 'planes than the enemy.' Edward barked a short, mirthless laugh and dropped into the sagging armchair in front of Bill's desk.

'You sent for me, why?'

'Your transfer, it came through this morning.' Edward leant forward, interest immediately lighting his eyes and going some way towards animating the grey boredom of his features. 'You have been selected to fly with the Royal Naval Air Services Expeditionary Squadron Number Four.'

'Sounds impressive, and where the hell are they?'

'In England,' he saw the light go out of Edward's eyes as he slumped back into his chair, before he added 'at the moment, but they are on their way to East Africa and, for some extraordinary reason, it seems they can't do without you.'

'What's the job?' Interest flared again in his voice.

'It doesn't say, Eddy, but my bet is it has something to do with the *Konigsberg*. They seem to be having the devil's own time in dealing with her.' Edward whistled through his teeth, leant back and swung his legs up onto Bill's desk.

'Jock was talking about that, the day before he died.'

'You will be under the command of a chap called Cull.' Purposely, he gave no indication of having heard Edward's last remark. 'You are leaving this afternoon on the R.E. convoy and if the buggers don't get lost you should be home in three days and, what is more, they have given you a totally undeserved week's leave.' Edward grinned and threw his goggles at him. 'You are to report to Cull at the R.N.A.S. Headquarters, in London, on the fourteenth.'

'How are we going to get out there?'

'No idea, you will just have to wait and see, as nanny would say.'

* * *

Eight days later, after interminable delays and considerable difficulty in obtaining passage across the Channel, Edward arrived in London already two days into his leave and booked into the Connaught. The next morning, he took a cab out to the R.N.A.S. headquarters and showed his credentials to the guard on the gate.

'You should find Flight Lieutenant Cull in his office, Sir, in D block. He rang through to tell me he was expecting you.'

'Thank you, Corporal. And where might I find D block?'

'Between C and E blocks, Sir,' and he laughed 'We are now all very regimented here, Sir, a place for everything and everything in its place.' He shifted from one foot to the other. 'It's straight ahead, Sir, The first block on your left after the Guard House is A, the next is B and so on.'

'Thank you, Corporal. You are not with the R.N.A.S. are you?'

'No Sir, I'm with the 2nd Essex, We just look after them.'

Edward saluted and walked through the guard house before the corporal laughed again. He reached D block and went into a small hall, leading to a long corridor with identical doors on both sides, at twenty foot intervals. Lieutenant Cull's was the second on the right. Edward knocked.

'Come in. Oh, there you are, we've been expecting you.' Edward paused at the door. 'Well, you are Eddy Meade?'

'Yes, and you must be Tommy Cull.'

'No, I'm Cull,' said a voice from over Edward's left shoulder. 'That one is Harry Watkins.' Eddy shook hands with Harry and turned to face Tommy Cull. They stood looking at each other for a moment, sizing each other up, and then shook hands.

'Welcome to the R.N.A.S.' His voice was deeper than Edward expected from someone so slightly built. He had dark hair and exuded vitality. His movements were quick and economical, and seemed to have that rare quality of innate leadership.

'Please sit down, we are very glad to have you with us. Harry and I have got a few things to finish and, by the way,' he added as he turned back to his desk, 'I have never seen the likes of the report Bill Benson wrote on you. You've got a hell of a reputation to live up to.' Edward grinned and sat down, happy with his new surroundings and, as the two talked, his interest increased. An orderly brought in a pot of tea and some biscuits and after he had left, Edward was drawn into the conversation.

'When are we leaving?'

'The day after tomorrow,' said Harry, 'on the SS *Persia*. They are loading her right now, down at Tilbury. We are taking out a couple of Sopwith sea 'planes with hundred horse-power engines, two thousand gallons of fuel and as many spare parts as we can get our hands on, to keep the damn kites flying.'

'How many will we be altogether, apart from the three of us?'

'Eighteen in all,' said Tommy, 'if we can get them together in time. They have had a lot of trouble on this job already due to local conditions, so we are taking a couple of chaps from Sopwith's works and an expert on propellers.'

'When do we arrive in B.E.A.?'

'Not until the end of February, Eddy, because we are going to Bombay first, unloading there to put the crates together and do some experimental work in tropical conditions. Then, we will reload the whole lot onto the *Kinfauns Castle* and head for Niororo Island.'

'Are we going to attack the *Konigsberg* or just do a recce. job for the Navy?'

'We are going to bomb the hell out of her.' said Harry enthusiastically and then added as an afterthought, 'if we can. We are taking more than enough bombs to do the job properly and the biggest of them weigh in at fifty pounds each but the infuriating thing is we just don't know whether the planes can lift the load in tropical conditions.'

'If they can't,' cut in Edward, 'then we spot for the Navy I suppose.'

'That's it Eddy, and that is where you come in. I'm hungry, will the two of you join me for lunch?'

On the twentieth of February the *Kinfauns Castle* arrived at Niororo Island and Number Four Squadron was unloaded, with their equipment. Their first flight was a fiasco. The seaplane, with two men, two bombs of sixteen pounds each, another two of fifty and enough fuel for four hours, stubbornly refused to leave the water. Finally, after four days, they managed to get one man and enough fuel for an hour up to a height of fifteen hundred feet. Three days later Harry Watkins crashed the other plane. For the next two weeks they tried every variation they could think of to improve the performance of the remaining aircraft. Petrol of a different density was brought in from Zanzibar and mixed with the existing fuel but, whatever they tried, including compressed air and oxygen, the monosoutape engine would not perform to their satisfaction and the demands of their mission.

CHAPTER 44

In the final month of her pregnancy, Adelaide had reluctantly agreed with her doctor that she would slow down a bit, and Jenny had gently but firmly made sure that she did. As a concession to her mother, she developed the habit of having her breakfast brought to her in bed. It had been a beautiful summer and many times she and Chadwyck had gone to the hill overlooking the vineyards for picnics and lazy siestas. It had been a bumper crop and Jan Viljoens predicted a good vintage.

The garden was at its best and the house was always full of beautiful flowers that Adelaide loved to arrange. There was a great feeling of excitement amongst the servants and field hands at the prospect of the new arrival. Chadwyck came through from his dressing room, sat on the edge of her bed and helped himself to a last cup of coffee, before going out to find Jan in the vineyards. Adelaide looked radiant, propped up in bed and wearing a beautiful silk nightdress, her dark hair cascading over her shoulders. She was going through a pile of mail stacked on the breakfast tray.

'Here's a letter from Eddy, Chad. How exciting, it's addressed to me.'

'Where is it from?'

'London.' she said and caught her breath, she moaned involuntarily and immediately Chadwyck was on his feet.

'What is it darling, are you all right?' She opened her eyes and smiled at him, there was a look of infinite love and understanding on her face.

'It's the baby, my darling, he's getting very restless.' For a long time they had referred to the child as 'he' because they were both convinced that it was a boy. She closed her eyes again and moved her hips, in an attempt to ease the pain. Too nervous to sit on the bed again Chadwyck knelt beside it, holding her hand. She closed her eyes and drew comfort from his strength.

'Do you want me to call Lea,' there was a note of alarm in his voice, 'or is there anything I can do?' She did not answer but slowly shook her head, her eyes were still closed and he could hear her grinding her teeth. It was an appalling sound that made the hair on the back of his neck stand on end. He moved closer and put his arms around her and noticed a fine sheen of perspiration on her forehead.

'For God's sake darling, what has happened, has it started, is he coming?' Her head was against his shoulder, her mouth beside his ear.

'I'm frightened, Chad.' She spoke in a hoarse whisper that sounded like tearing silk. She held him fiercely, her nails biting through the fabric of his shirt, deep into his arm. She hissed again in pain and tears were squeezed from the corners of her eyes. The bed beneath her felt wet and she thought it was blood. Panic-stricken, she tried to kick the bedclothes off her legs and cried out again in pain, as the baby moved inside her. 'I am bleeding Chad, please help me.' As gently as he could, he freed his arm and pulled the sheets back from her legs. They were soaked but there was no sign of blood, her waters had broken. He pulled the sheets up and held her tightly.

'It's all right darling, there is no blood but the baby is coming and I must go for help. I won't be a moment.' She clung to him desperately and pleaded with her eyes, for him to stay. He covered her ear nearest to him and yelled for the maid. Moments later there was a tap on the door and Lea came in. 'It is time Lea, stay with your mistress while I telephone Doctor Clarke and find Mrs Flynn.'

'No Chad, please don't leave me.'

'I must, my darling, just for a moment, to call the doctor.' Reluctantly she released her hold on him. 'Lea have you seen Mrs Flynn?'

'Yes Baas, she is in the morning room having breakfast.'

'Stay here Lea and I will be back in five minutes.' He took the stairs two at a time and almost collided with Isaac, the butler, as he crossed the hall to the library. The old retainer stepped back, concern showing in his gentle brown eyes. Nervously, he ran arthritic black fingers through his white peppercorn hair.

'What has happened, Baas?'

'The baby, Isaac please find Mrs Flynn and ask her to go up to our room, I must telephone the doctor.'

'Yes, Baas and I will fetch my wife too, as she has had many children and knows the way of these things. It will be all right Baas, it is God's doing.' After what seemed to be an interminable delay, Chadwyck raised the operator and got through to Doctor Clarke. It took the doctor two minutes to calm Chadwyck down, before he was making sense and when he understood what had happened he promised to be out there as soon as possible.

When Chadwyck got back to the bedroom he could see immediately that Jenny had taken charge and, with the help of Lea and Isaac's wife, they had made Adelaide as comfortable as possible. Leaving the two women by the bedside Jenny came over to the door and led Chadwyck out onto the landing.

'She is settled now Chad, she was frightened by the suddenness of it. I am afraid that, as it is her first child, she is in for a long confinement.'

'I must see her, Jenny. I promised I would come back immediately.'

'No Chad, come downstairs with me and we will wait for the doctor, I assume he's on his way.' He followed her downstairs to the library. 'Lea has changed all the bedding and Adelaide is now trying to relax, which is the best thing for her.' Although it was only ten in the morning Chadwyck poured two large glasses of sherry and gave one to Jenny, his hand was shaking. She smiled reassuringly at him, as she took the glass. 'Try to relax Chad, come and sit down over here and I will tell you how it was, when Adelaide was born.' An hour later they heard a car pull up and Chadwyck was out in the hall before Jenny had left her chair. Isaac was already at the front door and Chadwyck could see that Doctor Clarke was followed by a middle-aged woman, in a very starched uniform.

'Chadwyck, my boy, how are you? I am not too late am I? surely I haven't missed all the fun.' He clapped Chadwyck on the shoulder, who was totally oblivious to his sense of humour. He was a big, raw-boned man with long white side-whiskers and a trim Van Dyke beard. 'May I introduce Miss Marshall, the most competent midwife, I know.' Jenny had joined them, in the hall. 'This is Mr Meade and Mrs Flynn. How are you Jenny?' Nurse Marshall bobbed a curtsey to Chadwyck and nodded politely to Jenny, who led the three of them upstairs.

'Really no need for you to come up Jenny, I know my way and, as for young Chadwyck, he is bound to get under foot. Better if you both wait downstairs and I will see you after I have seen my patient.' Chadwyck resented his hail-fellow attitude and, had it not been for Jenny's reassuring hand on his elbow, he would have argued the point. With as much grace as he could muster he let them pass and returned to the library with Jenny. Before Chadwyck had finished his second drink the doctor reappeared, with a broad, confident expression on his face. 'Nothing to worry about, dear boy,' he boomed as he accepted a drink, 'the girl is as fit as a fiddle and should have no problems at all. But, being her first, it will be a long confinement.'

'I know doctor, Jenny told me.' cut in Chadwyck, irritated by his platitudes. Unperturbed by the interruption, Doctor Clarke beamed at Jenny.

'The young are so impetuous today my dear, I can see that the father is going to be more trouble than the mother.' He turned back to Chadwyck. 'You can go and see your wife now and you will see that I am right. Fit as a fiddle.' He repeated and refilled his glass from the decanter. Chadwyck left the room without a word, and when he came down again he was glad to find that the doctor had left.

'How is she?' asked Jenny, taking his arm and leading him through the French windows onto the terrace. They sat in rattan chairs under a pergola, the sound of bees loud on the still air.

'She was fine, almost asleep. Nurse Marshall has given her a sedative. Lea has gone about her duties but Isaac's wife refuses to leave the room.'

'Then Doctor Clarke's confidence was well founded.'

'It seems so,' said Chadwyck grudgingly, 'but I can't understand why Adelaide likes the man.'

'He has an impressive record and has long since lost count of the number of births he has attended.'

'Is he coming back or is it up to Nurse Marshall now?'

'Darling Chad, of course he is coming back but it will take hours yet, it always does with a first child.'

'For Heaven's sake Jenny, you are repeating yourself. Please tell me something I don't know.' He got up and went over towards her. 'I'm sorry, come on let's go for a walk, until lunch is ready.'

At five o' clock Doctor Clarke came back with another nurse that Jenny had suggested to him, and he found them sitting in Adelaide's room. He conducted a cursory examination of her abdomen, patted her reassuringly on the shoulder and left the room with Nurse Marshall. Shortly afterwards the nurse returned, alone. Chadwyck heard the doctor's car driving away and looked across at Jenny, who seemed equally surprised.

'Miss Marshall,' he said testily, 'perhaps you would be good enough to tell us what Doctor Clarke said.'

'He was in a bit of a hurry, sir and asked me to make his apologies.' She averted her gaze as she lied and Chadwyck warmed towards her.

'That's all right, Miss Marshall and I am sure my wife is doing fine or he would have said something to us.' They were talking in whispers, on the far side of the room.

'Oh yes, sir and you must not worry, sir.'

'Please Miss Marshall, do not ever tell me that again.'

'No sir, I am sorry.' For a moment he thought she was going to cry

253

but then added 'He gave me some laudanum for your wife sir, but at the moment she does not need it because the pain has passed and the contractions are not that frequent.'

'Thank you very much Miss Marshall, that is the first clear explanation I have had since this whole thing started.' She smiled and he noticed that she had very pretty hazel eyes.

'He also said Sir, that he would come back after dinner, unless the cycle shortened drastically and then I was to telephone him and he would come immediately.'

'Thank you, Miss Marshall.' He touched her briefly on the shoulder in appreciation and she blushed but he did not notice, as he had already returned to his chair.

Jenny and Chadwyck dined alone, and as they were finishing their coffee she opened her handbag and fished around inside. 'I had a letter from James I forgot to mention it before. It's odd how a change in priorities affects one's thinking.'

'Mine too. I cannot believe I never asked. How is he and what's his news?'

'Very well, by all accounts. He has been promoted to Captain.'

'Did he tell you anything about their operations?'

'Not much, but I suppose they have to be fairly careful, in case a letter falls into the wrong hands.'

'Let's go up and see Adelaide and then we ought to try and get some sleep.' The servants had made up a small bed in the far corner of Adelaide's room for the nurse and had finally persuaded Isaac's wife to leave. Nurse Marshall had gone to her own room down the corridor and the other nurse was rearranging Adelaide's pillows, when they walked in. A knotted sheet had been tied to the foot of the bed and lay there in readiness. Adelaide was very pale with dark smudges under her eyes and her hair was matted with sweat.

'Chad darling, please don't look at me, I must be a frightful sight.' He carefully sat on the very edge of the bed and took her hand.

'No you're not, you look beautiful. The most beautiful thing I have ever seen and I'm very proud of you.' She smiled and squeezed his hand with a limp, damp pressure. Suddenly the pressure increased enormously as air whistled through her teeth followed by a deep-throated groan, that was suddenly cut off on a higher note. Her eyes, which had snapped open, closed as the pain subsided. He held her hands, unable to say anything and appalled at the intensity of her distress. He watched numbly, as a pulse beat in her throat and was comforted when Jenny moved up behind him and put her hand on his shoulder. Finally Adelaide opened her eyes.

'I have lost count how many times that has happened, it's always the same and it is always a surprise.'

'How often does it happen?'

'About every hour, no less, more like every half hour.' He looked back at Jenny for reassurance.

'That's good,' she said, 'the shorter the gap, the nearer you are to the end.' Chadwyck glanced at the clock on the bedside table. Adelaide had been in labour for almost eleven hours.

'So we will wait, it cannot be much longer now.'

'No my darling, you are tired, you must get some sleep, and you too Mother, the nurse will call you, if anything changes.'

Nothing did change until six hours later, when Chadwyck returned to Adelaide's room and found Nurse Marshall and her colleague standing on either side of the bed and talking in low, urgent tones. Adelaide was so still and such a ghastly colour that, for one terrifying moment, he thought she was dead. Before he could reach the bed Nurse Marshall met him halfway and led him to the door.

'What is it nurse? I know something is terribly wrong.' She ushered him out into the corridor and closed the door, before answering.

'The contractions, which were down to one every ten minutes stopped almost half an hour ago, her pulse is faint and I would like you to call Doctor Clarke. There was no Sir and no please.

'What do you mean, faint?' alarm jangled in his voice.

'Weak, unsteady. Ask him to get here as soon as he can and tell him what I have just told you.' She turned back into the room and shut the door in his face, before he could say anything else. Jenny came out of her room as he reached the head of the stairs.

'You look worried, Chad, what is it? Is she all right?'

'I hope so Jenny, please go and see, I must telephone Doctor Clarke.'

When he arrived, Chadwyck was once again banished to the library and from there, heard the heart-rending screams as the doctor moved the baby, causing a violent contraction. When he came down to the library, he was his usual urbane self but he could see that Chadwyck was at breaking point and spoke to him in a kinder, more considerate manner.

'She is all right now, my boy, these things happen and, when they do, they are never pleasant for anyone involved. Nurse Marshall had it right but, to be on the safe side, she called me or rather had you call me,' he swung an arm around Chadwyck's shoulders in what he meant to be an affectionate way 'and quite right she was to do so.' Chadwyck eased away from his grasp and stood facing him.

'How is my wife? She looked ghastly when I last saw her.'

'She is very weak, but that is understandable, her pulse is now almost normal and within the next few hours she will give birth. When she does, I shall be here but now I must go, I have other patients waiting.' All morning Chadwyck wandered around the house, unable to settle anywhere. He wanted to be with Adelaide but was unable to sit and watch the pain, caused by the contractions, becoming more frequent. He knew Jenny was with her and somehow managed to convince himself that Adelaide would be more at ease with her than him. No sooner had he done so than he realised the real reason: he was afraid, and unable to bear Adelaide's pain for her. He felt totally ineffectual and, for the first time in his life, unable to cope. All he could do was fight against the debilitating effects of frustration, fear and anger.

Doctor Clarke returned at lunch time, although no one was thinking about eating, and immediately went to Adelaide's room, insisting Chadwyck remain downstairs. The contractions were very frequent and Chadwyck knew that it would not be long. Without realising he was doing it he started to pray aloud, terrified for Adelaide in her exhausted condition but without a thought for their child. For an hour he paced the long hall like a caged animal. He could hear the muffled voices of the women as they offered advice and encouragement and then the piercing, agonised screams of Adelaide. The sounds became increasingly louder and more frequent and, when he knew that he could bear it no longer, there was suddenly a terrible silence. He stopped dead in his tracks, spun round and ran for the staircase. Halfway up he heard the baby cry. Completely drained and overcome with relief he sat where he was, unable to go any further. Ten minutes later Doctor Clarke found him still sitting there, his head in his hands and tears seeping through his fingers.

'It is a boy Chadwyck, all nine pounds and eight ounces of him and both of them are doing well. Congratulations.' He stuck out his hand and pulled Chadwyck to his feet. 'You look awful,' he added, 'you ought to see a doctor,' Chadwyck laughed lamely, 'or better still you ought to go and see your wife and son. I must be off now, I will send you an impressive bill, later.' Chadwyck stood there and watched the doctor cross the hall and leave the house, slowly his strength returned to him. With the sound of the front door closing, he felt suddenly released from a great burden. He ran the rest of the way up the stairs and met Jenny coming out of Adelaide's room.

'I'm sorry Chad, you can't go in yet. Nurse Marshall is still waiting for the placenta and then, when Adelaide is cleaned up a little, we will both go back in and see her. Right now I need a drink, so let's go and celebrate and perhaps we ought to get something to eat.'

Half an hour later Nurse Marshall called them and they both went up to see Adelaide. She was supine, her matted black hair framing a wax-like, emaciated face. The baby was in his cot and Isaac's wife had returned with a wet nurse. Adelaide was far too weak to either feed or hold him. Lea was trying unsuccessfully to get her to take a few mouthfuls of consommé. Chadwyck walked across to the bed, as if on eggshells and Lea moved away so that he could be close to Adelaide.

Her hands were clasped together across her tummy. He took one of them and she opened bruised eyelids and gazed at him listlessly, from sunken eyes.

'We have a son, Chad.' The effort of forming the words was almost too much for her.

'I know and we both love you. You were marvellous and so very brave but you must rest now.' She closed her eyes and he sat there holding her hand for a long time.

One of the servants brought a tray of food for him but he left it untouched, he did not want to let go of her hand. He could feel her pulse fluttering beneath his fingertips and, after he had sat there for over an hour, he suddenly realised that it was no longer as strong as it had been. She had not moved, nor opened her eyes and he thought that she was asleep. He had shut out the rest of them, the sounds of muted laughter and happiness, as others came on tiptoe to see the baby. Without letting go of her hand, he looked round for Nurse Marshall and, prompted by the expression on his face, she crossed the room, gently disengaged his hand and moved him to one side. She held Adelaide's wrist for a moment and then, in a quiet firm voice, she asked the other nurse to clear the room, leaving only herself, Jenny and Chadwyck. She leant forward and raised one of Adelaide's eyelids, the pupil was dilated. With quick competent movements she drew back the bedclothes and Jenny cried out, like a wounded animal, at the sight of so much blood, as it spread across the bottom of Adelaide's nightdress and soaked the sheets.

'Call Doctor Clarke, Mister Meade, tell him to come immediately and that your wife is suffering from severe post-partem haemorrhaging.' Chadwyck could not move and Jenny ran out of the room, to telephone.

Nurse Marshall pulled Adelaide's nightdress up and started to massage her tummy in a desperate effort to get her flaccid uterus to contract. Unable to control himself Chadwyck again started to cry. Without breaking the rhythm, Nurse Marshall instructed her colleague to prepare several cotton pads and an injection of postignam. Chadwyck was appalled by the amount of blood that continued to spread across the bed. When Nurse Marshall had first started to massage Adelaide's abdomen a great rush of blood had flowed from between her legs. It had been collecting inside her, since the placenta had detached itself.

By the time Jenny returned, Nurse Marshall had given Adelaide the injection, in an attempt to contract the uterus. The two nurses, working in silence had done their best to pack it, in an attempt to stem the flow. There was nothing more they could do. Adelaide never moved again, not even to open her eyes. She slipped silently into unconsciousness and, just as Doctor Clarke arrived, she died.

CHAPTER 45

By midday Johnny had done everything he had to do in Jagersfontein, collected his mail and returned to the farm alone. He had noticed a well-handled envelope with James's distinctive handwriting and he looked forward to reading it, after lunch, in the comfort of his study.

Back at the farm he jumped from the wagon, rubbing his back where it was stiff, while Sesi led the horse away.

Throwing his hat into the chair on the veranda, he ran powerful fingers through tussled hair. God, he thought, the place was empty without Jenny. The children were all at boarding school and the big house rang hollow as he called through to the kitchen for lunch. Alone, he ate quickly, without interest in his food, while he glanced at the newspaper. Most of the news was about the war in Europe. He picked up James's letter and told the maid to bring him coffee in his study.

Opening the envelope with an ivory-handled knife, he pulled out three closely written pages wrapped around a photograph. An oddly assorted band of men stared back at him, some mounted while others stood squinting self-consciously. Johnny immediately spotted James and Jack in the centre and, standing towards the back, was Caachy. He grinned fondly at his son's image and memories of his own commando days, during the Boer War, came flooding back. He propped the photograph against the ink well and started to read.

Somewhere in German East Jan 16th '15

Dearest Father and Mother,

This is the first of, I hope, many reports of the shenanigans of me and my merry men, or rather Jack's, as he keeps reminding us that he is in command. I don't envy him a bit as I have never met such a rough bunch before, as you can see from the enclosed photograph, which was developed at R.N.A.S. H.Q. on Niororo Island.

When Caachy and I got to Zanzibar Jack had left me a cryptic message at Naval Headquarters about the rendezvous and I had to bribe an Arab to take us over to Bagamoyo in his dhow that night. We beached a mile south of the town where we were met by a guide, who led us inland until it got light. Then we had to hide all day to avoid being spotted by several German patrols.

Two nights later we met up with Jack and the main party, where they gave me a horse and bedding and, thank God, I had brought my own rifle, some of the team are armed with museum pieces. We are now camped, if you can call dugout burrows in the sand camping, on a small tributary of the Rufiji river, about four miles from the Konigsberg. Every night Jack sends out a patrol, on foot, to recce. the ship. There seems to be a lot of onshore activity and Jack thinks they are trying to remove some of the four-inch guns and convert them into field guns for Lettow-Vorbeck, in the north.

Our job is to stop them doing it, if we can, or at least get information out to Jack's superiors and the R.N.A.S. They are making an awful nonsense at the moment of aerial reconnaissance, trying to spot the Konigsberg so that the Royal Navy can destroy her by gunfire. Last month one of the R.N.A.S. seaplanes flew over our forward observation post, having suffered considerable damage from the Konigsberg's machine-guns and came down in the mangrove swamps, behind a small island. We saw it happen but, because of our main objective, we were unable to go to their aid. The pilot was captured but the Navy managed to retrieve the 'plane.

We are living on iron rations, which are foul as we obviously can't shoot anything. Caachy and one of the natives have been setting traps but, so far, without much success. Morale at present is good but if we don't get orders soon Jack will be forced to do something, just to keep the men happy. We have enough explosives with us to make a damn nuisance of ourselves should he decide to do so but the trick will be to get away afterwards. I am sending this out with the next runner taking Jack's reports to the R.N.A.S. in the fond belief that it will not take too long to reach you. I hope all is well with you at Rietfontein. I pray for Adelaide every day, as I know it will soon be her time.

Yours loving son, James

Johnny put the letter on his desk, by a photograph of James and picked up the weekly report from Red. He was due out at the mine in the morning and wanted to familiarise himself with the latest developments. He could not concentrate on the figures as his mind wandered back to James, in his trench on the riverbank. He wished he was with them. There was a tap on the door and Sesi came in.

'Telegram Baas just come, rider waiting Baas.' He handed Johnny the telegram and slipped out of the room. With a great surge of happiness Johnny tore open the flimsy and turned towards the light to read the message. At last, he thought, I am a grandfather and this confounded waiting is finally over. Although the words formed in his mind, he was unable to believe what he read. He slumped back into his chair and buried his head in his hands, the telegram crumpled against his forehead.

He sat like that for a long moment, unmoving, and then suddenly he reared to his feet, his face a terrifying mask ravaged by grief. His eyes burnt with an unholy fire and the muscles rippled and bunched along his jaw line. A low whistling sound escaped his lips as he bent to pick up an immensely heavy six-foot-long ironwood and glass table that stood in front of the sofa. He raised it high above his head and hurled it across the room, so that it smashed into pieces against the fireplace. At the same time he uttered a cry of such primeval fury it chilled the blood of all those that heard it.

'Adelaide,' he roared again and again, 'Adelaide, my darling, why in God's name did it have to be you?'

* * *

When Johnny arrived at Springbokfontein, exhausted physically and emotionally after the twenty-four-hour train journey, he found all despondent and shattered by Adelaide's death. They appeared to be moving in slow motion, as in a macabre dream sequence. Jan Viljoens met him at the station, unable to talk about Adelaide or, for the first time since Johnny had met him, anything at all.

They drove in silence to the house where Jenny, aged ten years in as many hours, was waiting with the twins and Sophie. She had collected them from their schools and told them, as gently as she could, of the terrible news, in a futile attempt to minimise the shock. The children hung back, as their parents clung desperately to each other. For the first time, since Adelaide had died, Jenny was able to cry in the safety of Johnny's arms. He tried to comfort her as best he could, stroking her hair and whispering reassuringly. His words sounded empty and seemed to drain him of the last of his strength.

'Where's Chadwyck?'

'I don't know,' she paused for a moment, then added, 'he went out to the vineyards after breakfast. I haven't seen him since.' She dabbed ineffectually at her eyes, with the great yellow handkerchief that he had given her. 'I am frightened Johnny, by the way he looks, not by his appearance so much but by the way he looks at us all. It is as if he didn't know us, almost as if he wished us all dead.' She started to cry again and he held her until she cried herself out, knowing that it would release some of the tension. Finally she looked up at him and he kissed her very gently on her mouth.

'I love you.' he said so quietly that only she heard him.

'Would you like to see your grandson,' she tried to smile, 'he is upstairs with his nanny. Doctor Clarke arranged for Chad to engage her. She is Scottish and very fierce. She is called Miss Mackenzie, I don't think she has a first name.' She tried to laugh and it wrenched his heart to see the effort made.

'Not now,' he said, rather too roughly, in an attempt to protect them both. He knew that, if they saw the unwitting cause of Adelaide death at that moment, it would be too much for them both. 'What's he called?' He added more gently.

'Johnny,' she said, pleased by the surprised expression on his face, 'after you or, to give him his full name, Chadwyck John Malcolm Meade. They somehow knew it was going to be a boy and we chose his names last week.'

Johnny smiled down at her with pride and pleasure in his eyes as he led her through the drawing room to the terrace. Unable to stand, feeling so weak and drained, she stretched out gratefully on one of the chaises longues. Johnny pulled over a stool and sat beside her, holding her hands, worried by the faraway look in her eyes. Finally he broke the long silence.

'Has Chadwyck said anything, I mean about his plans. What he will do?'

'Chadwyck?' she asked confused, her mind lost in memories of Adelaide as a child. 'No, not really, he has hardly spoken at all. I think he blames everyone and himself the most and yet, I think he knows it was no one's fault. He wants revenge and is looking for a target.' At that moment they heard footsteps on the gravel and Johnny looked round as Chadwyck climbed the broad flight of steps, to the veranda.

'Johnny.'

Johnny got up and held out both arms, as if to embrace him, but Chadwyck stood in isolation at the top of the steps, surrounded by an aura of palpable grief. Johnny checked himself and held out his hand which Chadwyck shook briefly. They looked at each other for a moment, unable to talk and Chadwyck dropped his gaze, crossed the terrace to a table set out with bottles and glasses and helped himself to a drink. He turned back to Johnny and, with an almost imperceptible nod, indicated that he should join him. After a moment's hesitation Johnny picked up a glass and Chadwyck filled it to the brim from the same whisky decanter. Without any salutation they drained their glasses.

'I have made up my mind, Johnny, to leave here immediately after the funeral. I cannot live here without Adelaide. I have arranged for Miss Mackenzie to take our son to Washington where my mother will look after him, until I return.'

'But Chadwyck, Jenny and I will look after him. He is as much our grandchild as Victoria's.'

'I know,' he rested his free hand on Johnny's shoulder, 'I know perfectly well that you and Jenny would take care of him better than anyone but I know I could not bear the pain, at least for some time, of seeing him in Jenny's arms.' He felt Johnny's whole body tense and he knew that he had been misunderstood, so he added as gently as he could 'She is so like Adelaide that it would break my heart every time I saw her.' He felt Johnny relax and, anticipating his next question, he continued, 'I am going to join the Royal Navy. I know I am shirking my responsibilities at the mine and I realise that with James away you will have to look after it alone, but Red is a good man and it shouldn't take too much of your time.' Johnny raised a hand in protest.

'It's nothing. My God, it will give me something to do. Can't you see I need that?' For the first time Chadwyck noticed the pain in Johnny's eyes and realised that his grief was equally as great.

'I'm sorry, when my father died I felt a loss of security, but now I feel a loss of life, mine as much as hers, and for you it must be the same. She had always been as essential to your life as she became to mine.'

'I will miss you Chadwyck, we will all miss you. When this bloody war is over you will come back and so will James and it will be just like old times, won't it?' They looked at each other for reassurance; both knew that it would never be the same again.

Immediately after the funeral Jan Viljoens took Chadwyck to the station to catch the train to Simonstown. It had been a very quiet and subdued family affair, held in the small village church on the estate. Messages of sympathy had come in from friends and family from all over the world and the church was filled with flowers and wreaths. The twins and Sophie, realising the finality of the occasion, were so stricken that Jenny was almost beside herself in her attempt to console them.

Chadwyck, washed out and fighting every inch of the way not to display any emotion, collected his single suitcase from the back of the car and shook hands with Jan Viljoens.

'Good-bye Jan and thank you for all that you have done for us during the last few days. Please take the children back to their schools tomorrow and then take Mr and Mrs Flynn to the station, so that they can catch their train home. I know you will take care of Springbokfontein as if it were your own. Whatever you think should be done please do it, knowing that you have my full authority. One day, when I can, I will come back and when I do, I know that I shall find everything as it should be.'

CHAPTER 46

A month before Adelaide had died, Admiral King-Hall had sent a small flotilla of steam trawlers and whalers from Simonstown to assist HMS *Chatham* in her blockade of the Rufiji river. Each vessel had been armed with either pom-poms or three-pounders and all had been fitted out for mine laying and sweeping duties. Their names, *Pickle*, *Fly*, *Salamander*, *Echo* and *Childers*, reflected their earlier use, rather than being dubbed with the usual glorious names of Royal Naval vessels. Their greatest value lay in their shallow draft and, unlike HMS *Chatham*, they were able to run in over the sandbars and penetrate far up the river.

At half past five in the morning, still dark, two of them under the command of Commander Bridgeman and Lieutenant Charlewood crossed the sandbar. They ran the gauntlet of the shore batteries on both banks of the Kikunja river, the most northerly and largest outlet in the Rufiji delta. Their orders were to rendezvous with Jack and his company of Grey's Scouts, six miles from the sea at a pre-determined spot on the north bank, a mile to the east of Pemba Hill and a mile and a half to the northeast of the *Konigsberg*. The wheelhouses, gun-mountings and hulls above the waterline on both trawlers had been reinforced with steel sheeting, capable of stopping small arms fire.

As the morning light flooded the river HMS *Chatham*, firing continuous salvos with her six-inch guns, pounded the German trenches on both sides of the river, ahead of the two trawlers. From previous attempts to reach the *Konigsberg* and from aerial spotting by Lt. Cutler the whereabouts of Lt. Commander Schonberg's shore defences were fairly well established. He had fewer than a hundred men, armed mostly with rifles, a few machine-guns and only four three-pounder field guns. He had made the most of the features of the delta to be able to bring the maximum amount of firepower on any British vessel attempting to reach the *Konigsberg*.

Within moments the German defences were in action. In the half light, white tracer from the machine guns poured across *Echo*'s bow, seeking her range and hoping to penetrate her armour. As soon as they found the range bullets ricocheted off the steel sheeting, making it almost impossible for the gun crews to fire back. Lt. Charlewood swung the wheel hard a port and steered to the south bank, to confound the enemy's aim. A three pounder directly ahead of them opened up and the first shell screamed over *Echo*'s bridge, tearing away the radio mast and landed in the river immediately in front of *Childers*, covering the foredeck gun crew in a towering cascade of water. *Echo* altered course again and her aft pom-pom opened up on the three-pounder's position.

With the flood tide in their favour the two boats covered the ground at more than fourteen knots, making it difficult for the gun layers on shore to find their range. A Maxim opened up on the north shore and raked the starboard side of *Echo* shattering all the glass on the bridge, forcing the skipper and his helmsman to dive for cover. HMS *Chatham* was still shelling both banks ahead of them, decapitating palm trees and shredding the mangroves in great gouts of vegetation. Half a mile ahead was a round island in the middle of the river and unless Schonberg had repositioned his defences, Lt. Charlewood knew that they would be comparatively safe behind it. At the same time he realised that HMS *Chatham* was firing at extreme range and was waiting for his signal to cease fire. Having come so far he did not want them both to be sunk, by their own cruiser. The pom-pom on the aft deck was firing furiously and, with his own radio out of commission, Lt. Charlewood ordered his bo'sun to semaphore *Childers* to radio HMS *Chatham*. With every moment that passed the two trawlers were closing the distance between themselves and the island. As the bo'sun stepped out onto the exposed part of the bridge, a direct hit from one of the shore batteries tore the pom-pom off the deck, killing both gunners instantly. The wheel was wrenched from the helmsman's hand and he swore in pain. The steering gear had been badly damaged and the boat was out of control. Leaving the bo'sun to make his signal, Lt. Charlewood, unable to be heard in the din of battle, grabbed the helmsman by his shoulder and the two of them leapt over the bridge rail. With machine-gun fire cutting the air around them, they jinxed across the deck and dove for cover, behind the aft railings.

Human remains were caught on the jagged edges of the ruptured deck where moments before the pom-pom had been and, below it, Lt. Charlewood could see that the port side steering gear chain had been severed. The rudder was jammed hard to starboard and *Echo* was going round in circles in the middle of the river. They both knew that if they could not free the rudder and shackle the broken chains together again, the three-pounders on shore would soon find their range and blow them out of the water. The last salvo from HMS *Chatham* screamed over their heads and then, for a moment, the comparative silence was unnerving. The enemy fire increased significantly and *Childers* was left almost alone as they concentrated on the easier target offered by *Echo*.

Sizing up the problem in a second, the bo'sun dropped his flags onto the deck and ran aft to help with the steering gear. One of the beams used to re-enforce the deck beneath the pom-pom had shattered and dropped down onto the rudder yoke, forcing it against the transom. All three men strained against it in the confined space until finally the end, jammed against the cabin sole, splintered and the rudder swung back to mid-ships. The bo'sun wrenched the lid off the steel toolbox in the aft cuddy and rummaged around until he found a shackle that would fit the steering gear chain. The skipper and helmsman forced the gallows over so that the rudder was hard a port and the bo'sun gathered both ends of the broken chain and shackled them together. The moment it was done the three of them ran forward to what remained of the bridge, the helmsman to the wheel and the skipper to wave off *Childers*, who had come alongside and was trying to put a line on *Echo*, to tow her out of danger.

It had only taken a minute and a half, from the time that the pom-pom had been blown off the aft deck, to get back on course. Another thirty seconds and they would have been swept by the flood tide onto the sandbars that ran down river from the island. A moment later both boats were in the lee of the island but still in immediate danger. Lt. Charlewood knew that with the improved visibility the enemy look-out on Pemba Hill would soon be relaying their position to the gun crews on the *Konigsberg*. As soon as they had that, the *Konigsberg* would lay down a withering fire with their four-inch guns, which would make all that they had been through before seem like a picnic.

* * *

As the sound of the first salvo from HMS *Chatham* rolled across the delta and the sky, far to the east of them, flared with the flashes from the muzzles of the great guns, James Flynn and Jack Ripon instinctively flattened themselves into the mud on the riverbank. The night was at it blackest, just before dawn and, although the *Konigsberg* was less than one hundred yards from where they lay, they were unable to see her outline. James could feel the mud oozing over the tops of his boots and the water, displaced by the weight of his body, trickled down his spine. All exposed skin had been chewed raw by the hordes of mosquitoes. The hippos and crocodiles that they had heard splashing in the shallows were silenced by the guns.

'Caachy should be back by now. Where the hell is he?' James whispered to Jack, who lay so close to him that their shoulders touched.

'Quiet,' said Jack 'I can hear him coming.' A moment later Caachy, doubled over to avoid detection and breathing heavily, appeared.

He was able to move a lot easier now that he had rid himself of the weight of the four limpet mines that he had just attached, below the water line, to the hull of the *Konigsberg*. Fifty yards to their left two other men had moved down to the stern of the ship, to attach four more mines as close as they could to the propellers and their shafts. Between these two points the rest of the Scouts had taken up their positions along the bank, prepared to retaliate in the event that the watch on board spotted the limpet parties. Two hundred yards behind them and slightly further upriver was a German camp of about twenty tents and two corrugated iron sheds, used for stores and supplies. The riverbank beside the *Konigsberg* had been cleared of mangroves, leaving an open area of some two hundred yards square. A track crossed it and led inland. Two shore sentries had been taken out by the Irregulars on their way in and everyone knew that with the bombardment it would be only moments before the camp came to life.

'They are well set, Baas,' said Caachy as he dropped on one knee beside him, 'all four of them at five feet intervals with ten-minute fuses, set about four minutes ago.'

'Did you see the other party?'

'No Baas, but I heard them.'

'Did you hear them leave?'

'Not before me, Baas.'

'How long do we wait, Jack? We are much too close to the Huns' camp for my liking and, if we don't move now, we'll be surrounded.' Just as they were about to leave there was a flat report from the *Konigsberg*'s bridge and a bright light burst directly above them, illuminating the whole scene. Everyone froze where they were. Just as the light began to fade someone at the camp started barking orders and Jack saw the other limpet party caught out in the open, less than a hundred yards from the *Konigsberg*. He searched the bank for their raft and saw it bobbing in the water, on the shore in front of them.

It appeared to him as prominent as a lighthouse but nobody on deck spotted it. He rubbed his eyes to adjust to the sudden darkness, tapped James on the shoulder and whispered loud enough for the rest to hear. 'Let's go, before they fire another flare.'

'Hold it, Jack. If we go now we'll lose the other two.' The sound of gunfire down river had increased considerably and James knew that the trawlers were already fighting their way upriver, to the rendezvous. He glanced at his watch and saw that there was only four and a half minutes to detonation. Without waiting for Jack's reply he grabbed Caachy's arm and whispered in his ear,

'Get down and find those two, then get back here immediately. We'll wait another two minutes before we pull out.' Caachy disappeared without a sound.

'The light is increasing, James, we can't wait any longer. They had their orders, they knew they had to get back and if we don't leave now, we will not make the rendezvous.'

'I told Caachy two minutes and two minutes it is. He'll be back then and I won't leave without him.' He was adamant and Jack knew better than to argue. The seconds dragged by and they lay there listening to the gunfire, down river. The camp was standing to and, by the sound of it there was at least a full company billeted there. They could hear an N.C.O. barking orders and, as the light increased, they could see the outline of the tents against the sky. Jack looked again at his watch: two and a half minutes to detonation.

'We must go James, they have probably been captured by now.' There was an edge to his voice but, before James could argue, Caachy returned.

'They are not there. They have gone straight down river.'

'You saw their tracks?'

'Yes Baas.'

'The bastards,' said Jack, 'I'll skin 'em alive if the Hun doesn't! Come on everyone, let's go.' He got to his feet and they followed. The light was increasing rapidly and they knew that if anyone looked their way from either the camp or the *Konigsberg*, they would be spotted.

They had bunched up instinctively and Jack ordered them to spread out. One mortar shell, at that moment, would have killed them all. They still had a hundred yards of cleared ground to go, before they reached the mangroves and less than two minutes before the mines exploded.

When they were sixty yards from the trees two more flares, fired from the *Konigsberg*'s bridge, burst over their heads. With the hot fetid air clogging their lungs they dropped to the ground as one, the fear of enemy fire upon them. Although less brilliant than before, because of the increased light, the effect was the same. A roar went up from the camp from several men at the same time, as a command from the bridge turned out the gun crews on deck. Those at the camp were the first to open fire.

'Run for it!' yelled Jack, as the flare died 'you all know the rendezvous.'

They leapt to their feet and scattered over the open ground to reach the comparative safety of the mangroves. Heavy rifle fire followed them from the camp, kicking up mud around their feet. Twenty yards from the trees James went down as if pole-axed, shot through the thigh. A heavy machine gun firing from the poop deck of the *Konigsberg* opened up with shattering intensity. It numbed their minds as it stitched a great swathe of destruction across the mudflats, where they had all just been. Without a second's hesitation, Jack swerved to one side to get out of the way of the man behind him and ran back to where James was struggling to his feet. He fell again just as Jack reached him and, with one fluid movement, Jack swung him over his shoulder. There was now enough light for the machine gunner on deck to see them clearly, as Jack struggled across the last twenty yards with James over his shoulder. The machine-gun opened up again and another of the Scouts, covering their rear and firing from the hip as he ran backwards towards the trees, was scythed in half.

Jack reached the first of the mangroves and dived headlong, without any thought for James's condition. Two of the other Scouts, who were already under the trees, returned fire on the machine-gun. Bullets ricocheted off the steel shield of the gun, distracting the German enough to spoil his aim. He recovered quickly and again the lethal trail of death swept across the open ground and raked the trees. At the same moment, the first of the limpet mines exploded and a great wall of water flared up the side of the *Konigsberg*'s hull and swamped the machine-gun.

Almost immediately the second of the four charges placed by Caachy exploded. Jack lay prone, fighting for breath and the strength to go on, while he waited for the other two mines to explode. Making the most of what little cover there was, the company medic cut away James's trousers and examined the wound. He applied a tourniquet above the bullet hole and twisted it tight with the handle of his knife. Without looking round, Jack shouted to James above the roar of gunfire.

'Are you all right, James? What's the damage?' The third limpet exploded and the troops in the camp increased their fire. James was in such pain he could not answer.

'It's a bullet wound, Jack, high on his right leg.' said the medic. 'It missed the artery and I think the bone, it doesn't seem to be broken.' The fourth mine exploded. A three-pounder, on the aft deck of the *Konigsberg*, opened up and a shell screamed over their heads tearing away the tops of the trees and exploding on the higher ground behind them.

'Jesus!' said Jack,' we've got to get out of here. Can he walk?'

'Not a chance, Corporate Symes and I will carry him.' A second shell thundered overhead on the same elevation and, with a great surge of relief, Jack realised that they could not depress the gun enough to bring it to bear on them.

'When you are ready, Sergeant,' he yelled, 'lead on and we'll follow.' He was still waiting for the other four charges to explode, on the stern of the ship.

While he and the rest of the Scouts kept up a steady fire on the camp, the medics bound James's wound in a field dressing and between them dragged him further into the mangroves. Jack watched the crews running forward to man two of the four-inch guns on the *Konigsberg*'s deck. He knew that there was now enough light on the delta for the observation post on Pemba Hill to spot the trawlers. Although he and everyone else, who had seen the preparations on the *Konigsberg*'s foredeck, were expecting the guns to open fire at any moment, none was prepared for the shattering effect and physical impact when they did.

The second group of mines had still not exploded and Jack realised that they never would; something had gone wrong with that part of the operation. He took a final look back towards the *Konigsberg* and was the last to leave their position. Considering the intensity of fire, he knew that it could have been a lot worse. Only two men would not leave, one just to his left, the top of his head torn away by a bullet and the other, twenty yards behind him and spread-eagled on the mudflats, where he had been almost cut in half by the machine-gun.

CHAPTER 47

It was bitterly cold in Washington and it had snowed heavily most of the night. Victoria, devastated by Adelaide's death and with the effect she knew it would have on Chadwyck, was busying herself with final arrangements for the arrival of her grandson and Miss Mackenzie. The SS *City of Athens* from Cape Town was due to dock in New York, early the next morning. Gerald had just left, having looked in to tell his mother that he was taking an early train, to be in good time for their arrival. But, from the way he was dressed, she knew that he had made other plans to amuse himself.

She was still shaken from their row about a missing equestrian statue made of solid gold. At first he had denied any knowledge; then, realising that he would miss his train if he was delayed any longer and, knowing that his mother would not let him go until she was satisfied, he had admitted with as much bravado as he could muster that he had taken it. After all, he had told her, *why not*. Had she not told them all on many occasions that everything of hers would be theirs, eventually. Shocked by his lack of shame, she had quietly reminded him that she was not yet dead. Totally unaffected, he had laughed infuriatingly and tried to hug her. She knew, without asking, why he had taken it but could not help herself – his words still echoed in her ears.

'Mother darling, *of course* I sold it. Why else would I take it?'

She wondered whether he ever knew or cared that it had been given to his father, years ago, for winning the only amateur point-to-point that he had ever ridden in. She dabbed at her eyes with a minute lace handkerchief and again went to check the extensive nursery and Nanny's apartment, totally redecorated for her grandson and Miss Mackenzie.

The following morning Betty came over to lunch with Charlotte and her Nanny. It was warmer than the day before and a lot of the snow had melted in the streets, spring bulbs were beginning to show and the cherry trees were in bud. The carriage arrived from the station and, when Wilkes opened the front door at Lafayette Square, Miss Mackenzie, bearing Chadwyck Jr. like the Olympic torch, strode into the hall. Shoulders squared and her uniform bonnet pinned at a no-nonsense angle, she preceded Wilkes into the drawing room, where Victoria received them.

'Good afternoon, Miss Mackenzie, welcome to Washington. I hope you are not too tired by your long journey.' Satisfied with what she saw, Miss Mackenzie, having subjected Victoria to close scrutiny, bobbed a short curtsy and smiled. It completely transformed the expression on her face, to one of great sweetness and kindness. Victoria was enchanted.

'Good afternoon to you too, Mrs Meade and thank you for your kind words. It has been a long and arduous journey and I am very glad to be here.' She spoke in the soft burr of the Scottish Highlands and gave an unquestionable impression of great character and resourcefulness. Victoria introduced Betty who stepped forward, unable to prevent herself from looking at the tightly bundled baby in Miss Mackenzie's arms.

'May I hold him please, Miss Mackenzie?' and added, to reassure her, 'I have a nine-month-old daughter, who is resting upstairs at the moment. I do hope that they will get on well together.' Reluctantly, Miss Mackenzie allowed Betty to take the baby, as Gerald came in and helped himself to a drink, without offering anyone else one. 'Gerry come and have a look, he is absolutely adorable.'

'No thanks, at that age they all look alike.' He took a swallow from his glass and sprawled out in one of the leather armchairs in front of the fireplace.

'You will find that your cases have already been taken upstairs,' said Victoria, 'perhaps you would like to go up now and I will show you your rooms. Gerald please tell Wilkes we will have lunch in ten minutes and ask him to send Miss Mackenzie's up to her room.' Victoria led the way out of the drawing room and the three women mounted the long, sweeping marble staircase. Gerald mockingly raised his glass to their backs, finished his drink and rang the bell for Wilkes.

Fifteen minutes later the three of them were sitting down in the dining room and one of the footmen, under Wilkes' supervision, was serving turtle soup from a silver tureen. Gerald looked at his watch and saw that it was almost two o'clock. He had a meeting with his father-in-law at three and, because of his present predicament, the prospect almost pleased him.

'Isn't he absolutely gorgeous!' enthused Betty. 'You are such a spoil-sport Gerry, why didn't you come over and see him?'

'I thought it would have been obvious my dear, I only see my own when I have to, so why should I go out of my way to see someone else's?'

'That's a beastly thing to say Gerry, I know you don't mean it. You are really very fond of Charlotte and when the next one arrives,' she patted her tummy, in triumph, 'which I know will be a boy, you will be absolutely besotted.' Gerald did not like being reminded that she was pregnant again. He waved away the footman in irritation when offered more soup and turned to his mother.

'I'm tired of working for Henry, he is such a bore,' he added, without any regard to his wife's feelings. 'I was speaking to Willy Speight, he writes for the *Washington Post* in case you were wondering and is not,' he added looking straight at Betty, 'one of my debauched and whoring cronies.'

'Gerald, if you use language like that again,' cut in Victoria icily, 'you will have to leave the table.'

'Don't tell me Mother, tell Betty, it's her expression.' He went on, rather than apologise, 'he is being sent to Europe next month to report on the War and he told me, that if I wanted to go, he could arrange it with his Editor. So I think I will go. I am seeing Daddy this afternoon,' he emphasised the Daddy, another one of Betty's words 'and I will tell him that he will just have to live without me.' Taken completely by surprise, neither Betty nor Victoria said anything while the plates were being removed. Gerald emptied his wine glass and motioned to Wilkes, to refill it. Victoria was the first to speak.

'Gerald, you are being totally irresponsible, as always. Have you no regard for Betty and the fact that she is expecting your child?'

'No, Mother, she's having the child, I've done my part.' he interrupted.

'Please let me finish. Then, have you no regard for me? Both your brothers are fighting in a war that is really not theirs. Obviously it has never occurred to you to consider how much that worries me and now you want to join them.'

'Come now Mother, be honest, you wouldn't miss me if I never came back, Chad yes, Eddy certainly, but not me.'

'Gerry, please stop. You are upsetting both of us.' said Betty. 'Let's say no more about it.'

'Just a moment, my dear, I don't think my Mother has finished yet.'

'Thirdly, Gerald you have no training as a journalist and no experience as a correspondent.'

'Correspondent or co-respondent, Mother?' Victoria's eyes blazed, angrily.

'You are being puerile and disrespectful. Washington must be full of experienced journalists who could make a much better job of it.'

'Thanks for the vote of confidence,' said Gerald bitterly. 'I am going to see Willy today and make my arrangements.'

'If you do Gerald,' said Victoria in measured tones, 'you do so expressly against my wishes and therefore in the full knowledge of all that that implies.'

'You are threatening me Mother and I will not sit here and be threatened, by you or anyone else,' he added, looking emphatically at Betty, before leaping to his feet and knocking the Chippendale chair on its back.

'I am not threatening you Gerald, I just want you to do the right thing, for once in your life.'

'From your point of view,' he shouted, glaring at them both, before storming out of the room. They sat there in stunned silence for a moment and heard the front door slam. Victoria then turned to Wilkes and, with remarkable control, she picked up her napkin and said,

'And now Wilkes, we shall continue with lunch.' Crying silently to herself, Betty was unable to eat.

* * *

'I have told you before, Henry, if you want to make money you have to spend it. If you want me to close this contract with the Government's agent, then I've got to show him a good time.' Gerald emphasised the last two words by banging on Henry's desk.

'Your idea of a good time is totally different to mine,' said Henry reasonably, in an attempt to placate him.

'Vive la difference Henry, you just don't know how to have a good time.'

'You must agree Gerry, chartering Vanderbilt's yacht for the day, probably without his knowledge, knowing you, and inviting half the cast from the Follies to an exorbitantly extravagant lunch is surely, even by your standards, overdoing it! I have here the bill from the caterers and here,' he stood up, paused dramatically and waved another sheet in Gerald's face, 'is the bill from the yacht's Captain for breakages, which is even greater than the caterer's bill and all this,' he added sarcastically, 'was to impress a little man from the Government. Here,' he waved another sheet of paper in Gerald's direction, 'is a letter from the manager of the Follies, threatening to sue me for lost revenue, as he had to cancel the matinée.' Gerald roared with laughter, and snatched the letter from Henry's hand.

'Let me see that, and for God's sake sit down Henry or you will have a heart attack.' Gerald paced the huge office as he read the letter, remembering the afternoon on the yacht. 'Let him sue you, and with the publicity you get every Government Department will want to sign a contract with us.' He threw the letter on Henry's desk and walked to the dummy bookcase, behind which he knew Henry kept a bar. He helped himself to a glass of whisky and sat back in a sofa, his feet on the table in front of it.

'You know I don't approve of drinking during office hours.'

'Then why the bar, Henry?'

'This can't go on Gerry, you must show more restraint because if you don't...'

'Are you going to fire me Henry? Because, if so, I will save you the trouble. I resign. I have had all I can take of your sanctimonious, pompous, social climbing ways.' He finished his drink, banged the glass down on the table and got up. He walked over to Henry's desk and, putting his fingertips on the edge, lent over him. 'This is goodbye father-in-law, to you and your rotten commercial life. I am off to Europe and a real life.' Gerald then went back to his office and put a call through to Lilly Swan, on his private line. 'Did I wake you?'

'Yes darling, I was having a siesta, who is it?'

'Me, who were you expecting?'

'Oh Gerry, darling, you of course. I miss you terribly' she added with more conviction.

'That is what I was going to say. I'm coming round. I'll be there in half an hour.'

'Oh no, darling! So soon?' He thought he heard a man's voice in the background but he wasn't sure, so he said.

'Yes, darling, so soon.' and hung up.

* * *

Mrs Meade,' said Sykes, coming into the drawing room, where Betty sat, still very upset, after coming home from lunch with Victoria. 'I am sorry to disturb you, madam but you are wanted on the telephone. It is Mr Wickham and he assures me that it is most important that he speaks to you.' Betty put her needlepoint on the table beside her and went through to pick up the telephone in the hall.

'Daddy, how are you and how's Mummy? I haven't seen you all week.'

'We are fine dear but I really must talk to you. I can't come round now, because I have a meeting in five minutes, so I am afraid I will have to tell you on the telephone.'

'Tell me what? You are frightening me, Daddy.'

'Gerry left here an hour ago, after some silly argument we had about expenses. He has resigned and plans to go to Europe.'

'I know Daddy, he said the same thing to Victoria and me at lunch. I have never seen Victoria so angry.'

'Do you think he is serious?' Before she could answer he went on. 'I was so worried by the way he behaved, that I had one of my clerks follow him. I am sorry, Betty, I didn't want to tell you this on the telephone but I have no alternative. I think it's something you should know.'

'What are you talking about, Daddy? You are not making sense.'

'My clerk just telephoned me and told me that he had followed Gerry to Lilly Swan's house and that Gerald is still there.'

'Who is Lilly Swan, Daddy?' There was silence on the line. 'Hello, are you there? Did you hear me? Who is Lilly Swan?'

'Not someone you would know, dear.'

'Obviously, Daddy or I wouldn't be asking.'

'I'm sorry, my dear, I probably shouldn't have mentioned it.' He was becoming flustered. 'I was just worried he would do something silly, and he did,' he added lamely.

'Daddy, for heaven's sake you are talking in riddles, please make sense.'

'I think I had better have your mother call you. Goodbye my dear.'

He hung up. Furious, she went back to the drawing room and tried to concentrate on her needlepoint but the fine stitching defeated her and she stared at the fire instead. When the telephone rang again she answered it herself, before Sykes could reach it.

'Yes Mummy, what is it?' There was a brief pause, and then Gerald's relaxed voice enquired.

'Betty, is that you? Since when do you answer the telephone?'

'Yes Gerald, it is me and I was expecting my mother to call.'

'How nice, give the old dear my best when she does.'

'Sarcasm doesn't become you. Why did you call?'

'Oh yes, I almost forgot, I won't be back to dinner tonight. I am at the office at the moment and I am waiting for a client to arrive. I am taking him to dinner at my club or perhaps,' he added, on reflection, 'we might go to a restaurant. It depends on the client of course, you do understand, don't you? So, I will see you later.' Suddenly, Betty knew exactly what Henry Wickham had been talking about.

'Who is Lilly Swan, Gerald?' There was a stunned silence on the line, followed by Gerald's not so relaxed answer.

'Who, dear?'

'You heard me,' she snapped.

'How on earth should I know, my dear?' He was almost on balance again.

'Ask my father, he just told me and I am sure he will tell you. As to seeing you later, I don't care if I see you later or, for that matter, ever again!' she slammed the telephone back on its cradle.

CHAPTER 48

The sun was just setting as the train pulled into Simonstown railway station. Chadwyck, carrying his own suitcase, having completed eight weeks of basic Naval training in Cape Town, was one of the first to alight and with a long purposeful stride soon cleared the platform. He surrendered his ticket at the gate and approached two uniformed naval officers, walking just ahead.

'I don't suppose you two are going to the Naval Dockyard, are you? My name is Chadwyck Meade and I have to report there this evening.' The two of them turned at the sound of his voice, they were both in their early twenties, one slightly taller than the other and both sporting sub-lieutenant's insignia. The shorter of the two grinned at Chadwyck and stuck out his hand.

'My name is George Haley, this is Sam Dobbs and yes, we are. Do you want a lift?' Chadwyck shook hands with them. 'With a bit of luck there will be a transport waiting,' continued Haley, 'and if we're really lucky, Lorna will be too.'

'Pay no attention to him,' said Dobbs, as he shook hands with Chadwyck, 'he has a one-track mind. Is that all the kit you've got?' and before Chadwyck could stop him, he scooped up his case.

Conspicuous in the melée of horse and oxen-drawn carts was a large blue Buick, an Admiral's pennant fluttering from its jack. Standing beside the car, one elegant foot on the running board while she straightened the seam of her stocking, was the driver.

'Lorna?' said Chadwyck.

'Lorna' they answered in unison. She turned to face them, when they were still twenty yards from her and a sensual smile spread across her generous mouth.

'Hello boys, who's your friend?' She moved towards them, holding out both hands. A small naval cap, tipped at a jaunty angle over her right eye, could not contain the vibrant auburn hair that had slipped from beneath and bounced on her shoulders as she walked.

'Mr Chadwyck Meade,' said Haley, emphasising the Mister, 'meet Lorna. Lorna this is Mr Chadwyck Meade, our newfound friend. Lorna, as you may have noticed, apart from being Lorna, of course, is Admiral King-Hall's driver.' Chadwyck smiled at her as they shook hands.

'Hello,' he said and added 'and where, or shouldn't I ask, is Admiral King-Hall?'

'I just left him at a dinner party, with the Military Governor.' Her voice was deep and provocative and, when she laughed at the expression on Chadwyck's face, her eyes laughed too. 'It's all right Mr Meade, if you don't tell him, I promise I won't. But let's get out of here before someone else arrives who outranks us all.' Chadwyck stepped forward to open the driver's door for her and she smiled again. 'No Mr Meade, in this man's navy, I'm supposed to do that for you.' The three of them piled into the back and Lorna drove them across town to the Naval Dockyard with practised skill. Ten minutes later they pulled up in front of the Officers' Mess, having made plans to meet an hour later for drinks and dinner.

At nine o'clock the next morning Chadwyck, splendid in his best uniform, sat with his feet crossed at the ankles reading the morning paper in the Admiral's anteroom. The previous evening the four of them had spent a most enjoyable time in the Mess, getting to know each other. Still unused to Naval drinking habits, Chadwyck had been lagging two or three drinks behind and as a result had been ragged, without mercy. The strangest and best part of all had been that not one of them had asked him a single question about himself or why he had volunteered. They had talked about themselves and what his life would be like in the future. He learnt that, after the interview, he would spend most of his waking hours in a round of naval indoctrination. In the fond hope, as they had said, grinning broadly, that he would know one end of the ship from the other before he was commissioned and sailed north with Admiral King-Hall at the end of May.

* * *

On 25 May, Sub-Lieutenant Chadwyck Meade with two hundred and eighty-six other officers and ratings, under the command of Admiral King-Hall, sailed out of Simonstown Harbour aboard the aged HMS *Goliath*, bound for Mafia Island, off German East Africa. The Admiral was to take over command from Captain Drury-Lowe, and Chadwyck, with George Haley, were attached to the Admiral's staff. Sam Dobbs, to his bitter disappointment, had been left behind at Simonstown to take care of new recruits.

There was a great deal of speculation on board, amongst the officers and men, about the nature of the operation. Rumours of the *Konigsberg* had reached Simonstown before Christmas but nobody seemed to know any of the details. For eight days they sailed north through moderate seas. Life on board was relaxed as everyone knew that there were no enemy ships abroad, in the Indian Ocean. As a result the endless rounds of gun and boat drills lacked any sense of urgency. Only the stokers were earning their pay shovelling tons of coal every day into the ancient fireboxes of the ship's boilers. For the rest of them, the passage was akin to a cruise. Forty miles south of Mafia Island, they were met by the armed trawler HMS *Salamander* and the Admiral welcomed Captain Drury-Lowe aboard and they retired to the Admiral's cabin.

'Sydney, it is good to see you again.' They shook hands.

'You too, Herbert, I'm just sorry to be leaving when we've almost cracked the nut.'

'I know. It's exciting times we live in. I was most impressed by your report on the joint ops. with the two trawlers and the Scouts. You must tell me more about it later. Let me introduce my two ADCs, Lieutenants Haley and Meade.' They shook hands.

'Meade?' said the Captain, 'any relation to Lieutenant Edward Meade?'

'My brother, Sir, I haven't heard from him since he left London at the beginning of the year.'

'Well I've got a surprise for you, my boy, he's right here on the Island doing his damnedest to defy gravity, with a bunch of other like-minded enthusiasts.' He warmed to the expression of pleasure that flitted across Chadwyck's face and added, with a twinkle in his eye and a wink to the Admiral. 'But I'm sure that you'll be so busy on board, that you won't have a chance to see him.'

'Come now, Sydney, I'm not that much of a tyrant. I'm sure we can both spare them a moment together at your dinner party tonight, which I'm looking forward to very much. Now we had better do something about our mooring before we run the old girl aground.'

The Cape Squadron turned out in force to welcome their Admiral. His launch left HMS *Goliath* and cut across the mile and a quarter of burnished sea towards the newly constructed jetty, on Mafia Island. They were heading directly into the sun, setting behind the distant hills on the mainland. Chadwyck, standing at the rail, noticed two Sopwith seaplanes bobbing at their moorings in the harbour. Beside one was a small launch and two men appeared to be working on one of the floats, while a third had his head under the engine cowling. A great deal of work had been done on the Island in the two months since a combined military and naval task force had wrested it from the occupying German forces. In the shade of the giant palm trees that lined the shore, mess halls and accommodation blocks had been constructed in timber, with corrugated iron roofs. All the material had been brought in from Zanzibar, as deck cargo on the colliers. Nearby, a large hanger with an adjacent workshop had been constructed for the seaplanes and from it a slip ran down into the water.

The Admiral and his two ADCs were piped ashore with Captain

Drury-Lowe. In the Mess with the other officers, with emphasis on informality, the Admiral, drink in hand, was led from one group to another by Captain Drury-Lowe. George and Chadwyck, who scanned the room for his brother, followed. The sides of the large room which were made of plaited palm fronds, now removed to allow a cool onshore breeze to sweep through making the paraffin lamps flicker and shadows dance across the ceiling.

'Now Herbert, you'll meet our aviators.' They moved on to another group. Squadron Commander Cull, may I introduce Admiral King-Hall who, as you know, is taking over from me.' The two men shook hands. 'Cull came out here to give us a hand, after Cutler was shot down and captured.'

'I've heard about you Lieutenant,' said the Admiral, 'and I'm most impressed with your efforts, under such difficult conditions.'

'Thank you, Sir, may I introduce two of my colleagues, Flight Lieutenant Watkins and Flight Lieutenant Meade.'

'Gentleman,' said the Admiral shaking hands with them both, 'may I introduce my two aides, Lieutenants Haley and Meade. You see Sydney,' he added, turning to Captain Drury-Lowe, 'that wasn't too difficult to arrange.'

'Eddy, how are you?' The two brothers shook hands warmly, seeing many changes in each other since they had last met.

'You look very dashing Chad. I had no idea you were going to join the Navy. What on earth did Adelaide say about it?' Even though he had anticipated this moment, Chadwyck found himself unable to cope with it. Edward, instantly aware of the pain in his brother's eyes, took a step forward and turned him away from the group. 'For God's sake, Chad, what has happened?'

'She's dead Eddy, she died in childbirth.'

'Oh Chad, I'm sorry, I'm so terribly sorry.' He paused for a moment and then added, 'and I never met her.' Thinking then that it sounded as if he would have been even sorrier had he met her he rushed on, 'James never stops talking about her and we had planned to take leave and go down and see you both at the end of the month.'

'James, is he here?' said Chadwyck, desperate to talk about anything else, 'and how is he?'

'Mending well, he was shot in the leg on their last operation, in one side and out the other, no serious damage. Yes, he'll be with us any minute now, just as soon as he gets his bunch of ruffians relocated on the other side of the compound. They had to move to make room for your lot, so he knows you're here. The Navy pulled them out almost three weeks ago in a couple of armed trawlers after they had had a crack at the *Konigsberg*.'

'Was Jack with them?'

Yes, it was he that carried James onto their rendezvous.' While he was talking he was watching his brother closely and could actually feel some of his pain. 'Leave it to me, Chad,' he touched his arm tentatively and hoped in some way to alleviate his grief, by sharing it. 'I'll tell him about Adelaide. We haven't heard anything here for months. We've all been waiting for HMS *Goliath* to arrive with the mail.'

'Thank you, Eddy, but I must tell him.'

'Well you can tell him now, because here he comes.' Chadwyck looked around and saw James as he worked his way across the room with a great grin on his face, as he swapped greetings with his friends. He was leaning heavily on a crutch and it was obvious to them both how much he was looking forward to seeing Chadwyck again. The Admiral and Captain Drury-Lowe had moved on to the next group of officers with George, who glanced back nervously in an attempt to reel in Chadwyck.

'Chadwyck!' boomed James, still ten paces from them. 'They told me you were here and I just wouldn't believe it until I saw for myself. How are you, you old dog? You look very snappy in your uniform.' He positioned himself in such a way that he could put his free arm around Chadwyck's shoulders. 'This is a great moment, it is the first time that the three of us have been together. I knew you couldn't sit on your backside forever while we were having all the fun. How's Adelaide?' He looked fondly at his brother-in-law and then back at

Eddy with an irresistible grin on his handsome face. 'Cat's got your tongue, Chad? I've never known my partner to be at a loss for words. I'd better go and say hello to the Admiral, then I'll find a steward and get us all a drink. On second thoughts, let's get a drink first and then I'll say hello to the Admiral.' He laughed, slapped Chadwyck on the back and left.

'You had better join the Admiral, Chad, I'll tell James when he comes back.' As Chadwyck turned to go he added, 'You never told me whether it was a boy or a girl.'

'A boy, Eddy, and he's now with our mother, in Washington.'

'A son and heir Chad, congratulations.' He was unable to convey any enthusiasm.

'Thank you, Eddy.' There was no pride in his voice, just infinite sadness.

CHAPTER 49

'Don't bother, I'm not going to change my mind, whatever you or Betty might think.' Gerald, finding it hard to keep his voice under control, paced up and down in front of his mother in the drawing room at Lafayette Square.

'Please sit down, dear and try to be reasonable. It's not good for you to excite yourself like this.'

'For God's sake Mother, stop treating me as if I were senile. I'm not.'

She rapped her folded fan across the arm of her chair, cutting across anything else he might have to say. 'I will not have you using language like that in my house. I see absolutely no point in continuing this conversation any further.'

'Conversation, Mother? This isn't a conversation, this is just the daily orders, that I've had to put up with all my life. The only difference is that I am now twenty-two and not twelve and I have to lead my life as I see it, and not as you do. Please let go Mother, and perhaps in time I'll be able to show you what I can do, rather than what you think I should do.'

He did not want to leave her like this, for, despite all of his bravado, he had considerable reservations about the wisdom of his impromptu decision. What, he thought, if he never came back and she was left to cope with his death and the bitter memories of their last encounter?

He suddenly realised, for the first time in his life, that he was thinking more about her than himself. He pulled up a chair, sat down beside her and took her hand.

'Mother, please try to understand my point of view,' he continued, 'This is a new phase in my life. I feel it very strongly. I cannot go on in a predetermined rut, however secure and comfortable it might be, when the rest of the world is in turmoil. Life as you knew it has gone and it will never be the same again.' With her free hand Victoria took a tiny lace handkerchief from her sleeve and dabbed at the corner of her eye. 'Please don't cry Mother, it's so unlike you and makes what I have to say so much harder. I feel that I'm missing out on life while remaining here in Washington. Last night I re-read Eddy's letter. and I realised that I am very dissatisfied with what I am doing here, frustrated by the realities of life. I want to become part of this metamorphosis, write about it so that everyone here at home can know what's going on. You will be all right here, you have your own life and friends, and,' he added with a boyish grin, 'think how peaceful it will be without me.' She squeezed his hand and caught her breath, unable to say anything. 'Please look after Betty for me. Whatever either of you might think, I really do love her and when I get back,' and he added with as much conviction as he could muster,' I will get back, Mother, I will prove it to her. I know that what lies ahead of me will stand me in good stead for the rest of my life and with the benefit of that knowledge I will no longer be a boy but will, hopefully, see life through a man's eyes.'

'Dearest Gerald,' she stroked his jawline with the tips of her fingers, 'I wish we had talked like this long ago and you would have saved me so much pain and anxiety. Go to France, as I see you must, and do so with my blessing. I will take care of Betty and I will try to make her see you as I now see you. She is hurt momentarily by your foolish indiscretions, as I was by your father's.' She laughed enchantingly at the expression on his face. 'Don't look so surprised, my darling, I wasn't. I don't think anyone other than me and perhaps one or two of his closest men friends ever knew and that is the difference. She will get over it, she loves you very much and believe me I, as a women, know these things. She is hurt because of the intensity of her love and not from the lack of it. I will arrange for letters of credit to be opened for you in a bank in Paris, as I know that a correspondent's salary will hardly pay for your daily boutonnière. Now, away home with you before I really do cry and make your peace with Betty.' She got up and led him to the front door, resting her hand lightly on his arm. 'Godspeed Gerald, I shall pray for your safe return.' She stretched up and kissed him gently on the mouth. When the door closed behind him, she went to the telephone in the hall and asked for Betty's number.

The next morning Gerald and Betty took the train to New York and checked into the Plaza Hotel. For the three days and nights prior to his departure they ate, slept and played as one, happier than they had been since their time in Paris. They went shopping on Fifth Avenue and were outrageously extravagant with each other. They dined at Delmonico and went again the next night as they had been so happy the first. On the morning of the fourth day, when Willy Speight, responsible for Gerald's posting, came to the hotel to collect him, Gerald and Betty were totally as one. She, not wanting to go to the docks to see them off, had arranged for her father, who had come to New York the day before on business, to take her to lunch and afterwards they would return to Washington together. As she said goodbye to Gerald in the hallway of their suite, she slipped a package into one of his pockets.

'What is it, my love?'

'You'll see soon enough but please not until after you've sailed. Feel me with you at all times, and should I fade in your memory this,' she tapped the pocket, 'will remind you.' He kissed her and tasted the salt of her tears on his lips. Her mouth was soft and warm and he savoured the moment until it was etched indelibly on his mind. He held her tightly and looked for what he needed to see in her eyes and, when he saw it, he kissed her again, but very gently.

'Goodbye my darling,' he said as his lips brushed hers, 'I love you.'

* * *

On their first night at sea Gerald and Willy went to their adjoining cabins to dress for dinner. The S.S. *New York*, although an American vessel, adopted the policy of most other lines and maintained a strict blackout at night to minimise the chances of detection by marauding German U-boats. Most of the damage to date had been done to Allied shipping, closer to British waters. As he hung his overcoat away, which he had thrown carelessly onto the bed, earlier in the day, Gerald remembered Betty's gift. He took it out and tore off the wrapping paper. It was a small, exquisitely tooled Moroccan leather covered photograph frame with gold corners and a gold clasp that held it together. He gently eased his thumbnail under the clasp and opened the frame. On the left-hand side was a hand painted photograph of Betty and, tucked beneath the glass in one corner, a tightly coiled strand of her hair. On the other side was exactly the same of their daughter. He gazed at the images fondly and recalled Betty's last words before placing it gently on the small table beside his bed.

After dinner, the following night, Gerald and Willy went through to the smoking room where they ran into two colleagues from the *New York Times*, friends of Willy. They too were bound for Paris and Gerald realised that it would be harder than he had first thought to convey to readers a fresh approach to the European war.

Very early in the morning on the last day of their voyage, only sixty miles west of their destination port of Cherbourg, Gerald was awoken by the sound of gunfire. Putting on trousers and a sweater over his pyjamas and sticking his feet into the first pair of shoes he could find he hammered on Willy's door and ran up on deck. Two miles off the starboard beam, indistinct in the diffused light of early morning, he saw two British destroyers herding a small convoy of eight cargo ships up the English Channel. A third destroyer, with a great trail of black smoke pouring from her funnels, manoeuvred in such a way as to lay a smokescreen between the convoy and an unseen enemy.

Willy appeared beside him on deck just as the convoy was

obscured by the smoke screen, but not before they had both seen the last ship drop back from the others, smoke and flames belching from her hold. It had not been gunfire that had woken him but the sound of a torpedo exploding against the hull of the crippled ship. At the same moment the liner altered course and increased her speed. Gerald and Willy ran aft down the promenade deck towards the stern so as not to miss the battle as it unfolded. The lead destroyer suddenly broke through the smoke screen and headed at maximum speed towards them. At that moment Gerald would have given anything to have had a pair of binoculars. He was convinced that he could see a U-Boat periscope breaking the surface, midway between the destroyer and themselves, less than half a mile astern.

Just as the liner altered course again they knew that the two forward guns on the destroyer had fired, because they could see the muzzle flashes followed almost immediately by the two shells landing in the sea and moments later the sound of the guns rolled over them, like thunder. As the guns fired again the liner altered course and the third destroyer, which had been laying the smokescreen, came around at maximum speed and headed on a converging course, to where Gerald had seen the periscope. Once on her new course she too fired her forward guns and her shells straddled those of her sister ship. High above them, the look-out on the portside flying bridge cried out in alarm.

'Torpedo three hundred yards, two points abaft the beam and closing.' With agonising slowness the great liner swung to starboard to avoid the torpedo. From where they stood, Gerald and Willy could see the white trail of it in the water. It was no more than fifty yards from the liner and now appeared to be running parallel. As they hung over the rail, mesmerised by the proximity of death, the look-out on the starboard flying bridge called out.

'Torpedo, four hundred yards astern.' Gerald knew that the Captain would have to wait critical seconds until the first torpedo had passed them before he could alter course again to port and break out of the pattern in which the U-boat Commander had locked them.

The moment the great liner started to come around to port again the starboard look-out reported a third torpedo on the starboard side and Gerald realised that, had they turned further to starboard, to avoid the second torpedo, the third would have run straight into them.

At the same time, the two destroyers converged on the spot where the submarine had last been seen and started laying depth-charges, systematically. Rack after rack were fired off the stern of each as they steamed back and forth over the area. The heavy crump of the underwater explosions, that caused sea water to rain on the destroyer's decks, merged into one continuous concussion. By now a great many of the passengers were lining the rails. A man standing next to Gerald was giving a running commentary on the action, as he saw it through a pair of binoculars.

'They're widening the pattern, wait a minute what's this? One of them has stopped firing. I don't believe it. Look! They've got it! I think they've got it! There are things bobbing around in the water I can't see what they are. Wait a minute… that's a man. There's a man in the water, waving. He's covered in oil. There's oil everywhere. They've stopped dropping depth charges. Look! There's another man… and another.'

'Let me see,' said Gerald, trying to take the binoculars from his companion, who hunched his shoulders and tightened his grip.

'One of the destroyers is lowering a boat.' The man continued. 'They've done it! They've sunk the U-Boat!' Just as he said it the sudden silence, after the almost continuous roar of battle, was broken by the staccato notes of the ship's sirens. A joyous declaration of victory, that brought a lump to Gerald's throat.

Three hours later, six hundred and sixty-eight very relieved passengers disembarked from the S.S. *New York* at Cherbourg. Most of them boarded a special boat train waiting to take them to Paris. By the time it left, Gerald, who had lavishly tipped the owner of a dockside cafe, had telephoned in his first story to the Paris office of the *Washington Post*.

CHAPTER 50

Mafia Island, British East Africa June 22, 1915

Dearest Mother,

Thank you very much for your last long, sweet letter and all your news about Chadwyck Jr. which finally reached me two weeks ago, after taking almost two months to get here, via South Africa. We have been so busy that I have not had time to write to you before now. Please forgive me, because I know you worry about us but you shouldn't, now that Eddy and I are both based here, we can look after each other.

You would not believe how difficult it is to get anything done here. Everything seems to be conspiring against us which, of course, it isn't but if one link in the chain breaks then everything comes to a grinding halt. The climate is so enervating that most of the work begins before sun-up and has to be done by eleven o'clock or else left for the last two hours of daylight. When there is a breeze the mosquitoes don't trouble us too much but when there isn't, they are unbearable. Snakes and scorpions are also bad and we have to check everything before either getting into it or sitting down on it.

Eddy is in great form, notwithstanding a little incident, which I will tell you about later, and very popular with everyone here. The R.N.A.S. have had the worst time of all, everything that you could imagine that could go wrong, has gone wrong. The 'planes literally fall apart in the heat. The glue holding the fabric together on the wings and fuselage loses its potency in the sun and the fabric is swept away which, as you can imagine, is very alarming when flying three thousand feet above a mangrove swamp.

The floats, with which they land on the water, are full of air. This expands in the heat to such an extent that it forces the seams apart, allowing seawater into the floats, thus preventing the plane from taking off. The engines, designed for British flying conditions, are quite unable to cope with the humid and heavy atmosphere here. They are constantly experimenting with various different aviation fuels and force-fed air and oxygen mixes, to improve their performance.

The day after I last wrote to you the radio shack on board HMS *Hyacinth* picked up a coded message between the *Konigsberg* and a German blockade-runner, called the *Kronberg*. Incidentally, I forgot to tell you, in my last letter, that I am still on Admiral King-Hall's staff and have been promoted to full Lieutenant! The Admiral transferred his flag to *Hyacinth* when HMS *Goliath* was recalled to the Mediterranean and sadly, according to information we received last week, she was torpedoed and sunk off the Dardanelles. The *Kronberg*, which somehow managed to slip through the north Atlantic blockade, round Cape Horn and find her way into these waters without being detected, almost eluded us. She was carrying two thousand tons of coal and other essential supplies for the *Konigsberg*. The rest of the cargo was made up of thousands of Mauser rifles and ammunition for General von Lettow-Vorbeck's army, which although out-numbered ten to one by our own troops, are fighting bravely and with great skill and determination.

Knowing where the *Kronberg* would have to pass us, we

patrolled the area all night, at action stations. When we spotted her at dawn we gave chase. It looked as if we would easily overhaul her when suddenly our starboard engine broke down completely and she pulled away. She disappeared through the narrows into Manza Bay, apparently totally unaffected by several salvos, fired from our forward guns It was typical of the problems we face. Without proper dockyard facilities and with an almost complete lack of essentials that we need to effect repairs, it is very difficult to maintain the fleet. With our port engine only we steamed on in pursuit into Manza Bay where, much to our amazement, we found the *Kronberg* beached on shore. Fire had broken out on board, which could have been a result of our shelling but more likely they had started it and great stacks of timber could be seen blazing on deck. Her crew had gone ashore in the ship's boats.

We, in turn stood off, lowered two of own boats and sent in a raiding party. They found that the sea-cocks had been opened and a fierce fire was raging through her holds. While on board the raiding party came under fire from the Germans on shore but suffered no casualties. Realising nothing could be done to save the ship or her cargo the raiding party returned to HMS *Hyacinth*. Not wanting the Germans to recover any of the cargo that might escape the fire, we opened up with our six-inch guns and laid down a heavy barrage on the stricken vessel. Three or four huge explosions occurred during the bombardment, which we assumed to be the ammunition. The loss of the two thousand tons of coal was a crippling blow to the *Konigsberg*. It was essential to the scheme of things, from their point of view, if she was ever to leave the Rufiji river again.

Eddy and Commander Cull went up in one of the Sopwith seaplanes on a recce. to see what the *Konigsberg* was up to and whether or not she had moved from her earlier position. They found her in the same place and looking very smart indeed, she had been repainted from stem to stern. Both the

Konigsberg and the *Somalia*, one of her supply ships, which had managed to rendezvous with the *Konigsberg* before our blockade was in place, opened fire on the seaplane. Eddy told me that Commander Cull was so incensed that he started shooting back at them, with his service revolver.

Eddy, not to be outdone, took the Very pistol out of its box, which was strapped to the fuselage and, as they flew back over the *Somalia* on their way home, he managed to get off two rounds at the bridge. Halfway back to base, the seaplane's engine failed completely and they glided down to land in the sea, seven miles from here. A bullet had torn away the air intake valves, closing the main oil pipe. It was very lucky that it did not happen sooner because, had it done so, they would have both ended up as guests of the Hun for the rest of the war.

Three weeks ago the two Monitors, HMS *Mersey* and HMS *Severn*, finally arrived after a very difficult voyage from England, via Malta and the Red Sea. They are extraordinary looking ships, really just floating gun platforms which look as if they would sink, in any sort of sea at all. They were originally ordered by the Brazilian Government before the war and requisitioned, before being delivered, by the Admiralty. Their greatest advantage from our point of view is that, although they are almost two hundred and seventy feet long and displace nearly thirteen hundred tons, they draw less than five feet. This will enable them to get near enough to the *Konigsberg* to engage her in action, which none of our cruisers can do. As I write, I can hear them doing gunnery practice out in the open sea while Eddy, flying above, talks them onto the target. Now that all our forces are finally assembled I am sure it won't be long before we have a crack at the *Konigsberg*.

Four days ago, the armed liner HMS *Laurentic* arrived here with much needed aircraft, crew and supplies for the R.N.A.S. team. Colonel McKye, with the Military Governor here, has rounded up every native and idle servicemen he can find to clear the ground and improve the original airstrip. They brought in a wooden and corrugated iron hanger from Zanzibar. They are going to put it up at the end of the airfield to house the two new Henry Farnums and two Caudrons. Hopefully these four new aircraft, of the very latest design, their spares and all other assembled kit will make life easier for Edward and his pals.

I hope all is well with you, Gerald, Betty and the children and I was very glad to hear that Miss McKenzie and you are getting on famously. There seems no end to this conflict and the news from Europe is appalling. I can't, with any honesty, tell you that I hope to be seeing you soon but at least the idea of it gives me something to look forward to. On the other hand, I do know that we will be here until this *Konigsberg* situation is resolved and after that our destiny lies in the hands of God and the powers that be. Both Eddy and I send you and your two grandchildren our love and want you to know that our thoughts are with you, at all times.

Your loving son,
Chadwyck

CHAPTER 51

An hour before lunch, on July the fifth, Chadwyck strolled over to find Eddy at the new hanger. There was a great feeling of expectation and excitement that affected everyone on Mafia Island. Although nothing had been said officially during the course of the almost constant briefing and debriefing that went on, it was generally felt that the raid on the *Konigsberg* was set for the following morning. The timing of the high tide was perfect. It would enable the Monitors to run into the river when still dark on the flood tide, do what had to be done and return on the ebb. As he rounded the corner of the hanger he could hear Edward's voice.

'Abdul! Where the hell are you?' Edward pulled his head out from under the engine cowling and looked around for the missing fitter. 'Oh, hello Chad, how's His Majesty's Navy today?'

'Spic and span, Eddy and raring to go. Who are you looking for? One of the local wallahs.'

'Yes. The man is always up to things he shouldn't be and never here when I need him. Pass me up that box at your feet will you, I'm changing the fuel filters on this old bus.' Apart from two mechanics, who were working on one of the Farmans on the other side of the hanger, the two brothers were alone.

'What brings you over?' asked Edward and added with a grin, 'not that I'm not always delighted to see you.'

'The Admiral's lunching in your Mess today and, finally, everything is set up,' he lowered his voice, 'We are going to attack the *Konigsberg*, before dawn tomorrow.'

'Thank God, about time too. We've been waiting for this for months. Let me finish here and we can talk about it. Where the hell is that bloody man? Sorry Chad, you're going to have to stand in for him. Hand me up that screwdriver, please, the one with the red handle.' They both looked up as they heard the guard marching past on the packed earth outside the hanger. On a command from the Corporal the six-man squad came to a halt in front of the hanger.

'Good morning, Corporal. Is it noon already?'

'Yes Sir, we've just relieved the old guard.'

'The spanner, please Chad, in fact give me both of them, those two beside each other on the bench. Have you seen Abdul, Corporal?'

'No, Sir.'

'Well, be a good fellow and have one of your men try and find him, will you?' The Corporal gave orders and Edward addressed Chadwyck. 'Funny thing Chad, him going missing just before an op. I would feel a lot happier right now if I knew his whereabouts.' He went on working for a while and then handed the tools down to Chadwyck. 'That's it. Just let me get cleaned up and we'll go back to my quarters, so I can get changed for lunch. I'll be up at the Mess, Corporal. Let me know when you find Abdul, or, what is much more important,' he added, on reflection, 'let me know if you *don't* find him within the next half hour.'

After lunch, the Mess was cleared of all officers, other personnel and servants who were not directly involved in the briefing. Only the Admiral and his two aides, the skippers of the *Weymouth*, *Hyacinth*, *Pyramus* and *Pioneer* remained, along with Captain Eric Fullerton of the *Severn*, Commander Wilson of the *Mersey* and the Captains of the *Trent* and *Laurentic*. The five skippers of the armed trawlers, *Fly*, *Pickle*, *Childers*, *Salamander* and *Echo*, were also present with Squadron Commander Cull and Flight Lieutenants

Watkins, Bridgeman and Meade. Guards were posted outside all doors, with orders to prevent anyone from entering.

'Gentleman,' said the Admiral, as he rose to his feet and glanced at his watch, 'It is now 1435 hours,' most of those present checked their watches, 'and at 0400 hours tomorrow we shall start our attack on the *Konigsberg*.' A growl of approval ran around the room. 'Please close in and Lieutenant Meade will lay out the chart of the delta on the table here, so everyone can see it. Eric, come in closer, I wouldn't want you, of all people, to get lost.' joked the Admiral, laughing at his old friend. Nervous echoes could be heard from the assembled company. Captain Fullerton, the Commander of the *Severn*, one of the most experienced naval officers in the Service, moved over beside the Admiral.

'Not much chance of that happening with you in charge, Herbert.' The Admiral, the ugliest man in the British Navy by his own admission, glanced at him shrewdly with steely blue eyes, scenting for sarcasm. Slightly off balance, he continued.

'I'm going to transfer my flag to the *Weymouth*, for this engagement, because she draws less than the *Hyacinth* and, hopefully, I can get in a little closer. I want the *Laurentic*,' he turned and addressed her skipper, 'to leave her anchorage an hour after dark tonight and sail for Dar-es-Salaam. An hour before dawn I want you to bombard the harbour as a diversionary tactic. Shoot for the ships bottled up in there and try to avoid hitting the town. I want you, Eric, to lead the two Monitors away from their mooring, alongside the *Trent* at 1845 hours today and make it look like a regular exercise. It'll be almost dark by then and I want you to take up a position, five miles east of the Kikunja estuary. *Pickle* and *Salamander*,' again he looked over his officers, until he found their two skippers, before continuing, 'will take up their respective positions, a thousand yards apart and two miles northeast of the estuary, as marked on their charts. You will hold your positions until daylight, showing only a masthead light. The Monitors can then take a back bearing from you, to navigate the estuary in the dark. Is that quite clear?'

'Yes Sir.' They answered in unison.

'I want you, Eric, to lead the attack, with *Mersey* four hundred yards astern of you, until you've reached the point that is already marked on your chart, east of Gengeni Island, some six thousand yards from the *Konigsberg*. You will be preceded by *Pickle* and *Salamander*, who will sweep the river for mines, closely shadowed by *Echo*, in reserve. You should be there shortly after 0630 hours, anchor and begin your bombardment. The *Trent* will remain at anchor where she is, as a hospital ship and all casualties are to be taken directly there, by the trawlers or by any other means available. Chadwyck, I am transferring you, for this operation, to HMS *Severn* under Captain Fullerton and you will co-operate with his signal officer and liaise with me direct, on board HMS *Weymouth*. Is that all right with you Eric?'

'Of course, Herbert and we'll do our damnedest to bring him back in one piece.'

'George, you will remain with me on *Weymouth*. We, with *Hyacinth*, *Pyramus* and *Pioneer* will take up a position east of the Monitors and move in as close to the estuary as we can, so that we're in a position to bombard the shore defences any time after 0500 hours. The bombardment will not start until the Monitors come under fire. We must maintain the advantage of surprise for as long as possible. *Echo*, *Childers* and *Fly*,' he looked at each of the skippers in turn, 'will follow at one thousand yards behind the Monitors and conduct themselves according to circumstances, at their skippers' discretion. We have the positions and ranges of the enemy's shore defences pinpointed, so we should not be shelling the river at all. If the enemy have moved their shore defences, or added to the ones we know about, I expect you, Chadwyck, to signal us and zero us in.'

'Will the R.N.A.S. be backing me up on this, Sir? My brother has told me that these gun emplacements are a lot easier to spot from the air, than the river.'

'Yes, as soon as it is light I want both Farmans in the air, one piloted by you Lieutenant Meade, without an observer, to bomb the enemy's artillery positions along the estuary, coinciding with our bombardment and the other piloted by Commander Cull with an observer, over the Monitors. Initially you will report any new shore defences you see to me, so that we can bring our guns to bear on them and then, when the Monitors are in position, I want you to zero their fire on the *Konigsberg*. Lieutenant Meade will return to base immediately after his bombing run and he and his observer, who will be waiting for him on the strip, will stand by to relieve Commander Cull. You,' the Admiral looked directly at Edward, 'will take off two hours after Commander Cull, so that you will be in position over the Monitors, in time to allow the Commander to return to base before running out of fuel. This turn and turn about tactic will be repeated for as long as the action lasts. Are there any questions?' He looked around at the assembled group and, one by one, they shook their heads.

'Well, that's it then. God be with you and good luck to you all. Eric, a word with you, if I may.' The meeting broke up and the Admiral and Captain Fullerton led the way out of the Mess. Chadwyck and Edward, as the two most junior officers, were the last to leave and were met by the Corporal of the guard outside.

'What is it Corporal?' asked Edward, 'you look worried.'

'That Arab, Sir, can't find him nowhere and one of them feluccas is missing from the harbour.' Simultaneously, the brothers realised what had happened.

'Call out the old guard, Corporal and anyone else who is off duty and find that man.'

'We've already done that, Sir and it's almost certain he has left the island.'

'Damn it,' said Edward, 'what the hell did we say in the hanger, before you arrived Chad, to make him so certain? I remember one of the mechanics saying that Ordinance had spent all day yesterday re-arming the Monitors but, with all the gunnery practice they've had recently, they do that almost every day. Anyway, we must tell the Admiral now. Will you do that, Chad?'

'Of course, Eddy and if I don't get back to you before the op.'

He paused for a moment and then punched him lightly on the arm, before adding, 'take care.'

'You too, Chad.' They grinned at each other and on impulse, shook hands.

At exactly four o'clock the next morning HMS *Severn* and HMS *Mersey* weighed anchor and left the harbour, on Mafia Island. They steamed out into the Indian Ocean, on a north easterly course, describing a wide arc until they were able to take a back-bearing on the two trawlers and then set a course for the mouth of the Kikunja river. By five-twenty, advancing very slowly and taking soundings continuously in the dark, *Severn*, closely followed by *Mersey*, reached the estuary. Suddenly, a gun opened up on the north shore, firing three evenly spaced shots.

'That was a signal,' said Captain Fullerton to Chadwyck, who was standing behind him on the bridge, 'you were right, Meade, they are waiting for us. Dark as it is, a sentry would never have seen us, unless expecting us.

'But why a signal, Sir, why not just fire on us?'

'God knows, but count your blessings because,' he added with a mirthless grin, 'you won't enjoy it when they do.' The two ships crept on in the dark, knowing that in another fifteen minutes it would be light enough for the shore defences to see them. Their only comfort was the knowledge that, when the light came, they would be able to increase their speed considerably. Peering forward from the bridge Chadwyck realised that he could see details on the foredeck that, moments ago, had been unrecognisable. The light behind was growing stronger and the gun crews on deck crouched expectantly behind their three-pounders.

The shore batteries opened up and at exactly the same moment, the first salvos from the fleet screamed over their heads. The three-pounders on board went into action and laid down a heavy fire on the enemy's positions. In the improved light, they increased their rate of fire and with rifle and Maxim bullets ricocheting and whining off the steel hulls of the Monitors, Captain Fullerton signalled 'Full

Ahead' to the engine room. Within moments the *Mersey* followed suit, closing the gap that had opened between them.

A field gun opened up on the south bank, tearing away a fifteen foot strip of railing, abaft the aft gun on HMS *Mersey*. The Gunnery Officer, having spotted the enemy's position, laid the aft three-pounders onto it and opened fire. His calculations were almost spot on, having allowed for their own speed assisted by the flood tide, which gave them a total of eleven or twelve knots over the ground. The first shells landed up-river of the shore battery but the second salvo, after a minor correction, destroyed it. At six-twenty the two Monitors were standing off Gengeni Island, having sunk three dhows and a launch that stood in their way, as they forged upriver. The two Monitors set their bow and stern anchors and hung between them, broadside to the river and brought their guns to bear on the *Konigsberg*.

The *Severn*'s stern swung too far round, so the anchor had to be re-set, to enable them to lay both guns on their target. By this time, a German look-out post had relayed their position to the *Konigsberg* and Captain Looff commenced firing. Her first salvo fell short, on the island between them but, in short order, the German observers corrected the *Konigsberg* fire and her 4.1-inch shells burst around *Severn*, swamping both her and *Mersey* with tons of water and, incongruously, the odd dead fish. Half an hour before daylight, Edward, in one of the Farmans, which was loaded to capacity, with sixteen and twenty five pound bombs, took off. He arrived, thirty minutes later, over the enemy positions, while it was still dark on the ground. The early morning light picked him out at an altitude of three thousand feet, making him an easy target for the enemy to spot from the ground. Immediately after the three-shot warning signal, one of the German Maxims opened up on him. Sluggish with the weight of the bombs he dropped five hundred feet, in a steep dive, to increase his speed and released two of his bombs over the machine-gun emplacement.

Surprised by his tactics, the gun fired futilely over the top of the

Farman and by the time the crew had corrected their aim he was above them and one of his two bombs had done its work. At this point the Monitor's three-pounders opened fire on both banks and the shore defences, diverted by them, paid little attention to the Farman. Edward had a clear run and dropped the rest of his bombs at irregular intervals every time he saw one of their artillery batteries. When he got back to Mafia Island, Commander Cull had already taken off to relieve him. The mechanics and fitters swarmed over his 'plane, re-fuelling it and checking the oil lines. They also had to patch the fabric of the fuselage, where over thirty machine-gun bullets had found their mark.

By 0745 hours the enemy observers had zeroed the *Konigsberg*'s guns in on HMS *Mersey* and, after several salvoes of near misses, she was hit twice, killing the gun crew on the foredeck, wounding several others and disabling the gun. Unable to move from her fixed position and knowing that the enemy would soon have a report of their success, the crew continued to man the aft gun. Every man on deck, apart from the gun crews, fought heroically to put out the blaze on the foredeck, before it could reach the magazine and destroy the ship. The other shell was a direct hit on the launch tied alongside. It was completely destroyed but, in being there, it cushioned the Monitor's hull from the direct force of the blast. Commander Wilson, knowing that his only chance of saving his ship was to move her out of the *Konigsberg*'s identified target area, signalled HMS *Severn* of his intention and weighed anchors. Just as he cleared the area, the enemy's next salvo landed in a close pattern on their last position. Commander Cull, flying his Farman three thousand feet above the battle, continued to direct the *Severn*'s fire onto the *Konigsberg*. Just before eight o'clock the *Severn* scored her first hit and disabled one of the 4.1-inch guns, on the enemy's foredeck. During the next fifteen minutes, the *Severn* scored six more direct hits and several fires broke out on deck. Black smoke poured from a great gaping hole amidships, just aft of the bridge and fire fighting details could be seen from the air desperately pumping water from the river, to put out the blaze.

Fifteen minutes later, having moved again, to confound the spotters on Pemba Hill, the *Severn*'s guns lost the range. Radio contact with the Farman was broken off, just as *Severn* took up her new position. When the *Mersey* relocated further downstream, most of the *Severn*'s shells were exploding without effect in the mangroves, behind the target. Commander Cull, desperately short on fuel, had returned to base even though Edward had not yet taken up his station to relieve him. Blind, HMS *Severn* continued to miss the *Konigsberg*.

Captain Fullerton, ignorant of the results of his shooting and acutely aware that the longer he stayed in one position the more likely he was to be hit, gave orders to cease fire and weigh anchor. Just as *Severn* came round under power to take up a new position, Chadwyck, still on the bridge wing, spotted a movement on the island. Bucking the violent motion of the ship he focused his binoculars with difficulty and made out two men on an improvised platform, high up in a tree. They were looking straight at him, through their own glasses.

They were three miles from Pemba Hill and Chadwyck realised that this observation post had been set up at the last moment, based on information that the Germans had received, after the attack had been planned. He knew that it was Abdul's work and not, as they had first thought, anything that had been said by Edward in the hanger. Somehow Abdul, knowing the express purpose of the Monitors, had got word to the Germans of the Admiral's arrival and they, based on this information, had assumed an attack was imminent. If the British ever caught Abdul, he would answer to a firing squad. A third man behind the two observers in the tree was operating a radio transmitter. Without taking his eyes off the target, Chadwyck called out the position to the Gunnery Officer.

'Enemy observation post in tallest tree on north shore, range five hundred yards.' The ship was swinging round and it was impossible for Chadwyck to give a relative position on the observation post. The Gunnery Officer stepped up beside him.

'Where man? Point to the bloody thing!' *Severn* continued to come round until she cut her own wake and Chadwyck, momentarily lost sight of the observation post.

'There! 'Guns.' He yelled, when the deck settled, pointing with his left arm, which was nearest to the gunnery officer.

'Got it,' he said and, holding the position with his glasses, he started to give orders to the gun crews, both fore and aft. Captain Fullerton stepped up behind them.

'Critical target, Harry, use your main guns. Well spotted Chadwyck, I wish we had seen the devils sooner.' The three-pounders soon found the range and shredded through the foliage and tree trunks, around the observation post. Yelling orders over the roar of their own guns and the deafening sound of the *Konigsberg* shells exploding all around them, the gunnery officer brought one of the six-inch guns onto the target, already identified by the three-pounders. Firing lyddite, the entire area for twenty yards around the observation post was obliterated. When the smoke cleared there was no sign of the tree at all.

Having lost their forward observation post, the *Konigsberg* was unaware of where HMS *Severn* had moved to, as both ships were now out of sight of the look-out on Pemba Hill. The Monitors were equally blind and, for almost an hour, they waited impatiently for one of the 'planes to return. Chadwyck was convinced that Edward had crashed or been shot down on his way out from Mafia Island. When he finally heard the sound of an engine he searched the sky to the east with his binoculars until he picked up the 'plane, flying at about a thousand feet towards their old position.

Spotting the Monitors, it banked sharply and swung round overhead and as it did so Chadwyck saw with great relief that Edward was at the controls. The two Monitors opened fire again so that the observer in the 'plane could correct their aim. They were both firing at extreme range and the results were very erratic. This was not helped by the confusion that soon developed when it became obvious to both Gunnery Officers that the pre-arranged signalling system did not make it clear to which Monitor the corrected range applied. During the next two hours almost a hundred six-inch shells were fired with little effect, and when Commander Cull returned in his 'plane, the confusion was compounded.

During the course of the afternoon almost eighty corrections were transmitted but no further hits were scored on the *Konigsberg*. Shortly before four o'clock, with the ebb tide in full flow, Captain Fullerton gave the command to weigh anchor and both Monitors steamed back down river, towards the estuary. The *Konigsberg* had been badly mauled but the officers on board both Monitors knew that the enemy was not beaten and that they would have to return to finish the job, on another day.

The return run past the shore defences seemed almost tame, in comparison to the shelling that they had received from the *Konigsberg*. The two vessels slipped out in the last of the light into the Indian Ocean, to be welcomed by the rest of the fleet with a whooping cacophony of sirens. Five miles off-shore, HMS *Severn* and the rest of the fleet took up their positions behind HMS *Mersey*, as she committed her dead, to the deep.

CHAPTER 52

Gerald was later than usual at his office in the Rue Louis le Grand, on the morning of 12 July. It was very hot and the pigeons were settling on the pavement in search of shade, beneath the plane trees. He and Willy had been invited the previous night to dine at the house of an aged and fading countess who had bored them rigid with her interminable recollections of the war of 1870. As soon as they could leave her and her equally archaic guests Willy went home and Gerald went slumming from one club to another, through Montmartre to Montparnasse. He drank far too much alcohol of a questionable quality and had been unable to find anyone who could hold his attention for more than a few moments. The churlish, arrogant side of his character had emerged and, at three in the morning he had gone home frustrated and in a foul mood.

'Good morning Gerry, you look awful.' Gerald threw his rolled-up newspaper at Willy who, sitting at his desk, swatted it aside and continued, 'thanks for waking me up when you came in last night, although you probably didn't realise that you had. In fact, I'm surprised you even found your way home. Don't tell me that you couldn't find anyone to play with?' He tipped back his heavy, leather covered chair and propped his feet on the scarred edge of his desk. He had been reading from a long length of paper ribbon, torn from the tele-printer. It was coiled in confusion in two heaps, one on either side of his chair. Michelle, the more attractive of their two secretaries, stuck her head around the door.

'Bonjour Gerry, oh, you look awful,' she laughed heartlessly, 'poor Gerry,' she continued with even less sincerity, 'would you like some coffee, or perhaps a Fernet-Branca would be more appropriate?'

'Coffee please, Michelle, and with lots of sympathy.'

'Liquid sympathy Gerry, with the coffee, or will you find the other sort later,' and added pointedly, 'from someone else?' She gave him a knowing, frosty smile.

'Ouch!' he said, when she had gone, 'Has the Old Man been in, yet?'

'You asked for that, why don't you leave her alone? She's a damned good secretary and we've already lost enough of them to your over-active libido. As to your question, I really don't know how you always get away with it, but the Old Man is at a meeting at Reuters.'

'About what, as if it mattered?'

'This, I imagine.' said Willy, waving the ticker tape.

'This,' said Gerald, testily 'what is this?' Willy ignored Gerald's remark and continued to read the print-out.

'For Christ's sake Willy, what's the matter with you?'

'Nothing that a little friendliness wouldn't cure.'

Gerald slumped down into the chair behind his desk, held his head in his hands and, after a moment's reflection, looked up.

'I'm sorry Willy, please tell me what it is as I'm sure it's important and I'll be the wiser for knowing about it. What other inhumanity is man inflicting on his fellow man?'

'Well, let me see,' said Willy, threading the tape through his fingers, 'the Austrian army, under the command of Archduke Joseph, is retreating out of Poland and the Russians have taken more than fifteen thousand prisoners at Lublin, along with a vast quantity of arms. Listen to this; 'Sir Ian Hamilton reports from Gallipoli that he has routed a Turkish attack on his position and the Turkish casualties exceed twenty thousand men killed, wounded or captured.'

'That's incredible! That's more than the entire population of a medium-sized town, destroyed in one action.'

'No more than the Allies lost in the trenches at Ypres on a daily basis. Here's something for you from Reuters. South Africa is going to organise and equip an army made up of volunteers, now that General Botha has accepted the surrender of the German forces in South West Africa.' Willy threaded more tape through his fingers and read on, in silence. 'Ah, this should interest you, more from Africa, which you might develop for our readers back home.'

'What on earth is it? Has somebody found King Solomon's mines?'

'No, just that your brothers have covered themselves in glory.'

'What on earth are you talking about?'

'Well it doesn't actually say so in so many words but it seems that the Royal Navy and the R.N.A.S. have finally had a crack at the *Konigsberg*, a German cruiser bottled up in the Rufiji river. From what little there is here, the outcome was far from satisfactory.' Before Gerald could reply, Michelle came in and told him that Abe Johnson, otherwise known as the Old Man, wanted to see him immediately in his office.

'Don't want to keep you from more important things Gerry, but sit down will you.' Abe Johnson, overweight and in his mid fifties with steel-rimmed glasses perched on a nose too big for the rest of his face, sat behind his desk chewing on one of fifteen cigars he would smoke that day. The overhead light, burning quite unnecessarily for such a bright day, made his baldpate shine like a billiard ball. Sarcasm was a way of life to him and so finely tuned that the unfortunate recipient was usually only aware of it, on reflection, later on. 'What are you doing, anyway?'

'I'm working on the *Konigsberg* story, Sir.' The use of 'Sir' sometimes helped if it sounded sincere enough, but not always.

'You must forgive my ignorance, Mr Meade, but what or who is the *Konigsberg*?'

'A German cruiser, Sir. She is bottled up in a river in East Africa and has just been attacked by a combined British Naval and Air force.'

'Why should this little incident be of interest to our readers?'

'Avenging the *Lusitania*,' hazarded Gerald, without much hope, 'showing our people that we can strike back, in the name of freedom!'

'For heaven's sake, Meade, you sound like William Wilberforce.'

'William Wilberforce, Sir?' said Gerald, blankly. Abe Johnson shook his head, in despair.

'It doesn't matter Meade, go on with what you were saying.'

'Well Sir, I have a personal involvement.'

'That's nice, I don't think I have ever seen you involved in anything personal or otherwise, since you arrived here.'

'My two brothers,' continued Gerald, 'fought bravely in the action, Sir.'

'Really? That should make a big difference to our circulation figures. I can see us selling at least another ten thousand copies a day with an enthralled public hanging on your every word, as they lap up one exciting sequence after another. Perhaps you think you should go out there, Meade?'

'Well, yes sir, I do think that would be a good idea.'

'Well I don't and that's final. But I do have something for you to do that will appeal to your macabre sensibilities.'

'Yes sir, ready to do anything you ask me.'

'I want you to do an article about the Catacombs, here in Paris, research the history of the whole thing and write it in such way to draw a parallel to the present carnage. I think the Romans were the first to bury their dead there and a lot of those interred died in the Great Plague, during the fifteenth century but check it out and try to make it interesting.'

'Yes sir, I'll do my best,' said Gerald, wondering how long he would have for such an assignment and how severely it would curtail his other plans.

CHAPTER 53

At six in the morning on July 11th, the same officers who had met there five days earlier gathered again in the R.N.A.S Mess on Mafia Island, to be briefed for the second attack on the *Konigsberg*. Although it was obvious to all that the Germans would be expecting their return at any moment to complete their destruction, Admiral King-Hall was determined to maintain secrecy and surprise for as long as possible.

'Gentleman, I shall make this as brief as possible. First of all, I want to thank you again for all you did on the first attack. Today we are going to finish it. All that can be done to repair the damage inflicted on HMS *Mersey* has been done, bearing in mind our limited facilities. Both Monitors are armed and as ready for action as they will ever be. As the tides are not ideal, the entire attack will have to be carried out in broad daylight. It is the necessity for immediate action that outweighs the advantages of a pre-dawn attack. At noon yesterday, a signal was transmitted to Cape of Good Hope Station notifying them of our intention to leave Mafia Island this morning for Simonstown with the two Monitors and a heavy escort, to effect repairs. This, of course, was transmitted in code but one we are sure the enemy knows. It will come as no surprise to them when their lookouts report that the two Monitors, towed by *Blackcock* and *Revenger* and escorted by *Hyacinth*, *Weymouth*, *Pioneer* and *Pyramus*, are seen to be heading south, in convoy.

Hopefully, if we are very lucky, they will think we consider the job done and have no further interest in the *Konigsberg*. We shall sail from Tirene Bay in one hour and be off the Kikunja estuary shortly after 0830 hours. At which point *Blackcock* and *Revenger* will cast off the Monitors, who will take the flood tide straight into the river, while the rest of the fleet take up their positions and start firing on the shore defences. Commander Cull and Lieutenant Meade will take off from here at 0900 hours, in one of the Farmans, so as to be over the Monitors at the same time as they start their bombardment of the *Konigsberg*. Well that's about it, any questions?' After a moments silence, during which he surveyed his command, he continued.

'Right gentlemen, that's all and good luck to you. I would like you to all go aboard your ships now, with the exception of the Captains of the *Severn* and the *Mersey* and Commander Cull and Lieutenant Meade and prepare for our departure at 0700 hours. Chadwyck you remain here and George please check, on your way out, that the sentries are still in position after the room has been cleared.' At his bidding, those designated, sat around one of the mess tables and the Admiral took a large silver cigarette case out of his pocket and offered the contents. Almost everyone helped themselves, and they could see from the Admiral's expression that he was not happy with what he was about to tell them.

'Due to a lack of detailed thought on my part, for which I take full responsibility, a great deal of confusion developed during our last attack, with regard to the guns' responses to corrections from the air. The fact that this is a new form of warfare is no excuse. We now know, from an aerial observer's point of view, that it is quite impossible, when two Monitors are firing at the same time, to tell which shell has been fired by which gun or even from which Monitor.'

'We are all equally responsible, Herbert,' cut in Captain Fullerton, 'we should have realised it, during gunnery practice. We didn't, I suppose, because only one Monitor was involved at a time.'

'Thank you Eric, but I don't think their Lordships would see it that way.' He subjected them all to a wintery smile and crushed out his cigarette in the ashtray. 'Today it will be different. There will only be one 'plane in the air at a time and the corrections will only apply to HMS *Severn*.' As he said it he looked up at the Captain of *Mersey* and, before he could say anything, he continued in a kinder tone 'Dickie, I have thought about this a great deal and there really is no other way to do it. You lost one of your six-inch guns, in the last action, reducing your fire power by fifty percent. I am convinced that you will be an invaluable contributor to the operation by setting yourself up as a moving target for the *Konigsberg*, while Eric sets his anchors and goes into action from a stationary position. So I want you, Dickie, to take the *Mersey* upriver towards the *Konigsberg*, posing a serious threat. I believe that if we do this she will concentrate on you and give Eric the valuable time he needs to find and destroy his target. Obviously, should you find any other target, such as one of the *Konigsberg*'s supply vessels, fire at will with all you've got.'

'Yes Sir.'

'Good, now I want you, Chadwyck, to join Captain Fullerton, as before. It is imperative that the 'plane is in position over head before HMS *Severn* is ready to commence firing, as a great deal of the success of the operation will depend on aerial spotting. If there is any doubt in your mind Commander, I would rather two 'planes were in the air, at the same time, just as long as only one is giving corrections at any one time.'

'We shall be there, Sir,' said Commander Cull, 'in good time. Lieutenant Watkins will be standing by with the Caudron and can be over the Monitors in less than thirty minutes, should he be needed.'

'I think you are right, Commander. There seems to be no point in having two 'planes in the air at the same time. In the event of engine failure or being shot down you, Eric, while Watkins replaces Cull, can weigh anchor and relocate. This will be to our advantage as it will mean that the enemy's spotters will have to start again, to get your range. Any questions gentleman?' After a moment's silence, he cleared his throat and continued, introspectively. 'I have never known so much time and effort devoted to a single action. It shows that the threat of the enemy and what they might do can tie up as much or more manpower and materials than would otherwise be the case if the threat were a reality and had to be dealt with as such. In other words, if we had sunk the *Konigsberg* in the Indian Ocean, at the outbreak of war when we had a chance to do so, none of this would have happened and all of us would have been able to direct our attention and efforts to other ways of bringing about the enemy's destruction. So,' and his voice hardened, 'let's make damn sure gentleman, that we put an end to it today. Good luck to you all.'

At exactly seven o'clock the fleet weighed anchor and, led by HMS *Weymouth* flying Admiral King-Hall's flag, they sailed out of Tirene Bay and set their course, in line ahead, south by south-west for Simonstown. An hour and a half later *Blackcock* and *Revenger* cast off the Monitors who immediately turned ninety degrees starboard and, preceded by the three trawlers, closed on the Kikunja estuary. The rest of the fleet positioned themselves, at equal intervals, across the mouth of the river and started an immediate bombardment of the shore defences. At 0855 hours HMS *Severn*, closely followed by HMS *Mersey*, crossed the sandbar, under withering fire from the now familiar enemy artillery positions and gave as much as they got. Gun crews on both vessels worked flat out to supply shells to the guns in a continuous stream to meet their insatiable demands.

Mersey was struck by two three-pounder shells almost immediately, one pierced the deck behind the bridge and exploded in the Captain's cabin, wounding two men there and blowing out the bulkhead. This in turn, threw the officer in charge of the aft six-inch gun into the scuppers so that, had he not caught hold of the ships rail, he would have gone over the side. The second shell hit the aft capstan, destroying it and scattered the sandbags. The stunned gunnery officer, unable to believe he had survived such an experience without a scratch, picked himself up and stumbled back to his post.

As HMS *Severn* approached the island, where she had destroyed the observation post on the previous attack, she altered course to avoid the sandbar. She then passed along the western side, so that she would be nowhere near her old position that had been so accurately targeted by the gunnery officer on the *Konigsberg*. An added advantage was that, in her new position, she was more than seven hundred yards closer to her target. HMS *Mersey* took the other side of the island and steamed on, towards the enemy's position. It seemed that the plan was working, the *Konigsberg*'s first salvo was high over the *Mersey* and quite a long way behind her. By this time she was in view of the observation post on Pemba Hill, whereas the *Severn* was not. The second salvo, a complete broadside of the remaining guns on the *Konigsberg*, landed closer to the *Mersey*.

Commander Wilson knew that the third salvo would almost certainly score, as the enemy gunners now had their range and speed, so he signalled full astern on the starboard engine and threw the wheel hard to starboard, to execute the tightest possible turn. The ship, heeling heavily to port, so that her rails were almost under and straining at every rivet, lumbered round painfully and steamed down river. The third salvo missed them and at the same moment Commander Wilson saw the Farnam high above his ship and heading straight for the *Konigsberg*. Simultaneously, HMS *Severn*'s guns opened up and he knew that his diversionary tactic had worked long enough for her to anchor and come into action. It was now only a question of whether she could find her target with the help of Lieutenant Meade and destroy the enemy, before they blew her out of the water.

Her first three salvos were high and way beyond the target, in the jungle behind her. On Edward's correction, the range was reduced by four hundred yards. Her fourth and fifth salvos were still beyond the target and to the left. By this time the Farman, only eight hundred yards from the *Konigsberg*, had come under heavy machine gun fire as she banked to fly back over the island, toward HMS *Severn*. Edward gave the next correction, bringing two six-inch shells screaming down onto the *Konigsberg*'s fo'c'sle. Craning back over his shoulder to make absolutely sure, he radioed the letters H.T. to confirm a hit and immediately two more shells landed squarely on the target.

The first pair destroyed one of the guns on the starboard side, killing the entire gun crew and most of the ammunition party. A shell fragment smashed through the bridge window and lodged itself high in Captain Looff's shoulder. It shattered his collar bone and threw him across the bridge so that he landed, semi-conscious, against the far bulkhead. His bo'sun, who had been standing by him at that moment, was decapitated by a large piece of flying glass. The second hit, which came less than a minute after the first, landed beside two large oil drums with petrol, used to run the donkey engines that raised the 4-inch shells from the magazine to the guns. These were shredded by the incendiary shell fragments which instantaneously ignited in a searing flash of flame that surged across the sloping deck and, like molten lava, poured down the hatch into the magazine below.

The thousand kilos of dynamite, that was carried to clear channels when needed, exploded, blowing out the bulkheads leading to the crew's quarters and the infirmary. Almost all of the patients, doctors and orderlies there were either killed outright or asphyxiated by the blast, while most of the remaining crew were on deck engaged in the action.

Just before the first hit, the gunnery officer on the *Konigsberg* had transferred his attention to HMS *Severn* and, ignoring HMS *Mersey* entirely, laid down two broadsides, which straddled the *Severn*. At the same moment *Severn*'s salvo landed on the *Konigsberg* and disabled one of the four remaining guns. Because of the chaos on deck and the break in the chain of command, due to the Captain's condition, a second salvo from the *Severn* destroyed another of the *Konigsberg*'s guns before she could fire again. Firing continuously, the *Severn* put a third gun out of action two minutes later. By this time, the fire on board the *Konigsberg* was raging from one end to the other and the ammunition party found it almost impossible to feed the remaining guns.

Captain Looff, slumped in his chair, continued to command his ship although he had been wounded again by flying glass, when the second gun had been destroyed. Blood streaming down his face closed one eye completely. Just as he gave the order to flood the remaining magazines there was a shattering explosion aft of the bridge, which tore through the deck. The pom-pom, which had been firing sporadically at the Farman was thrown over the side into the river, like a child's toy. The crew, who were shredded into parts so small that none were recognisable, died instantly.

Still the *Severn*'s six-inch shells poured into the stricken *Konigsberg* and, over the deafening noise of the guns, Chadwyck picked up a signal from his brother that the Farman had been hit. Standing on the bridge Chadwyck could see the 'plane losing altitude rapidly, as it tried desperately to glide out of the enemy area towards the Monitors. Chadwyck immediately informed Captain Fullerton, who ordered Lieutenant Watkins into the air. He then ordered Commander Wilson on the *Mersey* to stand by with a boat, to pick up any survivors from the 'plane. By extraordinarily skilful flying, Commander Cull cleared the mangrove swamps and slightly nose heavy, brought the 'plane down onto the water less than two hundred yards beyond HMS *Mersey*.

The 'plane somersaulted, broke Edward's belt and threw him over the pilot's head into the river. When Edward came to the surface, he could see only the floats of the 'plane showing and no sign of his skipper. With only a moment's thought for the crocodiles which were less than fifty yards away and launching themselves like torpedoes into the river, he dove beneath the surface in an attempt to free the pilot. His blood hammered in his head and his lungs felt as though bound in iron, as he struggled for almost a minute to free the inert body. With the last of his breath and with a raging pain behind his eyes, he finally managed to unbuckle the harness and drag his skipper to the surface. Strong hands hauled them both unceremoniously into the whaler, seconds before the first of the crocodiles reached them. The sub-lieutenant, commanding the boat, unbuckled his revolver and fired all six shots to discourage them.

Two sailors laid Commander Cull over the midship's thwart and pumped his arms rhythmically, in an attempt to get some of the water out of his lungs. After a few painful moments of coughing and retching he recovered enough to sit upright in the bottom of the boat. As soon as the two airmen were safely aboard, one of the crew jumped on to the 'plane's floats and attached a charge of gun-cotton, packed in a tin, to the engine block. Commander Cull had told Commander Wilson that the aircraft was unrecoverable, under the present circumstances. The whaler made back to the *Mersey* and, just as she was being slung inboard, the charge blew and the Farman disappeared beneath the surface.

During the whole of the recovery HMS *Severn* continued to fire over their heads into the *Konigsberg*, until her guns became so hot that she was no longer able to shoot. On Captain Fullerton's orders HMS *Mersey*, with the Caudron piloted by Lieutenant Watkins now flying overhead, steamed upriver and took up a position less than four thousand yards from the *Konigsberg*, set her anchors and went into action. Sustained machine gun fire from the shore, followed the Caudron as she flew towards the *Konigsberg*. Lieutenant Lloyd, the observer, could easily see the first shot from HMS *Mersey*, as it landed less than a hundred yards short of the target. After relaying two minor corrections to the gunnery officer, he reported a hit with her fourth shot.

Shortly after two o'clock he radioed Captain Fullerton that the target was destroyed. By that time, HMS *Mersey* had scored twenty-eight hits and the *Konigsberg* was burning out of control, from stem to stern. She lay on the bottom, listing heavily to starboard, with the river washing her decks and still the fires raged. Half an hour earlier, Captain Looff had ordered those members of the crew that could to carry the wounded, ashore. Shunning assistance himself he turned his back on his ship, with a feeling of infinite sadness. A great column of black smoke rose high over the delta and marked her grave. No longer was the *Konigsberg* a threat to Allied shipping and never would she be again.

CHAPTER 54

Both Monitors and most of their escorts made it safely back to Mafia Island, where Admiral King-Hall called a debriefing, at the end of which he asked Chadwyck to stay behind.

'Well done Chadwyck, Captain Fullerton speaks very highly of your conduct. I don't suppose you expected to see so much action as my A.D.C.'

'No sir but I was glad I was there, fighting with my brother. Without his corrections we wouldn't have been able to make such a good job of it.'

'So I hear, I must recommend him and Cull for some appropriate decoration.'

'Thank you Sir, is that all Sir?'

'No, sit down, Chadwyck, I have a new job for you. I'm afraid you're going to be split up, you and your brother. In about a week he will be heading back to Port Said and posted on to Gallipoli, same job, spotting for the artillery but with more opposition, and you are going to the western shore of Lake Tanganyika. You'll be leaving at about the same time as your brother and I will be taking the squadron back to Simonstown, so report to Captain Shaw and he will give you your orders. I'll see you before I go, to say good-bye.' Chadwyck stood up and replaced his hat, saluted and left the Admiral's office.

'You will be liaison officer between Commander Spicer-Simson, head of the Naval Expeditionary Task Force to Lake Tanganyika and Admiral King-Hall,' said Captain Shaw, sitting across his desk from Chadwyck, 'your orders are somewhat unorthodox. You will be travelling with the three Grey's Scouts who have been on this island since their land-based attack on the *Konigsberg*.'

'You mean Lieutenants Ripon and Flynn, Sir, and his native. I know them, in fact Flynn is my brother-in-law.'

'I thought so, the Admiral had mentioned something about that and I was very sorry to hear about your wife.' He rubbed his nose, self-consciously and continued,' I believe Ripon knows the country there and Flynn's native is a very good tracker, I'm told, so they should be a great help to you. You will be on your own from the moment you leave here until you reach Northern Rhodesia. Intelligence suggested that you hitch a ride on the railway that runs between Dar es Salem and Tunduna, on the German border with Northern Rhodesia. Our chaps have pretty sound information that the Germans have just started to build a new hospital for their wounded, at Mbeya. We have been told that there is a fairly constant stream of trains running between Dar and Mbeya, mostly at night. You will have to leave the train before it reaches Mbeya and cover the rest of the journey to the Rhodesian border on foot. You will be in German territory for the whole of your trip until you reach that border. You'll be leaving after most of the German troops have been withdrawn from the Rufiji river, as their reason for being there no longer exists. A local guide of ours will lead you up the Rufiji to its confluence with the Ruaha river and then on up that, to a point where it flows beneath a bridge carrying the railway line, near a place called Kiberege. There is a steep escarpment a few miles to the west of the bridge, which will slow down the train and enable you to board. It's about a hundred and thirty miles from the mouth of the Rufiji and will probably take you about eight days, if all goes well.'

'Will we have any porterage on the rivers, Sir?'

'None to speak of and you will be travelling light with only a few days rations. You will have to live off the land, just your rifles, bedding and minimal medical kit. You will be travelling in two light canoes, each with two paddlers and you will carry your canoes around any rapids you encounter. The distance from where you intercept the train to Mbeya is about four hundred miles and, depending on how many trains you have to use, it shouldn't take you more than a couple of days. Albertville, your destination midway up the western shore of Lake Tanganyika, is about another three hundred miles from the border. If you walk the whole way it will take you over two weeks, but you should find some transport with Rhodesian troops being moved up to join the Belgians at Nyunzu.'

'What will my companions be doing once we arrive at Albertville?'

'Flynn and his native will be scouting along the northwest end of the lake and reporting back to Spicer-Simson on any movement out of Kigoma, the German naval base, on the Eastern shore and Lieutenant Ripon will liaise between Spicer-Simson and the Grey's Scouts HQ.

'Is Commander Spicer-Simson at Albertville, now?'

'No, he and his expedition should be somewhere near Elizabethville by now and,' he added with a self-depreciating smile, 'I'm glad I am not with them.' Chadwyck was surprised by his candour but didn't want to ask why, but Captain Shaw had seen his expression and continued, 'In my view and this is just between us, the whole project is a little…' for a moment he was lost for words, '… unusual.' Chadwyck waited for him to continue. 'Very heroic,' he elaborated, 'and who knows, it might work.'

'What are their plans Sir, or shouldn't I know, yet?'

'No, of course not, I'm sure hundreds of people know about it because so many people have been involved. The Admiralty has decided, in an attempt to clip the wings of the two German ships on Lake Tanganyika, to send two forty-foot mahogany launches, originally built for the Greek government. They were sent, with their crews and stores, on one of the Union Castle boats to Cape Town and from there to Elizabethville by rail and native porterage. A chap called Lee, a professional elephant hunter, was engaged by the Admiralty to map a route from Elizabethville to Albertville, where they are presently building a naval dockyard. I believe the second leg of the journey involves building more than a hundred bridges. They will need at least four hundred natives to man handle the two ten-ton tenders that have been built for the two launches. I think each one is drawn by sixteen oxen, which will need to be constantly rotated.'

'Don't the Germans have two fairly good-sized ships on the lake? I know one of them, the *Hedwig von Wissenn*, is about eight hundred tons with some pretty heavy armament. What can two forty-foot wooden launches do against that?'

'I think you'll find the answer to that once you get there. Good luck.' He held out his hand and the briefing was over.

CHAPTER 55

At the beginning of the following week, two days after Edward and his RNAS colleagues had sailed for Port Said, Jack Ripon arrived on one of the squadron's armed auxiliaries to pick up Chadwyck, James and Caachy and run them up the Rufiji river to rendez-vous with the two canoes and their paddlers, laid on for the remainder of their journey to the railway line. All of them were dressed in the uniform of the Grey's Scouts because, if captured, they didn't want to be shot as spies. Once they had transferred to the canoes they managed to paddle for over three hours before it became too dark to continue.

They eased in towards the bank and pulled their canoes up under some thorn bushes. Caachy lit a small fire to warm their rations, while the four native paddlers made their own camp. They took it in turns to stand guard while the others slept. Before it was light enough to see properly, Caachy woke them with a steaming mug of tea and hard tack. As soon as they had had breakfast, they pulled the canoes out onto the river and continued upstream.

On the second day the river narrowed considerably between a gorge, causing a lot of white water and twice they had to go ashore and carry their canoes above the rapids. Once past the second rapids, they pulled the canoes ashore and made camp, even though there was still two hours of daylight left. The natives were exhausted and James wanted to see if he could catch some fish with his split-cane trout rod.

A brother officer on Mafia Island had given it to him a month ago and James had had some success fishing on the reefs around the island. He had brought it so that he could forage silently: they could never be sure when they might run into a German patrol. Using a small red and silver fly, he managed to land three good sized bream within half an hour. They were cooked by Caachy and divided between the four of them, the natives had their own biltong and posho. James produced some Portuguese cheroots and once they were lit, he turned to Chadwyck.

'Have you told us everything you know about this task force that we are meeting up with?'

'I think so,' said Chadwyck 'and the more I think about it, the crazier it sounds.'

'That's putting it mildly,' said James, 'with all the timber they have on the Belgium side of the lake and twenty good boat builders, they could knock up a much more effective vessel in one of the bays on the south western tip of Lake Tanganyika and bring in all the machinery and armament needed, from Elizabethville. Chad, do you know what guns these launches have?'

'I think a couple of three-pounders and machine guns,' said Jack.

'That's insignificant compared to what the Germans have. Nothing we've put on the lake so far has lasted because of German superiority. Did they tell you anything about Spicer-Simson?'

'Captain Shaw didn't but I found out quite a lot about him before we left, from one of our chaps who knew him back in London.'

'And?' prompted James.

'Well, most of it is pretty negative. He is a bully and a liar and I believe he has virtually no combat experience, whatsoever.'

'So why on earth was he put in charge of such a hazardous operation as this?'

'God knows, he must have pulled strings with the Admiralty. Also,' continued Chadwyck, 'I believe he is covered from his neck to his ankles with tattoos.'

'How extraordinary, he must be insecure, unhappy in his own

skin, one might say.' They laughed and Jack put another log on the fire. 'I'll take the first watch.' he said, 'We should get some rest now.'

Two days later they came to the confluence with the Ruaha river. Wide sand banks had been created by the current across the Rufiji and were festooned with basking crocodiles. They were more than halfway to the railway line and had not yet seen a single German askari. They knew that there would be more ahead of them than behind, and it took them until the afternoon of the third day before they saw the railway bridge, crossing the river ahead. They immediately pulled into the nearest bank and dragged the canoes out of the water.

'We're off the water Chad, so I am now in charge.'

Chadwyck grinned at Jack and said. 'I thought you were from the start, so what do we do now?'

'We wait here till it is dark because there is almost certainly a sentry on the bridge.'

'I'll go and scout out the situation with Caachy and see how the land lies to the west,' said James.

'We need to find somewhere to lie up next to the track tonight and tomorrow,' added Chadwyck, 'we should find the steep incline, somewhere west of the river, that Shaw told me about, which will slow the train down enough to enable us to board.'

They crept into the bush and waited until dark, when James and Caachy left. Shortly before midnight they returned.

'There is a small post on the east side of the river,' said James, 'with four men, that I could count, and you were right, Chadwyck, it seems that there is one on the bridge at all times. Caachy has found a good place for us to camp tonight and lie up tomorrow, it's just above the line, so if a train goes by and somebody is looking out, they won't be able to see us.'

'And what is the gradient like?' asked Chadwyck.

'Too flat to affect the train, but we don't know yet at what speed they travel. It might be possible from the hiding place we found to drop down onto the roof of the train, if it's not going too fast, and then climb down into one of the wagons.'

'That would only work if it is a freight train, forget it if there are troops on board.'

'This is the parting of the ways,' said Jack, 'Do either of you have any coins on you?'

Chadwyck fished in his pockets and came out with a few shillings and James added a few more to the pile.

'With what I've got,' said Jack, 'it should be enough. I am going to send the natives home.' He walked over to where they were sitting beside the canoes and spoke to them briefly, giving each one of them a few coins. Within minutes he was back, 'they are going to wait here until just before first light and then head off downstream. If there is a sentry on the bridge, he won't be able to see them at that time, from that distance. Make sure you have everything and leave nothing in the canoes and that none of your kit rattles. We'll move out in single file with Caachy leading, I'll bring up the rear.'

Two hours later, Caachy led them across the tracks and they climbed up onto the embankment, which stood about fifteen foot above the rails. There was a small depression along the top of the embankment, covered with thick thorn trees, a good defendable position that couldn't be seen from the air. They settled in for the rest of the night and Caachy took the first watch.

Early the next morning, before the others were awake, Caachy set out to find the right piece of wood to make a bow and some arrows. He would need it to shoot small game because it was too risky to fire a shot when they had no idea where there might be an enemy patrol. Caachy returned while the others were eating breakfast from their diminishing rations and started to make the bow and arrows.

'Chadwyck and I are going to go further up the line, and look for a better place to jump the train,' said Jack, 'if we can find it and an embankment like this, we'll make camp there and hopefully there will be a train through tonight. James, you stay here with Caachy and watch out for any German patrols going either way on the tracks. As soon as it's dark come on up the tracks with Caachy till you find us in a similar situation to this but on a steeper gradient, we'll keep an eye out for you.'

Ten miles west of the river, the tracks began to climb the beginning of an escarpment in a slow right-hand turn that ran between two steep embankments. Almost half a mile ahead of them, James could see where the tracks disappeared from view, as the ground levelled out. They had seen no one all day, neither Germans nor natives, nothing but a herd of zebra that had crossed the line, now some five miles behind them. It had been just before they came to a passing place where two tracks ran parallel for some two hundred yards, with points at both ends. Chadwyck, realising the risk of being caught in the cutting, waved James over to his side and they both climbed onto the top of the embankment and forced their way up through the thick bush to where the ground began to level out.

'This is where the train will be at its slowest,' said James 'so here is where we will jump it. It's just a question of whether this side of the line is better than the other. There doesn't seem to be much difference but here we have more cover from above although, who knows whether the Germans have any 'planes this far south.'

'I think the other side is better because it seems more open and it will be easier to run alongside the train, before we jump.'

'You could be right, let's go and have a look.'

Four hours after the sun had set, they heard a faint sound on top of the embankment, opposite to where they were lying which was almost immediately followed by a birdcall.

'It's James and Caachy,' said Jack, 'the crafty buggers have followed our tracks instead of wondering down the railway line.' He gave the same birdcall and within minutes the others crawled in beside them. He told Caachy to light a fire and cook the dik-dik he had shot, all grateful for the fresh meat after days of dried rations and the odd fish.

'We came across to this side of the line because it is more open,' Jack explained to James, 'there is a twenty-yard clear stretch and I'll show the three of you the best way to jump onto the roof of a moving train. We'll stand at the beginning of the clear run, one behind the other, Chadwyck first, then James, followed by Caachy. We should be able to run more or less at the same speed as the train, at two-yard intervals. Each of us must judge our moment and you must all twist in the air, so that when you land on the carriage roof you'll be facing the back of the train. This way, if you are not running as fast as the train you will fall forward onto your hands rather than your back and, hopefully there will be rails along both sides of the carriage roof. Do you understand what I am saying? If we don't all land on the same carriage, it doesn't matter, just make sure you don't land in between two carriages. If one of us falls off, we must all shin down the ladders at the end of the carriage and drop off the train before it clears the summit.'

And then what?' said James.

'We'll just have to wait for the next one. Is that clear? Now let's get some rest. Caachy you take first watch and go fifty yards back down the line to give us a bit of warning before the train gets here. Shout when you hear it, any noise will be covered by the engine and run back to us and take up your position. Do not unbuckle any kit while you sleep.' They each found a place to rest and Caachy left them to take the first watch. Just before dawn, James was woken by Chadwyck, who had taken the second watch, shouting, 'It's coming, I can hear the train!'

'How many carriages?' shouted Jack.

'I can't count them,' cried Chadwyck as he forced his way through the shateen back to where they were. 'There must be seventy yards between the engine and the rear light.' Moments later Chadwyck joined them and the engine steamed past, wheels screeching on the rails for traction.

'Go,' said James.

They started running. What luck, thought Chadwyck, that there aren't two engines, as he found himself running at the same speed as the train. Just before the end of the clear ground he jumped to his right, twisted in the air and landed towards the front of the third carriage, squarely on his feet. Flaying his arms, he managed to keep his balance and immediately dropped flat, stretching out a hand for one of the rails. He twisted around just in time to see James turn in the air above the train and land like a cat on his feet with his two hands in front. He was on the very edge of the same carriage and seconds later Caachy landed on the front of the next carriage. They had all made it and, thank God, thought Chadwyck, we don't have to get off and do it all again. As Jack had told them, they all lay where they were, silent, in the hope that no one on the train had heard them. A few moments later the train pulled over the summit, gathered speed and James crawled forward and lay beside Chadwyck.

'Wait here, I am going to the end of this carriage to see how we can get into one or the other. I don't want to go any nearer the end of the train, as there will certainly be a guard there. I've already told Caachy to follow us.' He crawled to the end of the carriage and disappeared over the edge of the roof. A minute later his head reappeared and he waved to the others. They had landed on a box car that could easily be opened from the outside and within minutes they had all squeezed in amongst the crates, stacked one upon another the whole length of the carriage.

'We must fasten the door from outside,' said James 'in case the guards see the clasp hanging open, when they stop to refuel.' He spoke to Caachy, who climbed onto one of the crates beneath the trap door, opened it and disappeared onto the roof, within minutes he was back with a broad grin on his face.

'Do you know, Jack,' asked Chadwyck, 'how often they stop for water and wood?'

'No, but I imagine it's about every hundred and fifty miles or so. Which means there will be either two or three stops before we get to Mbeya.'

'They won't be at regular intervals as it will depend on availability of water.' They settled down as the sun warmed the inside of the box car and an hour later they began to slow down. Chadwyck got up to put his eye to a chink in the boards and could see an elevated water tank beside stacks of cordwood. The train stopped just before they reached it, and moments later they could hear the two guards chatting as they walked along side of the train.

'What did they say,' asked James, after they had passed.

'They were arguing about a woman,' answered Caachy.

Five hours later they stopped again and Caachy listened carefully for any snatch of conversation between the guards, as they walked forward towards the engine. James raised an eyebrow and Caachy answered,

'They were talking about the war and how lucky they were not to be fighting.'

'Nothing about when we will get to Mbeya? We must know so we can get off before we get there and, we can only do that, immediately after we pull out of the refuelling stop before we reach Mbeya.'

Half an hour later, they heard the guards coming back, one was grumbling and obviously complaining about something and they heard the other slap him on the back and say something and then he laughed. Again, once the guards were out of hearing, Caachy translated, 'The older one is unhappy about having to work so hard and the other was laughing at him and told him there were only one more stop, before the end of their shift.'

'The answer to a maiden's prayer,' said James, smiling at them all. 'How lucky can we get? That means another five hours and by then it will be dark. We must all rest now and try to get some sleep. We'll jump off just after the next refuelling.'

Almost five hours later and about fifteen minutes after they had stopped for refuelling, James sent Caachy up onto the roof so that he could open the door, shortly after the train started to move and before it gathered too much speed.

'We must all jump together,' said Jack, 'and the moment we hit the ground lie absolutely still until the guards van is at least a hundred yards down the track. If they happen to be looking out from the back platform, they'll only see us if we move. This is vital. I think we are about sixty miles from the Rhodesian border and, if we walk all of tonight and the next two nights, resting during the day, we should have crossed it. There's enough moon to see what we are doing and we are less likely to run into a patrol at night. Now make sure you have all your kit strapped on properly because we should be jumping in the next ten minutes.'

* * *

At dawn on the third morning they could see a German patrol moving across their front. James calculated that they were probably fifteen miles southwest of Tunduma. They had crossed the Songwe river and the Nayasaland border shortly before midnight. As the light increased, they lay in line abreast on slightly elevated ground with good thorn cover behind them and James studied the ground ahead through binoculars. He was looking for patrols on both sides of the borders. He hoped that the German patrol, seen earlier, would continue on their way towards Tunduma and that, with luck, a Rhodesian patrol might appear, which, more or less, would show him the border. He conferred with Jack and between them they calculated the approximate distances between where they were and where they thought the border was, so that when it was dark they would know how to find their way across. They lay there all morning in whatever shade they could find, and finally Chadwyck picked up a mounted patrol on the Rhodesian side, approaching the border at right angles to it, coming straight towards them, in line ahead. 'Do you see what I see?' said Chadwyck.

'Yes.'

'I think there are about twenty of them and I think they are pulling a field gun. It looks like they are planning to set up a post on the border.' Within half an hour, the patrol had stopped and dismounted, with the exception of two who James presumed were officers. They separated and went in opposite directions, moving slowly in a rather haphazard fashion.

'They are looking for a good defensive position.'

When both riders were about five hundred yards from the group one of them called out and the message was relayed by the group in the middle to the other, who turned back to join his brother officer, telling the rest of the patrol, as he passed, to follow on. Both Chadwyck and James watched them dig in, fill bags with earth to pack around the gun emplacement and build parapets for the trenches, that ran parallel to the border. Their horses had been led back about four hundred yards behind the trenches to a small, shaded depression, where they would be out of sight of the enemy.

'Well now we know where to go,' said Jack 'but we'll have to think carefully how we'll approach. We will have to find a way to let them know who we are before some jittery Private uses us for target practice.'

'What was the name of the C.O. at Chipata?' James asked Jack. 'You know the one with all the whiskers.'

'Freeman wasn't it? Colonel Freeman?'

'What was his nickname?'

'I don't know it was months ago, I don't remember.'

'I do,' said James, 'it was Bottlebrush.'

'You're right,' said Jack.

'Well that's our password.'

Chadwyck laughed and they settled down and ate some of the cold meat from the Thompson gazelle Caachy had shot two days before. At nine o'clock they moved slowly forward towards the patrol and, when they were within three hundred yards they settled down to wait for one of the sentries to give away their position. After maintaining absolute silence for ten minutes, Caachy touched Jack's shoulder and, with his eyes, indicated the direction in which he had heard some sound. Silently, the two of them moved in the direction that Caachy had indicated. Every twenty yards, they stopped to listen and finally Caachy could make out the silhouette of a trooper sitting with his back to a tree. He was no more than forty yards away. Just ahead of them was a donga, now dry but cut deep by the rains, giving them the necessary cover. They dropped into it and could no longer see the sentry.

'Trooper,' called Jack in a voice that would just reach the sentry but go no further. 'I am Lieutenant Ripon, Grey's Scouts, part of the

Konigsberg special detail. Don't shoot. I am here with three colleagues and want to come in.' He heard the snick of a safety catch and at the same time, the rattle of a rifle bolt. So there were two of them. A second later, there was the crack of a bullet, at head height but about five yards to one side.

'Don't shoot, you stupid bastard or I'll have you on a charge before Colonel Freeman!' There was a stunned silence and then, 'You can't, he's been transferred.'

'Old bottlebrush?' said Jack, 'don't tell me he's been made a brigadier?' Jack could hear the two men talking and finally one of them called out.

'Just one of you come forward. There are two of us here and we have you covered.' Jack got up and walked slowly towards them, he had left his rifle with Caachy and he held his hands above his head. When he had halved the distance, the two troopers came towards him and one of them spoke.

'What was the name of the Chaplin at Chipata, when you left?'

'Cecil,' said Jack, 'Cecil, Cecil, fat as Friar Tuck, Swope, I think.'

'You'll do, where are the others?'

'I've got one with me, my tracker, and the other two are a few hundred yards further back.'

'Well, call them up Sir, and Bill here will take you back to our position.'

The patrol had eaten when they got there but the four of them were fed and settled in for the night and the next morning were lent four horses and escorted by one of the troopers back towards Nakonde, where the rest of the Third Rhodesian Irregulars were camped. The first two officers they met had been with the Fifth at Chipata with Jack and soon introduced the other two to everyone in the Officers' mess. Caachy had been taken by Bill to the Corporals' billets. That evening, Jack, Chadwyck and James sat down with the Colonel after dinner to work out the best way for them to continue their journey.

'I should be able to set up some motorised transport for you between here and Mbala, the road runs parallel to the border and we use it a lot. From there you can make your own way to Mpulungu where you should be able to pick up a boat to take you around the southern tip of Lake Tanganyika to Ndole Bay. I wouldn't recommend going any further north on the lake, because the Germans pretty much control the whole thing.'

'That must be pretty close to the Belgium border.' said James.

'It is, and from there you must head west past Lake Mweru until you reach Pweto. Alternatively, you could follow the lake and head north to Moba, but I wouldn't recommend it because you would have to cross the Marungu Mountains. That would be pretty heavy going and you would be entirely on your own. I've been told that the Belgians are moving a lot of their men north from Pweto to Albertville and beyond, in preparation for an attack on Kigoma, once the German fleet can be neutralised.'

'Well that sounds fairly straightforward Sir,' said Chadwyck. We'll hitch a ride when we can and we'll walk when we can't. At least we won't have to keep a weather eye out for the Bosch and we can shoot for the pot with impunity. I'm looking forward to it!' and he grinned at James.

'When do you want to leave,' asked the Colonel 'you can rest up here, if you like, until I find transport for you.'

'That's very kind of you, Sir.' said James 'We've been given very comfortable quarters and will await your orders.'

Three weeks later, having walked almost all the way from Ndole Bay to Pweto and at least half the remaining distance between Pweto and Albertville, they arrived, exactly three weeks to the day after they had left the Third Rhodesian Irregulars at Nakonde.

CHAPTER 56

On August 23rd 1915, the day that Italy declared war on Turkey, Edward landed at Mudros. His squadron of BB 2s, their crews, riggers and mechanics were part of the re-enforcements from England sent out to Sir Ian Hamilton, then G.O.C. the British Army in Gallipoli. From there, they moved to Sedd-el-Bahr, on the north side of the entrance to the Dardanelles and were attached to a French Division, under the command of General d'A1nade. General Joffre had sent the French Division to the Dardanelles, even though he considered it to be a lost cause, to strengthen his own position when persuading the British Authorities, on a quid-pro-quo basis, to co-operate with the French in the Salonica expedition. The squadron's orders were to spot for the land-based Allied Artillery, as well as the twelve- and fifteen-inch guns of the French and British Navies. They also had to intercept and discourage German and Turkish 'planes, who were spotting for their artillery and strafing the Allied trenches.

As a result of the developments in Salonica, the War Office decided to evacuate the three British Armies and their Allies from the Dardanelles during the month of December. A major factor in their decision was the unwarranted losses for so little gained, almost two hundred thousand killed, wounded, sick or missing. The weather was atrocious, winter conditions worse than they had been for many years and the enemy, partly through lack of appropriate clothing, were suffering more than the Allies. On 15 December, under the overall command of General Sir Charles Monro, the first of the three armies started their evacuation from Suvla Bay. Intricate preparations went into sustaining the daily barrages and combat unchanged, as well as in maintaining the highest level of secrecy. Edward and his Anglo-French Squadron were amongst the very few who were aware of the overall plan of evacuation. They had to know, as their job was to watch for and report on any enemy reaction to their manoeuvres.

The evacuation took place at night, and the enemy were convinced that whatever activity they did notice was no more than the arrival of re-enforcements. During the day the fighting continued as before, along the ridges of Krithia and Achi-Baba. Towards Christmas, the number of German Scouts in the air increased dramatically and, although Edward's Squadron was strengthened by other Allied 'planes, they were still under severe pressure. Because of the general conditions and constant bombardment on both sides, sleep was sporadic. Accumulative fatigue was wearing them down and they were losing that necessary edge, essential to their survival.

On Boxing Day, their third sortie seemingly over, Edward and the two others in his flight turned their noses towards home. It was not to be. Six German Fockers, the sun at their backs, swooped behind in a perfectly co-ordinated ambush. Edward's wing man was first in their sights. Edward threw his plane into a sharp turn, trying to come to the man's aid. But it left him oblivious to the approach of another German. All his attention focused on the dog fight ahead, Edward's first notion of danger came from that terrible sound of machine gun bullets tearing through the fabric of his own plane. The last round hit home, ripping through his left side just below the shoulder blade. The shock wrenched the stick from his hands. The bullet had nicked the edge of one lung, tore his gold cigarette case through the front of his flying jacket and on out the other side of the fuselage. Numbed by the shock, Edward struggled to regain control, dropping all the time, from seven thousand feet to fifteen hundred, leaving the fight above and behind. He fought the rising panic, his entire focus on trying to land the aircraft safely. There was blood everywhere and his left arm and hand would not respond. He realised that he was losing control of himself, as much as of his machine. The rudder was jammed and even using all his remaining strength, he could not bring the 'plane round towards his own airfield. He was heading straight out to sea, mercifully flying level but he knew he would soon have to ditch. The last thing he saw before he did was the blurred outline of a British destroyer, just as he cleared its funnels.

By the time he hit the water, a longboat was being launched to recover him. The evacuation continued, while Edward was transferred to the sickbay and later to the first troop transport ship scheduled to leave for England. By 9 January 1916, with virtually no casualties and in possession of almost all their guns, the Allies were evacuated from Suvla Bay, Anzac and Helles.

CHAPTER 57

By early October, Chadwyck and Jack had settled into the new Naval Base at Albertville, next to the native quarter. James and Caachy had been sent further north to Makungu and attached to a Belgium company, billeted three miles west of the lake, opposite the German Naval Base at Kigoma. There was a powerful radio station at Albertville which enabled Chadwyck to communicate with Admiral King-Hall in Simonstown, relayed through Bulawayo. Jack had been assigned to one of the Rhodesian engineer companies building the new port three miles south of their camp using surplus stone from the railway, just completed. When it was almost finished, a vicious storm destroyed about eighty yards of the southern breakwater. It was rebuilt with much larger stones from a new quarry, found near to the site, and soon completed by some five hundred native labourers working around the clock.

At the beginning of December, Commander Spicer-Simson and his entire expedition finally arrived at Albertville, having left the two boats three miles inland at Makala, concealed until the work on the new dock could be completed. Doctor Hanschell, who had accompanied the expedition from the start, was not pleased with the close proximity of the native quarter with its open drains. Commander Spicer-Simson decided to move the existing camp nearer to the new dock. Once he had settled in he sent for Chadwyck.

'I hear you are here to spy on me?' Chadwyck, taken aback by his greeting, saluted, removed his cap and stood in front of Spicer-Simson, who was seated at his desk.

'Not quite how the Admiral put it, Sir and how do you do?' Spicer-Simson got up and walked around his desk and stood behind Chadwyck, his rounded shoulders emphasised by the way he held his hands clasped behind his back. Chadwyck turned to face him and looked straight into his light grey eyes, two foot from his own. Spicer-Simson, Chadwyck's height and at least three stone heavier, had unusually close-cropped hair and a fastidiously trimmed Van Dyke beard.

'I don't give a damn how the Admiral put it, you're under my command now and you'll do things my way.' He spoke out of one side of his month with a pronounced nasal drawl, which Chadwyck found affected.

'Yes, Sir,' said Chadwyck, noticing for the first time that Spicer-Simson's uniform was different from his own, in several ways.

'Do you like it, boy?'

'What, Sir?'

'My uniform, of course, I designed it myself. All my officers, including you, will have to wear it, now that we are a separate Command.' And he laughed at the expression on Chadwyck's face and returned to his desk. 'That's all Meade, and nothing is transmitted without it first passing my desk, do you understand?'

'Yes, Sir,' Chadwyck replaced his cap, saluted and left the office. As he closed the door behind him, he bumped into a young officer, waiting to go in, who stepped back and said,

'I'm sorry. I'm Arthur Dudley, his number two and you must be Chadwyck Meade.'

'Yes,' said Chadwyck, 'and don't you say that I have been sent here to spy on you by the Admiral.'

'Is that what he said? He is not known for his tact but I'll make it up to you, over a drink or two in the mess, this evening.'

The next morning, Spicer-Simson summoned all his officers.

They stood in a semi-circle in front of his desk and, to Chadwyck's amazement, he found that Spicer-Simson was wearing a lavalava, a type of Polynesian kilt, below a white jacket.

'Good morning, Gentlemen.' He walked along behind them, looking at each one of them up and down, before returning to his desk. 'I have been told that the dockyard will be finished in the next few days and I want you, Wainwright, to organise a fatigue party and bring Dog and Cat down to the new dock.'

'*Mimi* and *Toutou*, Sir?'

'Whatever,' said Spicer-Simson, peremptorily, 'a stupid Naval tradition to dub all ships with female names, to me they are still Dog and Cat.' He went back to his chair and put his feet up on his desk and Chadwyck was fascinated to see the convoluted tattoos of birds and butterflies that completely covered his legs from his ankles to the hem of the lavalava.

'I have news for you all;, it seems we have more opposition than expected. Not only the *Kingani*, which was seen this morning steaming north and the *Hedwig von Wissmann*, which are here for us to destroy, but our Belgium brothers-at-arms have just told me that there is a third German vessel on the lake, newly built, of some eight hundred tons and goes by the name of *Graf von Gotzem*. Apart from the armament you would expect on a ship of that size, she is also armed with one of the *Konigsberg*'s four-inch guns, which you, Meade, failed to destroy on your first attempt. Once the launches are in their new dock, I want you, Wainwright, to post look-outs ten miles north and south of our base, to keep an eye on the Bosch and meanwhile, we will do some speed and gunnery trials.'

Three days later, the entire company, including Chadwyck, were paraded dockside, above where the two launches were moored. Spicer-Simson detailed a sub-lieutenant and four ratings to take one of the old tenders out, which had been rigged with a floating target. This they would tow a hundred yards behind them and the remaining officers and ratings were ordered aboard the two launches. When *Mimi* and *Toutou* had first been floated the mechanics and maintenance teams had found them both leaking badly because the seams had opened in the extreme heat, during the long overland journey. A lot of work had also gone into tuning the engines and realigning the propeller shafts, but now they were considered seaworthy. They were both powered by twin one hundred horsepower petrol engines, which had driven them at nineteen knots during the initial sea trial. They each had a three-pounder mounted forward and a Maxim machine gun, aft. Their petrol tanks were protected with additional plating against machine gun and rifle fire. The three-pounders could fire only dead ahead, due to the lack of support beneath the foredeck.

The previous day a measured mile had been set up between two buoys. The tender with the target steamed out to one, while Spicer-Simson, commanding *Mimi* and followed by *Toutou*, headed out for the other. *Mimi* swung around facing the buoy, while *Toutou* continued on a further half mile and turned back, to face the buoy. Sub-Lieutenant Wainwright stood beside Spicer-Simson with a flag in one hand and a stopwatch in the other. When *Toutou* had turned towards them, he held the flag above his head for a moment and then dropped it and *Toutou* headed towards them, gaining speed as she went. By the time she passed the buoy she was running at her maximum speed and Wainwright pressed the button on his stopwatch. *Toutou* tore on across the lake towards the other buoy and as she passed it, they heard a pistol shot and Wainwright pressed the button again, on his stopwatch.

'Well?' said Spicer-Simson.

'Just a moment, Sir,' said Wainwright, scribbling on a pad, 'just over fifteen knots, Sir.'

'Right, signal them to do it again and time them to see if the tail wind makes any difference.'

Toutou turned around a few hundred yards beyond the other buoy and then sped towards them. As she passed the buoy, Wainwright clicked the button on his watch the moment he heard the pistol shot. Spicer-Simson said nothing and, after a quick calculation, Wainwright looked up and said,

'Almost sixteen knots, Sir.'

'All right, flag them back here and now it's our turn.' *Toutou* pulled up alongside *Mimi* and Wainwright jumped aboard. 'Now we will see which one is the better boat,' said Spicer-Simson, 'anyone want to bet against me?' There were no takers and *Mimi* cut away to the starting point while *Toutou* took up her place by the buoy. Wainwright pressed the button on his watch when *Mimi* passed them and again when he heard the pistol shot. It was a half knot faster than *Toutou*'s time and he assumed the return would be the same.

'Well,' said Spicer-Simson, as *Mimi* drew up alongside, 'was I right?'

'Yes Sir, there was about half knot in it.'

'Right, then from now on *Mimi* is my flagship.' Chadwyck barely smothered a laugh. 'Something funny, Meade?'

'No Sir, I think I'm getting a cold.'

'Report to the M.O. and I'll have one less blighter to keep an eye on.'

The tender was already steaming out towards the middle of the lake and, as she went, she paid out the line on the floating target, until it was following in her wake.

'Right, Dudley, you take *Toutou* out first and position yourself so that the target is passing across your front and about one mile from you. Fire three shots, with the three-pounder as fast as you can, as you approach. If at least one shot doesn't hit the target, I shall want to know why.'

'Yes, Sir,' said Arthur and *Toutou* headed out into the lake, followed closely by *Mimi*. Chadwyck was standing close to Arthur on the bridge, while the gunnery officer and his crew loaded the three-pounder on the foredeck. Chadwyck could see the tender about a mile and a half ahead , travelling at about ten knots.

'What speed does the *Kingani* do, Arthur?'

'About fifteen knots, about the same as us but from guns' point of view, it makes little difference as long as one is within range. Fire when ready!' shouted Arthur through a megaphone. *Toutou* checked violently as the gun fired and both of them were thrown forward against the bridge rail. When they recovered, Arthur turned to Chadwyck, 'Now I know why they fitted the gun on fixed mounts, facing forward. If it had been mounted mid-ships and fired broadside, we would now be rolled over, keel upper most.'

The shot landed in line with the target but a hundred yards short. By the time they had reloaded, they had already covered that discrepancy and fired again without re-sighting. The second shot went through the right-hand corner of the twenty foot square target, knocking it so far over that they could both see the orange painted bottom, of the float. A spontaneous cheer went up from the foredeck. Because the relative positions between them were changing, Chadwyck noticed that the target and tender were becoming dangerously close to one another.

'Shouldn't we realign?' he said and Arthur nodded and spoke to the helmsman. Using their superior speed they came up level with the tender and about a thousand yards from it before turning towards it and firing the third shot. Used to the recoil, they both gripped the rail as the gun fired and were disappointed to see the shot land slightly to the right of the target and two hundred yards beyond it.

'One out of three is good shooting,' said Chadwyck but Arthur only grunted and waited for *Mimi* to come up alongside. It was *Mimi's* turn and Chadwyck knew that Spicer-Simson would be unbearable if he managed to hit two out of three.

* * *

After nearly two months of stultifying inactivity, James was ordered to take out a patrol from the Belgium post near Makungu and to head north along the western shore of the lake. They had rations for a week and their job was to report on any enemy activity on the lake north of Kigoma. They had had a report that the *Kingani* had been moving troops and stores over to the Belgium side of the lake. Within three days they were back at their post, having confirmed that it was just another native rumour; as was so often the case when the natives were offered money for information, they just made it up. To keep an eye on any possible enemy movement, James had left a corporal and two askaris in a fly-camp on the shore, with the remainder of their rations and orders to report back to their post when their rations were finished.

James had been given permission by his commanding officer to set up his own intelligence network, with the help of Caachy and a locally recruited askari, who spoke Bantu and other tribal languages. James changed the payment system, so that the native scouts soon knew that they would not receive any remuneration until the information had been substantiated. To begin with, native intelligence almost dried up but slowly James and his C.O. were able to build up a more accurate picture of what the Germans were actually doing and planning. Towards the end of December, a report came in that the armed German trawler *Kingani* was being refitted at Kingoma and was due to sail in a few days. This information was immediately radioed to HQ, at Albertville.

* * *

On Sunday, 26 December, *Kingani* appeared opposite the Naval Base, while Spicer-Simson was conducting a church parade. In the best traditions of Drake, he finished the service before sending his men to action stations. He allowed the *Kingani* to proceed further south to prevent her from returning to her base at Kigoma before he could intercept her. Spicer-Simson took command of *Mimi* and Arthur with Chadwyck, were in command of *Toutou*. In line abreast, they pursued the *Kingani* and when about two thousand yards astern of her, they opened fire, as they slowly shortened the distance.

'She is making a run for it,' said Chadwyck, as she swung about and headed north 'and look at the black smoke billowing from her funnel, she must be pouring oil into her firebox, to increase her speed.' Arthur immediately changed course, in an attempt to intercept her at closer range.

'We'll run up on her starboard quarter,' said Arthur 'and zig zag as we go, to avoid her fire. Go forward and tell guns' to fire on her every time we swing through her.' *Kingani* was firing back whenever she could bring her six-pounder to bear on *Toutou* or *Mimi*, who was copying *Toutou*'s tactics. As they approached nearer, a shell from *Toutou*'s three-pounder exploded on the foredeck of the *Kingani* just behind the six-pounder gun shield and within a minute a second shell from *Toutou* pierced the *Kingani*'s hull, on the water line. Their six-pounder had stopped firing and she started to list.

'She's sinking,' said Chadwyck.

'Better than that, she is surrendering,' this, they both saw at the same time, as the *Kingani* hauled down her colours. A cheer went up from the foredeck of *Toutou* and Spicer-Simson, waving wildly, ordered *Mimi* to cut across *Toutou*'s bows and head straight towards *Kingani*. Tate, the helmsmen, through inexperience and excitement, miscalculated the distance between the two boats and rammed *Kingani* amidships, throwing Spicer-Simson flat on the deck, where he had been standing in full view of the enemy, throughout the action. *Mimi* was badly damaged and started to take on water from the bows and a chastened Spicer-Simson ordered her back to the dock, while *Toutou* escorted *Kingani* at a slower pace, while her surviving crew worked frantically at her pumps to keep her afloat. When they got back to the breakwater, Chadwyck went on board *Kingani* with Doctor Hanschell, to take care of the wounded.

'Where is Spicer-Simson?' said Chadwyck as they climbed the gangway.

'Unavailable, I think,' said Doctor Hanschell. 'He was holding a bloodied handkerchief to his nose when I saw him as he stormed into his quarters, completely ignoring my greeting. What happened?'

'Well,' said Chadwyck. 'He did appear a little foolish to all of us on deck when he was thrown flat on his face, on impact with the enemy.'

'Hence the bloody nose,' said Doctor Hanschell.

'Yes,' agreed Chadwyck, 'and public humiliation, which I am sure we'll all have to pay for.' Doctor Hanschell laughed and moved across to the six-pounder gun. The remaining interior of its turret was plastered with blood and badly distorted by the explosion. Within, they found the remains of the Captain and two gunners, whose bodies had been ripped apart by the explosion. The only thing left alive on the foredeck, was a white goat tied to one of the stanchions and bleating, piteously. The remaining crew from below deck were taken ashore under guard and locked up. Arthur questioned the senior survivor and found out that there had been a total complement of sixteen, of which three were dead and two missing. Half an hour later, Spicer-Simson reappeared and went aboard *Kingani*. Two of Doctor Hanschell's orderlies were doing their best to sort out the dismembered limbs of the Captain and gun crew, to remove them for burial.

They all stood back as Spicer-Simson approached and watched silently as he bent forward and removed the signet ring from the Captain's finger and put it on his own. Doctor Hanscheel was about to say something when Arthur put a restraining hand on his arm and said to Spicer-Simson, 'When would you like to file the report, Sir?'

'I've already done it and dispatched it to the Admiralty.'

'But we haven't submitted our report yet, Sir.'

'Not needed,' said Spicer-Simson, 'I've made it all quite clear to the Admiralty and I am sure they will be well pleased with what we've done.'

'Yes Sir,' said Arthur, 'I'm sure. Is there anything else, Sir or may we go to our quarters?'

'Carry on.' he said and led the way ashore. Chadwyck and Arthur waited until he was well ahead of them before Chadwyck said, 'I would like to see that report.'

'So would I,' said Arthur. 'Let's see who is on duty at the radio shack.' Once Spicer-Simson was out of sight, they doubled back to the radio shack and found Signalman Hopkins in charge, who leapt to his feet, when he saw Arthur.

'At ease Hopkins, just come down to check that the Skipper's report went out to the Admiralty.'

'Yes Sir, I have the original here,' and he picked up a pad with Spicer-Simson's distinctive writing on it and handed it to Arthur. Chadwyck moved behind his shoulder and they read it together, neither of them said anything.

'Thank you,' said Arthur returning the pad, 'No problem with the transmission?'

'No Sir, none at all.'

The two of them left the radio shack and walked slowly back towards their billet. Neither of them said a word to begin with and finally Chadwyck, who couldn't contain his amazement and anger any longer, blurted out, 'I don't bloody believe it, I just don't believe it. How many hits did he claim?'

'Twelve,' said Arthur, 'out of thirteen shots. A total impossibility, that will be seen by anyone in the Admiralty, who reads the report, to be a blatant fabrication. Never, ever, in any action, has any vessels ever scored twelve hits out of thirteen shots.'

'I don't think *Mimi* scored a single hit,' said Chadwyck. '*Kingani* was only hit twice and both times by us, one shot after another and I am not sure if we weren't between *Mimi* and *Kingani* at the time, so she couldn't have hit her, let alone twelve times.'

'So who is going to write the damage report on *Kingani*?' said Arthur.

'I'm not, I'll not put my name to it.' They had reached the guard house, at the main gate and Arthur spoke to the sergeant, as they saluted.

'Sergeant Jones, I want you to detail a guard on the graves of the German dead, once they are buried, I don't want them to be dug up tonight by the Belgium askaris and eaten.'

'You're joking, Sir,' he said, incredulously.

'No I am not, Sergeant, half of their askaris have been conscripted from cannibal tribes.'

'As you say Sir, right away.'

* * *

The Admiralty was delighted with Spicer-Simson's version of events and substantiated his appointment as Commander. They also enclosed the text of a telegram from the King, congratulating them all. *Kingani* was repaired, re-floated and recommissioned as HMS *Fifi*. Her old six-pounder was removed and replaced with a twelve-pounder quick firing gun that had been sent by the Admiralty for the Belgium steamer *Baron Dhanis*, still in sections at Kabalo, waiting to be entrained to Albertville. Spicer-Simson and the Belgium Commandant fell out over their relative seniority and, after various signals between their respective governments, it was agreed that the Belgium Commandant was in command on land and Spicer-Simson on the lake. The Belgium steamer *Delcommune* was re-floated, renamed *Vengeur* and armed with the *Kingani* six-pounder, which still had some two hundred shells left.

CHAPTER 58

At the beginning of February, James was recalled to Fife by the C.O.
of the Northern Rhodesian Rifles. On their way south, he and Caachy
stopped at the Naval Base at Albertvillle to look in on Chadwyck.
Doctor Hanschell, who was concerned about the possibility of
deterioration in the general health of the company, had persuaded
Spicer-Simson to have a new camp built on the hill behind the
Harbour, with emphasis on hygiene and proper sanitation. Spicer-
Simson, very aware of the natives' growing deification of him, took
to bathing publicly, with great ceremony at precisely four o'clock on
Wednesday and Saturday afternoons. The natives surrounded his
canvas bath by the hundreds and watched in awe, while he stood
naked, soaping himself and flexing his muscles, so that the tattooed
snakes appeared to writhe around his body.

The morning after James's arrival, the *Hedwig von Wissmann* was
seen steaming south, four miles off-shore. The officers were having
breakfast in the mess, when Spicer-Simson called for action stations.

'Take me with you, Chad, this could be fun.'

'You shouldn't but I suppose you can come as a military observer,
my responsibility.'

'What will Spicer-Simson say, won't he have you on the mat?'

'He won't know in time to stop us.'

'Right skipper, lead on.'

'We'll get my kit first and join up with Arthur. We have been assigned to *Mimi* and Spicer-Simon will command *Fifi*.' Nobody paid any attention to James in the scramble that followed, as everyone was concentrating on collecting their kit and getting on board their respective vessels, as fast as possible. The *Hedwig von Wissman* was armed with two six-pounders, one forward and the other aft with a Hotchkiss machine gun, mounted on the transom. Knowing that he had the greater range with the quick firing twelve-pounder and believing *Fifi* to be a knot or two faster than the *Hedwig*, Spicer-Simson sailed northeast out of Kalemie to intercept. Arthur, Chadwyck and James followed in *Mimi*, *Toutou* was still laid up for repairs. The light was very tricky, with mirages causing chaos amongst the gunners over size and range. The surface of the lake was like a mill pond, making it almost impossible to differentiate between air and water. From the shore it appeared that all three boats were floating in the sky. At ten o'clock, Spicer-Simson fired the first shot at *Hedwig* and *Fifi* stopped dead in her tracks, as a result of the recoil of the twelve-pounder. The target image was so distorted that they were unable to correct their aim and Spicer-Simson realised that *Hedwig* was in fact slightly faster than *Fifi* and she soon started to pull away.

'We're going to lose her,' said Chadwyck, 'if we stay on station.'

'So we won't. Watch me show a clean pair of heels, to the old man,' said Arthur and he eased the throttle forward making *Mimi* surge ahead, past *Fifi*. Arthur ignored all of Spicer-Simson's frantic semaphore signals and *Mimi* was soon in range of *Hedwig*. Arthur opened fire and his intention was not so much to sink her but to force her to turn her six-pound gun on him, thereby slowing her down so that *Fifi* could catch up and destroy her.

Mimi's first shot fell just in front of *Hedwig*'s bow and once *Mimi* had reloaded she moved up closer, using her superior speed and fired again. Meanwhile, the machine gun on the aft deck of *Hedwig* opened up on *Mimi* and sent a stream of bullets clattering across the shield of the six-pounder. *Mimi* fired at the same time and the shell tore into the superstructure aft of the bridge, exploded and scattered debris over the aft deck. The machine gun crew stopped firing and dived for cover, as the *Hedwig* swung around to face *Mimi*, at five hundred yards. Her first shot cleared *Mimi*'s mast head by no more than twenty feet and Arthur swung the wheel to starboard before they could fire again.

'We'll circle them,' said Arthur,' make them pivot on the spot, until *Fifi* catches up.'

'I'm going forward,' said James, 'to join the gun crew on the six-pounder, I want to see how it works.'

'All right, but keep your head down.'

Mimi surged ahead and came around to *Hedwig*'s quarter, and when Arthur brought *Mimi*'s bow back to bear on *Hedwig*, the gun crew fired again. The shell tore over the bridge of *Hedwig* because, by then, *Mimi* was only four hundred yards from her and closing fast. Arthur turned the wheel to port to clear *Hedwig*'s stern and, as he did so, the machine gun crew on her transom opened fire again. The bullets arched across the gap between them, scything down beside the six-pounder and one of them caught James through the back of his head, just to the right of his left ear and came out through his forehead at the hairline, above his left eye. He has been standing behind, but just outside, the gun shield. He was thrown forward across the shell bin, rolled back onto the deck and caught up against one of the forward mooring stanchions. *Hedwig* was swinging around to face them and bring her six-pound gun to bear. Neither Chadwyck nor Arthur had seen James go down because they were watching *Fifi*, as she approached within range and opened fire with her twelve-pounder. The shell tore into *Hedwig*'s hull, amidships on the waterline and a second later her magazine exploded. She started to sink and Arthur continued to circle around her as the surviving crew leapt overboard. He was intending to move in and pick them up when Sub-Lieutenant Shaw shouted back to him, from the six-pounder.

'Lieutenant Flynn is hit, Sir!' Chadwyck went forward on the double, skidded to a stop near James and dropped to his knees. He could see a trickle of blood running down towards his left ear and he noticed that his right arm twitched repeatedly, Chadwyck put his fingertips to James's neck and felt for his pulse. He found it tapping gently and started to turn him over.

'Come on, old boy, say something, are you all right?' He stopped short as he saw the exit hole of the bullet on James's hairline, just above his left eye. Chadwyck took off his jacket, folded it several times and eased it between James' head and the deck. By this time, Arthur had handed the wheel over to the coxswain and gone forward, to join Chadwyck.

'Arthur, we must get him to the doctor as soon as possible, he's been shot through the head and probably suffered some brain damage, look at the exit hole. He is still alive but he must be operated on as soon as possible.' Without moving, Arthur shouted,

'Flags, signal *Fifi* that we're heading in!' and to Chadwyck he added, 'They can pick up the survivors. Lieutenant, call up the medic for a stretcher and some blankets.' He looked up at the bridge and yelled to the helmsmen, ' Fisher, head for home, maximum revs!' *Mimi* surged ahead and swung in a wide arc until she was pointing straight towards the Naval Dockyard and her bow wave streamed out behind her. By the time they reached the break water and pulled up at the dock, they had James cocooned in blankets and strapped to a stretcher. Chadwyck hadn't left his side for a moment and had noticed that his right arm spasmed occasionally and his eyelids fluttered in unison with his arm. Twice he had tried to speak but had managed nothing coherent. Two ratings lifted the stretcher off the deck gently, carried James ashore and headed up the hill to the hospital. Chadwyck ran ahead, shouting for Doctor Hanschell and found him attending his patients.

'James has been shot, Doctor, through the head, small calibre machine gun. They are bringing him up now, where can we put him?'

'Follow me,' and he led Chadwyck into the operating theatre, shouting for two assistants by name, at the same time. He immediately started to scrub up, put on a gown and wheeled a tray of surgical instruments from the sterilizer, towards the operating table.

'Over here.' he said, as the stretched bearers appeared at the door. 'Gently now, unstrap him, remove the blankets and ease him onto the table. Thank you, you can go now and you too Chadwyck but, before you do, tell me exactly what happened.' While his assistants prepared James for surgery, Chadwyck told Doctor Hanschell all that he could recall, in as much detail as possible.

'How long since he was actually hit?'

Chadwyck looked at his watch, 'a little over thirty minutes ago, I would say.'

'How rough was your return?'

'Dead smooth and at maximum speed.'

'How far did he fall, when he was hit?'

'I didn't see it happen but it could only have been his own length.'

'And he mumbled twice?'

'Yes sir, nothing I could understand but he was obviously trying to say something. '

'All right, that's it for now. Please wait outside, I'll be some time.' Chadwyck went back to the dock and found Arthur.

'How is he doing?'

'I don't know, I told the Doctor everything I could and he was totally non-committal. He asked me a few questions and then threw me out.'

'And there will be a lot more question when *Fifi* gets in,' said Arthur, waiving his hand in the direction of the incoming vessel.

'Don't worry,' said Chadwyck, 'I can sort out Spicer-Simson.'

'How?'

'I'll tell him I pulled rank, which I could have done and take full responsibility for it. He will insist I am recalled but that doesn't matter as I would want to go anyhow with James, if he lives. I know, it will go against the grain with you but you must back me up, or he will make your life hell. Will that be all right with you, Arthur?'

'But it is not true, Chad, I gave the commands and every man jack of the crew knows it.'

'And so you would have, because you were acting under my

orders. You must agree, Arthur because you know that if you don't, he will demote you, or worse.'

All right, but I don't like it.'

'I know, but nobody but the two of us will ever know and remember, our action might save James's life.'

'I hope they picked up all the survivors, God knows, how many were killed.'

'There must have been a lot of damage below the waterline,' said Chadwyck. 'I couldn't believe she went down so quickly. There was no sign of her by the time we were a mile from the action.'

Together they walked down to the breakwater and stood at the dock where *Fifi* would tie up. Spicer-Simson leapt ashore before *Fifi*'s lines were secured. He stood before Chadwyck and Arthur, with his shoulders rolled forward, his face beet red and spluttering incoherently until finally he managed to gain control of himself.

'I'll court martial you both,' he screamed, 'you're finished, I'll see to that. I'll report you both to the Admiral and meanwhile, have you thrown in the brig!!'

'So shall I, Sir,' said Chadwyck, when Spicer-Simson paused briefly to draw breath.

'So shall you what?'

'Report to the Admiral, Sir, that is my job. I shall tell him that I took temporary command of *Mimi*, which I was perfectly entitled to do as I outrank Lieutenant Dudley and ordered *Mimi* to return to base, with a critically injured man. It was my decision, Sir and mine only. No one on *Mimi* had any other option, including Lieutenant Dudley.'

'Is that so, Dudley? '

'Yes, Sir.'

'Look at me, man! Is that how it happened?'

Arthur looked straight at him and said, 'Yes, Sir, that is how it happened.'

'You disobeyed my direct semaphore signal to stop, Meade.'

'I don't think it was seen, Sir, and in any case, I would have had to countermand my order, before anyone else could have acted on your signal, had they seen it.'

'Don't play silly buggers with me, Meade, I also signalled you to pick up survivors, which you disobeyed.'

'I hope you managed to recover them all, Sir and I am sorry that we were unable to help but it was a critical situation and every minute counted. The patient is in surgery with Doctor Hanschell right now.'

'And who, might I ask, is this special patient?' his voice dripped with sarcasm.

'Lieutenant James Flynn, Sir, of the Grey's Scouts attached to the Rhodesian Rifles, who was on his way back to his unit in Fife.'

'And what, may I also ask,' there was a dangerous edge to his voice, 'was Mr Flynn doing on *Mimi*?'

'I invited him, Sir.'

'I see and I suppose you Dudley, didn't know he was there. '

'No, Sir, I gave my permission. We've taken Allied other services on exercises before.'

'Well you better hope he doesn't die, because it will be you who has to explain it to his CO.'

'Yes, Sir.'

'I see you have the *Hedwig*'s colours there, Sir.' said Chadwyck.

'Yes,' said Spicer-Simson, brandishing the flag that he has been clutching in his hand, 'a trophy that will go well on my wall. You were right Dudley, you did the right thing. Meade does outrank you so we'll say no more about it or that you overtook *Fifi*, against my semaphored orders, when you should have returned to your station. Your initiative made it possible for us to catch up and destroy the enemy.'

'Thank you Sir, will that be all?'

'Yes, for now but you, Meade will hear more from me, once I have heard from the Admiral.'

Chadwyck and Arthur sat for more than two hours outside the operating theatre, before Doctor Hanschell finally came out. They both stood as he walked towards them, stripping off his gloves and removing his gown.

'He's alive,' he said, 'but he still has a long way to go. Fortunately it was a perforated wound and the bullet went through the right frontal lobe tip, and out through the forehead. It was well above the lower regions, thus missing the brainstem, which would have killed him instantly. I had to drill a hole in his skull, it's known as trepanation, nothing new, it's a procedure that has been in use for thousands of years, to relieve the pressure caused by the passage of the bullet.'

'Will he live, Sir?' asked Chadwyck.

'I can't tell you that now, it depends on so many different factors. At the moment, he's in a coma and it is far too soon to know how long it will last.'

'So he can't be moved? He was on his way to join his unit at Fife.'

'Good heavens no, the next two weeks is critical. He must remain here, without movement and I will watch him like hawk. I have given him as much morphine as I dare and hopefully I can prevent any infection from developing. There are two good things in our favour. Firstly, you got him here as quickly as you did and secondly, I have at my disposal, in this God forsaken place, all the instruments and medication that I needed.'

'Thank you Doctor for what you've done. I have to make a report to the Admiral and would like to come back later to see him, if I may?'

'By all means, about six o'clock this evening, would be a good time.'

'Come on, Arthur, let's get our reports written.' They turned back towards the Officers' Mess.

'What are you going to tell the Admiral about James?'

'I don't know, I just don't know. If I underplay it and it conflicts radically with your boss's report. It could become complicated.'

'Complicated, like you could end up back on civvy street?'

'I really wouldn't mind if I did, it's not my war. I joined the Navy for the wrong reasons.'

'I know, because of Adelaide, but I think it soon will be your war.'

'You are probably right, but then I'll join the American Navy. I told you about Adelaide and how I reacted because' he paused and ran the fingers of both his hands through his hair 'but now if James dies...' he left the sentence unfinished.

'You will be indirectly responsible for two deaths in the Flynn family.'

'Succinctly put, Arthur, no sugar-coating, no beating about the bush, but you are right. I should never have let him come. But we are brothers in law, partners and damn it, Arthur, he saved my life just two days after I met him. I just could not say no to him.'

'When the outcome manifests itself, so too does the right choice but invariably too late.'

'Very profound, Arthur, but what do I tell my father-in-law? If James dies, it would devastate him and that, in turn, would destroy Jenny.'

'Nothing until the doctor has had his two weeks. There is no point in distressing them when we don't know. We just don't have the answers,' His tone softened. 'You, as a person, Chad have done nothing wrong, fate stepped in, leaving you to carry the can. You just made the wrong decision. Now let's get our reports done and get some lunch.'

* * *

'What did the Doctor have to say, today?' It was almost three weeks since the sinking of *Hedwig* and Chadwyck and Arthur were sitting on the veranda in front of the Officers' Mess, drinking sun-downers.

'He's gradually improving, Arthur, he is more responsive and if the Doctor can keep infection at bay, he has a chance of recovery but, to what degree, nobody yet knows.'

'What's happened to his native, I haven't seen him for some time.'

'He has been given quarters behind the hospital and hasn't moved since James was admitted. I've looked in on him several times and he is well taken care of, his needs have always been minimal.'

'And what about the other chap that came with you from the Rufiji? What was he called, Jack, I think?'

'He was seconded to the engineers while they built the new dock and then transferred to the Rhodesian Rifles, in Fife, when the dock was finished.'

'Have you heard back from the Admiral, yet?'

'Which one, yours or mine?' said Chadwyck with his glass to his lips.

'Yours,' laughed Arthur.

'Yes, he regrets my decision but understands my position. He made no mention of any report that your Admiral might have made. What about you, did he drag you over the coals? I can't believe nothing more is being said.'

'Nothing, he's playing his cards close to his chest, he's very uncommunicative since he let the *von Gotzen* sail past us, obviously looking for the *Hedwig*, without attacking her. Everyone thinks he was scared and I can understand why he could have been. The *von Gotzen* is about ten times bigger than anything we have, a lot faster and able to outgun us, at any level.'

'Perhaps he's frightened of blotting his copy book. With two victories to his credit, he obviously doesn't want a major reversal, which would have been the probable outcome, if he had tangled with the *von Gotzen*.'

'Could be, he's talking of bringing up another vessel from Boma, on the coast.'

'The Admiral told me, in his last dispatch, that next month they are going to build a sea plane base at Tongwe, which is about twenty miles north of here. They plan to use British sea planes with Belgium pilots and the idea is to destroy the *von Gotzen*, with bombs. When is Spicer-Simson going down to the coast?'

'Soon, I think, why do you ask?'

'I was just thinking it might be the best way to take James home. '

'Is that what you're going to do?'

'Yes. We could take the train to Kabalo and travel from there down the upper Congo river on one of the stern wheelers, join the Congo and take it all the way down to Boma, on the coast. There we can pick up a ship heading south to Cape Town and install James at Springbokfontein, where I can provide any medical treatment he needs. I would also see the Admiral at Simonstown and formerly resign my commission and then, when James is fully recovered, he and I can go up to Reitfontain and perhaps carry on working the mine.'

'That would certainly be a lot easier on him, than travelling overland and what about his parents, when are you going to tell them?'

'I'll tell them what Doctor Hanschell told me. He also gave me the name of a neurologist colleague in Cape Town to supervise James's treatment'.

'Now the two weeks are up and the Doctor has made his report,' said Chadwyck, 'I will write to them, with the whole story and invite them to Springbokfontein.'

Over the next three days Chadwyck made plans for their departure, without actually saying goodbye to anyone. He would do that when he was certain that James was stable enough to travel. Every day after that, James's condition improved and by the beginning of the following week Doctor Hanschell told Chadwyck that James was ready to travel. He added that he was sending one of his nurses, familiar with James's condition and treatment, with them till they reached the coast. That night, Chadwyck said his goodbyes and the following morning James, strapped to a stretcher, was transported to the station and he, Chadwyck, Caachy and the nurse boarded the train for Kabalo.

CHAPTER 59

On April 11th, coincidentally the same day that General Sir Charles Monro published his dispatch on the evacuation of Gallipoli, Edward arrived at Glen Lyon for four weeks' well-earned leave. He had spent the last three months recovering in a London hospital and, even with the best help available, he was still suffering from a certain immobility in his left shoulder. A month before he left the hospital he had received a letter from his mother telling him that Gerald was working for the *Washington Post* and was based in their Paris office. Missing him after so many years, Edward wrote and told him what had happened to him and that he hoped to see Gerald whenever he could get away. Within days he had had an answer from Gerald saying that he would wangle some leave once Edward knew when he would be discharged from the hospital.

Hector Macpherson met him at the station and as they drove back to the house he handed Edward a telegram, it was from Gerald, saying that he had managed to arrange two weeks' leave and would be arriving at Glen Lyon later that week.

'Great news Hector, Gerald is coming, I haven't seen him in almost three years, just before our father's funeral.'

'And we haven't seen you Sir, since then.' It was the first time that Hector had addressed him in such a way, he had always called him Master Eddy. Edward almost said something but changed his mind and asked instead.

'Are the salmon still in the river, Hector or is the spring run finished?'

'A few salmon, Sir but a lot of sea trout.' Everything seemed to remind him of his father's death and he knew it would be worse when they reached the front of the house.

'Did you build the monument, Hector, the one you suggested to my mother?'

'Yes Sir, it is between the stable block and the house, it's very simple and I think you will like it.'

'Thank you Hector, when I have seen it, I will write to my mother. Do you know I have not seen her since then. This beastly, bloody war, when will it ever end? I am so bone tired and sick to death of it all. I don't know how much longer I can keep going.' Hector's hands tightened on the wheel; he wasn't used to such unaccustomed and naked confidences. As the sun set, they turned in at the gates of Glen Lyon and pulled up in front the house. One of the gardeners appeared and took Edward's bags into the house.

'My wife has everything in readiness for you, you are in your old room, nothing much has changed since you were last here. I'll have her prepare Mr Gerald's room later.'

'Thank you Hector, I am very tired. Please tell your wife... no, I'll do it,' as he saw her standing at the top of the steps by the front door. 'Thank you for collecting me, I'll see you in the morning. I'll be up early and we'll have a crack at those sea trout you told me about.'

'I'll see you then Sir and welcome home. It is very good to see you again.'

The fishing was good and slowly Edward settled into the sedate rhythm of Glen Lyon and by the time Gerald arrived, three days later, Edward had managed to shed some of his lethargy. He was determined to re-establish the bonds of his youth with his brother. Edward had told Hector he would collect Gerald and after breakfast he set out for the station in the estate Daimler. It was a calm spring morning and, as he had two hours to spare before the train arrived, he decided to spend time in the church yard at Fortingall. There was nobody there and no sound except the blackbirds in the yew tree. He walked past the newest graves to the family plot, where his father lay buried. There were fresh flowers in a stone vase and he knew that Hector had arranged for them to be changed frequently.

It was three years since his father had died and Edward realised that this was his first proper reprieve from the constant demands of conflict, both passive and active. There seemed to be no end in sight and such a high price had already been paid. He ran through his mind an almost endless list of pilots that he had known in France and Turkey who were now all dead. A few had been with him for some months and some had died after only a few days of combat, totally unprepared to cope with the merciless demands made upon them. It seemed strange to him that the longer they flew the more likely they were to continue to do so. Some had been posted to other units and others, who just couldn't take it, had been sent home or transferred to the infantry. Having survived one near miss he wondered, dispassionately, when his number would be up. He then wondered why he was so resigned to the possibility but pleased that, for the moment, he should only be thinking of it as a possibility rather than a probability. The power of self-preservation still ran strongly through his veins.

He looked up at the sound of two voices and saw the minister and a woman he didn't recognise walking towards him. He stood up and they stopped in front of him; the minister extended his hand and Edward shook it firmly,

'Edward it is good to see you after so many years. This is Mrs. Black, my housekeeper, we have come to tidy up the church a bit.'

'It's good to see you too Mr McLeod, you're looking well and I hope to see more of you while I am here. I've been given four weeks leave and I'm now on my way to the station, to pick up Gerald.'

'Hector told me, he said you had been shot down in Turkey just before the evacuation. I was there years ago as a student and even managed to learn some of the language. I'll come up to the house one day and you can tell me all about your war.' He beamed at

Edward and led the way towards the church door, followed by his housekeeper, who curtsied to Edward as she passed. *My war*, he laughed mirthlessly, as he walked back to his car, I would happily give it to anyone who would have it.

He parked outside the station and went through to the buffet and ordered a pot of tea, picking up a copy of the *Telegraph* on his way. Since he had been able to read newspapers, in the hospital, he had always been surprised to see that each of them had had that day's date on them. He had become so accustomed, in Africa and Turkey, to be reading English papers that could be at least two months old. There was one other couple in the buffet talking quietly, at a table in the far corner. He scanned the pages of the paper, paying little attention to the headlines. He knew how heavily censored everything was to make the impact of the war less frightening to those on the home front. Only the families of those whose husbands and sons had come home on leave knew the true picture and strangely, as if part of some unspoken conspiracy, the men were loath to tell their families for fear of upsetting them even more.

He finished his tea, left six pence on the table and walked out onto the platform with the newspaper clutched in his left hand. He could hear the train approaching and watched it as it steamed around the long gentle curve through the edge of town and pulled up. A door opened in the carriage, immediately behind the engine tender and Gerald stepped out onto the platform. He somehow managed to wave to both Edward and a porter at the same time. The porter crossed the platform and Edward watched his brother organise his luggage. He's put on weight, thought Edward, the soft life in Paris. A tinge of resentment flicked through his thoughts as Gerald walked towards him. When five yards apart, Gerald exclaimed,

'Thank God I knew who I was meeting or I wouldn't have recognised you, Eddy,' he added, embracing him, 'it's so good to see you but you have changed so much, what have they done to you?' Eddy flinched, he couldn't help it, from the dual impact of his brother's words and embrace. Gerald instantly let go , 'what happened? I hurt you.'

'No, it's nothing, just my shoulder, it still hurts a bit.' Edward put his right arm around his brother's back, 'Come, I'm so glad you are here, I brought the car myself,' and the porter followed them through the station.

That evening, after dinner, the two of them sat opposite each other nursing large ballons of cognac. They had eaten well on a sea trout that Edward had caught that morning and the talk turned to Gerald's wedding and subsequent events. There was an awkward pause between them, partly because it seemed so long ago but was, in some way, undiminished by the lapse of time. Edward had found it very difficult to forgive his brother for all that had happened and for how it had happened.

'Father never knew that you had married but I think mother suspected it. I could never understand why you felt the need to. We had always been so close, you, Chad and me, well perhaps not Chad but certainly you and me. You never told me anything about your plans, when I was last home and that can't have been more than three months before your wedding. I know that we've known the Wickhams for years but you never seemed particularly interested in Betty.'

'And you, baby brother, never realised how hard our father was on me, he and I were constantly at odds. Now, I can see how he might have thought it was all in my own best interest but, at the time, I felt that he almost hated me. Chadwyck could do no wrong and you were the golden boy following in our grandfather's footsteps. I'm afraid,' he added with a disingenuous smile, 'it came down to simple economics. Without money I had to do what father wanted and with it, I didn't. Betty was the obvious answer and you wouldn't believe how easy her father made it. He couldn't wait to be associated, in whatever way, with our family. I am not particularly proud of it but I blame our father, as much as I blame myself. He never understood that we were not all the same.' Edward twisted in his chair to relieve the ache in his shoulder and sipped his cognac silently. There was so much he wanted to say but he couldn't because he had never been part of it, except briefly during the summer holidays.

'Say something, Eddy, it's obvious you disapprove.'

'No, I don't disapprove. It might surprise you, but I've never known a woman…'. In an attempt to ease the growing tension he added, 'and all they can do to us chaps.'

'I don't believe you, with all that you have done since you left school.'

'No Gerry, there just hasn't been either the time nor opportunity and that is the end of it. How is Betty, you haven't mentioned her at all.'

'Fine, just fine, I had a letter from her two weeks ago. Of course, I haven't seen her since I left Washington, almost a year ago and she has moved back with her parents because she felt lonely in our house without me. She seems happy and sees quite a lot of our mother.'

He emptied his glass and lent across to retrieve the decanter, 'can I top you up?' Edward offered his glass, 'what was East Africa like? I knew where you were, in fact, Betty and I sailed past Mafia Island before you ever got there.'

'It all seems so long ago,' said Edward, 'and so experimental, everything was so new and most of our kit kept falling apart because of the heat. Do you know Gerry, my only armament at the time was a service revolver and yet, less than a year later, I was shot down by a machine gun. If technology progresses at the same rate, it is inevitable that the death toll will increase accordingly. I'm so glad I'm in the air and not on the ground. You and I have no idea what the day-to-day life in the trenches is like on the Western Front but I shall see for myself soon, in my next posting.'

'Do you know where they will send you?'

'Not yet but I will let you know when I do. Have you ever been near enough to hear the guns Gerry, have you ever been on an assignment on the Western Front?'

'Not yet, most of the time I have been editing watered-down versions of enemy actions, for the American public. The French and British press corps are heavily censored by their own people but we seem to be less restrictive. I think Teddy Roosevelt tried to tell the

British government that they should ease up on censorship, and with good reason. If they don't, the problem is people might start believing the German press instead – it's always been available there. Ten million Germans live in the States, would you believe, either born there or of German extraction. That's almost ten percent of the entire population, Eddy. They might well swing things when it comes to decide if America remains neutral or comes into the war on the Allied side.'

'Well you should go to the Front, if it is at all possible and perhaps you will be more aware of the price being paid by both the French and the British. Thousands upon thousands of men entrenched in appalling conditions, being blown up by German mines, as we are doing to them or shelled continuously for days on end, before an attack that invariably goes nowhere. A stalemate, orchestrated by Generals, that seem to be completely out of touch with reality. Edward's voice trailed off towards the end and again he felt the bone-deep tiredness of unrelieved tension. Gerald hadn't noticed his brother's despair nor recognised it in the tone of his voice.

'I have an assignment when I get back to Paris. If I'm late the old man will string me up to the nearest lamppost.'

'What have they asked you to do?'

'Something that should interest you. A new squadron is being formed by a friend of the old man, a chap called Norman Prince, who is flying with the French at the moment. They are going to name it after the Marquis de Lafayette, who was involved in both the French Revolution and the American Civil War. Apparently most of the pilots are Americans. The old man thinks it is a ploy, a bit of propaganda to bring us Americans into the war.'

'What about our neutrality? I bet the Germans will have something to say about that.'

'You're quite right, they have already protested to the State Department. That's why they've changed the name from the original Escadrille des Americains to Lafayette and placed them under the control of the French Air Department. The squadron started life two months ago in Luxeuil Les Bains and now they are moving to Bar-

Le-Duc, which is about two hundred kilometres east of Paris, near a place called Verdun. Perhaps you ought to think of joining them and then I would really have something to write about.'

'Afraid not, Gerry, I'll have to go where I'm posted.'

'Pity, I could turn you into an American hero.'

'That's the last thing I want.'

'One of the pilots is a chap called Drexell, he is about my age and the grandson of Anthony Drexell who founded the university in Philadelphia. He is a member of the squadron and I have to go and interview him in Bar-Le-Duc, on my return.'

'I wish you luck Gerry but now I am for bed. Do you want to go fishing tomorrow before breakfast?'

'I'd rather not, I'm not very good in the morning. Why don't we go for a walk after breakfast?'

'Good idea, we can go up to the old war memorial on the hill behind the house and be back in time for lunch.'

The memorial stood high above them as they followed the dogs up the hill. It commemorated those of the local Highlanders who had died in the Boer War. On its fluted top stood a small statue of a Highlander in full battle kit and below, around its granite base, were four sandstone inlays with the names and ranks inscribed on all sides. Edward stood silently in front of the memorial and looked up at the Highlander. Why was war inevitable? It seemed that no sooner was one over than another began, so that every generation lost family and friends before their time. His eyes dropped to the names in front and he picked out those of his own uncle William, as well as Hector's younger brother, Allan, and Jersey McLeod, the head stalker. Those were just the men from Glen Lyon Estate, and there were many others from crofts scattered around the Glen.

'Why' said Edward, 'do the British consider soldiering as an integral part of their lives? As long as there are soldiers, there will be wars. Perhaps it is part of their primogeniture tradition, the first son inherits almost all, the second goes into the army, the third usually goes into the Church and any others head out into the world to make their fortunes, Empire building. We are all taught to fight from an early age, for what we want, for what we believe in and for what other people have and I think it's the last that ends up in war.'

'Come on Eddy, it's not that bad.'

'It is, it's worse than that, it's destroying me. You and I have a foot on both sides of the Atlantic and right now I feel a lot more British than American. It's inevitable they will come in but I don't know why they are taking so long to make up their minds. Of course, if they had only come in a year ago, it would probably be all over by now. I think it could be another year before they do and I don't think I can last that long.'

'Are you feeling sorry for yourself Eddy?'

'No, I am feeling sorry for everyone else. When I was at school, which now seems a hundred years ago,' he grinned at Gerald, 'I saw a great future for us all but that future depended on all of us making it so. You have no idea how many of those that left in my year are now dead and how many more will die before this war is over. We will lose almost everything, including those we need to rebuild what we have lost. I have had a lot of time to think about this, over the last three months and I have seriously considered resigning my commission with the RFC but that would be a personal defeat I don't think I could live with.' He stood there almost at attention in front of the monument but his shoulders drooped and he hung his head. Gerald couldn't believe how much he had aged since he had last seen him and regretted his remarks at the station, which he had thought funny at the time.

'Eddy, I think you should go home.'

'I am home,' and he spread his arms about him, encompassing the estate below.

'I mean Washington, mother needs you. '

'Not as much as my squadron does. '

'What are you talking about, you haven't got a squadron, you told me that it had been disbanded. '

'No Gerry, I must go on, I owe it to those who have died,' and he added as an afterthought, 'or at least as long as I can.'

CHAPTER 60

In mid April, Edward was ordered to report to Brooklands, having been promoted to Captain. He was now skipper of his own Squadron, flying Nieuport 11s. After six weeks' preparation, they crossed the channel to St Omer, it was 1 June 1916 and everyone was in high spirits.

An hour before sunset, Edward and his Squadron left St Omer and headed south for the short run to the airfield at Estrée-Blanche, where they would join two other squadrons and become part of the 22nd Wing of the RFC. Five miles before the airfield they flew past the Chateau d'Aval, which Edward already knew was to be his billet. Surrounded by mature ash and oak trees and back-lit by the setting sun, he admired its spectacular early 18th-century elegance.

As soon as they landed at Estrée-Blanche, Edward handed over his new 'plane to the mechanics and walked over to the Officers' Mess to meet the out-going Squadron Commander. Edward tapped lightly on the door and walked into the C.O.'s office. Major Robert Jenkinson was standing by the window watching a 'plane land, in the last of the late afternoon light. His stooped shoulders and silver hair gave him a worn and tired look. He was a regular soldier, near to retirement and had been seconded to the R.F.C. because of his exceptional administrative abilities. He turned and held out his hand.

'Welcome to Estrée-Blanche, Captain Meade. I watched you land

and a very pretty sight it was too.' They shook hands and Edward sat down in the chair that was indicated.

'I'm glad to be here Sir. It feels like I've come full circle. I first flew against the Hun two years ago, not so far from here.'

'It's all here in your file. You've certainly been about and, I might add, with great distinction. How were things in England when you left? Although,' he added ruefully, 'it won't be long before I find out for myself. I feel I've failed, not so much in what I've done, but more in what I haven't done.' He opened a drawer in his desk and pulled out a bottle of brandy and two glasses. 'Would you like a drink? It's not whisky, I'm afraid, haven't had any of that since I got here but it's a damn good cognac. The Countess gave it to me. You'll meet her soon, your Landlady you might say. Were you told that you would be billeted at the Chateau d'Aval?' He poured a couple of inches of cognac, a rich mellow colour, into the two glasses and handed one to Edward, and continued, 'I've been there for the last six months and very comfortable it is, too. Most of the fellows here are in and around the village, by the airfield and half a dozen senior ranks from here and Triezennes are staying at the Chateau.'

'Thank you, Sir. They did tell me where I'd be staying, but nothing in detail. How do you get back and forth and,' he added with a grin, 'what is she like?'

'The Countess or my car?'

'The Countess, Sir.' Edward laughed self-consciously, a little uneasy at the way the conversation was going. 'It seemed such a beautiful place, from the air,' and he added in an attempt to explain himself, 'I flew by it on the way in and I rather assumed, for God knows what reason, that a beautiful person must live there.'

'Well, you're right about that, my boy, beautiful she is but a little aloof or so she seems to me. Her husband, who I believe was quite a few years her senior, was killed at the beginning of the Turkish Campaign. As to how I get there, I have my own car which I bought from my predecessor, on his departure and which,' he added, with a speculative look, 'I'll sell to you for what it cost me. I've found it very

376

useful and not just for running between here and the Chateau. Many a time I've had to go out and collect one or more of my pilots when they prang on their way home.' Edward could hear the sound of a 'plane landing and Jenkinson looked at his watch. 'That's what I've been waiting for, they're all in now. So drink up and I'll take you out to the Chateau.' Edward picked up his kit, which he had left outside the C.O.'s door and they walked out together, Jenkinson returning greetings from various officers as they went.

'I met your adjutant on the way in,' said Edward, 'and he told me he'd take charge of billeting my squadron.'

'Good, then there's nothing here for us till tomorrow morning.' They went through a door at the back of the farmhouse, commandeered as the Officers' Mess and came to a gravelled area behind the house where a Leyland lorry, a motorbike and a handful of bicycles stood beside two cars. Jenkinson led the way to the furthest one, in the shadow of the lorry, and it wasn't until Edward climbed over the low door on the passenger side, that he realised it was a 1912 three litre Bentley. He tried, without much success, to curb his enthusiasm in case it affected the price that he had already decided he would pay, almost irrespective of what it might be.

'If this was mine, Sir, I wouldn't sell it. I'd take it back with me.'

'I can't say I didn't think of that but petrol is almost unobtainable at home and the car is a bit rich for my blood. I'm very glad to see that you obviously appreciate it for what it is, so take good care of it and I'm sure it will take good care of you.' He switched on the ignition, regulated the fuel and air mix. It started first time and the engine settled into a deep, melodious purr. They drove out of the airfield and in less than half an hour they swung off the road, through massive wrought iron gates and drove on between two ornamental lakes down a long avenue of mature lime trees.

It was now almost dark and all that Edward had seen so far had been vague and indistinct. As they left the car, with Edward carrying his grip, the front door opened and a shaft of light flooded out and illuminated the steps in front of them. Jenkinson led the way into a large, high ceilinged hall with an elegant free-standing marble staircase at the far end. It rose from the centre and then split midway into two and curved back upon itself and merged with a gallery that ran around the entire perimeter of the hall. An elderly, dark skinned maid closed the door behind them.

Halfway down the staircase stood a woman dressed in dark flowing silks who had stopped when she saw them with one hand resting lightly on the banister while the other swept her skirt away from her small, narrow feet. For a brief moment she and Edward looked at each other, and then she continued her descent and, with a delightful, musical tone, spoke to his companion.

'Good evening, Robert.' They were now both standing at the foot of the stairs. He took her proffered hand and briefly bobbed his head, in an awkward attempt at Gallic gallantry.

'Good evening, Countess. You look particularly beautiful tonight,' and suddenly realising the implication of what he had said added, as an afterthought, 'as if you don't always' and laughed, nervously. 'May I present,' he continued with a bold sweeping gesture, to cover his own confusion, 'my successor, Captain Edward Meade.' He glanced at Edward, stepped to one side and added formally, 'Captain Meade, may I present the Countess Giselle Mont-Lemaitre d'Aval.' Edward stepped forward, bowed very slightly and, with his eyes still on hers, took her hand and raised it to within an inch of his lips.

'Enchanté, Madame.' Her eyelids flickered for a moment, surprised by his almost flawless accent.

'Captain Meade, welcome to your new quarters. Please call me Giselle and hopefully,' she added, a suggestion of a smile playing at the corner of her mouth, 'I may call you Edouard,' she pronounced it in the French style and he was enchanted with the way she said it. His name had never sounded so attractive to him before and he was amazed at the impact on his own feelings. He could not believe that after only a moment in her presence he should want something so fervently, albeit his own name, as a talisman that belonged exclusively to the two of them. She retrieved her hand and smiled gently at him, knowing what he felt and suddenly realising that for the first time in years she too felt the same.

'I will have Marie show you to your room and then we will all meet for drinks with the others in the Library in,' she looked at the long case clock in the hall, 'let's say, half an hour.' She gave instructions to the maid, who picked up Edward's grip and led the way upstairs.

Edward waved Jenkinson on and stood at the foot of the stairs, while he watched Giselle cross the hall. As she opened the Library door, she half turned towards him knowing that he would be looking at her and she smiled again. He held her gaze for a moment and felt an irrepressible grin spread across his face. As she turned away, he admired the soft, creamy skin of her lovely bare shoulders. Her thick, lustrous black hair was piled neatly on top of her head and had accentuated the delicate line of her neck and throat. She wore no jewellery at all but, he thought, it would only detract from her natural beauty.

* * *

Major Jenkinson stayed on for the rest of that week to help Edward get the hang of things and introduced him to No. 60 Squadron, which was to remain behind at the same airfield, under the command of his adjutant Captain Charles Bishop. On his third day Edward found himself in the C.O.'s office with Charlie Bishop, the three discussing possible variations on standing orders, relating to new tactics.

'I think I'll leave you two to thrash this one out' said Jenkinson, 'I'm too much of the old school and will be leaving at the end of this week.' He got up and turned at the door, 'and anyhow it will be your office then, Edward.' He closed the door behind him and Edward sat down again.

'I don't even know how long you've been on this field, in fact, I know nothing about you, we have hardly had a moment together since I arrived.'

'Almost four months now,' said Charles, 'came out with

my squadron and found Jenkinson already here. He's a great inspiration to us all, with enormous experience, and he can be very understanding when it comes to dealing with the new chaps, a father figure to us all.'

'Would you like a drink,' asked Edward, 'I know it is a little bit early but it won't harm us.' He went over to the C.O.'s desk and pulled out a bottle of cognac and two glasses from the top drawer.

'I hear you were flying in Gallipoli and got shot down, what was it like? From the reports I heard chaos reigned, a total lack of communication amongst the top brass. The worst cases of incompetence, I believe, affected the Australians and the New Zealanders. Was it as bad there as it is here on the Western Front?'

'I never saw much of what was happening on the ground. I was zeroing in our artillery on the enemy gun emplacements and sometimes flying photo reconnaissance, the same as we are doing here. It was just before the evacuation that I was shot down, ditched in the sea next to one of our destroyers, so I was lucky to get fished out in one piece.'

'Were you damaged or just the 'plane?'

'Shot through my left lung and spent three months in hospital back in England.'

'Why, if I may be so bold, are you flying with us, you're an American aren't you, although you don't sound like one?'

'I was at school in England when the war broke out and all of my year joined up, it seemed the thing to do at the time.'

'So you have family over here, I mean in England?'

'No, my mother lives in Washington and my father died three years ago but one of my brothers, Gerald, is now in Paris. He works with the *Washington Post*, as a war correspondent, while his wife languishes in Washington.' The door opened and the C.O. stuck his head around it.

'Lunch is ready chaps, come and sit with me and tell me what *we* have decided.'

'Not much yet, Sir,' said Edward, 'but we will sort something out.'

During the first three weeks of his command Edward was able to build up a picture of what was happening from snippets of conversation garnered from various pilots of new 'planes, refuelling at Estrée-Blanche on their way to their own airfields. At the end of each day, which always started before dawn and rarely finished, at that time of the year, before nine in the evening, Edward drove the Bentley back to the Chateau, enjoying a time of relaxation, before dinner.

His fellow guests, three of which were from the airfield at Treizemies, usually managed to meet for dinner with Giselle. She was a perfect hostess, her witty conversation and sometimes gay laughter a great tonic. With each successive day, although his time at the Chateau never varied, he had the feeling she was spending more time with him, or perhaps it was that she had more time for him. During the previous week, one of his fellow guests from Treizennes had been killed in some stupid accident. His engine had failed just after take-off and he had turned too quickly in an attempt to regain the field and had crashed. Another guest had been transferred back to St Omer so, as a result, Edward had found himself sitting on Giselle's right at dinner.

* * *

After the last patrol of the day had landed and been debriefed, Edward handed over to Charles, who lived in a farmhouse adjacent to the airfield, and drove the Bentley slowly back, thinking of Giselle and marvelling at his good fortune. By some extraordinary quirk of logistics all five other officers at the Chateau had been transferred. He and Giselle would dine alone and, when he had left that morning, Giselle had told him about it in such a way that he was convinced she was looking forward to it as much as he was. When he got to his room he bathed, dressed in black tie and came down to the library to find himself alone.

It was just after nine and he helped himself to a glass of the Countess's seemingly limitless supply of cognac, with a splash of soda, while he waited. He stood by the window and watched the sun settling over the park while rabbits played along the hedgerows and he wondered whether Jules, the gardener, would be out setting snares for their dinner tomorrow. The library ceiling, as in the main hall, was very high and a narrow gallery ran around two sides of the room, which was literally covered with books from floor to ceiling. Elegant mahogany steps, with a beautifully carved banister, descended from one end of the gallery and made it possible to look at all the books without having to balance on a rickety ladder. He was just about to climb up to the gallery when the door opened and he turned expectantly to greet Giselle.

'Excuse me, Monsieur,' Marie said, bobbing a curtsy, 'Madame has asked me to make her apologies. Unfortunately the Countess is not feeling well and is unable to join you at dinner.' His disappointment was palpable and for a moment he was unable to answer; finally, 'What has happened Marie, where is she?'

'Madame is in her room, Monsieur.'

'I must go and see her, in case there is anything I can do for her.'

'Oh no, Monsieur, I don't think that would be appropriate. I will tell Madame of your concern.'

'Please tell her, Marie, that I am more than concerned and that I shall wait here for her answer.' Marie curtsied again and just as she was about to close the door, he added, 'Tell her too that I will leave immediately to collect the squadron medical officer, unless she will allow me to see her.' He put his glass down and for a few moments paced the room impatiently. He was on the point of following Marie upstairs when he suddenly heard a delighted laugh from above. He stepped back into the middle of the room and looked up to where the sound had come from. Giselle stood above him, leaning back against the books. Confused at first, he felt relief and then great anger, which was immediately replaced by an extraordinary feeling of deep happiness.

'It's you,' he said, 'How dare you do that to me!' She heard all she wanted to hear in his voice, stepped forward to the banister and, with another laugh, tossed a red rosebud to him. He caught it deftly and, passing it briefly beneath his nose, inhaled its scent.

'I wanted to see your reaction.' She walked, floated he thought, to the end of the gallery and slowly descended.

She was dressed in a bottle green, almost black, satin evening gown embroidered in gold over lighter green georgette. It had a slight pointed train, the last foot or so of which touched the ground behind. The hemline at the front was raised, so that as she took each step he could see her slender ankles. Her shoes were covered in the same material and also embroidered in gold. A small tortoiseshell and ostrich feather fan swung from a gold silk cord twined around her right wrist. All the time she watched him and, when she reached the last step, with her head still just above his, he noticed in her eyes a fleeting concern.

'Are you angry with me, Edouard?' He did not answer her and she continued, 'I knew yesterday that the other officers were leaving today but I didn't tell you because I wanted to examine my own feelings. I wanted to know whether I really wanted to be with you alone. It is strange but since I heard of my husband's death I have never, until now, been alone with a man. I thought about it most of last night and decided very early this morning that I did want to be alone with you tonight. So I told you so this morning and that is why I did what I did, just now. I had to be sure that it meant as much to you as it does to me. Now do you understand?' She took the last step and, as they had done every night till then, he kissed her proffered hand, but the difference lay in what he saw in her eyes. All the anger he had felt, albeit briefly, dissolved to be replaced by an overpowering feeling of strength and an almost unbearable need to hold her and never let her go. Instead he smiled, kissed the rose that she had given him and put it back between her fingers.

'No,' he said, in a voice that was almost normal, 'I'm not angry, I was for a moment but now, for the first time since this frightful war started, I feel a peace that blocks out everything else and leaves me in a world where all that seems to matters is you and us.' She kissed the flower and stepped closer until she was almost touching him before threading it into his buttonhole. Her eyes, downcast as she did it, were on a level with his mouth and impetuously he bent forward and very gently kissed her cheek. She looked at him for a moment, still searching and then seeing what she was looking for she raised her left hand and traced her index finger across his lips.

'Are you hungry?' and she laughed, shamelessly, at the almost comical expression on his face. She took both his hands and rocking back on her heels looked him up and down, from his confused eyes to his patent leather shoes. 'That's not what I meant but I can see you are. Dinner should be ready, let's go and eat.' She dropped one of his hands and led him by the other from the room. When they reached the dining room they found, to Edward's dismay, that their two places had been set at opposite ends of the long mahogany table. There was at least fifteen feet of burnished wood, three crystal candelabra, two decanters glowing with vintage claret, several salt and pepper cellars and two lovely, attenuated vases of sweetly scented dog roses, between them. Equally amazed, they looked at each other and burst out laughing.

'What, is that women up to? Marie, where are you?' She appeared from behind the screen that stood in front of the kitchen door. 'Ah, there you are. What is the meaning of this? Please set Captain Meade's place next to mine, on my right.' She turned to Edward, 'It's warm and stuffy in here, please help me open the windows onto the terrace.'

They stepped outside and, almost touching, stood by the mellowed sandstone balustrade that ran the full length of the Chateau. A long silvery reflection of the three-quarter moon, just clearing the tree tops, cut across one of the two ornamental lakes. In silence they listened to the frogs and crickets calling. Way over to their left a dog barked beyond the farm buildings and, unanswered, fell silent.

'The table is ready Madame, shall I serve the soup?'

They sat with their heads close together and Giselle talked about her life as a child. She told him that she had always lived in the country and had been brought up near Chantilly, to the east of Paris, where her father was a doctor. She went on to tell him of how she met Jacques, and how her mother had disapproved of the match. According to her mother he was much too old for Giselle and had what she had rather mysteriously, at the time, referred to as a reputation. Giselle suddenly stopped and looked at him with wide, clear eyes.

'You are good for me, Edouard, I don't think I have ever spoken to anyone like this before.' Marie removed the main course plates and brought them cheese and fruit, while Edward refilled their glasses.

'For me too, it's different,' he said. 'It seems that everything you say is the most important thing I've ever heard, and yet, I know it cannot possibly be so.' She laughed in delight and touched his lower lip.

'You're dribbling.'

'I'm not.'

'Then you're drooling.'

'Perhaps.' he grinned.

'No truly, look.' She held her hand between them and he could see a tiny piece of pear on her nail. He caught her hand and licked her finger. 'I see you're still hungry.' He nodded, they both knew what she meant and suddenly he almost panicked. He looked away, then quickly back again and what he saw in her eyes reassured him, steadied him, but still he prevaricated.

'Do you smoke, Giselle? I don't remember ever having seen you smoke.'

'Only when all else fails.' He was sure she was teasing him. 'Jacques used to but on you go.'

He took a pack from his breast pocket and a gold cigarette lighter that had belonged to Jock and lit a cigarette. He lay the pack down on the table and Giselle, whose hand was almost touching his, picked it up. She opened it and saw that it was nearly empty.

'Is this all you have left?' He nodded. 'I have some, or I think I do. They were Jacques's, they'll be very stale. They're probably in the sideboard drawer.' She got up and, as she passed him, she trailed her finger tips across his shoulder. He tried to catch them but they were gone, before he could move. She laughed, enchantingly. 'I can't help myself, you're irresistible.' She opened the drawer and looked inside, 'Ah, I thought so.' She came back and laid an exquisitely chased slim gold cigarette case on the table. 'Open it, it could be empty.' It was almost full and on the inside of the lid was engraved 'from me to you' in handwriting, which he assumed was hers and the date, September 15, 1914. 'I gave it to him for his birthday, just before he left for Turkey with his squadron.'

'How extraordinary, that was the day when I first arrived in France.'

'Do you have a cigarette case, Edouard?'

'I had but I lost it just before Christmas.'

'How?' She traced the back of his hand with the tips of her fingers and he looked up. 'I'm sorry, does it bother you? I can't help myself, I told you.'

'No, of course not.' He took her hand, turned it over and kissed her palm. 'I love it but I'm just not used to it.' She searched his eyes, hoping it to be true.

'How did you lose your case?' she asked again.

'When flying on patrol. I didn't move out of the way quickly enough and I got hit by enemy machine gun fire.'

'Mon Dieu,' her hands flew to her mouth. 'You were hit, you were wounded?' In the soft candlelight her eyes were huge. 'My poor Edouard, what happened?'

'A bullet went through the fuselage of the 'plane into my back, passed through the edge of one lung, broke a rib and smashed into my cigarette case which it tore out of the front of my leather flying coat and on through the other side of the fuselage, into the wide blue yonder.'

'Mon Dieu,' she said again and they looked at each other for a moment, suddenly silenced by a mutual feeling of déjà-vu. 'That's incredible. An inch or two to the right, and you would not be here.

I would never have met you and would never have felt the way I do now. Where was this?'

'Sedd-el-Bahr.'

'But Cherie, that is where the French were. '

'I know, I flew with them all the time.'

'But that is where Jacques was, when he…' She could not bring herself to finish the sentence and, as he looked, she started to tremble and two tears appeared in the corners of her eyes. Was it the memory of her husband, he wondered, or because of what he had just told her? 'You must have the case, I want you to have it. Even the inscription applies. It is 'from me to you' and the date is auspicious, not that I knew it at the time. But it was the day that you came to my beloved France and now,' she added as she dabbed at her eyes, with her napkin, 'to me.' She got up from the table and he followed her out onto the terrace, having put the cigarette case in his pocket. Marie came in and started to clear the table.

'Would you like to dance Edouard? I feel so sad with one half of my heart and so happy with the other. I want you to hold me and make the other half happy. I want you to dispel all that the war is and has been, to all of us, if only for tonight, I want it to go away.' She smiled brightly and took his hand, 'Come, there is a phonograph in the library. We can dance in there and later, perhaps, I'll show you where the gallery door leads to.'

* * *

He lay quietly beside her and listened to her gentle breathing and to the drone of bees in the honeysuckle outside the open windows while skylarks, high above the chateau, welcomed the dawn. He could just see the vague outline of the wardrobe against the far wall of her bedroom, as detail built on detail in the early morning light. His left arm was beneath her neck and her cheek rested gently on the scar on his chest. They had lain like that since last making love. Neither of them had moved at all, totally content and at peace. He gently sifted long tendrils of her hair through his fingers, not wanting to waken her but acutely aware of the time and the need to return to the airfield. He could feel the weight of her left leg across his and he felt rested, relaxed and somehow invincible. She had led him, as promised, into her dressing room through the small hidden door at the back of the gallery. It was cleverly disguised, with the leather book spines in neat rows, to blend with the real books on either side. They had undressed each other slowly and then, in his case, feeling an almost unbearable sense of longing, with greater haste and hunger.

She moved her leg, touching him gently with her knee, and he thought again of the expression on her face when she realised that it was to be his first time. She had changed dramatically and at first her need had softened. He had wanted her to lead and she had until a certain moment and then somehow, without words, she had managed to make him feel as if it were all his doing. When the end was near her need returned, greater than ever and overwhelmed them both. They had talked quietly of little things, seemingly of great importance, while the candles on both sides of the bed had burned themselves out. Then they had slept, woken, made love and slept again and now it was morning and he had to go. He pulled very gently on her hair, she moved again and when she felt him, she woke quite suddenly. He watched her with infinite tenderness in his eyes and, fascinated as he was with everything she did, he saw hers focus on him in the pale morning light.

'Edouard,' she said, softly and closed he eyes. Just his name and nothing more.

'I love you, Giselle,' he whispered, he couldn't help himself. He had wanted to say it, again and again, from the first moment they had made love. Having said it once, he said it again a little louder and would have said it again, had she not kissed him. She snaked her arms around his neck and pulled him on top of her.

'Then love me my love and make me feel you will never leave me.' She whispered to him, as he moved between her legs.

Before leaving her, they bathed together in her magnificent

Victorian cast iron bath that stood, on four lion's feet, in the middle of her marble floored bathroom. From where he lay, with his feet beneath the taps and with her kneeling between his legs he could see the dawn, through the window behind her. Sensing his mood and suddenly fearful of losing him she playfully lifted a huge sponge from between them and held it over his head, squeezing the last of the water from it. Her mood changed and for a moment she became serious.

'You have made me very happy, Edouard. For the first time in my life you have made me understand what it is to be a woman and for that I thank you.' He was embarrassed and elated at the same time and, not wanting to spoil the moment by saying anything, he pulled her down towards him and held her close. Although the sun was only just over the horizon, he knew that the dawn patrol was already airborne. Charles would have been there to see to it but still he felt the weight of responsibility.

'I must get back to my room and dress, Giselle. I should have gone long ago, but I just couldn't bring myself to leave you.'

'But Cherie, I understand. We have tonight and tomorrow and all the other tomorrows. I shall spend the whole day thinking of you and what,' she added, brushing her lips across his, 'I shall do with you tonight.'

'I'll come back to say goodbye, when I'm dressed.' He laughed, thinking of what she had just said and kissed her again. He eased himself out of the bath, wrapped a towel around his waist and dripping everywhere, went back to his own bedroom.

He dressed quickly in his double-breasted uniform jacket and, as he did up the buttons, he suddenly remembered the letter for Giselle that Jules had given him the previous evening. He took it out of his pocket and looked at it again. It was addressed to Giselle, postmarked Paris and dated almost two weeks ago. When dressed, he retraced his steps and found her sitting at her dressing table, running a silver-backed brush through her hair. She smiled at his reflection in the glass.

'That was quick and I know the day is going to be very long.' She made a face, like a spoilt child and then laughed with such happiness, that it squeezed his heart.

'This is for you,' He held the letter out to her 'Jules gave it to me last night. He found it outside and said the postman must have dropped it, I completely forgot to give it to you then.'

'Don't be sorry Cherie, please open it.'

'Of course not, it's addressed to you.'

'No, I insist you open it, I'm very busy,' and she laughed, having emphasised the very and continued to brush her hair. He ran his thumb nail under the flap of the envelope and took out a single sheet of writing paper. He started to read it and, as he did, he paraphrased its contents.

'It's from the War Office in Paris,' and, as he read on, his expression changed. Watching his reflection in the mirror, she saw it change and felt a sudden, terrible fear.

'What is it, Edouard? Why have you stopped? I can see that something awful has happened, what is it?' Without a word, he handed her the letter and turned away. He did not want to see her lovely face when she read it. He took the gold cigarette case out of his pocket and held it in his hands for a moment, then opened it and took out a cigarette. He heard her gasp and immediately afterwards he heard the hairbrush fall. He lit the cigarette and slowly closed the case, held it for a moment longer and then placed it gently on the table. He could hear her crying but could not bring himself to go to her, nor even say goodbye. Without looking back he left the room, ran downstairs and out of the front door, which he left standing open behind him. He jumped into the Bentley and, unconcerned for his own or anyone else's safety, within moments was tearing down the long, straight road to the airfield.

CHAPTER 61

All that day Giselle remained in her room and refused to come out. Marie begged her to come down and have something to eat, or at least accept a tray of food. The letter lay where she had left it on her dressing table. She must have read it a dozen times, so she knew it by heart. She was deeply hurt that Edward had left when he did. She knew perfectly well why he had and was even honest enough to admit to herself that, in similar circumstances, she would probably have done the same. But, it still hurt and she cried quietly until she could cry no more.

It was not until mid-afternoon, wandering aimlessly around her dressing room, that she found the cigarette case. She picked it up, opened it and ran her thumb across the inscription. He was so young, she thought, even with all that he had done he was still an innocent and so fiercely proud. She knew that he too must be hurting as much, or even more than she was. Instinctively, she had believed him when he had told her that he loved her. She had expected him to say it but, when he did, there was something in the way he said it that made her know he meant it.

Perversely, she envied him the intensity of his feelings. She had never felt anything like it when Jacques had first taken her. Nor had she since, during the infrequent times that they had made love before he had gone; she looked again at the letter, somehow hoping it would go away and him with it. It surprised her that, when she thought of him dead, she could cry a little and feel a certain loss but, when she thought of him alive, she realised that she was totally reconciled to his death. Would she, she wondered, feel this way had Edward not appeared in her life?

* * *

Edward arrived to find the airfield almost deserted. All three squadrons, his own, Charlie's and Number 56, with the delightful Arthur Rhys-Davids and Jimmy McCudden, were all still out on patrol. Tactics had changed considerably since last he was operational. The old way of sparring in small numbers, the haphazard dog fight, shooting at each other with pistols, was a thing of the past. Patrols were now full squadrons, each of three flights made up of five 'planes and, with the beginning of what was referred to as the second battle of Ypres, both Germany and the Allies were going flat-out to achieve supremacy in the air. Parking the car, without kindness, in the courtyard behind the farmhouse, Edward stormed through the mess to his office, barely acknowledging the salutes of the ground crews. There was a pile of messages stacked on top of his desk and, to one side, de-briefing reports of the previous evening's patrol. Charles had done a good job in his absence. He was still working at his desk, having refused breakfast, when he heard the first of the 'planes returning.

Feeling claustrophobic in his office he strode outside and impatiently paced up and down while, singly and in pairs, the 'planes came in. Subconsciously, he checked off those of his own squadron, one by one, as they landed. He could tell by the erratic sound of some engines and the obvious damage to other 'planes, that they had seen some fierce fighting. Charles was almost the last to land and, mother hen as always, he was shepherding the new boys home. At this stage, because of the insatiable need for new pilots, some of them were joining front-line squadrons with less than fifteen hours solo flying time. If they survived their first week they increased their chances considerably of surviving the next two. So, to a point, the more they flew the more likely they were to continue to do so.

'How'd it go, Charlie?'

'Fine.' Good old Charles, thought Edward, laconic as ever.

'Doesn't look so fine to me, from the damage I can see from here.'

'Well, we did have a bit of a scrap. The Hun came at us, in Eindeckers, out of the sun as usual, while we were behind their lines doing our best to spoil their breakfast.'

'What happened, any kills?'

'Three of theirs are down but one will probably fly again, I saw it land.'

'And us? There has to be an us Charlie, or you wouldn't have said theirs.'

'Phillips.'

'Christ! He only got here yesterday.'

'I know. I got the Hun that got him but sadly too late for Phillips. I was right behind them both, we were at twelve thousand feet and I saw Phillips go down in flames. Before he had dropped a thousand feet I saw him jump. He died when he hit the ground and, even though he had a minute to think about it, assuming he didn't pass out, it's better than being incinerated.' He shook his head, as if to clear it and added, 'I'd use this, before that.' He tapped his revolver and they walked on in silence until they reached Edward's office. An orderly brought mugs of strong, sweet tea for them both.

'Thank you for doing my job for me.' Edward sat behind his desk, picked up the forms and handed them to Charlie.

'My pleasure old boy. But if I may say so, you don't look too happy about something. Do you want to talk about it?'

'No,' and then, less abruptly, 'But thanks anyway. I must write to Phillips's parents but God how I hate doing that. You'd think Charlie, after all the letters I've written, it would be easier than it is.' He tipped his chair back and swung his feet up on his desk and closed his eyes. With his right hand moving in the air, as if writing, he continued, 'Dear Mr Phillips, It is with deep regret that I have to inform you that your son John died today, fighting gallantly for his country.' It's a bloody lie, Charlie. He didn't die fighting gallantly for his country. He had little idea of what he was supposed to be doing and no time to learn. He was a child we pushed up there in a 'plane he could hardly control, to be murdered by someone who was fortunate enough to have had a little longer in the air and thus the edge. I'm sorry Charlie, I'm not very good company at the moment, I'll see you at lunch.'

That evening, all three squadrons went up again and Edward, in a state of suppressed frustration, led A flight. He regretted not having accepted Charlie's offer to air his other problem and it had been no better at lunch. He just could not bring himself to talk about what was going on in his head. At ten thousand feet he led them across their own lines, over no man's land and turned to the north-east, towards Ypres. Cloud formation was heavy and it had taken some time to break through into bright sunshine. The great banks of dark cloud stretched beneath them and covered the ground as far as the eye could see. He knew that soon it would rain, which would break the stifling heat and would make life more bearable, except of course for the infantry. For them it would be even worse than it was already.

As he thought of them, the rain started and gaps appeared in the clouds below him, revealing patches of brown and blasted earth. He flew on and his mind drifted from one random thought to another, past and present, but always returning to Gisele and how he had left her. Suddenly he realised he was looking at a small enemy squadron about two miles to his right, tiny black dots against the indigo sky. His mind snapped back into focus, he waved to his two wing members and started to climb. His squadron responded immediately and, with the sun still behind them, they climbed another 2,000 feet, while closing with the enemy, until one of the enemy broke away and the rest of their squadron splintered in all directions. They were a contact patrol of AEGs, looking for trouble. Edward picked out their leader and, gunning his engine, went into a steep dive in pursuit.

A hundred yards behind the AEG Edward opened fire with his Vickers and, because he was diving at the time of the attack, his speed was considerably greater than the enemy's. Within seconds the gap between them had closed to twenty yards and yet the Hun still flew on, without trying any evasive action. At the very last moment, when Edward realised that he had left it too late to avoid the AEG, it side-slipped sharply to the right. As he passed over it, he could see the observer clawing his way over the gun ring in a desperate attempt to reach the pilot, now slumped forward over the controls with the whole of the back of his head blown away.

As Edward levelled out of his dive, banked and started to climb again he knew, as he looked back over his shoulder at the plummeting 'plane, that he would have run into the back of it had it not altered course at the last moment. He wondered whether that was, at least subconsciously, what he had wanted at that moment. The more he tried to identify his feelings, the more evasive they became. Two miles below the AEG hit the ground and Edward could see the pin-prick flare as it burst into flames. He closed the gap with the rest of his squadron, still engaged, and forced himself to concentrate on nothing except the fight ahead. He knew that if he didn't and let his mind wander, for just one moment, it would be in that moment that the enemy would destroy him. As he got nearer, the remaining Huns were breaking off and he could see that there were three fewer of them than there had been. Not a bad morning's work, he thought, three to us and none to them. The squadron fell in behind him and, without further incident, they returned to Estrée-Blanche.

After the de-briefing Charles stayed behind in Edward's office. He stood quietly by the window watching the riggers and mechanics swarming over the 'planes, refuelling, repairing and re-arming. After he had been there a while Edward spoke, a peevish edge to his voice.

'What's the matter Charlie, haven't you got anywhere else to go? Be a good chap and run along, can't you see I'm busy.'

'Not till you've told me what is the matter with you. We have all been warned of mid-air collisions, I've even seen one and it is nearly always head-on. But I was watching you, Eddy, and if that AEG had not slipped at the last moment, you would have run straight into the back. I want to know why and that is why I'm still here.' He sat down, straddling the chair in front of Edward's desk. He took out his cigarette case and offered it to Edward.

'Thank you,' said Edward. Fished for Jock's lighter and lit them both. Neither of them spoke. They let the silence build and lie like a fog between them. Charles finally scratched his neck and was about to speak.

'I'm sorry Charlie, you're quite right. I'm guilty of the cardinal sin in our game, allowing one's emotions to override one's concentration. Would you like a drink? I still have some cognac left, courtesy of my loving landlady.'

'Ah, hah!' Charles stood, to emphasise the point.

'Ah, hah! What the hell do you mean by *Ah, hah*?'

'You know very well Eddy what I mean; it's just a question of whether you want to talk about it.' Edward stood up, poured the drinks in silence and handed one over. They stood across the desk, and as Charles watched he could see tension gradually draining from Edward's expression, until finally he grinned and raised his glass.

'To the cause of it all. Giselle, Countess Mont-Lemaitre d'Aval.' They touched glasses and drank. 'Sit down Charlie, and thank you for being such a good friend. I'll try and tell you what's happened. Up until yesterday morning, me and five other chaps were billeted at the Chateau, where we all lived uncommonly well and were graciously cared for by the very lovely Giselle. When I say lovely Charlie, I really mean lovely, she's absolutely, breathtakingly beautiful. When I first saw her, when Jenkinson took me there just three short weeks ago on my first day here, I couldn't believe nor understand the effect she had on me. Since then, I'm not ashamed to say, at least half my waking hours have been spent thinking about her.' The bottle of cognac stood between them on the desk and Charles refilled their glasses.

'Her husband, who co-incidentally was fighting the Turks long before me but in the same area, was reported missing, believed dead. As the months passed with no news of him by the beginning of this year, she became convinced that he was dead. Last night, because the others had all been posted elsewhere, we were alone at the chateau and, in what was to me the greatest thing that I've ever experienced, we became lovers.' They sat in silence, engrossed in their own thoughts until finally, just as Charlie was about to prompt him, Edward continued, 'The old gardener, who does just about everything around the place now that the others are away in the war, gave me a letter when I arrived yesterday evening. It had been dropped by the postman, that morning and the gardener had found it. It was addressed to Giselle and I put it in my pocket and it wasn't until early this morning, just before I left to come here, that I remembered it.' Again, he lapsed into silence.

'And?'

'I gave it to her and she asked me to read it. I refused but she insisted.' Again Edward paused and the expression on his face hardened and then closed to the point where Charles thought he would not continue, but finally he said, in a voice almost inaudible, 'He's coming back, Charlie.'

'Who's coming back, the husband?'

'Yes. I opened the letter and read it as she asked. It was from the French War Office in Paris. Her husband had been in a prison camp, when the Turks withdrew. They had abandoned the prisoners to their own devices and eventually her husband had managed to make his way back through Greece to France. He will be at the chateau within the next few days. I don't know what to do Charlie. I love her, I told her so and then I treated her so badly. She was crying when she read the letter and, thinking only of myself and what I was feeling, I left her there alone. I'm not going back to her tonight because I can't. I'll stay here and they can put up a cot.'

CHAPTER 62

Giselle stood at her bedroom window wearing a black peignoir, without make-up and with her hair undressed. She was listening for the sound of the Bentley, as she had done many times before, but had never told him. It was way past his usual time and she found herself making excuses. She appeared colourless and she felt totally exhausted, her eyes swollen and red-rimmed from crying most of the day. But there was still enough of the woman left to raise a self-depreciating smile when she thought what he would think should he see her now. Feeling tired, she moved a chair towards the window. She sat down finally, accepting that he wasn't coming, and yet wanting to be there in case he did.

She had not eaten anything all day and she felt light-headed, almost ethereal. It was at least an hour since Marie, tapping hopefully again at the door, had tried to get her to take something. She no longer thought of the way in which he had left her that morning, not because it was less painful to forgive him but because she could understand the depth of his own pain. The sound of an engine cut across her thoughts and, for a brief moment, she thought it was Edward. She soon saw that it wasn't and listlessly watched as a car pulled up in front of the chateau and two officers got out, took their luggage and walked out of sight into the house. She could hear Marie's voice below, welcoming the last of her five new guests.

She had telephoned the Paris number on the letterhead and, after interminable delays and being disconnected several times, she had finally found out that her husband was temporarily stationed at a barracks near Lyon. He was awaiting transportation home and she was told by the effusive and well-meaning clerk that, if she could contain herself for another three days, or possibly four at the most, she would be re-united with her husband. Then the clerk had added the unkindest twist of all, telling her that she must have believed that her husband had died, that she would never again be happy.

Nothing would be the same ever again; nothing could be the same after what had happened last night. All afternoon she had thought of how she had felt when first told that Jacques was missing in action, believed dead, and she found it very hard to recreate the moment. Whatever sense of loss had long since dissipated as, month after month, she had waited in vain. As she had entered her second year of supposed widowhood she had become totally reconciled to her new status. Although there had been a constant stream of officers through her house, some dashing and others not so dashing, she had remained content within herself, or at least she had until Edward had arrived. She thought again of his expression that first night as he stood at the foot of the staircase, when she had looked back and smiled. She started to cry, again.

* * *

Before it was light next morning, Edward and all the other pilots on the field were woken for the dawn patrol. He had hardly slept, he had lain there longing for Giselle, feeling incomplete without her touch and tantalising scent. His head ached as he struggled into his heavy sheepskin boots and sipped hot, syrupy tea from a large, cracked mug that had been put on his desk. He could hear the engines being run up by the mechanics and other sounds of the still sleepy voices of his brother officers gathering outside and someone laughing at an unheard joke.

When he joined them he could see that cloud cover was almost complete, as there was no sign of the last of the stars. It had rained heavily during the night and he thought again of those in the trenches when he saw how slick and flat the grass was around his feet. He started to walk out to his 'plane alone, doing up the last buttons on his heavy leather coat and pulling on his leather helmet, which he strapped beneath his chin.

'Eddy!' It was Charles, trailing behind him. Edward stopped and waited for him to catch up.

'What? '

'Grumpy, aren't we?'

'I'm sorry Charlie, I've hardly slept and I feel like hell. What did you want?'

'It's not very important old boy, I got this in the post from the C.O. yesterday.' He fished an envelope out of his pocket. 'It's about new tactics and I wanted you to have a look at it, when you have a moment, before I answer it.' Edward took the envelope and slipped it into his flying jacket pocket and Charles headed for his own plane.

Edward tapped the engine manifold for luck, as he always did, nodded wordlessly to his mechanic and, with his goggles in his left hand, swung himself up into the cockpit. Five minutes later all three squadrons were airborne and they began the laborious climb over their own lines to clear the clouds at twelve thousand feet, before heading east to take on the enemy.

* * *

Unable to remain in her room any longer and not having slept at all, but with her mind finally made up, Giselle dressed quickly and went downstairs to the kitchen. She had heard the rain during the night and she noticed that the roof was still leaking over the servants' hall. She made a mental note to talk to Jules about it and, as she did, she saw him sitting alone at the kitchen table, dunking a rough crust of bread into a mug of steaming coffee. He stood up the moment he saw her and pulled the beret off his grizzled head and let it hang by his side.

'Bonjour Madame, How are you? I am pleased to see you. The sincerity in his slow voice was obvious and she was touched by his concern.

'I am very well, thank you Jules.' There was a new determination in her voice. 'When you have finished breakfast, please bring the car round because I want to go to the airfield at Estrée-Blanche.'

'But Madame, we have no petrol.'

'Then get some, Jules, ask one of the drivers of the officers I saw arriving last night. Siphon it from their tank or whatever one does and may I have some of that coffee, please?' He shuffled forward and filled a cup that Marie had set out on a tray the night before. Giselle took it and thanked him; the coffee was strong and aromatic. 'Oh, by the way, the ceiling in the servants' hall is leaking again. Please do something about it. That is, of course, after we get back from the airfield and,' she added as she left the kitchen, carrying her coffee, 'I'll be in the morning room, when you are ready.' He stood there, beret in one hand and the coffee pot in the other, and listened to the sharp tapping of her heels, diminishing down the long flagstone corridor. Slowly he put the coffee pot down and scratched his neck. He whistled softly to himself, replaced his beret and went back to his breakfast.

The light was bad and was not helped by the renewed rain. The long straight road, tapering to a point in the distance, was dressed on both sides with a single line of tall, pointed poplars. The road was badly cratered and getting worse every day, with the increasing military traffic. The rain lay lifeless in every pot-hole, moved only by the passage of the car. Giselle sat in the back and tried to arrange her thoughts and feelings into some sort of coherent order. She was certain of one thing: she was in love with Edward and that precluded all else. Her husband had died and she had accepted that. She had mourned him and observed conventions in the proper manner. She had then convinced herself that fate had taken a hand and prevented

Edward from giving her the letter when he might because, had he done so, she knew that they would never have become lovers. But they were and they had because, as she kept telling herself, it was meant to happen. A new life lay ahead of her, a life with Edward. Her old life had died, even if her husband had not, and there was no going back. They were stopped briefly by the sentry at the entrance to the airfield, but once Giselle had identified herself to his satisfaction, they were waved on. They could see a great deal of activity going on to one side of the field. There was a line of open-ended, canvas-covered hangers, where mechanics were working on dismantled 'planes, repairing damage and replacing parts as needed.

An orderly showed Giselle into Edward's office and asked her to wait, saying that it would be about half an hour before the squadrons returned. He offered her coffee and a week-old copy of *The Times*. She looked around the sparsely furnished room, trying to find something personal to Edward. There was nothing but two photographs on his desk, one obviously of his mother and the other of a family group that must have been taken before the war. Over in the corner stood the still unmade cot, where she now knew he had spent the night. When the orderly had left and closed the door she went over and sat on the cot, to feel for any remaining warmth. There was none, he was gone but soon he would be back. Within a few minutes she heard the first faint sounds of the 'planes returning.

She dropped the unread newspaper and went outside. Jules was standing patiently by the car. She could not understand why the beat of the engines was so erratic, not knowing several were flying on the very last of their fuel. The pilots dropped in quickly, grateful to be down in one piece. She could see several of the 'planes were badly damaged. One landed late, ran on beyond all the others and crashed into a small wooden shed at the end of the field, tearing away half of one wing. Giselle moved forward to intercept the pilots as they walked in, muffled in their protective clothing and some with goggles still in place. They all seemed the same to her but, even so, she knew that Edward was not amongst them.

It started to rain again and she suddenly felt very cold; it was a premonition, instantly associating rain and tears. No more 'planes landed, but still she stood, without her umbrella, unable to shake her fear. Finally, and with a great effort, she turned to go back when she heard another 'plane approaching. Suddenly the engine stopped and then cut in again. The 'plane came in very low, missing the trees in the adjoining field by a few feet and landed short, on one wheel. Its wing-tip clipped the ground, the 'plane cart-wheeled onto its back and the engine died instantly, as the propeller dug into the sodden field. Without thinking she ran forward across the field, losing her shoes as she went and was one of the first to reach the 'plane. The pilot was hanging upside down, unable to release his harness and, over the pervading smell of wet grass, she could smell petrol fumes. One of the mechanics grabbed her by the arm, just as she lunged forward to help the pilot.

'We'll do it Miss, you be a good girl and stay here. You never know, it could catch fire at any time.' He left her and didn't hear her cry out, deep in her throat. The next moment he and another man had released the harness and the pilot fell onto his back beneath the 'plane, rolled to one side and cried out, involuntarily. He staggered to his feet, holding his right arm with his left, pain etched across his face. Giselle ran forward – a few feet short she stopped when she saw it was not Edward.

'Where is he?' she cried, desperately.

'Who, Madam and what are you doing out on the field?'

'Edward.'

'You're wounded, Captain Bishop,' said the mechanic at the same moment. 'I'll call a medic.'

'Not here Bill, I'll see him inside. Let's get out of this rain.' He turned back to Giselle and with his good hand, took her arm. 'Please, Countess.'

'You know me?' Surprise showed in her eyes.

'Yes, Edward told me last night.'

'Where is Edward?' He did not answer but led her towards the farmhouse.

'Captain Bishop,' she cried, 'He called you Captain Bishop. Please tell me, where is Edward?'

'I'm sorry Countess, my name is Charles and I should have introduced myself. He held out his left hand and they shook hands, awkwardly. For the fourth time she asked him but with her eyes only.

'He was shot down.' She stopped and stared at him. He had tried, as they were walking in, to think of a way of softening the news, to somehow make it seem more palatable. He had almost laughed aloud at the absurdity of his thoughts; there was nothing palatable about war. He watched her closely and she did not react at all. She just stood there in silence, as if waiting for more. Her beautiful cornflower eyes were fixed on his, and huge. The rain increased and Charles's arm throbbed painfully but still they stood there in silence, just looking at each other. Her hair, now completely straight, hugged the sides of her head and neck and her dress was plastered to the contours of her body. For the first time he noticed that she had lost her shoes.

'We must go inside, Countess.' He took her arm again and led her gently through the farmhouse, until they reached Edward's office. The medic had arrived with his first aid kit and hovered in their wake. He put down his bag and helped Charles out of his coat and then his tunic, the right arm of which was soaked in blood down to the cuff.

'I'll have to cut it off, Sir.' He heard her gasp and added, 'The sleeve that is,' and smiled, reassuringly at her before adding, thoughtlessly, 'the bullet has torn too much of the cloth through the flesh to allow me to remove the shirt.' Charles sat on the edge of Edward's desk and, with his good hand, fished out a packet of cigarettes.

'Would you like one Countess?' Suddenly, her hand started to shake so badly that she couldn't hold it to her lips. He took it back, lit it for her and she accepted gratefully. Holding it in two hands she inhaled deeply. While the orderly worked on his arm, Charles told her what had happened.

'We were outnumbered more than two to one, but that is not unusual. By the time we had cleared the cloud cover at six thousand feet, No. 56 squadron, which had moved north-east during our ascent, was away in the distance and suddenly we saw, in the blinding sunlight, two staffeln, stacked one on top of the other of Albatroses and DFWs, they were waiting for us and they held all the cards.'

'I saw Edward go for the leader of one flight, attacking from below, just as they were about to drop on us. It was the last thing they expected and, having recovered the advantage, Edward managed to shoot down the leader and the others scattered. I picked up on one of them and managed to get a few bursts into him with my Lewis gun but then lost him in the cloud. I came back to join the squadron and immediately two Huns attached themselves to my tail and I couldn't shake them off. I dived below our squadron, for speed, to manoeuvre and I saw Edward dis-engage from another 'plane. He then got onto the two on my tail and shot down the one nearest to me, while the other broke away.

We had just re-grouped on the edge of the main area of combat, when another staffeln suddenly appeared out of the sun, all guns going and both Green and Hislop were blown to pieces in a matter of seconds. As they turned to come back on us Edward dived on their leader, who broke away and dived. I could see Edward gaining on him and then I suddenly realised he had fallen into a trap. The other members of the staffeln had throttled back until they had Edward between their leader and themselves.

At the same moment that I realised what had happened, Edward must have too because he tried to spin out, but he was too late. Two of them had him caught in a crossfire and I saw him take brutal punishment. He increased his dive and smoke from the engine trailed behind him in a long thin ribbon, but there were no flames. There was a break in the cloud and I could see the trenches far below us and, just before the Hun attacked us again, I got this,' he nodded towards the orderly, who was still working carefully on his arm, 'I saw Eddy reach the ground, about two or three miles behind the enemy lines I could see the movement of the falling 'plane, rather than the 'plane itself and then nothing. If a 'plane catches fire on impact with the ground one can always see it, a brief flare, even when one's at a greater altitude than we were.' The cigarette had dropped from her fingers to the floor, between her bare feet. She stared at it as it burnt, while the smoke rose towards her tragic face.

'Oh, Edouard,' she said and hugged herself as her tears fell to the floor, beside the smouldering cigarette; finally she looked up at Charles. The orderly had finished dressing his arm, now strapped across his chest in a sling. The cigarette had gone out, extinguished by one of her tears.

'Can a man survive such a fall?' She asked so quietly that he strained to hear.

'Sometimes.' She looked down at her hands, which hung between her legs and twined her fingers. He waited, wanting to light another cigarette, until she finally spoke again. 'He's dead, I know he's dead, I feel it here,' she touched her breast and looked directly at him, naked pain in her eyes, 'I can no longer feel him with me.'

The medic left the room quietly as Charles crossed over to where Giselle was still sitting, head bowed and crying silently.

'Please don't Countess, we just don't know what happened but we will soon.' She looked up at him waiting for more.

'I don't understand,' she said, 'what more is there to know, he is dead.'

'Not necessarily, it depends a great deal on what he hit and how.' She flinched at the thought of the impact.

'May I have a cigarette please?'

'Of course.' He offered her his case and took one himself, lit their cigarettes and went back to his chair. 'Almost every time one of our pilots goes down behind enemy lines we are told by the Germans who it is and what has happened to him. Quite often they fly over our fields and drop messages, and other times our artillery somehow finds out and lets us know. So we must wait and probably by this time tomorrow we will know what has happened.' He had almost said whether he is dead or not, for he was thinking about his newest pilot who had just died and the letter he must write to his parents.

'But, if he is alive then what would happen and what can we do?'

'If he is hurt, the Germans will put him into one of their hospitals, they are good at that. If he is not, he will be made a prisoner of war and, either way, we will be formally notified.'

'You talk as if you think he is still alive.'

'No, I just hope he is and, until we know…' he shrugged and immediately regretted doing so, '… we don't.' She got up and walked towards him.

'Do you have a blanket, I am suddenly very cold.'

'Of course, how thoughtless of me.' He crossed the room in two strides, stripped the blanket off Edward's cot and wrapped it around her shoulders. She smiled gratefully at him and hugged herself. He saw renewed hope flicker in her eyes.

'If he is in hospital, would I be able to go and see him?'

'No, I don't think so.' He went back to Edward's desk, sat down, stubbed out his cigarette and lit another one. 'Did you know that Edward has a brother in Paris. He is a war correspondent for the *Washington Post*.'

'No, we never talked about his family, but why do you ask?'

'I was just thinking that perhaps he might be able to help us in some way but I'm not sure how. Now Countess, before you catch your death of cold, I think you should go home and get out of those wet clothes, and the moment I have any news,' he emphasised the any, 'I will let you know.' He got up and stubbed out his cigarette and, putting his arm around her shoulders, walked her out towards her car. 'Keep the blanket.' She tightened it around her shoulder, knowing that Edward had been the last to use it.

CHAPTER 63

Edward realised his mistake and that the outcome was inevitable. He rolled into a dive and at the same moment felt the machine-gun fire cutting across the fuselage in front, into the engine. Immediately his dive accelerated and the plane did not respond, so he knew that his aileron wires had been severed by the bullets. He was already two thousand feet below the German, who had caught him in the crossfire. A long trail of smoke streamed from the engine cowling but there was no sign of fire yet. He pushed down hard on the rudder bars, first one and then the other in an attempt to slow his descent and he succeeded in bringing his nose up slightly. He continued to fall at a reduced rate, rather like a sycamore seed. He could see the German trenches below, zig-zag formation clearly defined, and realised that he would crash behind their lines. At three thousand feet the German infantry started shooting at him, but it wasn't until he had dropped another thousand feet that a burst of machine gun fire tore through the fuselage, smashing his legs together up against the far side of the cockpit. He could see the fuel line rupture and petrol sprayed across his head, at any moment he could be engulfed in a fire ball. He was well past the enemy trenches and, with the last of his strength, he tried to keep the plane level as he flew over a small wood and the roof of a barn just beyond. Surprisingly, the barn was still intact and his undercarriage clipped the roof and he felt the plane bounce slightly on impact, before plunging into a duck pond on the far side. He was thrown violently forward onto his harness, his head smashing against the grips of his Lewis gun. He lost consciousness, releasing him from the agonising pain in his legs. The tail of the 'plane sank slowly and settled into the soft mud of the pond with the nose on the far bank; the cockpit was only half submerged when the 'plane came to rest.

Slowly Edward's head cleared and he became aware of his surroundings and felt great pain in his legs. He looked down at them and saw that he was sitting in a pool of diluted blood. His forearm was badly cut and blood was running from a deep gash on his forehead, which had closed his right eye. He could hear a sizzling sound and realised that it came from the engine and wondered why. He raised his arms to the sides of the cockpit and tried to lever himself up but his straps held him in place. He fumbled for the harness buckle and realised that he was waist deep in water. His goggles had been knocked off his head on impact and he had difficulty removing his helmet because part of it was embedded in the gash on his head. He tried again to lever himself out of the cockpit but couldn't and became aware of two voices, a man and woman talking rapidly to one another, in French. He tried to turn his head to see where they were and thought he was going to lose consciousness. He heard splashing behind him and felt his shoulders lifted in a firm, strong grip, he cried out in pain. The Frenchman had climbed onto the fuselage behind him.

'Laissez-moi vous aider!'

'My legs,' said Edward and pointed towards them beneath the blood stained water. He realised that his seat had sheared from its mountings and was tipped forward in the cockpit and that he wouldn't be able to get out without having it levered back into its original position. Without much difficulty he conveyed this to the Frenchman who immediately jumped off the wing and returned with a crow bar, which he used to force the seat back into its place, at the same time telling his wife to bring one of the window shutters from the house. The Frenchman straddled the fuselage behind Edward and, as gently as he could, with his hands beneath Edward's arms, attempted to drag him from the cockpit onto the fuselage. Edward screamed and fainted but not before the Frenchman had seen the awful damage to Edward's legs and knew how much blood he had lost and how little time there was to stem the bleeding. He then realised that Edward's feet were trapped beneath the rudder bars and as both legs appeared to be badly broken, there was no way he could free Edward without freeing his feet.

The Frenchman jumped down from the 'plane and ran to the barn shouting for his wife to bring sheets and a knife. Within moments he was back behind the engine with an axe which he used to cut through the fuselage above Edward's feet. As soon he had freed them he returned to the fuselage behind Edward and at the same time his wife reappeared with the sheets and the shutter. He lifted Edward again, as gently as he could and told his wife to slide Edward's legs and feet from the cockpit. Between them they succeeded and managed to ease Edward onto the shutter that they had placed between the bank and the lower wing. Edward was still unconscious as they carried him higher up the bank and laid the shutter down on flat ground. Immediately the Frenchman set to work with the knife cutting away Edward's breeches and boots. At the same time, his wife produced a pair of scissors from her apron and started to cut the sheets into rudimentary bandages and tourniquets, knowing that if they didn't stop the bleeding soon, Edward would die.

They both heard a convoy, coming away from the Front, at the same time and, leaving his wife to continue with the tourniquets, the man ran to the road to intercept the vehicles. As he had expected, it was made up of ambulances ferrying German casualties back to the nearest field hospital. They were moving quite slowly and, running alongside the last ambulance, he managed to persuade the driver to stop. There was a doctor sitting on the front bench beside the driver who followed the Frenchman back to Edward's 'plane, leaving the remainder of the convoy to continue on their way. Grasping the doctor's arm, the Frenchman urged him towards where Edward lay, by then partially bandaged and losing less blood. The doctor immediately went to work on Edward. He injected morphine for the pain, straightened his distorted legs in preparation for the splints and tied sutures wherever possible, to enable him to loosen the tourniquets. As the doctor worked, the Frenchman led his wife to one side while two orderlies ran over from the ambulance carrying a stretcher and other medical supplies between them. The Frenchman spoke quietly to his wife and she slipped away and went into the house. Within minutes she was back again bringing something wrapped in a white cloth. With the help of the orderlies the doctor set the splints on Edward's leg, moved him onto the stretcher and covered him with a blanket. The orderlies picked him up and carried him back to the ambulance. The Frenchman took the package from his wife, unwrapped it and handed a bottle of Calvados to the doctor.

'Pour vous Monsieur, et merci beaucoup.'

* * *

From a great distance, Edward's mind began to focus on his surroundings. Slowly, as the effect of the drugs faded, he became aware of increasing pain in both his legs. His body rolled from side to side in the narrow hammock that he was strapped into, on one side of the ambulance. The dominant sound was that of an engine and briefly he thought he was still flying, before he realised his mistake. There was someone standing above him, washing his face with cold, carbolic scented water in an attempt to remove the dry and crusted blood from his eye. Some of the water ran into his mouth and he realised that the carbolic scent came from the nurse and not from the water. She was making soothing sounds but he couldn't understand what she was saying, he raised his hand to her arm and she pushed him gently back down on the cot and exchanged the flannel for a towel, to dry his face. He managed to open his eye and looked at her while he tried to orientate himself.

'He is awake doctor,' she said in German and he raised his head slightly and saw the doctor leave his seat in front of the ambulance and move back towards them. The nurse shifted to one side and the doctor took her place, raised Edward's wrist in one hand and glanced at his watch.

'You're lucky to be alive,' he said in English, 'your legs are badly damaged and I don't know if you'll ever walk again but that is not my job. We've got a very good orthopaedic surgeon in the hospital at Lille, who might have a more optimistic opinion.'

'Is that where we are going?' said Edward.

'Yes, it's one of the two old hospitals in Lille that survived the shelling two years ago.' He took a syringe from a tray above Edward's head and filled it from a small bottle 'I am giving you more morphine for the pain, which will make the transfer to the hospital more bearable.'

'Am I a prisoner?'

'Technically yes, we'll let your people know,' he added, anticipating Edward's next question.

'Your English is very good and you have a Scottish accent.'

'I did two years postgraduate work at Edinburgh University, before the war.'

'How will you let my people know?'

'There is an established informal exchange of information of captured or killed airman and sometimes our flyers drop messages on your airfields as do yours on ours, when the pilot is well known.'

'I'm not…'

'I know. Your name is Charles Bishop, you have a letter in your tunic, a bit bloodstained but still legible.' Edward raised his right hand.

'No, you are mistaken. I…'

'Steady there, calm down. I'm Sascha Schackmar,' said the doctor and shook Edward's hand, as he eased him back onto the stretcher, a small smile playing at the corner of his mouth. Edward could feel his body relaxing as the morphine took hold, closed his eyes and mumbled

'Delighted to know you…'

CHAPTER 64

Charles left the Mess immediately after lunch and went out to where the Bentley was parked, checked to see if he had enough petrol, while he convinced himself Edward wouldn't mind. He started it up and headed in the direction of the Chateau. He had good news for the Countess and looked forward to passing it on. The unexpected intermittent rain had stopped and he thought briefly of the men in the trenches and how it would, to a certain extent, make life easier. Once again he felt the same comfort he always did when comparing his lot to theirs and understood, in part, why the infantry resented the lifestyle, as they saw it, of the RFC. He turned into the gate of the Chateau and saw the Countess crossing the courtyard towards the stables and, at the same moment, she saw him and started running towards the car. When they were twenty yards apart she stopped in her tracks, her shoulders slumped and her joyful expression changed to one of bitter disappointment, she raised her hands to her mouth as he pulled up beside her.

'I thought…'

'I know, I'm sorry I didn't think of that but I have good news.' Immediately, she lifted her head again and looked at him, hope flaring in her eyes, 'He is alive. I heard this morning that the Germans have him, under my name, in a hospital somewhere on their side of the lines.'

'Thank God I was wrong, I don't know why, I was certain he had died. I am so confused, I have heard from Paris and Jacques will be here the day after tomorrow. I don't suppose you know where Edward is.'

'No they never tell us.'

'How can we find out?'

'It won't be easy.'

'We must find a way, please come inside. Have you had lunch?'

'Yes, but thank you, we eat fairly early in the mess.'

'Perhaps a glass of cognac?' Charles left the Bentley where it was and walked across the yard and together they went through one of the side entrances into the Chateau. Giselle called to Marie and told her to bring them coffee and cognac in the library, where they sat in front of the fireplace in deep leather armchairs, with Charles in the same one Edward had sat in just three days before. Marie brought the coffee and poured it out for them and Giselle filled both their glasses with a generous measure of cognac. Silently they toasted each other, both deep in thought, in pursuit of the same solution.

'Have you ever asked for further information, in a similar situation?'

'Yes, on several occasions, but I've never had even a reply and none of us want to upset the status quo because it is better to know what they do tell us than to be completely in the dark.'

'Then I must find a way of getting behind their lines. I have an old school friend who lives in Lille or at least she did when she last wrote to me.'

'It would be very difficult and very dangerous, everyone in occupied France has been issued with identity papers which would be very hard to obtain without the official sanctions or knowing where to obtain forged documents.' They lapsed into silence and all that could be heard was the steady sound of the eighteenth-century long case clock, ticking away the time like grains of sands slipping through the waist of an hour glass.

'His brother,' she said suddenly, 'you told me about his brother, a war correspondent, surely he can cross the lines. I must go and find him, I must go to Paris,' she continued breathlessly 'my sister lives there. I'll go and stay with her. I must go now,' she added full of renewed hope. She also realised that if she did, she wouldn't be at the Chateau when Jacques got home. She stood up, transformed with energy and went over and stood beside Charles's chair.

'Can you take me to the station? I can be ready in fifteen minutes. Please Charlie, you don't mind me calling you Charlie, do you?' She said, with the first smile he had seen on her lovely face.

'Of course, I would be delighted to but who knows when the next train will be.'

'It doesn't matter, I will take some sandwiches that Marie can make while I pack and I'll sit there until one arrives, the first that takes me in the right direction. If I leave now I might be in Paris before nightfall.'

Half an hour after they left the Chateau they pulled up in front of the station; luck was with her: there was a train due shortly bound for Amiens that would connect with the Paris express so that, all being well, she would be in Paris by eight that evening. She bought a single ticket, fleetingly aware of its significance, said goodbye to Charles and made her way through to the platform to wait for the train. There was only one other couple on the platform and an old man sitting on a bench in the sun who didn't move when the train arrived.

With only ten minutes to make her connection, she hurried across the station at Amiens realising that there would be no porters to help her, all of them absorbed into the insatiable military maw. She thought briefly of sending her sister a telegram but decided against as she didn't want to miss her train and, if her sister wasn't there, she could always take a room in a hotel nearby. The train arrived, to her surprise, within a minute of the appointed time and she saw it as a good omen. She felt she was on the right track, the Gods were with her. The train was packed with soldiers on their way to the eastern end of the front, near the Swiss border. They are all so young, she thought, all laughing and joking and appeared to be happy having finished their basic training, ready to face the Bosch, in action for the first time. They were standing, massed along the whole length of the corridor but somehow managed to allow her through. One of them opened the door to the first compartment and immediately the man in the corner seat stood up, took her bag, swung it up onto the rack and offered her his seat. With a smile she sat down, and he stepped out into the corridor and slid the door closed behind him. Just before eight the train pulled into the Gare du Nord and Giselle remained seated while the troops disembarked and fell in on the platform. They were still laughing and joking and those of them who had stood for the whole journey seemed totally unaffected. After they marched off, she carried her bag out into the street and hailed a cab.

'Rue Milton please, probably easiest if you take Rue de Maubeuge and it's just off Rue Lamartine.' The driver was not amused to be told his way around Paris by someone just off the train from Amiens. Within minutes they turned into Rue Milton and she called out, 'Number 29 please, towards the end on the left.' She stepped down, paid the driver and looked up to the first floor and saw light shining in the window. She crossed the pavement and rang the bell, she could see a light coming down the stairs reflected in the fan light and the door was opened by a maid.

'Madame la Contesse, we weren't expecting you, Madame is having dinner at Chez Henri, on the corner,' she pointed down the street, 'with Madame Faubert. Shall I run down and tell her you are here?'

'No,' she racked her brain for the maid's name, 'Please take my bag and coat, I will be staying for a few days and let me go and surprise my sister.'

The restaurant was full and brightly lit, they must have received fresh produce from the country, and when that happened word spread very quickly in the immediate area. She could see her sister sitting with another woman at a table near the kitchen door. A white-haired sommelier, with stooped shoulders and carrying a bottle, was shuffling across the room towards them. They were in deep conversation and hadn't seen him. Giselle crossed quickly to his side and, with a dazzling smile, persuaded him to surrender the bottle. She moved on to her sister's table.

'Shall I pour Madame Delon?' her sister looked up in surprise and cried out with delight.

'Giselle, what on earth are you doing here and what are you doing with that bottle?'

'I have a new job.'

'Don't be ridiculous, this is Nicole Faubert. Put that bottle down at once and sit down.'

'Yes, Babette.' She hasn't changed a bit thought Giselle, always the elder sister and always telling me what to do.

'When did you arrive in Paris?'

'Just now.'

'Don't you have any luggage?'

'Yes, I left it at the house, what is your maid's name? I couldn't think of it.'

'Amelie, I hope she has the sense to make up your room. Have you eaten, of course not, we're having lamb, it was brought up from Henri's farm this afternoon and do ask the waiter for another glass.' She turned to her companion, 'Nicole, this is Giselle my baby sister, she thrives in deep country, married a man almost as old as our father which caused considerable distress to both him and our mother.'

'Babette that is not fair, he is only fifteen years older than me.'

'Sixteen.'

'Well sixteen, then,' she admitted, 'But he didn't look it the last time I saw him.'

'What does it matter, he is dead anyhow.' Nicole flinched at her candour.

'No, he is not.'

'What do you mean? You told me he was dead. He died in Turkey or some such place.' Nicole's eyes were swivelling like gun turrets from one sister to another.

'That's what I was told and believed for more than a year, but now he is coming back. In fact he might even be in Paris right now.'

'Ah ha, so that's why you are here.'

'No, in fact he doesn't know I'm here, he is expecting to find me at home when he arrives there sometime tomorrow.'

'Then, why are you here, Cherie?'

'That's a long story, which I will tell you tomorrow. But tell me now what you have been doing since I saw you last.'

Nicole tried to hide her disappointment and turned to Giselle, 'Where do you live?'

'A place called Estrée-Blanche, north of Amiens, very near the Front.'

'How exciting, can you hear the guns?'

'Yes, sometimes very loudly but it depends to a certain extent on the wind direction.' An hour later the party broke up and Nicole, who lived on the same street, left them at their door and continued on home.

'Come up to the drawing room, you must tell me everything, you must tell me why you are here in Paris, I can't wait to hear what you have been up to,' and added, 'a little adventure perhaps?' and she squeezed her sister's arm, conspiratorially. 'Amelie,' she called out to the maid's retreating back, 'Bring us some coffee and cognac, please.' The two sat side by side on a sofa and, to Giselle's surprise, Babette put her feet up on the brass fender in front of the fireplace.

'Don't look so shocked, try it, you might enjoy it.' She reached across and took her sister's hand, now tell me all about him, it must be one of your aviateurs. But when I was there they were all as old as Jacques.'

'Well this one isn't.'

'Ah ha, so it is an aviateur, tell me all about him.'

'I have to find him.'

'What do you mean, have you already lost him or did he run away?'

'No, Babette this is serious. He was shot down three days ago and

I found out this morning that he wasn't killed but is being taken care of in some hospital behind the Germans' lines.'

'How do you know that?'

'They have some reciprocating system of letting each other know when one of their pilots is down behind the other's lines.'

'So the Germans told you that they had shot him down? How extraordinary!'

'No, they told the C.O. of Estrée-Blanche and he told me.'

'How very civilised, so all you have to do is ask them where he is.'

'I'm afraid it is not that easy, I had the same thought and the C.O. told me it never happens.'

'So what are we going to do?' Giselle felt an immediate surge of gratitude for her sister's choice of words.

'The only lead I have is his brother.'

'Who's brother, the C.O.'s brother?'

'No, Edward's brother.'

'So his name is Edward.'

'Yes.'

'How long have you known him?'

'Not long, about four weeks.'

'I can see you're smitten.'

'It's more than that Babette, I love him, I am in love with him.'

'Poor Jacques, you are in a pickle.'

'I know, but I also know that to me Jacques is dead.'

'That's ridiculous and he is still your husband.'

'Yes, but I have mourned him and accepted his death and even if I hadn't met Edouard, I'm not sure I can go back to where I had been with Jacques.'

'You know that's not true, you are just saying that to justify your feelings for Edward. Anyway, who am I to stand in judgement.' she added, as if she had never strayed before.

They drank their coffee in silence, Giselle uncertain how to continue. Babette got up and crossed over to the double full length windows that led out onto the balcony.

419

'It's stuffy in here' she said, turning back to Giselle, 'and why did you stop telling me about Edward?'

'I need your help, I need to find him.'

'I know, you're repeating yourself.'

'The only lead I have is his brother, he's here in Paris.'

'You have already told me that too. What is his name?'

'Gerald.'

'Is that all?'

'No, Gerald Meade, like Edward Meade.'

'I don't believe it. What time is it?' Giselle looked at her watch.

'Almost half past ten. Why?' Babette lent across the table and picked up the telephone, dialled the operator and asked for a number.

'Claudine, it's Babette, not too late am I?' Giselle could hear the other voice on the telephone but not what was said. 'What was the name of the man you brought round here the other night? He sounded like an American.' Again, an indistinct answer, 'I thought so, when will you be seeing him again?' Giselle was hanging on her every word. 'He just left? Why, no don't answer that,' she added before Claudine could say anything. 'Hang on a moment, I have my sister here.' Babette put her hand across the mouth piece and turned to Giselle. 'They are meeting for lunch tomorrow. Do you want to join them, I can invite us.'

'Of course, what an extraordinary coincidence.' Babette smiled and turned back to the telephone.

'May my sister and I join you for lunch tomorrow? Thank you, where are you lunching? Of course, at what time? Fine see you there then. Good night.' She turned back to Giselle. 'I thought so. Claudine, one of my best friends, brought Gerald here last week and, if Edward is anything like his brother, I admire your taste. We're lunching with them tomorrow at Fouquet.'

'How do they know each other?'

'How should I know? He is probably taking care of Claudine while her husband is at the Front.'

'Oh,' said Giselle, not sure how to continue, when she realised the hypocrisy of her thoughts.

'You must be tired, and I've got my dressmaker coming at ten tomorrow, so I think it is bed time, you know where your room is.'

'Yes and thank you.' Giselle lent across and kissed her sister's cheek. 'I have so much to tell you.' Babette touched her lightly on the arm.

'Tomorrow my dear, now off to bed with you.'

CHAPTER 65

'There they are,' said Babette, 'and they're early.'

'No Babette, we're late.'

'Well not by much, it was my dressmaker's fault.' Gerald stood as they approached and took Babette's hand,

'So good to see you again Babette and your sister,' he added, turning to Giselle. Babette kissed Claudia on the cheek briefly, taking care not to dislodge their hats.

'Claudia, this is my sister, Giselle, I don't think you have met, she is a friend of Edward, Gerald's brother.' She turned to Gerald as he held a chair for her and sat down. 'My sister lives in the country, north of Amiens near where your brother is stationed.' Gerald moved around the table smiling at Giselle and held out a chair for her.

'You know Edward? Forgive me for being so rude but I haven't seen him since we had leave together in Scotland. I know he is somewhere in France but he is playing his cards close to his chest.'

'I didn't know you were in Paris, either. Edward never mentioned you. In fact, we never talked about his family and it was only yesterday that his C.O. told me about you.'

Claudia had already taken her place. The head waiter approached with four menus, closely followed by the sommelier, who left the wine list on the table beside Gerald and withdrew.

'Lucien,' said Babette, 'how nice to see you, busy as ever I see.'

She turned to Claudia, 'You would never think there was a war on, would you?' She opened the menu, 'What do you recommend today, Lucien?'

'The fish is very good, Madame Delon.'

'Trout, I suppose.'

'No Madame, halibut, it came in overnight from Saint Brieuc.'

'Marvellous, I'll have that and you, Lucien, can have the menu.' She handed it back to him. 'How about the rest of you?' Lucien looked from one to another, his pencil poised above his pad.

'Same for me,' said the two women in unison and Gerald fell in with the majority.

'Well that's settled' said Babette. 'Lots of vegetables, Lucien, with an avocado salad and a dozen oysters each, to start with. And you Gerald must pick a really good wine and this is my treat.'

'How very kind, Babette but you are all my guests or,' he grinned at each of them in turn, 'I should say guests of the *Washington Post*.' Lucien left them and the sommelier returned for Gerald's order.

'A magnum of Montrachet would go down well, 1907 if you have any left.'

'Oohhh one of my favourites,' said Babette, clapping her hands. 'Giselle, tell Gerald all about Edward, he must be dying to know.' Giselle picked up the edge of her napkin unsure whether to talk about Edward's arrival at the chateau or of his being shot down and decided on the former. She turned to Gerald.

'He arrived at my house last month with the C.O., also staying with me. There were five officers staying there at the time but, as in most cases, they were only there for a week or so, hardly time to get to know them, but with Edward it was different. He had been my guest for some four weeks and sometimes he was late back to dinner, depending on when they returned from their patrol, but three days ago he didn't come back at all, so the next morning I went to the airfield to find out why not. He had been shot down and had crashed somewhere behind the enemy's lines.' It was out before she had had time to prepare him. 'He is all right Gerald, he is in a hospital in occupied France but that is all I know.' She was now twisting her napkin between her fingers and when she realised what she was doing she spread it on her knees. She hadn't meant to tell him so abruptly but her need to express herself overruled any caution she intended.

'Well, there you are Gerald,' said Babette, 'you have it in a nutshell, not quite how I would have put it but nothing like going straight to the nub of it.'

'That's all right Babette, he is a survivor. I am sure he will find a way out of his predicament.'

'That, Gerald, is what I had hoped you might be able to help me with. I've told you all I know.'

'Don't upset yourself Giselle,' Gerald wanted to lean forward and take her hand but thought better of it. 'We'll think of something. It rather depends on how badly he is hurt.' He saw her flinch and took her hand, anyhow. 'If he is seriously injured, they won't have taken him far. If it is just a scratch, he'll be moved eastward with the Allied infantry prisoners.'

'Unpalatable options,' said Babette, 'either there is a good chance of finding him and he is badly damaged or he is not and he will be irretrievable. I put my money on the first option, because of what I know of this beastly war, those that drop from fifteen thousand feet don't usually walk away with just a scratch.' Gerald was still holding Giselle's hand and was surprised by the strength of her grip, on his. He smiled at Babette.

'It seems you don't pull your punches, either.' Claudia laughed and immediately covered her mouth with her napkin, as Lucien returned with two waiters carrying four plates of oysters.

'Some bread, please Lucien,' said Babette, 'and lots of lemons, cut in quarters, not those silly ring things.' With relish, they started on the oysters and one of the waiters brought bread while the other laid finger bowls on the table in front of each of them. The sommelier drew the cork and poured a small amount into Gerald's glass, as another waiter appeared behind him, with a large silver ice bucket. Gerald sipped the wine and beamed with pleasure.

'It's very good,' he said to Giselle and nodded to the sommelier, who filled their glasses before replacing the bottle in the ice bucket. Gerald raised his glass, 'here's to us, to the end of the war and most importantly to Edward's recovery, medically and physically.' They all raised their glasses and drank. Not much was said until their plates had been cleared away but not before Gerald had offered each of them a second dozen. 'I've been thinking,' he said, 'there is something I can do, my editor is always on about my lack of inspired contributions, so I was thinking it might be possible to persuade the German press liaison officer to allow me behind their lines to write something about, I don't know, about how well they treat their prisoners,' he finished with a flourish. 'That's it, I could give them some spiel about how well they treat our chaps and how the American public would enjoy reading about it.'

'What a marvellous idea,' said Babette, 'inspirational. Now tell me Claudia, what happened to your sister in Marseilles?' Claudia looked across at Giselle and smiled.

'That is really not very important Babette, this is much more interesting,' she said, managing to cut Babette off, in full flow.

'But do the Germans let Allied war correspondents behind their lines?' asked Giselle.

'Sometimes, if it's to their advantage and it's mostly our chaps they let through, because they want to be painted in a good light. Their fear of America coming in with the Allies increases daily.'

'But how about censorship,' asked Claudia, 'surely you are not allowed to write what you want.'

'It's pretty severe with the French and English correspondents because the powers that be believe that the truth, in all its grizzly detail, would demoralise their respective people, back home. Our chaps have a freer hand because most of the American public don't want to hear war news from the German point of view, which would be the only other alternative.'

'So,' said Giselle, 'if they gave you a pass you would be allowed to go from hospital to hospital to interview Allied pilots and German doctors? And, if Babette is right, Edward is most likely to be within fifty kilometres of where he was shot down.'

'It will be quite a job, my dear, there will probably be at least a hundred field hospitals in that area but, if my luck holds, there may not be more than ten permanent hospitals and it would be quite possible to have them all included on my pass.'

'And if you find him, when you find him, what can we do then?'

'That my dear, we'll think about when it happens.'

'That's wonderful Gerald, you're so brave,' he inclined his head, 'what happens if something goes wrong and they keep you on their side of the lines?'

'Then there will be two Meades to be recovered but I will do my best not to let that happen.' He smiled reassuringly at her. 'When I get back to the office this afternoon,' he continued, glancing briefly at Claudia in time to see her disappointment, 'I'll talk to my editor and get him fired up because it is he that must apply for the pass. I'm sure he'll do his best, if only to have me out of the office for a while.'

'Have you been behind their lines before, Gerald?'

He turned to Babette with a sardonic grin. 'Not me but Benson, one of the chaps in our office spent two weeks there doing an article on how the Germans conscript local French women as nurses and he got back in one piece. What is the nearest large town in occupied France, to where Edward came down?'

'Lille,' said Giselle.

'Then I'll start there and will let you know the moment I have any news. We have an office code so we can send messages through official channels, which aren't understood by the Hun.'

* * *

That afternoon Gerald walked into his editor's office, 'Good afternoon Abe, I've got an idea I want to run past you.'

'As hare-brained as the last?'

'No sir, it is a human interest story, which should appeal to our readers back home.'

'I can hardly wait.'

'I can see the headlines, 'Allied pilots in German care.''

'Go on,' an encouraging spark of interest flashed briefly behind his specks.

'I picked up a lot of information when doing the Lafayette article, giving details of how the Germans treat the Allied pilots that are brought down behind their lines. Both the Germans and the Allies go to great lengths to let the other side know what has happened to their airmen, whether dead or injured.'

'That seems very civilised, amidst such carnage, but do go on.'

'I thought it might be a good idea to go behind their lines and interview the doctors and their patients, in several different hospitals.'

'And how do you propose to do that, assuming I sanction it. How are you going to get behind their lines?'

'Quite simple Sir, we have to apply for a pass, as we did in Benson's case six months ago, from the German liaison officer at the Paris press office.'

'That was different, they asked us to send someone.'

'Exactly, a two-way street and in this case, I think they will be delighted to give us permission because they will think it will show them in a good light, to our readers.'

'I was just about to say the same thing, surely that is not in our best interest.'

'But it will be Sir, it's all in the way I'll write it. I'll end my article by pointing out that the Allies are doing just the same for the German pilots that are brought down behind our lines. The only difference is that I will show that we are doing a much better job of it than they are.'

'OK Gerry,' he rarely called him that, 'Make the application and I'll sign it.'

'Thank you, Sir,' Gerald stood up and left the office before Abe changed his mind.

After almost a week in Paris with Babette, Giselle felt that she had to return to the Chateau and face Jacques. Babette begged her to stay a bit longer because she was enjoying her company and introducing Giselle to all her friends.

'No Babette, I must go, I am sure Jacques is home by now and I should be there.'

'What are you going to tell him?'

'I don't know, the truth, probably. I don't want to hurt him but I no longer feel anything for him and, on reflection, I wonder if I ever did. He was protective and worldly-wise and when we married, I felt safe with him.'

'Weren't you safe with us, your family?'

'Of course, but it was another kind of safe, I had moved on from being a child to a woman. But there is really nothing there now and certainly nothing like what I have with Edward. No, I'll tell him the truth and if he throws me out I'll be back in Paris. You'll have me won't you?'

'Of course darling, I would love it, you can stay here as long as you want, even when my husband comes back, because that would really annoy him.' She laughed and continued, 'Go on, pack your things while I check the train times and then I'll take you to the station.'

'May I ring Jacques and tell him I am on my way, so he can come and collect me.'

'Of course, the operator will put you through but you may have to wait a little while.' Almost an hour later, the call came through and Marie answered.

'Marie, how are you? I'll be home soon. May I speak to my husband, please.' Giselle listened to Marie's answer and turned to Babette and held out her hand. Babette moved forward and took it, concern showing in her eyes.

'What is it?' she said in a whisper.

'Thank you Marie, I will ring again when I have the train times.

Please have Jules meet me.' She put down the telephone and Babette took her other hand.

'What is it cherie, you're very pale.'

'He's not there, he left this morning. Marie told me that he arrived two days ago and he left this morning,' she repeated, 'but why?'

'Is that all she said?'

'Just that and that he had left a letter for me. I feel cold Babette, somehow he knows about Edward and me but that's not possible.'

CHAPTER 66

Marie had prepared a late supper for Giselle but she couldn't face it. She had been given Jacques' letter but hadn't opened it. She went through to the library, poured herself a generous helping of cognac and curled up in the leather chair where Edward had last sat. She slid a silver letter opener under the flap; a single sheet of headed writing paper lay within, behind it an envelope addressed to her in an unfamiliar hand. She unfolded the letter from Jacques and started to read.

My dear Giselle,

By the time you read this, I will have left here and re-joined what remains of my old squadron. I think it is best for both of us and you will see why soon. I was surprised and very disappointed not to find you here when I returned. I thought it would have been the least you could have done, after we have spent so much time apart but, having read the enclosed letter, I can understand why and I make no apologies for having opened it.

I know you were told that I was missing in action and were then led to believe that I had most probably been killed but I can't understand why, in less than two years, you should have given up on even the remotest chance of my returning to you. You probably won't believe that it was the thought of you and our eventual reunion that sustained me through all that I suffered at the hands of the Turks. I still love you, in my own particular way and I will wait and see, however long it might take, what you decide to do. Stay on at L'Aval, if you want and, when this war is over, we will see where we stand.

Your loving husband,

Jacques

Her bottom lip trembled and two tears ran down her cheeks and splashed onto the letter. She put it down on the table beside her and withdrew the other envelope. She looked at it for a long time, bizarrely admiring Edward's handwriting, before she opened it and started to read.

My love,

It is very late and I am sitting on a cot in my office as I can't sleep. I can hardly breathe, your presence leaves no room for me to think or move freely in neither my mind nor body. I have never felt like this, so confused, yet so clear headed about my feelings for you and my memories of last night. How you managed to turn me from boy to man in a glorious but so brief a time and I will never forget the expression in your eyes, when you realised that I had never known a woman before. Nor will I ever forget the way you showed me what to do without my realising, at that moment, that that was what you were in fact doing.

Please forgive me for leaving when and how I did, I should never have done it in such a way, a coward's way but I couldn't face the thought of losing you. I know what I must do, now that we both know that your husband is alive and will soon be with you. I will never forget you and will always love you.

Edward

She clutched the letter in her hand and pushed herself out of the chair and ran up the steps to the library gallery, through the secret door to her bedroom and threw herself onto her bed. She didn't cry, she was almost laughing as she grabbed one of her pillows, hugged it to her breast and rolled onto her back.

'Oh Edouard, Edouard,' she exulted, 'you really do love me.' She had believed him when she had first heard it but not as she did now, having read his letter. She smoothed it out between her fingers and read it again before putting it down on her bedside table. She picked up her pillow again, 'I will find you my love.' She confided to the pillow, 'I will not rest until I do and when I do, I will never let you go.'

CHAPTER 67

Gerald swung his feet off the editor's desk as Abe came into his office.

'You sent for me, Sir?'

'Yes, dear boy.' He's in a good mood, thought Gerald. He must have heard from the German Press Office. 'They've finally sanctioned your trip to Lille and, thinking about your ideas on this, I can see where it can reflect well on us. They have given me a list of hospitals that you are allowed to visit, in and around the town.'

'I thought it would never happen, it's been more than two months since you applied. Meanwhile, I've been finding out what I could about Lille, Sir. It seems it was badly knocked around by the Germans in October '14, heavily shelled, causing a lot of damage.'

'Yes and at the beginning of this year there was a massive explosion in a German munition dump at Dix-huit Ponts, in the old town ramparts near Porte Valenciennes. Hundreds of German troops and some civilians were killed, a great many of them blown to pieces beyond recognition. The Germans suspected sabotage and many residents were arrested and shot.'

'I'll have to keep my wits about me. Who will my contact be in Lille, Sir?'

'You are to report to a Captain Max von Stosch at the Kommandantur after you have checked into the Ermitage Gantois. These are your papers and don't lose them.'

'How do I get there, Sir?'

'Take the old Citroën from the office pool and a couple of cans of extra petrol because you may find it difficult to refuel.'

'Which route do I take, Sir, to cross the Front?'

'Head for Soissons and onto Laon where you'll cross the Front and then onto La Capelle, Maubeuge, Valenciennes and finally Lille. It's about seventy-five miles from here to the front and another hundred onto Lille. It's all written down here with your papers. You leave first thing tomorrow morning.'

* * *

Checked in and with his car safely parked, Gerald walked round to the Kommandantur. Two guards stood in front of the studded doors and one stepped forward and held out his hand.

'Your papers,' he said in French, barring the way.

Gerald removed his papers from his pocket and handed them to the guard. 'I'm an accredited American war correspondent and I'm looking for Captain von Stosch.'

As Gerald climbed the stairs he could see a German officer casually leaning over the banister, dressed in an immaculately tailored uniform with leather boots polished to a high gloss. They shook hands when Gerald reached the top of the stairs and introduced themselves.

'I hope you had a pleasant journey, without too many delays.' He spoke fluent English with an almost unnoticeable German accent.

'Not bad,' said Gerald. 'Just a bit of trouble when I came through the Front because the registration number of my car wasn't on my papers.'

'Typical. It's the simplest oversights that cause the biggest problems. I do apologise on behalf of our Press Office. I can see you were about to comment on my English, taken aback, you might say, but too polite to mention it.' Gerald laughed and relaxed as Max continued, 'I was up at Oxford when this whole thing started, reading Classics and making some progress with a delightful young girl in the town. I also speak French, which is probably why they sent me here and, having done eighteen months on the Front, in the thick of it, I can tell you I'm much happier here.'

'This is my first time anywhere near the Front, all very exciting.'

'The office is about to close, and it's too late to get your I.D. card, which you will need while you are here.'

'Then, if it is all right with you,' said Gerald 'perhaps I might go back to my hotel and rest. I'm rather tired after the journey and I'll report back here tomorrow morning.'

'No, let's have a drink at your hotel at about six. I have a few things to finish here and then we will have a bit of time together before I have to have dinner with the Kommandant. Don't get caught out after curfew, especially as you haven't yet got your I.D. You can dine at your hotel, it's better than most places and you'll be quite comfortable there.' They shook hands and Gerald retraced his steps out past the guards and headed back towards his hotel.

Once he had rounded the first corner, out of sight of the Kommandantur, he changed direction and headed towards the Place de la Nouvelle Aventure, off which he would find the Rue de Flandre. Giselle had told him that a school friend, Pauline Lazaro, lived in number 3, a house that had belonged to her husband, killed in the first few months of the war. He found it without difficulty and knocked on the door. There was no answer and after a moment he knocked again louder and while he waited he noticed a list of names pinned to the door. Nobody answered, so he assumed that Pauline was not yet back and took a seat at a table on the pavement, of a café across the street. Just as he was about to order he noticed a woman approaching, walking with quick nervous movements, on the other side of the street. He got to his feet and called out.

'Pauline?' She turned towards him and stood poised, ready to run. He quickly crossed the street and she, dropping her shoulders, continued to her door. He held out his hand. 'I'm Gerald Meade, a friend of Giselle Mont Le Maitre d'Aval. Don't be frightened, I need to talk to you.'

'You can't come in. It's not allowed. You're not on the list.'

'List? What list?'

'This!' she said, pointing to the door. 'Everyone who lives inside has to be listed outside, it's for the German police, you know.'

'Well then come and have a drink with me, across the street.'

'No, not there. There's another bar around the corner.' She led the way and when they were seated inside, away from the neighbours' prying eyes, he ordered absinthe for them both. 'How is she? I haven't seen her for years. We were such good friends. We had a lot in common, including our mutual distaste for school discipline. At times we were very naughty,' and she laughed.

'She is very well. I saw her in Paris last week. We need your help.'

'Of course I will help you, if I can but it's very difficult here now, with the Germans. They control everything. When did you arrive?'

'About an hour ago.'

'Where are you staying?'

'In the Ermitage Gantois.'

'Do you know about the curfew. It starts in about half an hour and they are very strict.'

'Yes, I know, Captain Stosch told me.'

'You know him?' Her eyes flicked to the street, as if she expected to see him.

'Yes, I just met him. He is organising my visit. I am here ostensibly to write an article for the American people on German medical treatment of Allied prisoners. But it's just a cover, my real reason is to find my brother and try to get him back into unoccupied France.'

'You think he's being held here in Lille?'

'It's possible. He was shot down almost three months ago, between here and Estrée-Blanche, where he was stationed. The Germans notified his squadron at the time that he is alive and badly wounded, so it's logical to assume that he will be in some hospital in or near Lille.'

'Well there are the two old ones, in the centre of town, which you could try first but there are several new ones that have sprung up in the old school buildings, damaged during the early bombardment.'

'I have to meet Max at the hotel at six, so we haven't much time. My plan is that Giselle is dropped in by 'plane from Estrée-Blanche, somewhere near Lille and walks in with the other daily workers from the countryside.'

'You know she will need an I.D. card to get into the city.'

'Yes, is there any way you can help with that and if we can get her here, can she stay with you?' Pauline looked around the café and lowered her voice.

'Her name would have to be on the door but just a moment, let me think. Malthide Guibert's name is still there and she was one of the people blown to bits in the Dix-huit Pont explosion, earlier this year. She was never identified and, probably because of that, her name has not been removed, her room is still vacant.'

'So Giselle could take that room' said Gerald 'and she would take her name, as her new identity.'

'Exactly and the I.D. card shouldn't be too difficult, because I work in the new Town Hall.' Gerald lent across and squeezed her hand.

'You are a great friend but please be careful. Why is it new, what happened to the old one?'

'The old one burnt down in April of this year. It was in Place Rihour and was the old Palais Rihour and had been the Town Hall since the late seventeenth century. It was a great loss to the City because all of the eighteenth-century records were lost and a good part of the City library. We are now set up in the Boulevard de La Liberte, which is about a fifteen-minute walk from your hotel. Do you have a photograph of Giselle?'

'Yes, I have one here for my brother, should I find him.' He took another look around and removed a small envelope from one of his pockets and slipped it into her hand.

'I will try and do it tomorrow. How long will you be here?'

'Until I find my brother. At least a week I imagine. There are quite a few hospitals on my list.'

'Let's meet again here at the same time, the day after tomorrow and hopefully I'll have the I.D. card for you.'

'Where have you been? I've been waiting for you.'

'Sightseeing, I was looking for background material for my article.'

'Come and join me at the bar and we'll have a drink and I'll tell you about the plan for tomorrow.' Gerald sensed that Max's initial suspicion was allayed as he followed the immaculately clad officer into the bar. 'What would you like to drink? Don't say Scotch, they won't have it, even I can't get it, with all my contacts.

'Brandy and soda will be fine.'

'My drink too' said Max with a smile 'or at least for the duration of this infernal war.'

The bar was almost empty and they went over and sat in two comfortable leather chairs next to the rather feeble fire. Max stretched out his legs and crossed one ankle over the other. The firelight glinted on his boots. 'I'll have your card for you tomorrow but I need a photograph, I suppose you've got one?'

'Yes it's in my bag, I'll nip up and get it.' When he got back he handed the photograph to Max, sat down and picked up his drink.

'Have you any preferences as to where we start?'

'Not particularly' said Gerald 'I'll follow your lead but perhaps, on second thoughts, the best plan would be to start with the nearest and work outwards, in concentric circles. Do any of the hospitals have more Allied patients than any other? If so, that would be the first to feature in my article. Especially if they have more advanced equipment and better qualified doctors.'

'The nearest one fits that bill, on both counts. It's called St Sauveur and can't be more than fifteen minutes' walk from here. I have one or two things to do in the morning and I'll pick you up here at nine o'clock. The doctors will be doing their rounds when we get there so we'll be able to tag along with them and that way you'll meet both doctors and patients at the same time. '

'How many patients do they have?'

'There are about three hundred beds, it's the largest hospital in

Lille and it's been there for ever, founded in the thirteenth century, I think but what's there now was built in the seventeenth and eighteenth century. It's a good place to start because they specialise in shrapnel and artillery damage to our men in the trenches. They also have a few of your pilots, both French and English, that were shot down and survived.'

'I suppose some of the doctors will speak English but weren't all Oxford men' he added with a grin. Max demurred.

'Yes, in fact most of them do. A lot were trained in America as well as in Great Britain before the War and they have all benefitted from the great strides that have been made recently in skin grafting and orthopaedic surgery. Now, I must go, the Kommandant calls.' He drained his glass and stood up. 'Don't get up Gerald, I'll see you tomorrow.' He raised the tip of his swagger stick to his forehead and turned on his heel.

* * *

Just before nine the next morning, Max found Gerald waiting for him in the lobby.

'How was your dinner?' asked Gerald.

'Ghastly,' said Max 'it always is and I dread it every time he invites me but I have to go. He's such a snob and only a few of us know that he came up through the ranks. You'd think he was the Kaiser's brother, by the way he behaves.'

Gerald laughed. 'I won't tell a soul and it won't appear in my article.' Max swung his arm around Gerald's shoulder.

'Come on, a brisk fifteen-minute walk will do us both good.'

They left the hotel and headed towards the Grand Place, continued down the Rue de Paris past the Church of St Maurice, until they reached the Porte de Paris, crossed the Place Ruault and walked into the main entrance of St Sauveur hospital. Max returned the salute of the guard on the door and walked briskly across the flagstone lobby to a long desk. The clerk stood at his approach.

'I would like to see the administrator.' There was no equivocation.

'Yes Sir, one moment please.' The clerk spoke briefly into a telephone, 'Gentlemen, please will you sit over there. Monsieur Lappin will be with you in a moment.' Supressing a grin, Max turned in the direction indicated and Gerald followed him. Almost immediately a door opened on the other side of the lobby and a small, bespectacled man in a rather tight suit scampered across the floor with his heels clicking in a staccato rhythm.

'Gentlemen I understand you want to see me,' he lisped through prominent teeth.

'I am Captain von Stosch from the Kommandantur and this is Mr Meade, an American war correspondent who is writing an article on Allied casualties in our care. We would like you to allocate somebody to take us round the wards, to interview the patients and their doctors.'

'It would be my pleasure Sir, give me a moment to let my secretary know' and, without waiting for an answer, he scuttled back. Max and Gerald looked at each other and burst out laughing.

'Priceless' said Max, 'he can't be called Lappin, all that's missing are the twitching whiskers!'

'This way, gentlemen' and they followed Monsieur Lappin to the wards.

'Do you,' asked Max, 'have a ward set aside for Allied pilots, or are they spread throughout the hospital?'

'We do indeed Sir. They're both French and English and most of them are in the old ward beyond the chapel, part of the original hospital.'

'So let's start there' said Max 'lead on!'

At the end of the long corridor Monsieur Lappin turned right into a smaller passageway, at the end of which was an old iron-bound, bow-headed door.

'We'll go this way Sir, through the chapel. The ward is on the other side.'

The door opened into the chapel, with the altar to their left and a beautifully carved sixteenth-century rood screen to their right. Beyond it they could see two long rows of beds backed onto the outer walls, a broad passageway running between them which was cluttered, in an apparently haphazard way, with camp beds, in a desperate attempt to keep up with the endless stream of casualties. Bright autumn light streamed in through the high broken arch windows on both sides and threw angular shadows of the traction frames on the beds, across the floor. Two doctors, walking with their heads close together and deep in conversation, approached.

'Doctor Leboyer' said the administrator, 'a moment of your time, if you please. These gentlemen would like to talk to you and meet others of your colleagues and, with your permission of course, interview some of the Allied patients.'

'Of course, Monsieur Lappin' and the doctor turned to his companion. 'Jean, we'll finish this later, after our rounds' and he turned back to Max and Gerald. 'Gentlemen, how can I be of help?'

'Mr Meade is writing an article for the American public about how kindly and efficiently we treat our enemy. I know you have several French and English pilots here in your care and Mr Meade, who speaks passable French, would like to interview some of them. Monsieur Lappin has very kindly offered to take us round but I must excuse myself as I have other matters to deal with in my office. Gerald, I may be able to get back before you leave but if not, please join me for lunch at your hotel. I'll be there at one o'clock and we can go on to La Comtesse Hospital in the afternoon.' He clicked his heels and retraced his steps back onto the street.

'Would you like me to come with you Mr Meade?' asked Doctor Leboyer 'I'm rather busy, so perhaps we could meet later, when I've finished my rounds.'

'Of course' said Gerald 'I'm sure Monsieur Lappin will manage.'

They started down the right-hand side of the ward; Gerald was appalled by the distressing condition of most of the patients and the almost overpowering smell of disinfectant and putrefaction that permeated the whole room. Each patient had his name written in bold script on a card attached to the foot of his bed and, after walking slowly along the line, Gerald stopped at the foot of a bed with the name Lt John Webb.

'I'd like a word with this man, Monsieur Lappin' and Gerald took a notebook and pencil from his pocket 'but there's no need to delay you any further, as I'm sure you're a very busy man. I will work my way around the ward and when I'm finished, I'm sure I'll be able to find the doctor.' Monsieur Lappin, obviously distressed by the conditions in the ward, nodded in agreement and excused himself. Lt Webb appeared to be asleep and on closer inspection Gerald could see that he had lost one of his legs. His eyelids fluttered and opened on two piercingly blue eyes that held Gerald's with disconcerting intensity. 'My name is Gerald, I'm a war correspondent working for the *Washington Post* and I'm here to interview some of the Allied pilots to find out if there's any way my American readers can help. There is a lot of work going on there now, raising funds to alleviate the hardships that are suffered by the Allies.' What a pompous little speech he thought, why am I so keyed up? 'I'm sorry' he continued 'that sounds silly. It's just that there are an awful lot of people back home who want to do something to help and can't and it was my editor's idea that this article I'm writing might give them a focus.' The patient closed his eyes and drew a deep breath.

'What can I tell you, I was shot down a month ago and lost my left leg but others are in far worse shape than me.'

'Where were you stationed?'

'Estrée-Blanche and I'm not the only one from there. The skipper's on the other side of the ward.'

'What's his name?'

'Charlie Bishop.'

That's impossible thought Gerald. 'When did he come in?'

'Almost three months ago, I'm told.'

'That's impossible,' said Gerald 'A mutual friend of ours saw him two weeks ago at Estrée-Blanche, we spoke about him last week in Paris.' Again the eyes opened and held Gerald's for a mesmerising moment.

'If you know that then there's no harm in my telling you that it's not Charlie Bishop in that bed over there, it's Eddy Meade. We joined the squadron together and there was a mix up when he came in because he was carrying a letter addressed to Charlie and, for some reason best known to himself, he never bothered to tell them his real name.'

'Just as well' said Gerald as he lent forward and showed John Webb his I.D. card. 'I'm his brother and I'm here to find him, as much as anything else. Forgive me, but I must talk to him now because I don't know how long I've got before my liaison officer returns. I'll be back when I can.' Gerald turned away and threaded his way through the camp beds in the aisle. Most of the patients were lying listlessly, some with limbs stretched at unnatural angles in traction and others swathed in bandages, but most followed him with their eyes as he searched their faces. He reached the end of the line and still hadn't seen this brother; then realised that there was a bed on the other side of the rood screen. They had been no more than twenty feet apart when he and Max had first arrived in the ward.

CHAPTER 68

Springbokfontein,
Cape Town,
9 July, 1916

Dearest Mama,

I hope this finds you well and in good spirits. I wrote you from Fife and told you about James and the sinking of the Herzog, but I am not surprised I haven't heard back from you because I am now back at Springbokfontein and the Rhodesian postal service is chaotic, at best.

James is improving, and his wound has healed cleanly and without any infection, thanks almost entirely to Doctor Hanschell's careful treatment and preparation for our journey to Capetown. James is still in hospital, and I see him almost every day. He is regaining strength and it seems that he has full movement and use of his limbs. He still has the same way of looking at me and, so far, his memory seems unaffected. The only difference I can see is that he now stutters. Not badly, nor detrimentally, but it has taken a bit of the bounce out of him. Doctor Drummond, who seems not much older than me, came out from London in July with all the latest procedures, and is a brilliant neurosurgeon. He is looking after James and he, Cecil, as he insists I call him, tells me that if all goes well,

James can come home in two weeks. More tests have to be done, but he is very optimistic. When I told James he would soon be as good as new, hinting that Doctor Hanschell had told me that as there was nothing between James's ears to be damaged, he didn't know what all the fuss was about, James laughed in his old way. This made my heart sing, because none of this ghastly business would have happened, if I had said no.

Johnny and Jenny were waiting for us when I reached Springbokfontein, having settled James in hospital. They had come down the moment they received my cable from Boma. Jenny was devastated by James's condition, but now, almost four weeks later, she is happier with his progress. Johnny had to go back to the farm, and left after the first week.

The Admiral called me in and tried to persuade me to withdraw my resignation. He made a very convincing argument, including immediate promotion and almost irresistible long-term career prospects. I stuck to my guns and repeated what I had put in my letter, that I wanted to be available to the American navy, when they came into the war. He agreed that that was now inevitable, within the next few months and reluctantly accepted my resignation. Entre nous, Mama, it's not the whole truth. As you know, my original reason for joining the Royal Navy was not patriotic, and once I realised what I had become during the Konigsberg action, I knew that, at least in part, I was masquerading. Killing Germans and seeing our chaps being blown to bits around me was not going to distract me from my grief by one iota. It just made me understand my own failings. I had abandoned my son when I should have done the opposite. He was, or is, the only real tie to Adelaide that is left to me. Thank you for doing what I should have done, and thank you for not trying to tell me where I was going wrong, because you knew that I had to find out for myself.

James, of course, is the other tie to Adelaide. And I now

feel very responsible for him. When Doctor Drummond tells me there is nothing more he can do for him, I will take James and Jenny back to Rietfontein and stay with them until I know I can leave, rather than run away again. We must decide what to do with the Ant Bear Mine. I will give James fifty percent of my shares, and retain twenty per cent of the company and this will give him a higher percentage of the profits, for doing most of the work.

Then I will return to you, and when this war is over, I will stir up all of Papa's directors, trustees and lawyers to find out where I fit in and what I should do.

Your loving son,

Chadwyck

CHAPTER 69

Gerald stood for a long moment at the foot of Edward's bed. He appeared to be asleep but, even with his face in repose, Gerald was shocked by how his brother had aged since last they had been together, not so long ago at Glen Lyon. Edward had suffered more in three years of this war than most do in their entire lives. The noise and the smells of the ward receded as he continued to stand there while images and memories of their childhood tripped one after another through his mind.

'Captain Bishop,' said Gerald in a low voice. There was no response. Gerald wondered how his brother was wounded by what he could see beneath the frame that straddled his legs and supported a grey blanket. His hands were lying above the covers alongside his body and Gerald moved forward and took hold of one and squeezed it gently. 'Eddy, it's me, Gerald.' Slowly Edward's eyes opened and Gerald watched them focus.

'Gerry, is that you? What are you doing here? I was asleep' he added, confused.

'I'm sorry I woke you but I don't have much time.'

'It's so good to see you, but why are you here? How did you find me?'

'The purpose of my mission, but I never expected such a short search. I wangled a pass behind the German lines with their press office on the pretext of writing an article on their admirable care of Allied casualties.'

'Well they have done a good job on me. I was lucky to be picked up by one of their ambulances bound for this hospital, after I crashed, with an English-speaking German doctor on board, to boot. I think they had me here in about an hour and a half and operated on my legs immediately. I don't remember much about it because they filled me full of morphine. I had lost a lot of blood and they told me later, in gruesome detail, how they replaced most of it through a tube from bottles of plasma, that they hung above me in the ambulance!'

'How did you lose so much blood?'

'My 'plane was badly damaged in a scrap, more than fifty 'planes in all and I partially lost control. I tried to glide down to land but couldn't help crossing their lines and I got caught by a burst of machine gun fire from their trenches, two bullets went through my right thigh and another broke my left tibia.'

'So you've been bed bound since you arrived?'

'That's right but tomorrow they are going to start teaching me how to walk again and, once they succeed with that, they'll ship me back to Germany as a P.O.W. They told me when I got here I would never walk again because the wound in my thigh became so badly infected they wanted to take both my legs off. A new doctor, who had just joined the hospital from Berlin, saved them, he just wouldn't give up.'

'I met a Doctor Leboyer on my way in and told him I would find him when I'd interviewed some of the Allied pilots, it was John Webb who told me to look for you over here.'

'How is he? He lost a leg. One of the nurses told me. They're mostly French you know with one or two senior German Sisters. I don't like the German nurses, they're callous and understandably treat the German patients far more kindly than us. You haven't told me why you decided to look for me here, in Lille.'

'Giselle told me it was the most likely place, the biggest town to Estrée-Blanche, behind the German lines.'

'You've met Giselle? How is she?'

'She's fine. It was she that started all this. Charlie Bishop told her that he had heard from the Germans that you had been shot down and badly wounded. It was she that guessed that you would be in a hospital in or near Lille. It was my idea to write the article so that I could convince the German Press Office in Paris to allow me behind the lines. They took forever to sanction my assignment. My editor put in the application about two weeks after you were shot down and the permit only came through five days ago.'

'Tell me about Giselle.'

'She loves you very much. Her husband knows about you and has re-joined his squadron after he read your letter to Giselle. He got back to the chateau before she did and opened it. He then wrote a letter to her admitting that he had read it and acknowledged that it was probably over between them but that they could decide if they had any future together, after the war was over.'

'I must get out of here. I must get back to her.'

'That's what we're working on, Eddy but it's easier said than done. She will want to come here now that I've found you and from what you tell me about the French nurses working here and, I assume, they are all local women, it might be quite easy to get Giselle on the staff. How long do you think it will take you to walk? How long did they tell you it might take when they saw you yesterday?'

'About four weeks but my leg muscles are very wasted and I don't think I will be able to put much weight on my broken leg for some time. How would you get her into occupied France?'

'I've already spoken to her school friend Pauline who will put her up in her own house without much difficulty and she is arranging now, as we speak, an I.D. card, with a photograph I gave her last night. I haven't really thought about how we can get her into Lille, I was more concerned in finding you. Perhaps Charlie Bishop could bring her over, my Editor tells me that the RFC quite often fly agents in behind the German lines. Allied 'planes are often over occupied France during combat and reconnaissance, it would just be a question of finding a suitable place to land and not being seen doing it. I have to go to Estrée-Blanche after I get back to Paris to give Giselle her I.D. card and I'll talk to Charlie Bishop then. We won't be able to tell you when she will get here but I think we can make it happen. You must have spent a lot of time thinking about how you could get out of here. Have you any ideas?'

'One, but it's pretty gruesome, I'd have myself removed with the dead bodies that are taken out every night from the mortuary to the East Cemetery. There's a French orderly here, ironically called Jacques, who has become a good friend of mine and he suggested the idea. He's in charge of one of the two squads responsible for the grisly work and they operate on alternate weeks.'

'How does it work?' asked Gerald.

'Simple, when a patient dies, two of Jacques' colleagues carry the corpse to the mortuary, which is somewhere in the basement, and when the morning shift comes on at seven o'clock they stack the bodies in a lorry, driven by Jacques, who takes them out to the cemetery. His idea was to stop in a dark street before reaching the city gate and let me out but I'd be on my own and in a very vulnerable state.'

'It might work and I could arrange a return visit in four weeks' time to do a follow up story on my first article which' he added with a grin 'by then, will have been seen and well received by the German Press Office in Paris. I'll allow myself a few days' leeway and insist on returning to St Sauveur on some pretext and we can finalise the details. All being well I can get you accredited as my photographer and take you back through the Front, before the balloon goes up.'

'What will happen to Giselle, how will we get her back into unoccupied France?'

'I'll think of something, I always do but now I've got to go Eddy and see the doctor and one or two other patients before I meet Max for lunch, that is,' he added as an afterthought 'if he doesn't walk in now and catch us together, which would be about the worst thing that could happen. I won't be able to contact you again between now and your escape so I'll be back here on November 1st, give or take a day or two and see you then. Please try to time your recovery to that moment, give them the impression that you aren't progressing as well as you are, we don't want them to send you to Germany before I get back!'

They shook hands and Gerald made his way back to John Webb's bedside. After a brief chat, he moved to another pilot's bed, on John's recommendation. By twelve o'clock he had interviewed three English pilots and one French one when Doctor Leboyer came to look for him.

* * *

'Your key Sir and there's a message for you from the Kommandantur.' Gerald ripped the envelope open and saw that it was from Max, excusing himself from lunch and hoping to find the time to meet Gerald at La Comtesse Hospital if not, he would be at the hotel at eight and they could have dinner together. Gerald handed the note back to the concierge, who dropped it in a basket.

'I would like to lunch out, where would you suggest I go?'

'The food is very good here Sir.'

'I know. I had dinner here last night and I'm having dinner here tonight, so I'd like to try somewhere else.'

'Oh' said the concierge 'of course Sir. Might I recommend Chez Maurice, a small bistro owned by my cousin.' The concierge removed a card from his waistcoat pocket and handed it to Gerald. 'Give them this when you arrive.'

'And ask for Maurice' added Gerald.

* * *

'God, what a day! If it goes on like this, I'm going to ask for a transfer back to the Front.' Max had arrived at Gerald's hotel at exactly eight o'clock, immaculately dressed, without a hair out of place. They had gone through to the bar and were sitting comfortably in the same chairs as the night before, by the fire. 'How did it go at La Comtesse?'

'Very well. Not so many Allied patients as at St Sauveur but I met a very interesting German doctor from Hamburg who works in both hospitals. You might say his speciality is reconstruction. He rebuilds men that have been literally torn apart. He was telling me that in the last two years, since we've been at each other's throats, enormous strides have been made in surgical disciplines. I hadn't realised, until I became involved in this assignment, the frightful responsibilities shouldered by all senior doctors. They have to make, in a matter of moments, a decision on the probable outcome of the use of available medicine, that amounts to whether a patient lives or dies.'

Max savoured his brandy and soda and re-crossed his ankles. 'What's his name? I probably know him.'

'Doctor Albert Koenig.'

'Yes I do know him. As you say he's very good and very new to us but we're lucky to have him. He's still keen, not yet jaded by the repetitive grind of hopeless cases.'

'What plans do you have for us tomorrow?' asked Gerald 'will you have time to accompany me?'

'Perhaps for part of the day but the two hospitals I want you to visit are new, beyond the old City walls so I'll make my driver available to you all day and, if I can, I'll join you. He knows the way to both of them and speaks some English.'

'Do you want to see my notes, so far? I can see how the article is taking shape. I think with another two hospitals, the day after tomorrow, I will have all I need to know.'

'So you will be going back to Paris on Friday?'

'I see this assignment in two parts. I want to write the first article, assimilate the readers' reaction from back home and then return to Lille in about a month to write a sequel, incorporating their comments on my theme, which, as you know, is to show the Americans how well Allied prisoners and patients are treated by the Germans.'

'That's not a problem, I'll be signing your application. How long do you think it will be before the Americans come in with the Allies?'

'From how you ask the question, you must think it's inevitable but it probably won't be for another six months or so and I agree with you, it will happen.'

'Let's go through to dinner' said Max 'before I express my true feelings, which I'm sure I would later regret.'

* * *

Gerald cut short his visit to a hospital in the outskirts of Lille on the following afternoon because there had been only two Allied patients to interview. Max's chauffeur had dropped him back at his hotel by four o'clock. Half an hour later, having tried to wash away the pervading hospital smells in a tepid bath, he was sitting at the café behind Pauline's house, waiting for her. He had ordered a glass of red wine and was revising his notes when he suddenly realised she was standing beside him.

'I startled you.'

'Not really but you move very quietly.'

'One needs to now, it's a habit,' she said, 'may I sit down?'

'Of course, what would you like to drink?'

'I'll have wine, like you. How's it going? That's a fat note book. Is there anything in it?' He grinned reassuringly and noticed that she was much more relaxed than she had been at their first meeting.

'It's almost full. I've been very busy and the more I see the more appalled I am by the conditions in the wards and the severity of the casualties. The smell is overpowering, a mixture of disinfectant and putrefaction, that clings to one's clothes and nasal passages.'

'Poor Gerald, you've had a hard time of it but I've got some good news.'

'You've got the I.D. card?'

'Yes, push your note book across and I'll slip it inside.'

'Well done, Pauline and thank you very much, you took a great risk and it can't have been easy.

'Have you found your brother, yet?'

' Yes, by extraordinary good fortune, he was almost the first

Allied patient I saw. I found him in St Sauveur yesterday morning and managed to be alone with him long enough to make some plans for his escape. He has a broken leg and has suffered very badly from infection in a wound to his other leg but the doctors have told him that he is ready to start exercising and will start to move around the ward on crutches, within the next few days. They told him that it will take some four weeks before he is able to walk, he needs to build up his muscles and gain strength and balance.'

'But when he does they'll send him to Germany, as a prisoner, I'm certain of that.'

'I know, so timing is critical. I have told Max I will be back here in four weeks. Do you think it will be possible to get Giselle accepted as a nurse by St Sauveur?'

'It will be easy, they're desperate to find anyone who will work in those conditions. A neighbour of mine works there and she will introduce Giselle to the Matron.'

'Well, that's it then. I will be leaving for Paris the day after tomorrow. I have two more hospitals to visit tomorrow and I will write the article over the weekend and then go down to the chateau on Monday to give Giselle her I.D. card. I have told Edward that I will arrange with a brother officer of his, to fly Giselle into a field near Lille. That will probably be on Wednesday of next week, so you will know when to expect her.'

'But how will she get in from the countryside?'

'She will walk. Max told me that dozens of countrywomen walk into Lille to work every day. She will have her I.D. card and will join other workers, that live nearby.'

'That is a good plan. Tell her to come here at this time and not to go to the house. I will be here from Tuesday onwards every evening until she arrives.'

CHAPTER 70

'Good Morning Giselle, this is Gerald. How are you? I'm back in Paris.' He listened for a moment and then continued 'I found him in the first hospital I visited, extraordinarily good luck. He is recovering well and we have a plan for his escape.' Again he listened. 'Of course it involves you, that's why I'm coming down to see you on Monday.' 'No I can't come down before then, I have to write the article and have it on my Editor's desk before Monday morning. I'll leave early and be with you by mid-afternoon.'

* * *

Gerald drove through the gates and was impressed by the ornamental lakes and the long drive to the chateau. He noticed an old man tending a deep herbaceous border to the right of the drive and waved as he went past. The old man removed his cap and bowed. He pulled up in front of the broad steps that led up to the front door, took his valise off the back seat just as the door opened and Giselle stepped out to greet him.

'Welcome to my humble abode Gerald, you have made good time.'

'Humble abode!' said Gerald 'this we would call a cottage in Palm Beach.'

'I know. I was there with Jacques the year before War started, we were staying with the Munns. Come in and Marie will show you to your room.'

'I'll leave my bag in the hall, if I may and, if you're ready, we should go onto Estrée-Blanche now rather than later and I can tell you everything that has happened, by the time we get there.'

'Of course, I'll get my coat.'

Half an hour later, they pulled into the airfield at Estrée-Blanche, parked their car next to Edward's Bentley and Giselle led the way through to Charles' office.

'Charlie, it's lovely to see you again. This is the redoubtable Gerald Meade.'

Charles got up from behind his desk and shook hands with Gerald. 'Welcome to Estrée-Blanche, home to those with a short life expectancy' he laughed mirthlessly and continued 'you must have found Edward or you wouldn't be here. Take a pew, would you like a drink?' The ubiquitous bottle of brandy appeared on the desk and Charles filled two glasses, Giselle had declined.

'Yes he's in St Sauveur, the biggest hospital in Lille, that's why I chose it to start my search.'

'How is he?' asked Charles.

'As well as can be expected and a lot better than most.'

'What's your plan, I'm sure you have one?'

'In principle, I do but not in detail. It depends on his recovery time.'

'I assume you're planning to get him back into unoccupied France?'

'Of course and it involves Giselle. She and I have been talking about it on our way over here and she's as keen as mustard to go.'

'Go?' said Charles 'Go where?'

'To Lille, to be with Eddy. She can get a job in St Sauveur, as a nurse.'

'And how, although I think I know the answer, do you intend to get her there?'

'Well, we rather hoped you would take her.'

'I thought as much, but let me think about it for a moment, it's been done before but it's very dangerous, both for the pilot and the passenger.'

'Please Charlie, I have to go. I have to see him again and I know I can help him escape.'

Charles took a gulp from his glass, refilled it and pushed the bottle towards Gerald. He got up and walked across to a large map spread across most of the wall behind his desk.

'It can't be too far from Lille because Giselle will probably have to walk in and it can't be too close because I don't particularly want to get peppered. Let me see now, there's a place here called St Marguerite which is about five miles north of Lille, it's a tiny village with open country around it. I will go and have a look at it tomorrow morning, when we go out on patrol and, if I like the look of it, I'll take you tomorrow afternoon at about this time. In the meantime, I really want you to think about it Giselle, we could both be killed in the attempt.'

'Thank you Charlie, I won't change my mind and we will see you tomorrow afternoon.'

* * *

An hour after returning to the chateau, Giselle and Gerald were dressed for dinner and sitting opposite each other at the long table in the dining room. Marie had managed to procure a chicken, and with that and a selection of vegetables, lovingly tended by her husband Jules, they ate well and enjoyed a bottle of wine from the diminishing stock in Giselle's cellar.

'I thought you would have other guests staying' said Gerald 'Eddy told me there are always six or eight billeted here from the airfields nearby.'

'Not since last month, they built officers' quarters at both of them so it's very quiet here and I miss their company.'

They finished dinner and Giselle asked Marie to bring them coffee and brandy in the library. They settled into the two armchairs in front of the fire and Giselle poured them both a generous tot.

'At least we've got plenty of this still left. I don't even know how old it is. Marie fills the decanters from old barrels that have been in the cellar for ever.'

'It's very good.' said Gerald. 'Are you sure you want to go to Lille tomorrow? Do you realise the dangers involved? You've got your I.D. and I think you'll be all right once you're there but I'm worried that something might happen to you on your way.'

'Gerald, how sweet of you to be so concerned. Of course I'm going, if Charlie will take me. Eddy is now my life and without him, I have nothing.' She leant forward and re-filled their coffee cups 'Do you ride, Gerry?' she asked suddenly and, without waiting for an answer, she continued 'we'll go riding tomorrow. I haven't ridden in ages.'

'It will be my pleasure to ride with you.' She checked at his choice of words.

'We,' we she thought, who are 'we' with Jacques gone? 'have only two old horses left, the army took the rest.' She finished her coffee, got up and stood behind her chair. 'I'm off to bed.' Gerald got up and moved towards her. 'No, please stay here and finish your brandy. I've told Marie that you will be staying here tomorrow night, before going back to Paris. She will spoil you, I'm sure. Good night.' Before he could answer, she turned and walked over to the gallery staircase. Gerald followed her but stopped, with his hand on the bannister, when she paused briefly at the top and waved. 'Good night' she said again and headed for the secret door.

'Good night' said Gerald, in two minds and with a rueful shrug he returned to his chair to finish his cognac.

* * *

After lunch the next day, Gerald and Giselle returned to Estrée-Blanche and were shown into Charles' office.

'I've found a good field a few hundred yards south of St Marguerite, it has a very tall church spire, still standing, which makes a good landmark. The field is about four miles north of Lille.'

'Sounds good, Charlie, so you are game to go?' said Giselle 'and it won't be too far for me to walk into Lille tomorrow morning.'

'Seems so, I have asked for a pack of sandwiches and some coffee in a thermos for you tonight, which we'll take with us. I see you've sensibly brought a very small bag, I'm sure you'll be able to find more clothes in Lille.'

'Where will I spend tonight?'

'I saw a barn in the north-west corner of the field, which should do the trick.'

'That's fine, I'll be all right. I will start early and, with luck, will have joined up with other workers, before we get too close. That way, I will be less noticeable.'

'Don't go to Pauline's house' said Gerald' but go straight to the Bar Soleil, which is behind her house, at about five o'clock tomorrow afternoon, she will meet you there. You will have most of the day to kill, so spend your time in one bar after another, for an hour or so at a time. Don't spend too much time on the streets.'

During the next half hour, Charles fitted Giselle out with a flying coat, boots, goggles and a helmet and, as the sun dropped towards the horizon, the three of them walked out to Charles' 'plane. Gerald helped Giselle into the forward cockpit and then went round to the front of the 'plane, to swing the propeller. When the engine caught, he moved to one side and waved as the 'plane slowly taxied forward, gained speed and took off into the setting sun.

CHAPTER 71

It had been a long day for Giselle, killing time in Lille: by half past four she had visited most of the cafes around the Citadelle and had reached her eighth of the day on Rue Colbert. She paid the bill and walked to the corner of Rue Leon Gambetta, turned left and walked into the Place de la Nouvelle Aventure. She crossed to the church, in the middle of the square and sat on a bench where she could see the Bar Soleil, on the far side. As the church clock struck five she left the bench, crossed the square and took a table inside the bar, beside the window, picked up a copy of the day's paper and immersed herself in the local news.

'Have you been waiting long?' It was Pauline, Giselle started and recognised her immediately, although they hadn't seen each other for at least eight years.

'No, I've just arrived.'

'It's so good to see you but you look very tired.'

'I've been on my feet most of the day and drunk a week's ration of what they're pleased to call coffee, God knows what it's made of.'

'Don't ask, let's go round to my house and get you settled in. Beatrice will be there soon and she has to be home before the curfew. She is an old friend of mine and has been a nurse at St Sauveur for years, long before the war. It is she that will take you in tomorrow and get you enrolled.'

The three of them sat in Pauline's kitchen and Giselle watched Beatrice as Pauline explained the situation. When she had finished she turned to Giselle and asked her 'Have I missed anything? Is there anything you want to add so that Beatrice knows the whole story?'

'I don't think so' said Giselle 'I'll do anything to be with Eddy, any type of work they give me. What would you suggest Beatrice? If I'm given a choice, what should I ask for?'

'Night duty. Nobody wants to do that and you'll have a much better chance of being alone with Edward.'

Pauline looked at the clock and, before she could say anything, Beatrice got up.

'I'll come and collect you on the street in front of the house, at six forty-five tomorrow morning, but I must go now.' She leant over and kissed Pauline on both cheeks and waved to Giselle as she left the room.

* * *

By half past seven the next morning, Beatrice had managed to complete the nurse's enrolment forms in the administration office and had taken Giselle through to the hospital laundry, to find her a uniform.

'It probably doesn't fit very well but it'll do for the moment, at least you will look the part.' Giselle glanced down at herself and pulled the full-length skirt up to her knees.

'It's so heavy and restrictive, must I wear all these under garments?'

'No, I don't, at least not now but when it gets colder, you will be glad to have them. Come on, we must go through to the ward and start our shift. Matron has made me responsible for you so if you get it wrong, I'll be the one to get the stick.' Beatrice grabbed Giselle's hand and they left the locker room, passed the mortuary and went up to the Wards.

'I'm not in Edward's ward but we can go through it on our way to my ward and at least you'll catch a glimpse of him and he'll know you're here.'

They turned off the long corridor and went through the chapel into the ward. There was a nurse standing beside Edward's bed giving him an injection as Beatrice stopped for a moment to exchange a greeting.

'Steady, Charles, or you'll break the needle. It can't have hurt that much. New blood?' asked the nurse, nodding towards Giselle, who fought to contain her emotions and her desperate need to throw herself into Edward arms.

'Yes' said Beatrice 'but she's made of strong stuff, so she may last the course. We'll be lunching at twelve, hope you can join us in the canteen.'

They moved back into the centre of the ward and worked their way past the camp beds, to the far end.

'Pull yourself together Giselle, I mean Mathilde, you look like you're about to faint.'

'I thought I would. I've never felt like this before, I must be with him.'

They moved on and soon reached Beatrice's ward, where they were met by a German Sister with arms akimbo and a thunderous expression on her slab-sided face.

'You're late Chevalier, your cap is crooked and who is this?'

'A new recruit Sister, her name is Mathilde Guibert.'

'It's Guibert from now on and you will address me as Sister. Do you have any nursing experience?'

'Only what we were taught at school, Sister.'

'Totally useless. You're responsible for her, Chevalier and your cap is still crooked. I'll hold you accountable.'

'Yes Sister. Come on Guibert, we start with bedpans.'

All morning, Giselle followed Beatrice around the ward, learning her duties and, wherever possible, the shortcuts. The entire ward was filled with German patients who had been wounded in the trenches by artillery fire and shrapnel. Most of them were dismembered and some horribly disfigured, wherever she could see their features through the swathes of bandage. She knew very little German but understood a great deal from what she could read in their eyes. Almost all of them were younger than her and a lot of them were still in their teens. By twelve o'clock she was exhausted and very grateful to Beatrice when she led her away from the ward, for their half hour break in the canteen.

They joined the queue and when their turn came each collected a bowl of soup with a small chunk of bread and a mug of coffee. They sat down at a table, which already had two other nurses eating there.

'I can't see your friend.'

'Don't worry, she may be here soon and at least we'll have time to say hello, before we have to go back to the ward.'

'How soon can I apply for the night shift?'

'You won't be able to until you've learnt the rudiments of nursing.'

'How long will that take?' and before Beatrice could answer, Giselle continued 'what is this?'

'It was called Kriegsbrot, which wasn't bad but now it's made mostly from potato meal, Indian corn and buckwheat, don't worry, you'll get used to it.'

'If you say so, I don't dare ask what's in the soup.'

'Wise decision, it'll keep you going until Pauline gives you something more nourishing tonight.'

'I interrupted you, you were telling me about my training.'

'Yes, if you apply yourself, you should have the basics within a week. There's one thing in your favour, most people don't want to do night duty. In a few days I'll speak to Matron and tell her you'll volunteer for it. She will easily find someone to swap places with you but the trick is they have to come from Edward's ward.'

'Aren't most of the English patients in Eddy's ward?'

'Yes, in fact I'd say they all are.'

'Well then tell Matron, when you see her, that I speak English and can translate for the French staff that don't.'

'That might put you on the ward but not necessarily on night duty.'

'Tell her I'm an insomniac,' and they both laughed.

'I'll do what I can but we must get back to the ward or Sister will string me up.'

* * *

A week later Giselle was deemed fit to work on her own, without supervision and was summoned by the Matron.

'Come in and please sit down. Your good friend Chevalier has spoken well of you and told me that you have mastered some skills and, more importantly, you have the right attitude. She tells me you want to transfer to night shifts and that you speak English. If that is so, you will be best suited to the Chapel Ward, where all the Allied patients are accommodated. You will be working alone but not as a nurse, you will be what we call a ward assistant, a general dogsbody, you might say, at everyone's beck and call.'

'Thank you Matron, I'll do my best.'

'No child, we should thank you. We've had quite a lot of problems with English patients who don't understand either French or German. We've already got a nurse on that ward during the day, who speaks all three languages and we need you there, at night.'

Giselle was exultant and felt like throwing her arms around the Matron's neck but bobbed a curtsey instead, thanked her and left.

CHAPTER 72

'Edouard' she stood by his bed and watched him wake. It was after midnight and her first opportunity to be alone with him. She leant over and put her fingertips to his lips, he grabbed her wrists and kissed them.

'Darling Giselle' he said and kissed her palms 'I've dreamed of this moment ever since Gerald was here.' He tried to sit up but she eased him back onto the pillows.

'Don't move, I'll be back in a moment. I'm going to change your sheets and we will be able to talk, while I do it.' Before he could say anything, she was gone.

During her first week's work with Beatrice, Giselle had only managed to get the occasional glimpse of Edward, when she and Beatrice found some excuse to pass through Chapel Ward, but never long enough to exchange a few words.

'Lie still, I'm going to remove the frame from your legs.' She turned back the top blanket, towards the foot of the bed, grabbed the frame in both hands and lifted it towards her. It was heavier than she expected and the corner caught in her skirt, lifting it well above her knees. Edward saw that she was wearing nothing beneath her skirt and slipped his hand between her thighs. She gasped and dropped the frame back on the bed, grateful for the support it gave her, while she pulled the blanket back over it. At the same moment, without conscious thought, she edged her hips towards him, until she felt his fingertips on her clitoris. She moaned and bit her bottom lip to stop herself crying out. Very gently he moved his hand until the knuckle of his thumb was against her clitoris and two of his fingers were inside her. With one hand she held him there and with the other, hung onto the frame.

'Edouard, oh Edouard' she whispered 'don't stop, please don't stop, …a little lower, …oh yes, there, yes' and a moment later 'I can feel it coming.'

He felt her contracting around his fingers and a creamy liquid ran across the back of his hand and down her thigh. Slowly he removed his hand and licked his finger-tips 'you taste delicious, just as I remember it.'

'Edouard!' She wasn't shocked but he felt that she thought she ought to be. 'Thank you, that was absolute heaven and exactly what I needed and now, my love, it is your turn,' and she added, with a mischievous grin, 'perhaps I should do it before changing the sheets.'

* * *

Two weeks after his cast had been removed Edward was walking with the help of crutches. All of his massage and rehabilitation treatment was carried out during the day shift but, when she could, Giselle brought him his crutches and helped him walk around his end of the ward. They had found a small vestry off the chapel, full of brooms and buckets. It had a solid oak bench attached to the back wall wide enough to allow both of them to lie down and, after some hazardous and hilarious practice and, with considerable care, they had become adept at lovemaking. Edward had taken to calling her Mrs. Meade and she responded in like manner.

They were both worried about getting caught, but once they had tried it on several occasions, without interruption, they became more confident and sometimes Edward would go there alone and wait for her. A week after their discovery of the vestry and having made love,

Edward pulled Giselle back on top and said, 'You seem heavier than you were Mrs. Meade.'

'To be expected Lieutenant Meade, I'm pregnant.' It was finally out, she had been dying to tell him but wasn't sure how he would react.

'That's wonderful' he said 'how do you know so soon?'

'I've known for some time, it happened that first night, at home.' She rolled off him and he held her close, between himself and the wall, while he ran his fingertips through her fine chestnut hair.

'I think that is the most wonderful news I have ever heard. Do you think it will be a boy or a girl?'

'I don't mind, as long as it is healthy and we can get away from the War.'

'Perhaps it will be one of each.'

'No, I don't want that. The idea of twins frightens me.' He held her tighter and kissed her for a long time. He could feel her heart beating rapidly against his chest and he continued to hold her until she relaxed.

'So now we must plan our escape.'

'Have you spoken to Jacques again?' she asked. She couldn't resist running her fingers across his tummy until she reached his pubic hair but stopped short of distracting him.

'No, but I will tomorrow when I see him, which I do on most days. The man on the other side of the rood screen was taken away this morning. Gerry will be here in two weeks, so Jacques should be back on duty again by then.'

'Yes, but what happens if Gerry is held up and Jacques is not on duty when Gerry is here?'

'Gerry mentioned a five-day leeway. Don't worry, he will be here and if not, I'm sure we can think of something else.' She propped herself up on her elbow.

'Be serious Eddy, we won't have another opportunity so this one must work and now I must get you back to bed.'

'I am in bed.'

'Don't be silly.' She rolled over him and got to her feet, picked up his dressing gown and crutches and held out her hands. 'I can't expect Therese, you know the one I mean, the blond assistant on my shift, to cover for me all night.'

'You shameless wench, you have told her about us?'

'Of course not, well, some of it I suppose, she's a romantic and loves being part of the whole thing.'

* * *

'You're doing very well Charles' said Doctor Leboyer 'we're all very pleased with you' and he looked at his two colleagues, standing on either side of his bed. 'In the last week you have made great progress and I agree with Doctor Braun that we can safely discharge you by the end of this month.'

'So soon, Sir?'

'Probably. Captain von Stosch was here yesterday making a list of German and Allied patients for transfer to Germany.'

'And I'm on that list, Sir?'

'Only if we say so.' Doctor Leboyer could see the trail of emotions flit across Edward's face, apprehension, even alarm, followed by stubborn resolution. Edward closed his eyes and clasped his hands together, until his knuckles showed white. 'I know Charles, you are a pilot and the idea of being a P.O.W. is the last thing you want but, think on the bright side, you will be safe and will survive the War.' Slowly Edward's hands relaxed and he opened his eyes.

'Did Captain von Stosch say when this train is leaving?'

'No. As I said, it will be during the first week of next month and most of the passengers will be wounded German infantry, being repatriated for convalescent leave.'

'My left knee is still swollen, Sir and painful when I walk. Have they told you, Sir, I still can't walk without my crutches?'

'There'll be many men with crutches on the train, Charles, but we'll have another look at you over the weekend, before we make a final decision.

468

CHAPTER 73

Gerald found Abe in his office, sitting at his desk with a cloud of blue cigar smoke drifting around his head.

'Come in Gerald and sit down.' Since the success of Gerald's article and the favourable German Press Office's reaction, Abe had looked on Gerald with a more kindly eye. 'Who is this Miles Stanway, photographer, par excellence, that you want me to accredit?'

'He was recommended to me by a reporter I know, who works for *Le Monde*. I met Stanway the other day. He's about my age, a bit younger. He's an American and has been working freelance, as a photographer, in Paris since before the War.'

'This application is dated October 21ˢᵗ and today is the 26ᵗʰ·'

'It's been on your desk since the 21ˢᵗ Sir.'

'Why not use our own photographer? '

'He's on assignment Sir, you sent him to Marseille on Wednesday.'

'So I did, I must see Stanway's passport before I can sign this.'

'Yes Sir, I'm seeing him this evening and will bring it in tomorrow. Have the German Press Office sent over my permits, yet?'

'No.'

'But tomorrow is Saturday, Sir and I'm due to leave on Wednesday. I told Max I'd be in Lille that evening, he is expecting me.'

'You can't leave without your permits. Wait until Monday and, if they are not here then, I'll have a word with their Press Office.'

CHAPTER 74

Edward was awake and heard the church clock strike three. He hadn't seen Giselle since midnight, and they hadn't been able to talk since the previous night, but she had promised to be back as soon as possible. He was about to get up when he saw her approaching from the other side of the rood screen. She was carrying his crutches and within moments they had reached the vestry and she had shut the door behind them.

'Tell me Eddy, what did they say?'

'What did who say?'

'The doctors. You're playing with me, Eddy.' She was angry and tense.

'Whenever you want, my love' he said, 'starting now' and he untied the ribbon at the back of her apron.

'Please tell me Eddy, what did the doctors say this afternoon?'

'It will be a close run thing.'

'What will?'

'Whether the Germans get me before Gerald does.'

'They're going to discharge you, send you back to Germany, as a prisoner?'

'Yes. Von Stosch was here yesterday, making up a list to fill a train with wounded Germans and they might put me on it too.'

'Oh God Eddy, Gerald won't be here for at least another three days. What can we do?'

'Well, first I will finish unbuttoning your uniform and then we will take it in turns to decide what is best for each of us.'

She turned round to hit him but he caught her wrist and kissed her.

'Eddy, please stop this.'

'Stop what? Answering your question? Or undressing you?' He could feel her relax in his arms and he continued with and finished what he had started.

He lay beside her and watched her breathing gently, totally relaxed and with a gentle smile playing on the edge of her mouth. She was asleep and he didn't want to wake her but he knew the risks and instinct told him he should be back in his bed. He blew on her eyelids gently until she opened her eyes and focused on his face.

'I love you' she said.

'I know, I love you more. There's something important that I haven't told you.'

'Not now, Eddy, not when I feel like this. It's bad news isn't it? Why didn't you tell me before?'

'I didn't want to spoil the moment, we were having such fun.'

'What is it? It's something to do with Jacques isn't it?'

'Yes, how did you know?'

'I didn't, just call it female intuition.'

'Well, you're right, he came to me this evening and told me he can't go ahead with our plan. He's frightened, perhaps paranoid but he has a point, they'll shoot him and his family if we're caught. You can't really blame him, he has a wife and God knows how many children, so we'll have to think of something else.'

'Eddy, I can't believe it, everything seems to be going wrong.'

'Well it could go wronger and wronger if I don't get back to my bed soon, we've been here over an hour.' He got up without her help and picked up her uniform from the floor, where he had thrown it. 'Time for you to get back into your Mother Hubbard, Mrs. Meade. Let me help you. I've had plenty of practice taking it off, but this will be a first' and, with a broad grin, he held the uniform up to his chest.

'You step into it, I'll button it up and then I'll decide whether to let you go or not.'

'Eddy, I've got an idea.'

'I know, you don't want to get dressed.'

'No, listen, please, I really do have a brilliant idea. We will dress you up as a nurse, I can see it so clearly, we dress you in a spare uniform at the end of my shift and you leave with me and all the other nurses, safety in numbers.'

He held the uniform between them and looked at it, 'It's too small.'

'There are bigger ones, the laundry and locker room are full of clean ones of all sizes.'

'It could work,' he reversed the uniform and held it up to his chin, 'but wouldn't I need a pass to get out of the building?'

'Yes, we could use Beatrice's or, better still, I could steal one from one of the girls on the incoming shift. We'll do it the moment we know Gerald has reached Lille.'

'The sooner the better, as far as I'm concerned and you will have to tell Pauline or Gerald, when you see him, of the new plan.'

CHAPTER 75

Giselle checked her watch and saw that it was just after ten to seven in the morning. Working alone, she wheeled the screens out to Edward's bed and went back to collect the clean sheets and bedding, in which she had hidden the nurse's uniform. Once the screens were in place Edward stood up, paused to get his balance and took a few tentative steps.

'Are you all right?'

'Yes, it's always difficult first thing in the morning but they'll soon ease up.'

'Put these on and I'll make up the bed.' She handed him the nurse's uniform.

Within minutes, he was dressed and had rolled up his pyjamas and dressing gown which she put into the bed with his crutches, to look like his body. The clock in the courtyard struck seven and they could hear the day shift coming on duty. She took some lipstick and rouge from her pocket and he sat on the remade bed.

'Don't move' she said, 'and look at me.'' She deftly applied a light coating of rouge to his cheeks and lipstick to his mouth, she had already shaved him earlier.

'Are you ready?' He nodded. 'Do what I do and we'll wheel the screens to the side of the ward together, then follow me into the nurses' room and we'll mix with the outgoing shift. We will have to wait until the first of the day shift have gone onto the ward, because I'm going to steal a pass from one of their lockers.' They then joined the queue of nurses going off duty, filing out of the door onto the street. As each one passed the gate, they showed their pass to a sleepy guard, who seemed totally uninterested in his job. Once on the street, they turned right and Giselle took his arm.

'We're free Edouard' she whispered. 'We're free!' she repeated and squeezed his arm.

'Not yet my love, we still have a long way to go.'

'How do you feel? Can you cross the square?' He nodded and she could see that he was in considerable pain. They walked to a café on the far corner of Place Ruault, just around the corner from the Porte de Paris. It was just opening, with the owner and his wife carrying chairs and tables out onto the pavement. They went in and sat at a table at the very back of the room and ordered coffee and brioche. A young girl took their order and scampered behind the counter. At the same moment, they could see Gerald pulling up in his car across the street, in front of them. He got out carrying a parcel under his arm, crossed the street and walked into the café, ignoring Edward and Giselle as he passed them, on his way to the toilettes. The girl brought their coffee and brioche and Gerald returned, without the parcel and took a stool at the bar and, when the girl returned, he asked her for coffee.

'My turn' said Edward with a grin and excused himself. Five minutes later, he walked out of the toilettes wearing the clothes Gerald had left him in the parcel, just as two workmen walked into the café, distracting the girl's attention. Edward left the café and crossed the street, passed Gerald's car and went into another café beyond it, where he took a seat in the window. The owner and his wife, having finished laying out the tables and chairs, joined the two men at their table by the window. Gerald suddenly appeared to recognise Giselle, finished his coffee and crossed over to her table.

'How are you? What a lovely surprise to see you, are you expecting someone?'

'No, I'm with a colleague who is in the toilettes' and she nodded her head in the direction of the door.

'And I have to move my car or the police will fine me. Come with me and we can talk and then we can come back and join your friend.'

She got up and followed him to the bar, where he paid both bills. Eddy watched them from the other side of the street and, as they crossed, he left the café and got into the back seat of the car, just as Gerald opened the driver's door for Giselle. Gerald then went round to the front of the car and swung the starting handle, as Giselle adjusted the mixture. On the second swing, the engine fired and settled into a steady beat. Giselle slipped across to the passenger side and Gerald got in and they drove off, in the direction of the Porte d'Ypres.

'Your *Washington Post* press credentials are in your jacket pocket' said Gerald without looking back. You are now Miles Stanway and you are my photographer and, as such, you will address me as Sir.'

Giselle laughed and turned round to look at Edward. She grabbed his hand and pulled him forward so that she could kiss him.

'Are you paying attention, Miles?' She licked his fingertips, let go of his hand and faced forward.

'Your camera equipment' continued Gerald, 'is in the boot, with your valise.'

At the Porte d'Ypres, they joined a short queue of vehicles leaving the city and when they reached the guard, they all had their documentation ready. Gerald showed him his laisser-passe from Max von Schloss and, without further ado, the guard saluted sharply and waved them through.

'I swear he flinched when he saw the document' said Giselle. 'What is it, a letter from the Kaiser?'

'No' he laughed, 'it's an authorisation for a plan I cooked up with Max, a few days ago.'

'Max? who's Max?'

'He's the liaison officer appointed by the German press office in Paris to look after me. '

'And what plan have you in store for us?'

'To inspect a field hospital out at Bondues. It was on my original list of places to visit where I might have found Eddy. It's also in the same direction as the field where you were dropped and where Eddy will collect you. So now, my girl, you're the navigator and here's the map.'

Gerald followed Giselle's directions, back-tracking the road she had walked when she first arrived, until they reached a point on the road that was nearest to the field. They could just see the barn on the far side, indistinct against the woods beyond.

'Right my girl' said Gerald. 'This is where we go our separate ways. There are some sandwiches and wine in a bag on the back seat; Pauline prepared them for you. Hide up in the barn until Eddy returns this evening and don't forget to have the farmer and his wife waiting with you when Eddy arrives, because you will need them to turn the 'plane around.'

Edward got out of the car and opened Giselle's door. They stood there for a moment in each other's arms and said nothing; all had been said before. Gerald came around to their side of the car and Giselle slipped out of Edward's arms and turned to Gerald and kissed him briefly on the cheek.

'Thank you Gerry, you are a brave man and I look forward to seeing you again in happier times.' Then without another word, clutching her sandwiches, she crossed the stile and followed the path around the edge of the field.

'Hop in the front, Eddy. We're going to identify some landmarks for you. It wouldn't do to end up in the wrong field.'

They drove slowly along the road until they came to a crossroads. Eddy memorised the layout and noted a tall church spire directly to the North. They came to the next crossroads and turned left so that they would pass the northern end of the field and, as they did, they drove over a small hump-back bridge, with a stream running almost north-south.

'That's all I need' said Edward. 'It will be easy to find as long as I'm here before the light goes.'

'Right then, let's cross the line.' Gerald turned the car in the direction of Frelinghein with its bridge over the river Lys. 'Our story is that we're going to an Allied hospital at Hazebrouck which is about 20 miles beyond Frelinghein to interview some German prisoners, mostly pilots. Max thinks it's a good idea and, with the same laisser-passe, we should have no problems with the German guards at the Front. I am supposed to return to my hotel by six this evening, with the story. My editor doesn't know about you, but I'll ring him once we reach Estrée-Blanche.'

'What do you mean he doesn't know about me? How did you get me accredited?'

'Well, Eddy, that's a long story, but we'll soon be approaching the Front and I'll tell you about it later. Having crossed the river Deule, at Quesnoy, they entered Frelinghien and found themselves blocked by a convoy of lorries and were unable to pass, because of another convoy coming in the other direction.

'They must be preparing an offensive' said Gerald, 'Keep your eyes peeled for anything that might help our chaps, when we get to the other side.'

Eventually, they reached the bridge and were the only car pulled up in front of the barrier. A guard stepped smartly out of a sentry box and demanded their papers. Two other guards appeared and stood on either end of the boom that blocked the road.

'Turn off your engine' said the guard in French.

'I can't' replied Gerald in the same language. 'I have trouble starting it.'

The guard shrugged, took their papers, and walked back to a small building just off the road. They waited and watched the two other guards watching them, with a strange combination of indifference and arrogance.

'They don't look too friendly, do they?' said Gerald.

'What were you going to tell me about my papers and why your editor doesn't know I'm with you? No, on second thoughts, don't bother, I already know, they're forged.'

'Well, dear chap, that's putting it a bit bluntly.'

'Yes or no Gerry, just tell me, so I know.'

'I suppose yes would be the right answer. I tried but they couldn't do it by the time I needed them, so I asked a dear friend of mine to help out.'

'Well now we're about to find out just how good they are because here comes the guard, with his boss.' The officer approached and, in impeccable English, addressed Gerald.

'The guard understands you are having trouble starting your car, but please switch it off and both of you accompany me to my office. Mr Stanway's papers do not appear to be in order. I know Captain von Stosch and, if there is any problem with the car, I am sure we can sort it out.' He smiled expansively and clicked his heels.

Gerald slammed his foot down on the accelerator and the car leapt forward into the boom, shattering it and scattering the two guards into the ditches, on either side of the road. A third guard ran out of a hut and jumped behind a machine gun that was mounted on a parked vehicle, to one side of the road. The gun's cocking handle jammed as the guard brought the barrel to bear on the speeding car and, by the time he had the gun working, the car was on the other side of the bridge. Simultaneously the two guards scrambled out of the ditches and began to fire at the car with their rifles. The officer ran out into the middle of the road, firing his pistol and screaming orders. The moment the car was over the bridge, two allied machine guns opened up on the German post and the guards scattered for cover. Once round the first corner, Gerald pulled up by a squad of Highlanders, on their way to change the guard at the bridgehead. Gerald stopped the car to inspect the damage and found that two bullets were embedded in the luggage rack and three more had gone through the canvas roof. Luckily there was no damage to the wheels or petrol tank. A Captain from the Cameron Highlanders approached.

'Been very quiet here until now. What did you two do to deserve such attention?'

'Left hospital without paying the bill' said Edward and the Captain laughed.

'Are you all right? You look a bit shaken.'

'I'm fine' said Edward, 'it's just my legs, I was shot down a few months ago and they were badly damaged. I'm only just up and about again.'

'Where were you flying from?'

'Estrée-Blanche.'

'So, I suppose you're going back there now?' Edward nodded and the Captain continued 'before you do, is there anything you can tell me about troop movements on the other side?'

'Yes' said Gerald, 'we passed at least ten convoys going in both directions on the far side of Frelinghein. Mostly artillery and further back, nearer the river Deule, there was a large infantry camp.'

'Could you estimate the number of men?' asked the Captain.

'Not easily," said Gerald, 'but it must have been at least 400 yards by 200 yards, mostly tents, with some pre-fabricated buildings.'

'Good show' said the Captain, 'very useful! I'll pass the info up the line. Brigade will almost certainly send some of your chaps over to do some aerial reconnaissance.'

CHAPTER 76

An hour later, Gerald and Edward drove onto the airfield at Estrée-Blanche and found Charles Bishop in his office.

'Good morning Charlie, what are your plans for today?'

'Good God! Eddy! How are you? Where have you come from?'

'From Lille and this is my brother, Gerald.'

'We've met' and they shook hands. 'I knew vaguely about your plans and whatever it was, it seems to have worked. Well done! Eddy, sit here by my desk, they told me you were badly damaged.'

'Much better now, Charlie, thank you, but I will sit. Let's have some of that stuff in the top drawer.'

Charles filled three glasses and they sat around his desk. 'It's very quiet here' said Edward. 'Are you short or are they all out on patrol?'

'A bit of both' said Charles. 'we've taken quite a beating recently. Higgins, Simpson, Jones and Nightingale have all bought it in the last three weeks. The rest, with the replacements who are hopelessly under-trained, are out doing a reconnaissance around a place called Frelinghein. They've just left.'

'That doesn't surprise me,' said Edward, 'we triggered it. But what does surprise me is how quickly the Brigade reacted.'

'What do you mean? You triggered it.'

'We broke through there an hour and a half ago, over the bridge on the river Lys. We had seen a massive build-up of troops and artillery and had reported it to a Captain of the Cameron Highlanders. They were posted on our side of the bridge and had fired back at the Hun once we were over it. Gerry needs to ring Paris. Is that possible from here?'

'Should be, if the lines aren't down. What's the number? I'll give it to the Corporal and see what he can do.'

Within minutes, the telephone on his desk rang and Charles nodded to Gerald, who picked it up.

'Good Morning, Willie.' He paused before adding 'no, not now, I'll tell you about it later. Put me through to the Old Man.' Gerald covered the mouthpiece, and grinned at the other two.

'This should be fun,' he said, as he moved round the desk and sat on the arm of Eddy's chair, holding the telephone a foot from his own ear, between the two of them.

'Gerald, where the hell are you?' Abe's voice carried to all three of them.

'Estrée-Blanche, *Sir*, an Allied airfield fifty miles due west of Lille. Mission accomplished, you might say, *Sir!*'

'Mission accomplished? What mission are you talking about? If we weren't already at war, you would have started it with what you have just done! I've had the head of the German press corps in Paris on the line three times this morning, since you smashed your way through one of the few remaining exchange points and killed one of their guards. They are threatening to close down the entire reciprocal system! Do you realise what that means?' he roared.

'No Sir, but I'm sure you'll tell me.'

'We'll be back in the dark ages, you raving idiot! You, single-handedly, have jeopardised any future exchange of information, on which we rely so heavily, to build up a picture of what the other side is up to. You were on a legitimate assignment and you used it to your own ends, to the detriment of everyone in this office and the American press corps in general. General von Graevenitz, himself, has demanded that we hand you over to them.'

'On what grounds, Sir? You just said it was a legitimate assignment.'

'Espionage and God knows what else. They'll try you and whoever was with you, for spying and probably shoot you both.'

'Well, we can't have that, Sir, can we? What do you intend to do?'

'Absolutely bloody nothing except denying all knowledge of your existence or whereabouts. You are not, I repeat not, under any circumstances, to return to Paris. You must make your way, as soon as possible, to one of the Atlantic ports in north-western France, where you will take passage on the first American-bound vessel. You will report to Head Office on arrival, where I hope *they* shoot you.'

' I say Sir, that's a bit steep!' The connection broke and the line hummed, there was no one there.

They sat in stunned silence for a moment, each with their own thoughts until Charles got up and refilled their glasses.

'Well, I don't think you'll change his mind' said Edward with a grin, 'so we'd better see you on your way. You've got your car. I assume' and he looked at Charles, 'we have plenty of petrol, and I suggest Le Havre as your most probable port of embarkation. What do you say Charlie?'

'Yes, on the petrol, and I agree on Le Havre, and if that doesn't work, there are plenty of other ports to the west of it.'

'So, this is goodbye Eddy, at least for now. I'll see you next time round. After all you've been through, you must be due leave?'

'Absolutely' said Charles, 'I was speaking to the C.O. about it the other day and he was saying that, if you weren't packed off as a P.O.W. into Germany and we managed to get you back, you would get at least two months' convalescent leave.'

'That's what I told Giselle' said Edward 'but I haven't told you about her, Charlie, I have to go back for her this evening, to the same field where you left her.'

'I'll go' said Charles, 'I can easily find it again.'

'No Charlie, I must go, but thank you for offering, that means a great deal to me.'

'Well, if this mutual admiration society has had its say, I must be on my way.' Gerald stood up and looked down at Edward before pulling him to his feet and embracing him. 'Take great care Eddy.' Smiling shyly, Edward broke the embrace and punched his brother on the arm.

'You too take care and make sure you pick the right boat, there are a lot of U-boats out there, right now.'

'I will, and I'll leave your bag with the Corporal. You can keep the cameras, a present from Abe Johnson.'

'I'll see you out,' said Charles ' and you, Eddy, must rest or better still lie down. You can use the bed in my room. I'll bring you some lunch later but you need to get as much rest as you can, if you insist on flying back over the lines this evening.'

He and Gerald left the office to procure sufficient petrol to get Gerald to Le Havre and Edward sat down again and nursed his drink.

CHAPTER 77

Just before sunset, Edward and Charles walked out to where the BA2C was parked on the side of the runway. There was a mechanic standing at the top of a ladder with his head beneath the engine cowling.

'How's it going, Harry?' asked Charles. 'Tanks and ammunition drums full?' He turned to Edward and continued. 'I know it's flying well because I took it for a spin this afternoon.'

'Don't forget you haven't got the ceiling of the Nieuport but the old kite is much more suited to short landings and take-offs, ideal in fact, for what you need.'

'It will probably be dark by the time I get back. Please arrange to have flares set up to guide me in and do I need a coat and the rest of the gear for Giselle?'

'No, she has it there. I left her with it when I dropped her.'

'Well that's it chum, I'd better be off. I'll see you soon.'

Edward crossed the lines at six thousand feet and, with the setting sun behind him, flew towards Lille. There was no sign of any enemy aircraft around. He was so intent on looking for them that he was almost past the church steeple before he realised that he had reached the field. Far away in the distance, he could see a long convoy moving slowly along the road between Menem and Lille. There were still no other aircraft in sight so he banked sharply, went into a dive and pulled out at five hundred feet. Half a mile ahead he could see the field with the church spire directly behind it. When he had halved the distance he spotted three figures standing together on one side of the field and they ran towards him, as the 'plane touched down. He hit the ground harder than he had expected and bounced badly twice, before running on. A searing pain ran all the way up his left leg and he almost fainted. Edward slumped forward over the stick when the 'plane stopped at the far end of the field, twenty yards from the wood. Within moments, Giselle appeared beside him with a stocky, solidly built man and a young boy, running close behind her. A trickle of blood ran down the side of Edward's face from a small gash on his forehead, where he had banged his head on the Lewis gun.

'Eddy, what has happened to you? Are you all right?'

'I will be, not one of my best landings' he shouted 'I can't get out, so you and the other two must turn the 'plane around. Tell the man.'

'Jean.'

'Tell Jean to take the tail and pick it up and you and the boy take a wing each and spin her round, it's easy. Also tell Jean that the moment you are in the forward cockpit, I will run up the engine and he and the boy must hang on to the tail skid, for as long as they can. It shortens the take-off and please thank them both for their help.'

Giselle buckled herself in and felt the engine thundering at her feet. Jean and the boy, unable to hold on any longer, let go of the skid and the 'plane leapt forward and gathered speed rapidly. Within seconds they were airborne and Edward turned towards the setting sun and started climbing, as fast as possible. There were still no signs of any enemy aircraft anywhere and he couldn't believe his good fortune. As they rose to six thousand feet, the sun appeared to be stationary on the horizon, half above it, and half below. He continued to climb and, fifteen minutes later, they could see the German trenches ahead of them and almost immediately their anti-aircraft batteries opened fire.

Giselle was terrified as the shells burst around them with great clouds of black smoke. Nothing was close enough to do them any serious damage and, by the time the guns had found their range, they were already over their own lines. In another twenty minutes they would reach Estrée-Blanche. Giselle unbuckled her harness and turned round in the forward cockpit, to face Edward. He waved her back down but she just laughed and, delighted with the feel of her hair that had escaped her helmet and was flapping around her face, she reached back towards him. He leant forward and just managed to touch her glove. She tried to describe how she felt and ended up blowing kisses instead because she knew she couldn't be heard.

He reached down and retrieved the slate and chalk hanging beside him. Balancing it on his knee, he wrote. Please buckle your harness. She turned back into her cockpit and found the other slate.

No. I won't be able to see you, if I do.

There is a rear view mirror on the front of your cockpit. She scrubbed off her last message with her sleeve and wrote.

Not the same thing.

I'll take you back to the field outside Lille.

That's blackmail! she added, made a face and blew him another kiss before dropping into her seat.

Ten minutes later they started to lose altitude as Edward made his approach to the field at Estrée-Blanche. They touched down gently and, as they taxied back to the farm buildings, a small group of ground crew, led by Charles, trotted out to meet them.

'Welcome back. How did it go? You have a few rips around the tail.'

'Flack from their artillery when crossing the front.' Charles helped Giselle down and folded her into his arms.

'You are a very brave woman. I can't tell you how happy I am to see you back here in one piece. You too, Eddy,' he added, almost as an afterthought, while wrapping his other arm around his shoulders. They started walking back to the farm, Edward leaning on Charles for support.

Charles led the way into his office, waved them to chairs and brought out the bottle of cognac from his desk drawer. He poured them all a drink and raised his glass: 'Your safe return, now and always.'

'And our future happiness' added Edward 'How would you like to go to Scotland, Giselle?'

'What a wonderful idea, I've never been there.'

'You'll love it, we'll go to Glen Lyon. Wild countryside, great fishing, lovely people, good food, no Germans and plenty of whisky. Charlie, you can look after the Bentley until we get back…' – a flash of apprehension crossed Giselle's face as she realised the inevitability of Edward flying in combat again – '… won't you, old chap? '

'Of course, nothing I'd like better but I think the powers that be intend to keep you in England, to teach your tricks to the new pilots. So you had better take it with you.'

'You think or you know?'

'I know'

Giselle smiled.

'Signals flying all over the place, including one about your promotion, Captain Meade and your D.S.O. It has taken forever for it to come through but both you and Cull have been awarded the D.S.O. for your part in sinking the *Konigsberg*, so now you co-rank and out-medal me.'

'Nonsense, you have a bar to your M.C. and two M.C.s almost', he emphasised the word, 'out-medals one D.S.O.'

'What on earth are you two talking about?'

'Gongs' they said in unison, as the Mess gong summoned them to dinner.

Bio

Simon Munro Kerr was born in Scotland in 1940 and educated in England. He toured Canada and America in the late '50s and returned to Scotland and served with the Cameron Highlanders until their amalgamation in '61 with the Seaforth Highlanders. He studied acting at the Stanislavsky Studio in London in '61 & 62, worked in b&w television, theatre and films there as well as in Germany and Spain.

He gave up acting when in Hollywood in '68 and moved with his wife, Cecilia and their two daughters to Nova Scotia and became a commercial lobster fisherman and a restauranteur. Followed on to Italy in '71 with a third daughter and opened another restaurant in Porto Santo Stefano.

Returning to Spain in '73 he worked for Court Line until their spectacular collapse in the summer of '74. He stayed on in Spain exporting cement to Nigeria and in '77 joined Interbras in London, developing new markets for Brazil in West Africa.

In '82 he and his family moved to Scotland where he and Cecilia worked on upgrading and decorating small country hotels. In '87 Cecilia died tragically, and he sold the house in Dumfriesshire and bought a Stevenson Lighthouse keepers' house, on the Isle of Jura.
There he worked on rebuilding and restoring the house, which hadn't been lived in since '49, when the light went automatic. Once the house was finished, he started work on the first draft of this book, buying over a hundred books of the period for research, being as it was before internet and because the nearest proper library was a day's journey away in Glasgow.